I Dream of Danger

D1010239

Books by Lisa Marie Rice

Fiction

HEART OF DANGER
NIGHTFIRE
HOTTER THAN WILDFIRE
INTO THE CROSSFIRE
DANGEROUS PASSION
DANGEROUS SECRETS
DANGEROUS LOVER

E-Novellas

HOT SECRETS
FATAL HEAT
RECKLESS NIGHT

I Dream of Danger

A Ghost Ops Novel

Lisa Marie Rice

AVON

An Imprint of HarperCollinsPublishers

This book is a work of fiction. The characters, incidents, and dialogue are drawn from the author's imagination and are not to be construed as real. Any resemblance to actual events or persons, living or dead, is entirely coincidental.

HarperCollins books may be purchased for educational, business, or sales promotional use. For information please write: Special Markets Department, HarperCollins Publishers, 10 East 53rd Street, New York, NY 10022.

FIRST EDITION

Library of Congress Cataloging-in-Publication Data has been applied for.

ISBN 978-0-06-212180-6

13 14 15 16 17 OV/RRD 10 9 8 7 6 5 4 3 2 1

This book is dedicated to my beloved husband, my personal hero

Acknowledgments

Thanks once again to my great editor, May Chen, and my great agent, Ethan Ellenberg.

I Dream of Danger

Chapter 1

Burial of Judge Oren Thomason
St. Mary's Cemetery
Lawrence, Kansas
January 10

He came.

She knew he'd come. Somehow she'd known.

She dreamed of him last night. She often dreamed of him, dreams so vivid she woke with tears on her face, aching for him.

Elle Thomason rose from where she'd thrown dirt onto her father's coffin, before the two undertaker's assistants covered it with earth and he would finally, finally be at peace—and that was when she saw him.

He was outlined against the chilly winter sun on the small hill where the chapel stood. He was only a dark figure against the dying sun, but she would recognize him anywhere, anytime.

Nick Ross. The boy she'd loved so much, now clearly a man. The dark outline against the pale winter sun was tall and broad-shouldered He'd been lean as a boy, like a young panther. Now he was a lion.

He saw her. He didn't wave to her or nod. Neither did she. She simply watched as he walked down the small hill toward her, eyeing him hungrily. She'd waited five long years for this moment.

In all the dead years, the years of caring for her father as his mind died long before his body, she'd yearned for this moment. As everything else fell from her life, as she lost everything, as her life was taken over by the daily care of a man who no longer controlled anything about himself, the only thing left to her was her imagination. And in her mind, she went wild.

In her mind, she and Nick were together.

Her favorite daydream was meeting him in some sophisticated city. New York, Chicago, San Francisco. Even better, London or Paris. Of course, she was sophisticated herself. She'd had a number of love affairs that had taught her a lot. She was well-groomed, successful, utterly in control.

Turning around in an expensive restaurant, there he'd be.

In her fantasies she could figure out what she was—poised and successful and happy. But she could never figure out what Nick was. What he'd become. She only knew he'd be handsome and he'd love her. She couldn't get beyond that point—that he still loved her, after all these years.

She'd ask why he'd disappeared so suddenly. It was still unfathomable to her. One night she'd gone to bed teasing him that he'd grow up to be Commander Adama of *Battlestar Galactica*, and the next morning he was gone. Completely disappeared. His things were still in his room. The only articles missing were two pairs of jeans, some T-shirts, a winter jacket, and his gym bag.

She'd been frantic. She wanted to call the cops, report him missing, but her father had gently taken the phone from her hand and flipped it closed. He never answered her questions and soon, very soon, he became incapable of answering any questions at all.

Not a phone call, not a letter, not even a postcard. It was as if Nick had dropped off the face of the earth, taking with him her entire existence. From a carefree teenager, the beloved only daughter of a respected and wealthy judge, her life plunged into the pits of hell. Her father started losing his mind day by day, darkness descending, and Nick wasn't there.

How many evenings she stared out the window, pretending to read, her father having finally exhausted himself enough to nap in an armchair. Going out on a date was unthinkable. There wasn't enough money to pay a nurse for evening hours. She'd had to earn extra credits over the summers to graduate at seventeen because she could see the day coming when the money would run out and she'd have to stay home all day to nurse her father, and she wanted at least a high school certificate.

Dating was out, going to movies with girlfriends was out, having friends over was definitely out. What she got was a nurse coming for a few hours a day in which she could rush to do the shopping and rush to the library to stock up on books. What she got was staring out the window, waiting for Nick.

Hoping for Nick.

Yearning for Nick.

Who never came.

So in her daydreams, when she finally did meet him, utterly by chance in a big city, she got to choose how it would be. He was either immensely rich and handsome or powerful and handsome. He was never a loser, a drunk, or an addict. That wasn't Nick.

Hello, he'd say, stepping back in admiration. *Aren't you beautiful?*

Thank you, she'd answer. *I hope you're well. I'd love to stay and chat, but I need to get back to my—*

Here Elle's imagination struggled a little. To what? Get back to what? What could possibly be more important than Nick?

But it didn't really matter because then he'd say:

—Have a drink with me. Please. Just five minutes. I'm so glad to see you.

And, well, this was *Nick*. And so she would. And then he'd say he loved her and would never leave her again.

It was a fine daydream and it had to be because it replaced more or less everything a young girl should have—school, friends, first love, dreams, plans . . .

The details wavered but the core of it was always the same. He found her whole and happy and successful. Beautiful and elegant and self-assured.

Not the miserable creature she was now. Pale and pinched from the last four nights of watching her father die when she hadn't slept at all. Wearing a too-thin jacket that didn't protect in any way against the cold because the only winter coat she had was ripped along the sleeve.

It wasn't supposed to be this way at all. But it was.

She simply watched as he walked toward her, and everything about her was numb except her heart. Her treacherous, treacherous heart, leaping in joy to see him.

He didn't hurry down to her, but his long legs seemed to carry him quickly. He had on a big heavy jacket that came down to midthigh; his gloved hands hung by his side.

Elle was aware of her own hands, gloveless, almost blue with cold. Embarrassed, she stuck them behind her back.

And that was how they met, Nick towering over her, face in shadow, looking down at her. The sun was at his back, huge just before sunset, an enormous pale disk. They stood and looked at each other. Elle was struck dumb.

He was here, right in front of her.

How she'd longed for this moment and here it was, by the side of her father's coffin.

She should say something, she should—

"Miss?"

Elle turned. She'd completely forgotten the attendants. "Yes?"

"You're going to have to stand back, Miss. We're going to cover the coffin with dirt."

"Oh." She stepped back and Nick stepped with her. "Of course."

She and Nick watched as dirt covered the coffin of her only living relative. She didn't cry. She'd shed so many tears over the years. There were none left. Her father had gone long before this. What had been left behind was a shell of a person, human meat.

Her father had been witty, well-read, strongly opinionated, charming. That man had died years ago.

So she watched as they covered the coffin, quickly and efficiently. It was cold and they wanted the job over as fast as possible. When they finished, they put away their tools and faced her.

There was a gash in the ground now, raw and red. Someday it would be covered with grass as the other graves were, but for now it was clear that the earth had recently claimed one of its own. A tombstone would come, eventually, when she could afford it.

The funeral home director had quoted figures that made no sense to her. The cheapest one cost over two thousand dollars. It might as well have cost a million. She didn't have it.

She didn't have anything.

One of the gravediggers pulled off his hat. "Real sorry about the judge, ma'am. You have our condolences."

Elle dipped her head. "Thank you. Um . . ." She opened her purse and peered inside, though she didn't need to look to see what was in it. One bill. Not a big one, either. She pulled out the twenty and handed it to the man, well aware of the fact that it should have been a hundred-dollar bill, fifty each.

He picked it up gingerly, looked at his mate in disgust, stuck it in his pants pocket and glared at her.

Elle understood completely. They had done a hard job. The ground was frozen and they'd toiled. The funeral director had let her know clearly that the cheap option she'd chosen didn't cover the diggers and that she would have to recompense them herself.

This was so *awful*. She felt so raw and exposed, reduced to ashes, to dust. All of this was playing out right in front of Nick, who was observing everything.

She remembered how observant he was. He always had been. He was seeing her humiliation in 3D HD, up close and personal.

Elle cleared her throat, reached out a hand toward the gravedigger, then stuck it in her pocket. "I'm sorry it's not more," she said quietly. "Perhaps—"

"Here." Nick handed over two bills. Her eyes widened when she saw Benjamin Franklin's face twice. "Thanks for your help."

The cap came off again, both men thanked him, nodded to her and walked off.

Elle stared at the ground, breathing through her pain. Nick had left many years ago, and for all those years, not a day, not a *minute*, had gone by in which she hadn't missed him so fiercely she thought she might explode from it.

All this time she'd yearned for Nick.

And here he was. At her lowest point.

"He loved you very much," she said, looking at the ground.

"I know," he said quietly.

His voice, already deep as a boy, had become deeper, rougher. The voice of a man.

He was a man. He'd been mature beyond his years when he'd come into their life, a runaway her father found in their backyard one winter evening. He was lying in the snow with a broken, badly infected wrist, dying, so emaciated her father was able to pick him up and carry him in his arms to the car to take him to the hospital.

From that moment on, Nick Ross belonged to them.

Until he left them, inexplicably, another cold winter night.

She looked up at him, hungry for the sight of him. How she'd dreamed of him over these past years! Her dreams had been so vivid, often unsettling. She'd seen him shooting, jumping out of planes, fighting.

She'd seen him with other women. That had been so hard because her dreams had the bite of reality. She'd seen him naked, making love to women, harsh and demanding, impossibly sexy.

The Nick standing next to her looked just as he had in her dreams—hard, tough, fully a man. Dark eyes that gave nothing away, close-cropped dark hair, broad shoulders, lean muscles. A formidable man in every way, even though the last time she'd seen him he'd been just on the verge of manhood.

"He was . . . sick?" Nick's voice was hesitant.

"Yes," she replied, looking down at the raw gash in the frozen earth. "For a long time."

Since you left, she thought to herself. *He was never the same, and then he started his fast decline.*

"I'm sorry." The deep voice was low, as if murmuring for her ears alone, though there was no one else on the cemetery grounds. There had been about thirty people at the funeral itself, but they left immediately, as soon as the service was over. Everyone had jobs, places to be, things to do. Nobody stayed for the interment. They'd paid their respects to the man her father had been and left. Her father had been dead to the town long before his body left this earth.

She nodded, throat tight.

"It's cold. You should have worn something warmer."

Elle huffed out a breath that would have been laughter in other circumstances. The cloud of steam rose quickly and dissipated into the frigid air. Yes, she should have worn something warmer. Of course.

"Yes," she murmured. "I, um, I forgot."

Why are we talking about coats? It seemed so surreal.

"Where's your car?" Nick asked in his rough voice. "You should get home. You're freezing."

Elle looked back up at him in panic. *He's leaving already?* That couldn't be!

Her throat tightened even more. He couldn't leave, he couldn't. He couldn't be that cruel.

The words tumbled out without her thinking. "I don't have a car. The undertakers were supposed to give me a ride home." Nolan Cruise, the DA, had driven her to the edge of the cemetery and dropped her off, apologizing for not being able to stay.

She looked around, but they'd gone. The cemetery was utterly deserted. Obviously, the two men had thought she already had a ride home. With Nick.

Oh God. The first time she saw him in five years and she needed to beg a ride home from him. She straightened, pulled her light-weight jacket around her tightly, trying to wrap her dignity around her too.

"That's okay. I—" Her mind whirred uselessly. Saying she'd walk would be ridiculous. Nick knew perfectly well how far home was. At least a two-hour walk. She was trying to invent someone who could plausibly give her a ride home when he took her elbow in a firm grip and started walking toward the exit. "Let's go."

Elle scrambled to keep up. Nick, always tall, had grown another couple of inches. His long legs ate up the grassy terrain. In a few minutes they were outside the gates of the cemetery, walking under the arched stone sign with *Requiescat in Pacem* engraved on the front.

Yes, indeed. *Rest in peace, Daddy.*

His last years, as his mind went, had not been peaceful. They had been dark and despairing as he felt himself slip day by day. Even after his mind had gone, she'd sensed the lingering despair.

He's gone to a better place, the few people who'd come to the funeral had said. The old truism was right. Wherever he was now, it couldn't be worse than the life he had left behind.

She and Nick were walking along an empty driveway, which

was always full of cars on Memorial Day and was mainly empty the other 364 days a year. Nick pulled out a remote and a big black expensive-looking car lit up, the doors unlocking with a *whomp*.

"Nice car," she ventured. There was so much to be said, but his face was so forbidding, so remote; she could only make the blandest of comments.

"Rental," he said tersely and held open the passenger side door for her.

A thousand questions jostled in her head but she simply sat, holding her jacket tightly around her while he got into the driver's seat and took off. A minute later, warm air was washing over her and the trembling she hadn't noticed eased off.

He knew exactly where to go, of course.

He might have forgotten her, he might have forgotten her father, but he wouldn't have forgotten where they had all lived together. That was another thing about Nick. His amazing sense of direction. The last few years before he ran off, whenever they went on an outing together, her father had counted on Nick to guide them. And for the last two years, after he got his learner's license, to drive them all where they needed to go.

The judge had probably started dementing already, though there were no signs of it then. He had been, as always, ramrod straight, with iron gray hair brushed back, always elegant and collected. The opposite of the shambles of a man she'd buried.

It helped to think of Daddy and not to concentrate on Nick, driving with careless expertise. He'd always been superb behind the wheel, right from the start. The instructor had told Daddy that he hadn't had to teach Nick anything. It was as if he'd been born knowing how to drive.

Elle stared straight ahead, doing her best not to take peeks at Nick. It was almost impossible. He was like a black hole, pulling in gravity toward him. Impossible to ignore, yet impossible to look at directly.

A thousand words were on the tip of her tongue. *How are you how have you been where do you live now do you like it there* . . . Empty words really. Because what she wanted to know, she couldn't say.

Why did you leave us? Why did you leave me?

The unspoken words choked her. She was afraid to open her mouth because they would come tumbling out. She had no filter, no defense mechanism. Plus, she'd lived alone so long with a father who could neither understand her nor respond to her, she'd grown used to saying exactly what she thought.

She wasn't even fit company anymore.

But *something* should be said. They hadn't seen each other in five years. Five years, seven months, and two days. Each minute of which she'd missed him. Even in her sleep.

She concentrated on practicing the words. If she said them slowly, one at a time, surely nothing else would escape her mouth. *How have you been?*

How. Have. You. Been?

There, she could say that. Four simple words. And he'd answer and she'd try really, really hard not to push. She could do this. She could—

"We're here," Nick said and swerved so that the vehicle was parked outside the garage.

She hadn't even noticed that they'd made it home.

She swallowed. The garage had been left open. Her mistake. She'd rushed in to get slippers for Daddy's last visit to the hospital, and in her haste hadn't closed it. There were no cars. Daddy had always kept a Cadillac and a Toyota, but both had been sold two years ago. She took the bus to the few places she had to go.

Nick didn't bother putting the rental inside the garage.

He wasn't staying.

Elle swallowed the pain and turned when he opened the passenger door. He held out a big hand. She didn't need help. But . . . this might be her only, her last chance to touch him.

She put her hand in his, and in a second, he guided her down to the gravel, dropped her hand, then held it out again, palm up.

She looked at it blankly, then up at him. *He wanted to hold her hand?*

"Keys," he said tersely.

Oh.

Numb with cold and pain, she opened her purse and gave him the door keys. She didn't have to rummage. Her purse held a now-empty wallet, a cellphone with very few minutes left, an old lipstick, and the keys.

In a moment, Nick had the door open and was standing there, waiting for her.

He watched her walk the few short steps to the porch and up to the portico. Lucky thing he wasn't looking around.

The grounds had always been a showpiece. When Nick disappeared, Rodrigo was still coming twice a week to take care of the extensive gardens. The drive had been flanked by seasonal flowers in large terra-cotta vases. The vases and flowers were long gone. There were no flowers anywhere and the hedges had long since lost their shape.

Elle had received three official notices of "abandonment" in the past six months.

Nick didn't seem to notice, thank God.

Inside the house, though, it was worse than outside.

The house had always been immaculate. Ever since her mother had died, when she was five, the house had been ruled by a benevolent tyrant, Mrs. Gooding, who kept it polished and fragrant with the help of a maid several times a week.

Mrs. Gooding was long gone, as was the maid.

Elle had done her best, but the house was big and the last months of her father's life had required round-the-clock care from her. She napped when she could, exhausted, and did the best she could to keep a bare minimum of cleanliness.

Her father had taken ill during the night, and they'd rushed to the hospital. She kept vigil by his side for four days and four nights. Then the funeral.

The house was a mess. A freezing cold mess, because she hadn't turned the heat on, knowing she'd be away all day.

This time Nick noticed.

He stopped inside the foyer and she stopped with him. His neck bent back as he looked up at the ceiling of the two-story atrium. Once there had been a magnificent Murano chandelier with fifty bulbs that had blazed as brightly as the sun. Now there was simply a low-wattage lightbulb hanging naked from a cord.

The rest of the foyer was naked too. Watercolors, the huge Chinese rug, the console with the ornately carved mirror atop it, the two Viennese Thonet armchairs on either side of the Art Deco desk with the enormous solid silver bowl full of potpourri—gone.

Nick didn't react in any way. His face was calm and expressionless.

What was he thinking?

Later, after he'd disappeared, one of her high school classmates said that he'd been earning extra money playing poker with lowlifes, and that he always won because he had the best poker face anyone had ever seen.

She was seeing that now. There was no clue to his thoughts.

Perhaps— Perhaps she'd hoped to see some softness or gentleness when he looked at her. But no.

She gestured awkwardly toward the back of the house. "Would you . . . Would you like something to drink?"

He nodded his head briefly without saying anything. She turned and walked into the kitchen, knowing he didn't need her direction. He knew the way.

His showing up had scrambled her brains, but now she forced herself to think, to reason things out. Where had he come from? Had he traveled a long time? Would he stay the night?

Her heart gave a huge thump in her chest at the thought.

"So"—once in the kitchen Elle turned to face him, plastering a smile on her face, making a real effort not to wring her hands— "what can I offer you?"

Oh God.

Too late she realized that there was very little to offer. If he wanted alcohol, there was none in the house. Her father had had a fine collection of whiskeys, but they had gone years ago and she had never bought another bottle. There was no food, either, she suddenly remembered. Only a last frozen pizza in the freezer.

"Coffee would be fine." His voice and eyes were so calm. She tried to cling to that, to calm herself down, but it was hard. This was *Nick*. Nick was here, right now, in her kitchen.

"Coffee. Right." There was coffee. Enough for one cup at least.

She turned and tried to keep her hands steady as she opened the cupboard to get the coffee. To her horror, except for the glass canister with an inch of grounds, the cupboard was bare.

Exactly like in some horrible fable.

She closed the cupboard, making a louder noise than she wanted, then set about making coffee with trembling hands for Nick.

Nick.

Who was here.

Preparing the coffee, setting out the pretty Limoges cup and saucer, part of a set that she hadn't sold because there were only four pieces, setting out a silver spoon and the Wedgewood sugar canister calmed her down a little.

He was still standing, and that was another blow to the heart.

This had been his kitchen once too. He had once been completely at home here. She remembered the thousands of evenings Nick had teased her and made her father laugh in here while Mrs. Gooding prepared dinner.

Now he was standing, needing her permission to sit. Tears

blurred her eyes but she willed them back. She'd had a lot of experience at that. She could do this.

"Please sit." She pulled out a chair.

He took off his jacket, hung it on the back of the chair, and sat. Underneath the jacket he had on a heavy flannel shirt.

Oh God. She should do the same, of course. Except she was still cold, and underneath the jacket she had on only a thin sweater. She did still have a few thick sweaters, but her mind had been so befogged by the exhaustion of the last days of her father's life, and the funeral arrangements, that she'd simply grabbed the first thing that came to hand. As luck would have it, it was a thin cotton sweater.

But she could pretend with the best of them. She hung her own jacket over the chair and sat down across from him.

They looked at each other mutely.

The coffee machine percolated. Elle sprang up and poured him a cup.

Nick hesitated. "What about you? Still don't like coffee? You always liked tea. Can I make you some?"

"No!" Elle cleared her throat. "No, thanks." She'd kill for a cup of tea, but it was in the cupboard above the stove and that was bare too. Two bare cupboards—it was too much for Nick to see.

Nick blew on the cup and sipped. As always, the delicate china looked out of place in his large hand, but she knew from experience that it was safe. His hands were huge, had always been huge, but he was far from clumsy.

They sat in silence until he finished half the cup, then looked up at her. "How long had he been ill?"

Elle didn't sigh, but she wanted to. "Several years. But his doctor thinks, with hindsight, that the illness started five years ago, only he managed to hide it."

Something—some faint expression crossed his face.

Oh God. He'd left them five years ago. It sounded like she was accusing him of precipitating her father's decline.

"Must have been hard. For you."

Elle simply dipped her head. *Yes, hard. Very hard.*

"So—what will you do now? Go back to college?"

"I wasn't enrolled in college."

That surprised him. It took a lot to surprise Nick, but she'd done it. "What do you mean you're not in college? You were a straight-A student, always had been. Or have you already finished college?"

She had to smile at that. She'd had anything but straight As while she struggled to deal with her father's eccentricities. It would be another year before she understood he was ill. She'd missed almost every other day her sophomore year.

"No . . . I, ah—it's complicated."

Nick was frowning. Okay. That was easier to deal with than that look of pity he'd had.

"Well, now there's nothing holding you back, is there?"

Well, if you didn't count no money and medical debts, and put like that . . ." No, there isn't."

The answer seemed to relax him. He looked around again, then back at her, his dark gaze penetrating.

"You're too thin. And too pale. You need to eat more and get outside more."

That *hurt*. Nick had been in her heart always, since he had first come into their lives. She'd only been seven, but she loved him the moment she laid eyes on him. She'd been a girl then, but she was a woman now—and everything womanly in her was concentrated on him, his handsome face, those broad shoulders, the outsized hands.

Every female cell in her body was quivering. And he spoke to her like an elderly aunt would.

Eat more, get out more. Don't be so pasty-faced and thin.
Yeah.

Next thing, he'd be telling her to bundle up warmly.

"And Christ—what's the matter with you, going out in this weather dressed like that?"

There you go.

How she'd *dreamed* of this moment! For years. And now here he was, sitting across from her, so close she could touch him if she simply reached out—and they were talking about her wardrobe.

"Don't," she said softly. "I had to get dressed in a hurry. But I don't want to talk about this. I want to hear how you've been doing. Where you've been."

And why you disappeared without a word.

But she couldn't say that. He was here. Right now she wanted to fill the empty years with images. She could only do that if she could imagine where he'd been, what he'd been doing.

Once upon a time, he'd told her everything.

Nick settled more deeply in the chair, frowning. "I can't really talk about that."

"Because you're in the military?"

He straightened, shocked. "How did you know that? Who told you?"

Nick sounded actually angry. It had slipped out of her mouth without her thinking about it, which went to show how tired she was. She never let slip things she shouldn't know, but did. She'd learned that the hard way.

She'd seen him. In her dreams. Not normal dreams—that floating phantasmagoria of disconnected images most people had during the night. She had those, too, like everyone else. But she also had *Dreams*. She went places in these Dreams, and it was like being there. Frighteningly, *exactly* like being there.

She'd visited Nick, without a clue as to where he was, but so real she felt she could touch him. He was exercising with a hundred other men, doing jumping jacks and climbing ropes and crawling under barbed wire. Shooting. Shooting a lot. Jumping out of planes.

And with women. That had been the worst of all. She'd watched, helplessly, as he made love to a series of women, rarely the same one two nights in a row. Elle would be looking down from the ceiling, watching the muscles of his broad back stretch and flex, his buttocks tightening and releasing as he moved in and out of the woman. Usually, he held himself above the woman *du nuit* on stiff arms, touching her only with his sex.

Those nights, as she watched from the ceiling, she would wake up with tears on her face.

A part of her thought she was crazy. And another part of her thought she could somehow travel outside her body.

Whichever it was—and maybe it was both—she'd said the wrong thing to Nick.

He reached across to clamp his big hand over her wrist.

"Did someone tell you something?" he demanded. "Someone spying on me?"

His grip was tight. Not painful, but definitely unbreakable. Nick had always been strong, even as a boy. Now he was a powerfully built man.

Slowly, unsure if her touch would be welcome, Elle laid her hand over his.

"No one told me, Nick," she said gently. It wasn't the first time she had to answer how she knew something she shouldn't. And it wouldn't be the last. When he lived with them, Nick had never known. Her father hadn't known. *She* hadn't known. "You have the bearing of a soldier, and your hair is cut military-short. There is a pale patch on your jacket. Where there would have been an insignia. You look like you're doing well, but you're not in a suit. You've got combat boots on. They're sold in stores, too, but taking all these things together—" She shrugged.

Nick relaxed, smiled. Oh, how she'd missed that smile! It had taken him almost two years to smile when he first came to live with them. She'd been only a child, but she understood instinctively that he'd come from pain and cruelty and she'd made it her personal challenge to make him smile.

Once he started, he smiled often. He was breathtaking when he smiled.

Like now.

He shook his head. "I forgot how smart you are. How perceptive. So you put all that together and came up with military, hm?"

It hurt that he forgot anything about her. She hadn't forgotten anything about him.

"Yes, but I wouldn't want to guess which branch of the service and how far you've climbed." She tilted her head, studying him. "So . . . was I right?"

"Bingo."

Elle relaxed. She'd reasoned her way out of the trap. "Which branch are you in?"

A cloud moved across his face, but he answered calmly enough. "Army."

A word flashed across her mind. She didn't even know she'd had it in her head, but the information she gleaned in her Dreams had its own agenda. The word came out of her mouth before she could censor it. "Rangers?"

Nick straightened, frowning. "Now, how the hell would you know that?" His look was keen, penetrating, impersonal.

There was no sense now that she had a special place in his heart. None. Ever since Nick had arrived in their lives, she knew he had a soft spot for her. That she could take risks with him. Like a puppy that could pull a wolf's tail with impunity.

Not now. She had no feeling at all that she was allowed liberties with Nick. His frown was deep and serious, and a little scary.

She swallowed, and started on the lies. She'd never had to lie to him before. "Sorry. That was stupid of me. I have no idea what's going on with you. There was a movie on TV the other night and the main protagonist was an Army Ranger. That's what they called him, in fact. Ranger. That's all. I don't even really understand what it means."

Even if she hadn't Dreamed that he was a Ranger, she'd have wagered money that if there was a special place in the army, Nick would have achieved it.

He relaxed slightly. "A movie hero? That's not me."

Oh, but it was. Nick was much more handsome than most of the actors she saw on TV. Most actors had a softness about them that was reflected in their faces. They might spend eight hours a day at the gym, but their faces were puppyish.

Not Nick. Nick had known real tragedy. Wherever he'd spent the first eleven years of his life before he came to them—and he never spoke a word about it—they had been hard, tough years. He'd had the bearing of a man even when young. As a teenager, he'd been wise and tough beyond his years. The other kids in high school either worshipped him or steered clear of him. No one *ever* tried to bully him. They wouldn't dare.

There was no actor on earth who could look as tough as Nick at twenty-three.

He'd had a rough life, which had made him hard. The military had taken him and made him harder.

He frowned at her. "How come no one was at the graveside? The judge was well known and respected. I'd have thought there would be thousands of people."

Elle didn't want to talk about that, about the past. She wanted to talk about the here and now. But he wanted to know, and she was hardwired to give Nick what he wanted.

"There were people at the funeral. Some. Not many. They couldn't stay for the interment." She swallowed. "Daddy . . . was sick for a long time."

Nick narrowed his eyes. "Yeah, you said that. So?"

"He also hasn't been a judge for a long time. I think . . . I think people sort of forgot about him."

Nick was really frowning now and Elle understood completely. When he'd left— *Wait*, use the right term. When Nick *abandoned* them, her father, Judge Oren Thomason, had been one of the most important men in the county. Nick had felt her father's natural authority firsthand. When she and her father had found him behind the house, in their backyard, starving and with a broken wrist, the judge had taken care of everything. Within a month, Nick had become his ward and was regularly enrolled in school.

Nick had often said his real life began the day the judge found him. He seemed to forget that Elle had been there too. A tiny girl, only seven, but it seemed her real life began that day too.

Nick had lived under the judge's protective aura. So Elle could understand that he found it hard to understand his last years.

"Daddy . . . declined. Mentally. He was forcibly removed from the bench via an injunction." She swallowed. Her father had been beyond understanding exactly *what* had happened, but he had understood very well that something important had been taken away from him. He'd been agitated for an entire year.

"Alzheimer's?" Nick asked.

She hung her head.

"Tough," he said.

You have no idea. She lifted her head, nodded.

They sat in silence, looking at each other. Finally, he gave a sigh and shifted in his chair. Elle panicked.

He was leaving already! He'd just arrived, and she hadn't seen him in five years. She was still gulping up details about him every time she dared to look at him. The hard cut of his jaw, the two wiry white hairs mixed in the thick black hair of his temples. His hands, bigger than she remembered. Clean but callused, with a strip of thick yellow callus on the edges. Judo calluses, or some kind of martial art. She'd read about that.

The shoulders that stretched beyond the shirt seams.

Nick was unshaven, his stubble thicker than she remembered. He was now one of those men who should shave twice a day.

That was new. So many things about him were new.

Including the fact that he was sexy as hell.

That was new, for her. As a child, as a young girl, Nick was . . . *Nick*. The person she loved most in the world after her father. Always there, always dependable, always fun. With a natural authority that made her feel safe and protected. The two men in her life, looking after her. Her father, with his understanding of the law, his status as a well-respected judge—nothing in society could harm her while he was around. And Nick—always strong and tough, with quick reflexes, always alert for trouble. Nothing in life could hurt her while he was around.

It was only now, alone, that Elle understood what a privileged childhood she'd had. And Nick had been a big part of that.

Nick wasn't her brother. She had no idea what feelings you could have for a brother because she'd never had one, but she instinctively understood she never thought of Nick as one. Nick was her friend, her protector.

She thought he'd always be there. How foolish. It hadn't even occurred to her that someday he'd fall in love and leave. She didn't know if he'd fallen in love, but he'd certainly left.

He'd definitely had women. Tons of them. She'd never seen male genitalia in person but in her Dreams . . . Nick was the epitome of maleness. She'd seen him with women, she'd seen him in bed pleasuring himself—

She swallowed, hoping she wasn't turning red. She'd always been an open book to him. Please God, let him not understand that she was remembering the violently arousing image of him having sex with other women and with himself.

Sitting across from him, she totally understood why women

fell for him. As a girl, her feelings had already started turning. But now she was a woman, and what he evoked in her was sexual desire—of a scale and intensity she didn't know how to handle.

Nick shifted in his chair, huffed out a breath. "Well," he began. "I guess I'd better be—"

"Where did you come from?" she blurted.

"What?"

"Where were you today? Or yesterday? When you decided to come?"

"Are you asking why I came?"

"No." And she wasn't. Why he came was clear, to her at least. They were linked by a thread that had become thin and stretched over time but still held. She'd needed him desperately and he came. That was bedrock for her. She didn't even question it.

He wasn't answering her question. She tried another tack. "I can't let you leave without feeding you. Dad would . . . Dad would have been appalled."

His hard look softened. "Honey, it doesn't look like you have much food in the house."

Elle swallowed, lifted her head. "Dad was very, very ill the last couple of weeks. I didn't have time to do any food shopping." She pulled her cell out of her pocket. "I can call Foodwise, though. Jenny would gladly send us a meal. Promise you'll stay at least to eat."

There were still a couple hundred dollars left in the checking account. The undertaker's bill would come later and plunge her into the red, but for the moment she had more than enough to cover a meal. Two meals, even. She didn't even think of ordering a pizza or a burger and fries. Nick deserved better than that.

He dipped his head. "Okay."

Elle beamed at him. He wasn't leaving right this minute. She still had time with him. There was so much to memorize. The lines beside his mouth, brand-new, that disappeared when he smiled. How the tendons in his neck stood out when he turned his head. How she could see his pectorals through his shirt.

How utterly handsome he was.

How he heated her blood.

She had to memorize this effect he had on her, because it wasn't coming back, not without Nick. She knew herself that well, at least. This was her one shot at feeling sexual desire and it would leave when he left.

Everything about her was aroused. Her skin was supersensitive. The small hairs on her forearms and on the nape of her neck prickled against her sweater. Even the lightest touch against her clothes seemed to burn her skin. It was hard to breathe, as if oxygen had suddenly mutated into a liquid. She had to concentrate to keep her lungs filled.

The biggies. Her breasts, never large, now felt immense and heavy. Her nipples brushed against the cotton of her bra. Between her thighs—that unmistakable feeling of heaviness and heat and emptiness she had when she woke up from ordinary dreams of Nick.

The changes in her body excited her and scared her. Excited her because, well, heat and pleasure were novelties. She'd been cold and hollow for a long time. These tingling sensations, as if her body were waking up after a long sleep—they were wonderful. They also scared her because as far as she knew, only Nick could make her feel this way.

But he was staying for dinner, or as much dinner as she could muster.

Take this second by second, she told herself. *Enjoy every second*.

She watched him as she dialed the number. Jenny herself answered. She had a soft spot for them. Once, when she was a young girl, long before Elle had been born, the judge had kept her out of trouble. Jenny herself had told her; the judge had never said a word.

"Hey, hon." Jenny's smoky voice, as always, was warm. Elle could imagine her leaning against a wall on a cigarette break, short gray hair brushed back, her long, lean, elegant frame slightly slouched. "I'm so sorry I couldn't make the funeral. We had to cater two luncheons. I'm really sorry, honey. If I'd had advance notice . . . but that's not the nature of funerals, is it?"

"No, it's not." Elle smiled. Trust Jenny to say the exact right thing. No doubt in the days to come she'd have thousands of people apologizing for not coming, though in most cases it was simply that the judge had fallen off their radar. He wasn't off Jenny's radar. If she'd been free, she would have come. "That's okay, Jenny. Dad knows you loved him."

"I surely did, hon. So what can I do for you? Can I send you a dinner over?"

Oh, bless her. "Yes, thank you. Today's special." She hesitated. "For two people."

Jenny didn't pry. "Two specials, you got it. I'll send them over around seven, with a nice bottle of wine. All on the house."

"Thank—" Elle stopped. It was an incredibly generous offer. Dinner would be at least seventy dollars, plus the wine and tips. But . . . that was the beginning of a long slippery slope straight to hell.

So far, Elle had kept up appearances. No one came to the house anymore, so they wouldn't notice that almost everything that could have been sold was gone. But Jenny knew, or suspected. If Elle started accepting charity now, it would snowball. The wives of former friends of her father would start sending over used clothes—*Just wore it a few times, Elle sweetie. You're welcome to it.* Maids would start leaving casseroles on her front doorstep.

It didn't bear thinking about.

Not to mention the fact that Jenny's smoker's voice came over loud and clear, and Nick had undoubtedly heard every word.

She injected confidence in her voice. "That's kind of you, Jenny, but not necessary. I'll give the delivery boy my credit card. But thanks for the offer."

She could barely look away from Nick's dark eyes. It took her a moment to realize Jenny was taking a long time to answer.

Finally— "Okay, hon. That's fine, then. But the wine will be on the house."

Yes. That was acceptable. A gesture of solidarity, not charity. "Thanks, Jenny."

"I loved that old man," Jenny replied and Elle nearly burst into tears.

That was what her father had been. The kind of man other people loved because he'd done such good in the world.

"Yeah," she whispered, forcing the word out, and broke the connection before she broke down.

She raised her eyes to Nick.

"I loved him, too," he said quietly.

And that broke her. It was like a sharp punch straight to the heart. Reaching past skin and bone in a nearly fatal blow.

"Then why did you leave us?" she whispered as tears began rolling down her face.

Chapter 2

Oh fuck.

That was the last thing Nick wanted, to make Elle cry. She was sitting across from him, crying her heart out without making a sound and it nearly brought him to his knees.

She nearly brought him to his knees.

She'd been a beautiful little girl when they'd found him that winter night. He'd run away from his fourth foster home. The last one had been the worst of all, run by a true sadist. Everyone in the household walked around with scars and hollow eyes. How the fuck the authorities managed to avoid reading the signs was beyond him. But they did. They kept shipping kids to Carlton Norris, and Old Man Norris just kept taking them in and cashing the checks. His beaten-down wife fed them shit food and did just enough housekeeping to keep cockroaches at bay, then would disappear into her room when the old man got that crafty look in his eyes.

It wasn't rage, it was addiction. He fed off other people's pain. He didn't feed off Nick's. Nick was five foot ten by the time he was eleven years old and he kept himself strong. No one messed with him. Norris didn't want to mess with him, anyway. Norris liked the smaller kids.

One night Nick stopped the beating of a small boy, Tim, who had that look about him. The look of someone who wasn't going to survive much longer. There wasn't anything Nick could do to help the kid's long-term survival, but by God he was going to survive this beating. Nick swung at Norris and connected well. He pulled the punch at the last minute so all Norris got was a black eye. It could have been a shattered jaw.

Nick woke to blinding pain. Norris had taken a hammer to his wrist and was shining a blinding light in his eyes. Just past the light Nick saw a gun barrel.

"You run, boy," Norris growled. "You run as fast as you can because in an hour I'm calling the cops and reporting a dangerous juvenile on the loose. He beat me up, and he beat up a younger boy. And don't think for one minute that little worm won't rat on you and say you gave him the scars and bruises."

No, Nick knew enough of the world to understand that Tim would be too terrified to contradict Norris.

The safety went off the gun. "Run, you fucker."

He ran.

He ran and ran. He hitched rides, was a stowaway on long-haul trucks, and once hid in the luggage compartment of a Greyhound bus. He didn't even know where he was going. He survived on stolen food and water bottles from service stations, but in the end his wrist blew up like a balloon and infection set in.

He dropped—in an affluent part of a town—unconscious with, as he was later told, a temperature of 104.

He came to very briefly to see an angel looking at him, so he knew he was dead. She was beautiful, a tiny sprite with light blue eyes, fair hair a halo around her head, screaming, *Daddy, Daddy!*

That's nice, he remembered thinking. *I died and went to heaven. Fucking A.*

Only he hadn't died and gone to heaven, he'd gone to Lawrence, Kansas. And his life split into two, because he was picked up by the finest man on the face of the earth, Judge Oren Thomason.

He was taken to a hospital where the little blond angel rarely left his side, and when he was better, he was taken home to the kind of home he never even knew existed. Calm and gentleness reigned there, along with love and respect.

The angel turned out to be Elle, a beautiful little girl who became his shadow. Nick had never been loved before, but Elle made up for that. She loved him fiercely. He went home with them—to his own room! With a bed with clean sheets, a closet full of clean new clothes, books, and a laptop on a desk. All his own. He'd gone from the hospital straight into bed, still too weak to stand up for long. Elle ferried in trays full of food she could barely carry and stayed with him until he finished every bite, then read to him, endlessly, from books he'd never heard of but which fascinated him. A wizard called Harry Potter. Lions and witches and wardrobes. A whole world called Middle-earth.

And in the meantime, Judge Thomason was working his own wizard's magic. By the time Nick was on his feet, he was a ward of the judge and enrolled in middle school.

Kindness like a warm, gentle tsunami washed over him, a strong and utterly irresistible tide that carried him forward.

Somehow Nick Ross, mongrel dog, had been folded into this loving family and he simply lapped it up.

Until his body betrayed him. He had just turned eighteen and had a man's body. One summer evening, Elle came in from the garden. Overnight, it seemed, Elle was turning into a woman. She'd been a beautiful little girl and was turning into a spectacular woman. Right then, on that summer day, with a sundress that outlined her small perfect breasts and tiny waist, shiny pale blond hair rippling down her back, she dazzled Nick. From being Elle his little shadow, she had suddenly morphed overnight into Elle a stunning girl on the verge of womanhood—and his body reacted instantly, instinctively.

He'd been having sex for a couple of years, but none of his bed partners had looked anything like Elle.

Before he could think, before he could shake himself from staring at her, he got a massive hard-on. Right then Elle was the most desirable sex partner any man could ever want and before he could will his dick down, before he could even be ashamed of himself, he caught the judge's hard gaze. Nick was wearing sweats and the judge could clearly see the effect Elle had on him. A boner big as a house.

And his life split into two once more.

No words were spoken. None were needed.

That afternoon, the judge called Nick into his office. The huge safe was open, empty. A stack of bills in plastic-wrapped bricks sat on the judge's desk.

The judge was sitting behind his desk, his gaze stern but not enraged. Nick understood completely. The judge had a beautiful and innocent young daughter to protect. Nick would have done the same. Actually, being more hot-blooded, if he had a daughter like Elle to protect, he would have beaten the mongrel to a pulp if he saw the guy get a woodie staring at her.

The judge shoved the bricks of hundred dollar bills across his desk and pointed to an open sports bag on the floor. Inside were some of Nick's clothes, clean and ironed, but most of the space was for the money. Nick stacked the bills inside, looked at the judge, nodded, and walked out of the study, out of the house, and out of that life.

In the bag, he later counted twenty-five thousand dollars in cash, obviously all the cash the judge had at hand. More than Nick deserved.

He'd headed south, to Fort Bragg.

Why did you leave us? Elle asked. He'd left because he was unworthy to stay in that house one more minute, but Nick didn't know how to say that.

He also didn't know how to watch Elle cry. It unmanned him, made his stomach swoop with distress. Worse than that first jump out of a plane.

"Why?" Elle asked again, and reached out for his hand.

There was no resisting her. He wouldn't have done anything five years ago. She'd been a young girl. His body had betrayed him. Luckily he'd known better than to give his body what it wanted.

But now? She wasn't a young girl, she was a woman and blindingly beautiful. She was no longer the pretty girl of privilege, she was a beautiful woman who had suffered. Overly thin, unsmiling, stunning.

Absolutely irresistible.

When her small hand closed around his, he felt an electric shock go up his arm and his body betrayed him all over again. A nuclear reaction he was totally unable to control.

He stood up so fast his chair fell over, pulled her into his arms so hard he could feel the breath leaving her body, but it didn't make any difference because she could breathe through his mouth, through him.

And oh, how she tasted. Like honey. All those years of fucking other women and he hadn't allowed himself once to wonder how Elle tasted. Not once, not while he was awake. His dreams—ah, that was something else. In his dreams he wondered . . . in his dreams he sometimes felt her presence, but this was nothing like his dreams; it was a million times better.

She was struggling against him, but he was so blasted with lust it took some time for him to catch on. She was fighting him, trying to get away . . .

Oh God.

It was his worst nightmare, worse than when the judge caught him staring at her and getting an erection. Because then it was just between him and the judge. Now he was getting the message from her, from Elle, and he was a hairsbreadth from coming while being intensely ashamed.

This was *Elle*.

He lifted his mouth, opened his arms, stepped back, feeling like shit.

"I'm so sorry, honey," he began when she threw herself back into his arms, mouth awkwardly searching for his.

Oh. He'd been holding her arms down and she wanted to hold on to him.

She'd been standing on tiptoe to kiss him and dropped back down onto her heels. Nick looked down at her, nearly blinded by the fact that she was so beautiful and . . . she was *Elle*.

Her hair had escaped the French braid and formed a soft pale blond halo around her head, just as it had all those years ago.

She lifted a hand from his shoulder to cup his jaw, then her fingers traced his face. From forehead to cheekbone, down over his jaw and neck. "Nick," she whispered.

He braced himself for more questions but she didn't say anything, just lifted herself back up to his mouth. He took the kiss over from there.

She tasted so fucking good. So good he was hard as steel. There was no way Elle could miss it either, plastered up against him, rolling her hips against him—groaning as she felt a woodie so hard it hurt.

Which was crazy, because he'd been getting laid on a regular basis at the training camp in Fort Benning. Everyone told him to get as much tail as humanly possible during training because there were no opportunities on ops, and even if there were, he'd be too strung out and exhausted to take advantage. So he'd been on a tear.

Right now, it felt like he'd never had sex before in his life.

Elle was like a cat in his arms, open to him in every way, rubbing sinuously against him. He put a hand under her ass, lifted her a little and groaned when he felt her heat against his cock. He was holding her so tightly he could feel her mound through the thin layer of her pants and panties. She was a furnace there, emanating heat like a sun. He shifted her a bit and felt the lips of her sex open over him. She swung her hips forward and rode him, driving him crazy. If they hadn't had clothes on, he'd be inside her.

Maybe he should dial this down a notch? It was crazy—they were practically fucking in the kitchen he'd eaten so many meals in, in this cold house on a cold January afternoon. And they'd reached this point in about a minute flat. Lips eating at each other, hips grinding together, one hand under her ass, the other cupping her small breast.

Their breathing filled the room, the sounds of their mouths catching, lifting, coming together again, echoing—and he was grinding against her, his mouth and his hips . . .

Down boy! he told himself. *Jesus, act like the gentleman you're not.* He was about ready to loosen his arms, put her back on the floor, step back, give them time to think this through when she said, "Take me to bed Nick."

And he was lost.

It was exactly like in her dreams. The phantasmagorical ones, the ones other people had. *Exactly.* Except of course for the circumstances. They were never in her kitchen and it was never so cold, but everything else—oh yes, everything else was the same.

No. Better.

Because she hadn't realized how *alive* this would make her feel. Hot and buzzing with life right down to her fingertips. These past years she knew she was alive because she ate and drank and cared for her father, but she hadn't felt alive, not in any way. Colors were muted, food tasted like cardboard, eating something she had to force herself to do. She had to remember to eat and drink and go to bed.

She had to work really hard to get up in the morning.

And now? Now she was one with the earth. Now she could leap mountains, breathe fire. Now she could fly.

It was her first, but she'd known instinctively how to kiss Nick. Her mouth had known. Her breasts had known to rub against his strong chest because they knew better than she did how good it would feel. And her hips all by themselves knew to move back and forth and feel him as he grew.

He grew erect because of *her!* He was excited by *her!* She turned him on—that was the greatest turn-on she could possibly imagine.

It was what she thought it would be—except better, and hotter, and more exciting.

Kissing him—no wonder she'd never tried to kiss anyone else. How could any man's kiss compare to Nick's? Every time his tongue touched hers, her skin prickled with electricity. Every time she felt that hard club rubbing against her stomach, the muscles in her thighs pulled and her vagina clenched, as if seeking to pull him inside her quickly.

It was fast, but it felt like she'd been preparing her entire life for this, for feeling Nick against her, soon inside her, for him to be a part of her in the truest possible sense.

The words came out of her mouth without any volition on her part, low and sexy, so unlike her voice it took her a second to recognize the fact that she was the one who'd spoken. It felt like it wasn't her vocal cords that spoke but her belly, the area between her thighs. The words simply welled up from deep inside of her.

"Take me to bed, Nick."

This was the way it was supposed to be. At her lowest point, after years of grayness, merely existing, watching her father's decline, at precisely this point Nick came back. As if the gods had sent him, as if the earth and the sun and the moon had sent him. An emissary from the forces of life to drag her back from the verge of death. She didn't question it anymore. He was here. He was supposed to be here. And they were supposed to be together.

Elle had never felt anything this strongly in her life. Nick was hers, she was his.

Waiting made no sense whatsoever. Not to mention the fact that her body was on fire.

Nick looked down at her and she memorized his features all over again. His face had been so clear to her that all she had to do was close her eyes and she could conjure him up. But this new Nick was even better than the old Nick. Not just handsome but fully a man. Face filled out more, a few lines around his eyes, jaw more prominent. She studied every feature eagerly, because this was the Nick that was going to be hers. This hard man with a hard face, looking at her with tenderness in his dark eyes.

"To bed," she whispered, just in case he hadn't heard her.

His lips curved. He was devastating when he smiled. Her heart simply turned over.

"Yes, ma'am," he said and bent his knees slightly to swing her up in his arms.

Oh yes. Yes-yes-yes.

She'd dreamed of this for *years*. For half her life, it seemed. Nick and her, heart to heart. Him carrying her wherever he wanted her to go. And she wanting to go wherever he took her.

Maybe this was a dream, after all, because it felt like Nick floated up the stairs with her in his arms instead of climbing them. His movements were smooth and effortless, not at all as if he were carrying an adult woman. Her arms were around his shoulders and she could feel the power in his muscles as he carried her—a deep strength, greater than that of any other man she'd ever seen. All the other men she'd ever seen in her life faded to background noise, pale simulacra of men.

Oh God. This was *Nick*!

In a sudden burst of joy, she leaned forward and kissed him, deeply, fully. Everything she needed to know about kissing, Nick had taught her in an instant. She'd simply followed his lead, and every second of it was pure joy. She opened his mouth with hers, tightening her arms around his neck, licking into his mouth, trembling. One hand moving through his short hair to hold his head tightly against her, though he wasn't making any signs of wanting to be pulled away.

Her back hit the wall as he swung her around and pressed into her, taking over the kiss. Possessing her, mouth eating at hers, tongue tasting her deeply.

It was overwhelming, she could hardly breathe, hardly think. Pleasure swamped her as she panted.

Suddenly Nick lifted his head and she could see the changes the kiss had made in him. His dark hair stood up and the half-smile had gone. His eyes were narrowed, serious; the skin over his cheekbones flushed. His mouth was dark red, swollen, wet. He looked dangerous.

Now he looked as if he was having trouble carrying her, but it wasn't that. He was aroused. His breath came in and out in short pants and she could feel him trembling.

She'd done that. *Oh yeah.* She'd smile at the thought, but it wasn't a moment for smiling. It was too big and too serious.

"You do that again and I'm having you right on the stairs," he said, voice low and dark.

For a second she didn't understand what he was saying and then she did. Her thighs clenched at the image his words conveyed, both of them naked and writhing on the stairs.

"Uncomfortable," she gasped. "Bed."

His head jerked in a nod. "Right."

And then he flew. In a second they were in her bedroom and he was setting her down on her feet, though her legs would barely hold her.

Elle held on to Nick as if she were holding on to a log in a raging river. He bent on one knee, as a knight does to his lady. She was immensely touched, reaching out to lay her hand on his head, fingers digging into his scalp. His hair was so dark the warmth came as a shock.

From this angle, looking down at him, he was foreshortened, like an art manual on perspective. He was all dark lashes, high cheekbones, sexy stubble. Insanely broad shoulders and huge hands, which were—*oh*—she smiled to herself, at her whimsy that he'd fallen to his knees before her. Nope. He was unlacing her boots and sliding them off, first the left then the right. She braced herself on his shoulders as he lifted her feet, fingers digging into the solid muscle. Even this was thrilling.

Boots off, Nick rose, so close to her she had to tilt her head back to look into his eyes. With the thrill of possession, she held his rib cage while he swiftly unbuttoned her thin sweater. With a swipe of his big hands, it fell off her shoulders. He reached around and unhooked her bra and she leaned into him, just to feel those heavenly muscles against her.

"Let go of me," he muttered as he worked her pants and panties down off her backside. *Let go of him?* Never! She'd just found him again, so why—

Oh.

Elle let go of Nick and the sweater and bra simply slid to the floor, as did pants and panties. He lifted her effortlessly and she kicked her clothes off and away. He held her around the waist with one strong arm and reached down to pull her wool socks off. There was a hole in one sock, but he wasn't looking at her feet—he was looking at her face.

And now she was naked. The first time she'd ever been naked with a man. There was no heat on; she should be cold, but there was no question of feeling cold with Nick looking at her like that.

"God." His jaw muscles clenched as he looked her up and down, slowly. "You're beautiful."

She didn't look down at herself; she knew what she looked like. "Am I, Nick?" she asked softly, watching his eyes.

"Oh, yeah." He nodded his head in a quick jerk. "Get under the covers. It's cold in here."

Standing so close to him was like standing next to a man-high radiator, but under the covers meant the *bed*, and getting in bed meant they were going to make love, so she obediently pulled back the bedclothes and slid in.

And, oh, he was stripping fast and he was just so beautiful, he seemed unreal. She couldn't even tell what clothes he had on, really. Whatever he was wearing was dark and it all drifted to the ground, and then he turned and she had a view of him, full on, so heartbreakingly beautiful she nearly closed her eyes.

He'd grown a few inches and had put on a lot of pounds, and it was all muscle. He was so finely built, exactly what she imagined a man should look like. A perfect man. Broad, thick shoulders, lean waist, long, strong legs. The vee of hard tendons running from belt level to the groin.

It looked like his penis weighed several pounds all on its own. It was fascinating, long and thick and upright, dark tan with a dark red tip shiny with his juice.

Even more fascinating, when her gaze drifted down from his face, over his chest, to fix on his penis, it swelled even larger. *Oh my God.* Just her *looking* at him aroused him!

It was huge, lying almost flat against his belly. She could see his heartbeat there.

This was pure magic, something so extraordinary she hadn't even thought to dream it. How on earth could she have known it was like this? How could she have guessed that it would feel like this?

Two kinds of heat—one slipping through her veins like a flow of warm honey and the other, almost painful, a prickly heat flashing over her skin. And her breasts and her sex—they felt like sources of heat themselves. Hot and swollen and, in the case of her sex, wet.

Her eyes drifted back up Nick's body and fixed on his face. He looked serious, almost grim, was narrow-eyed and unsmiling, a muscle twitching in his jaw. If a thousand books hadn't told her that a man's erection spelled pleasure, she would have thought he was in pain.

Well, she sure wasn't in pain. This was, hands down, the most glorious moment of her life. It was as if pain had been banished from the world and only pleasure existed.

She pulled her hand out from the covers, astonished that it didn't feel cold. Cold had been banished from the world too. She curled her fingers in the universal *come here* gesture.

Just in case he didn't get it, she said the words, "Come to me, Nick."

Her words seemed to release him from some invisible bonds. In a second, he was slipping on top of her under the covers and, oh, she nearly fainted from the sensory overload. He felt so damned *good*. It was all so new and so incredibly enticing. The heavy weight of him, the rough hairs sliding against her skin, the hard muscles. Elle didn't know what to do, but her body did, without any help from her.

Her body just naturally opened to him, in every way possible. It offered itself to him, naturally, as if it had been born to do this with Nick. Her mouth was already open when he bent, smiling, to kiss her, a heated, deep kiss that melted her bones. Her back arched, so her breasts were crushed against the cut pectorals of his chest, the rough chest hair tickling her breasts. Her legs slid apart, lifting slightly, the inside of her thighs hugging his lean hips. The wiry black hairs around his penis felt harsh in contrast to the velvety smoothness of his penis. She was open completely to him there, feeling empty, wanting him to fill—

And then there he was, sliding into her, so hot and hard, and there was pain, yes, but life was pain and joy, she knew that, but there he was, inside her, and this was Nick. Nick inside her and it felt so wonderful, tears gathered in her eyes.

And then the wonder stopped because Nick withdrew from her, pulled out, pulled away, and instead of there being heat and strength against her entire body, there was nothing but cold and emptiness.

It was shocking. All of a sudden she was freezing, bereft. Trembling.

He was sitting up, the noise of the sheets shifting loud in the silence of the room.

"N-Nick?"

Oh God. She'd done something wrong. Whatever she'd done it had been *wrong.* The wrong thing to do. She thought she'd been moving so naturally, but clearly she'd done something she shouldn't. Or hadn't done something she should.

And now he was angry. She chanced a peek at his face. Or . . . if not angry, then something. Whatever, he wasn't happy. That was clear.

Nick swung his long legs over the side of the bed and sat, hands gripping the edge of the mattress, head slightly bowed.

This was frightening. What kind of mistake could she have made to have him so cold and remote, all of a sudden? "Nick?" she whispered.

He was turned away, so all she saw was his broad back, the dips and hollows of the muscles, the strong neck. She had no idea what he was thinking, feeling. None at all.

What to say, what to do? She had no idea. She was suffering from whiplash, going from extreme pleasure to extreme distress in a few seconds. It was hard to keep up, even to know what she was feeling.

Cold and alone, that was what she was feeling.

Nick turned to her and she couldn't know what he was feeling either. The smile was gone and all that was left was an impersonal remoteness.

"You're a virgin." His voice was distant, flat. He gestured down at himself, at his erect penis that had some blood on it. Her blood. "Were a virgin."

Well . . . yes. Of course. It had never even occurred to her that Nick might think otherwise. Of course, he couldn't know that these past five years there'd been no question of dating anyone. She'd graduated from high school by a miracle and, frankly, by the indulgence of her teachers, who knew what was happening at home. A boyfriend had been out of the question.

But beyond that, well . . . no boy and no man had ever attracted her, in any way. She'd been waiting for him.

How pathetic was that? He wasn't happy she'd waited for him. He was . . . what? Annoyed? Impatient? Exasperated?

She made a noise in her throat because she had no idea what to say. Words weren't coming to her. Words had completely fled her mind.

His dark eyebrows came together. "Why the f—." He stopped himself visibly, Adam's apple bobbing as he swallowed the word. "Why didn't you tell me?"

Why the fuck didn't you tell me? What he really wanted to say hung there in the air.

Oh God. He was edging toward angry.

Elle sat up, clutching the sheets, bringing her knees up to her chest. Where before she delighted in feeling his bare skin against hers—such a mind-blowing pleasure—now she felt naked. Naked in every sense.

She opened her mouth but no words came out. Not even air. She coughed and tried again. "Sorry."

She should say something else, but nothing else would come out.

And then his face changed, almost melted. "Pixie," he said. All of a sudden that deep voice was liquid with tenderness.

Pixie. His pet word for her. Usually accompanied by a tug of her hair. Elle's muscles relaxed; she gasped in a big breath of air, let it out again on a sigh.

He was back. Nick was back.

The tip of his forefinger ran over her cheek. "You really should have told me. I'd have done it differently."

Elle blinked. There was another way? She shook her head sharply, quite beyond words.

Nick sighed and lifted his head as if he'd suddenly heard something. In a second, he was in her en suite bathroom, the one he'd teasingly dubbed Fairyland when she was a kid. It *was* a little over the top. Her father had redecorated when her mother died. Her bedroom was an ode to frills, and her bathroom—candy cane pink and cream, with roses hand painted in the washbasin—was embarrassing as an adult.

Her senses expanded back out as she watched Nick walk naked into her bathroom. For a few seconds she'd imploded on herself, a black hole of negative gravity threatening to suck her through it, totally incapable of thought and observation.

But watching him walk across a room, she was getting a little more relaxed, capable of feeling a little electric thrill of delight. His buttocks were firm as apples, round and tight and absolutely delicious.

So utterly different from her father's flaccid muscles as she tried to wash him in the last months of his life.

No. No thinking like that.

Her father was dead and wherever he was, he was truly in a better place. That was the past, this was now. A better now than she'd even dared to dream of just this morning. A magnificent now that held threads of hope for the future. A future with Nick in it, of watching Nick, listening to him, just being with him.

He hadn't bothered to close the bathroom door and she could see him, all rough male in her ridiculously prissy bathroom like a foreign species. He'd taken a washcloth from the pile by the sink and was washing himself. Washing his penis briskly, drying off, wetting another washcloth and walking back to her.

It was impossible to decide which was the better view. Maybe from the front with that rock-hard penis lying against his rock-hard belly.

Yes, definitely.

He stood by the bed for a moment, looking down at her. "Lie back down, honey," he said softly and she did, immediately, that "honey" ringing in her ears. When he looked at her like that, called her "honey," she'd have obeyed him if he'd said, "Put your hand in the thresher, honey."

He sat on the side of the bed, making it dip, and just looked at her, perusing her carefully, from her face, over her breasts, belly, down her legs to her feet, then back up again.

He sighed and she stiffened.

"God, you're beautiful," he said and smiled at her. "Now open your legs."

She smiled back and slid her legs apart.

He applied the washcloth between her legs and she winced to see it turn red and then pink. His eyes followed his hands as he cleaned her. His movements were impersonal, prosaic, and she was immensely turned on.

"I never even thought you might be a virgin," he said and stopped for a moment, almost indignant. "I mean, look at you! You're a beautiful young woman. What's the matter with the guys in this town? Are they blind? How the f— How the hell was I supposed to guess that you hadn't done this before?"

Elle rolled her eyes. "First of all, Nick, you can say *fuck*. If we're going to fuck, you can say fuck."

He stopped and his eyes widened in shock. His mouth fell open. She laughed. It took a lot to shock Nick. Or maybe not, if hearing her say "fuck" made his jaw drop.

"Fuck." He breathed, and she laughed again, then he shook his head. "Okay, my vocabulary aside, please tell me how someone who looks like you has never—" He stopped instinctively. "Has never—" He couldn't complete the sentence.

"Fucked," she offered.

"Okay." He sighed. "So how can someone who looks like you never have fucked."

Never kissed either. She was really glad he hadn't figured that one out.

She gave him the easy version. "Daddy started getting really sick in my sophomore year. It had been sort of funny before. Losing the keys, forgetting where he put his glasses even though they were on top of his head. Then he said he took early retirement. I only found out later that he was forced into it. There was no way he could sit on a bench. But then it got worse, very fast. One night the police knocked on the door at three in the morning, holding Daddy between them. He'd wandered off. They found him in his bathrobe on State Street and brought him home. They were really nice. They were a little less nice the tenth time that happened. And downright angry the thirtieth. It—It's a terrible disease, devastating. I had my hands full. I was young, but it was as if I had four small kids. There isn't a boy on earth who'd put up with that, and no one did."

The hard version—she was never even remotely tempted by anyone but Nick. He filled her head and her heart and no one came even close. Certainly not the callow, shallow boys in high school. And then they all left for college and she didn't even have a chance to turn dates down.

"Assholes," Nick said prosaically and startled a laugh out of her.

"Yeah." Yes, they were assholes. It was liberating to think of it that way.

"So." He'd finished cleaning her up and was simply looking at her, washcloth in hand. "Here we are."

His voice, his face were neutral.

Well, she wasn't neutral. Not a bit. "Yes, here we are. I'm naked and you're naked and we've already done it—sort of—so what are you waiting for?"

He shook his head, smiling. "Pixie," he said, his deep voice low, "what am I going to do with you?"

"If I have to tell you, Nick Ross, then there's no hope for you at all. I would think you'd know exactly what to do, since clearly I don't. You do know what to do. Don't you?"

The smile deepened, and his famous dimple, the one she'd teased him so much about, appeared. "Yeah, I guess I do. Except—"

Her eyes widened. "Except?" *Oh God, what now?*

"Except I've never done it with a virgin before."

Oh no. Elle rolled her eyes. "Actually, I'm not a virgin anymore, so that isn't a problem."

"No? You think it isn't a problem?" He touched her, between her legs, eased his index finger inside her opening. She wasn't expecting it. It hurt, just a little, and she winced.

"See?" His eyes bored into hers.

"It's fine." She shook her head without looking away from him.

Nick's hand smoothed back down over her thigh, the skin of his fingers rough. She shivered and all of a sudden the cast of his face changed completely. His eyes sharpened, became hot, the skin tightened over his cheekbones. He looked slightly older, utterly male. Even if he weren't sitting naked in front of her fully erect, she'd have known he was aroused.

"Let's take this slowly," he whispered, his gaze never leaving hers, cupping one big hand around her thigh and separating her legs even further.

"Let's," she whispered back. She was so completely open to him, everything she was, laid bare. Not just physically. She could actually feel her heart opening to him, like a flower unfolding instead of a chunk of muscle. To deal with her father, she'd had to close her heart up like a bank vault otherwise it would have been unbearable. She hadn't allowed herself to feel anything at all for so long.

And now she *felt*. Everything. Inside and out. She felt the lines of attraction between her and Nick, strong, almost visible. She was connected to him. What he wanted, she wanted. He could do with her whatever he wished.

And her body was open too. In the few yoga classes she'd taken way back when, before Daddy got sick, the instructor had told them that there was an invisible line running through the center of the body. She was open on either side, fully available to him. Her shin was resting against him, against the hard muscles of his side. She rubbed her leg against him, just a little. It wasn't just the female thrill of feeling a hard male, it was that Nick was so fully alive. Just touching him made her feel fully alive, too, vital and warm and strong.

And she realized by comparison that she'd felt already dead and buried for so long.

As long as Nick was with her, as long as she could touch him, she was alive too.

His rough finger began circling around her, up and down, touching her lightly, and where he touched her, the skin sparked to life. Gently, lightly, his finger opened her, moved slightly inside.

She sighed, and felt goose pimples along her arm.

"You like that?" Nick murmured, and she felt his words resonate in her diaphragm, ripple along her skin.

She was beyond words. She nodded jerkily.

"And this?" His finger penetrated deeper, still circling, as if to widen her up.

And he was. Oh God. He was opening her up so he could put his penis back inside her. The image, the very thought, made every single muscle clench in anticipation, including *down there*.

Nick's eyes narrowed even further. "Whatever you just thought, think it again. Because you just got wetter."

Yes, of course. Her body was preparing itself for him, becoming liquid. Not just her vagina. Elle felt like everything else was opening up, softening, becoming liquid. She felt like she could float away on some warm rocking sea.

She was slick now, she could feel it and she could hear it. It could have been embarrassing hearing the sounds her vagina made as he moved his finger in her, but she wasn't embarrassed. She was miles away from embarrassment, beyond even thinking of it. The pleasure swamped any trace of that from her head.

His finger was moving in and out and not just around, swirling in her, opening her up. And then his thumb moved and caressed another part of her, and it was as if he'd plugged her into something.

"Oh!" she stiffened. "What was that? Do it again!"

"Clitoris," he muttered, and did it again.

For a second, the word didn't penetrate her heated head, and then she understood. What romance novels called the pearl of desire. Nubbin of pleasure. It wasn't a pearl or a nubbin it was a *button*. Press it and you switch a woman on.

She'd washed herself a million times, right over that specific spot, and nothing like that had ever happened.

Nick's finger and thumb were working their magic, and he bent to her. She smiled, instinctively opening her mouth, but it wasn't her mouth he wanted. He bent lower and grazed his teeth along her breast. Lightly. Then he bit her and she jumped.

He lifted his head, smiling. "Yeah, that worked."

Elle ran her hands through his hair. "It all works, Nick. Everything you do to me. It all works."

"Yeah?" He bent to her again. "Let's see." He licked her nipple, long sensuous strokes, then started sucking and each pull of his mouth went right to her groin in a line so straight it could have come out of a geometry class. Exactly in tune with the tugs of his mouth. He suckled lazily for what felt like hours, certainly beyond any notion of time she had. The part of her head that marked time simply quit. *Poof.* Gone. Now she was on Nick time.

Each time he pulled at her breast, her vagina pulled at his finger, in sync, like a little ballet her body was doing. His thumb was stroking her clitoris, but that was off the beat, out of tune, a quite dissonant heat.

Nick took her nipple between his teeth, very gently, and pulled. It was just a tiny bite of pain, nothing really, but it was that tiny sting that pushed her into complete overload. Time stopped, suspended, then rushed back in as her body convulsed, long hard pulls of her vagina muscles and belly and thigh muscles, her entire body pulling toward the center of her, where Nick had his hand.

Her back arched, her toes curled, everything spiraled inward then . . . exploded.

She gave a great cry as her body convulsed, pulsing in time with her heartbeat, and in one of those pulses Nick slid on top of her again and into her again and just as the pulses were dying down, they started again, only more intense this time, on the razor's edge of pain.

He was moving in and out of her slowly, in time with the beats of her body. She was wrapped around him, arms, legs, and heart.

When her body subsided, finally, her hands fell to her sides, palms up. Her legs loosened their hold on his hips and her knees fell apart. She opened her eyes and stared at the ceiling, completely and utterly sated, thinking of absolutely nothing and feeling alive in every single cell of her body.

Nick placed his mouth close to her ear and whispered, "Uh-uh." She blinked. *Uh-uh? No?*

He bit her lobe and something sparkled again, right under her skin, like a dying engine fizzing to life for one last second, sparks flying.

"It doesn't work like that." His lips were caressing her jaw and she could feel him smile against her skin.

"It doesn't?"

"Nope." He settled on her more heavily, big hands smoothing down the backs of her thighs. Then, surprisingly, he lifted them so her knees nearly touched her chest. "You don't get to stop, not yet." With her legs so high, she was completely open to him. He tightened his buttocks and slipped deeper inside her, and, oh God, the tingling and the *heat*. . .

Nick had been rocking inside her, short, gentle thrusts, but soon he was moving strongly, long, deep thrusts with the full power of his muscles behind them, so strong she was surprised he wasn't hurting her, but he wasn't. Not in any way. His body took over hers; there was no other way to describe it. She moved to his rhythm, to his beat, completely insensible to anything outside the bounds of her skin and his. He'd laid his head next to hers, his mouth close to her ear, and she could hear his breath soughing in and out, gasping, as if running a four-minute mile. He was slamming into her now, making her bed creak, then making the headboard beat against the wall in a fast and faster rhythm, moving so hard and fast inside her it was a miracle she wasn't catching fire down there from the friction and then, oh my God, she did catch fire, everything in her simply went up in flames.

It wasn't like the previous orgasm, which had been pleasant. Fun, even. This was earth shattering, some outside force taking over her body, as unstoppable as a freight train as she convulsed, over and over again, fingers digging deeply into his heavy shoulder muscles because it felt as if clinging to him was the only way not to shatter into a thousand pieces.

With a shout, muffled by the pillow, Nick's movements became frenetic, no longer those heavy measured thrusts, but out of control writhing inside her, as if he were hammering his way to her heart with his penis.

She felt him swell, and with another shout he started coming. She'd never felt this before, had barely read about it before, but it was unmistakable. He was jetting semen into her until she was wet, they were both wet, to the groin.

Finally, with a groan, Nick collapsed onto her and she realized that he hadn't been putting all his weight on her. Now he was, and he was heavy as a horse. She could feel her ribs bending slightly with the weight of him and wheezed.

Nick was still breathing heavily but at the sound of her wheezing, he planted two large hands by the side of her head and prepared to lift himself off her.

No!

Elle grasped him tightly around his back and twined her legs around him, the body movements as clear as words. *Don't go.*

With a groan, Nick subsided and she made sure she wheezed quietly.

Because she loved this. Everything about it.

Nick's immensely heavy weight grounding her after she'd felt as if she'd fly apart into a million pieces. They were plastered together all along their fronts because he'd sweated heavily and she supposed she had too. It was hard to tell.

They smelled, mainly of Nick. It was an intense, pungent earthy scent she'd never experienced before—human sex—but recognized instantly. Another example of her body knowing things, instinctively, that she didn't. Her entire groin area was wet with what was causing that smell—his semen, her juices. Mixing together in a unique mix.

He was still hard inside her, which flummoxed her a little. He'd had an orgasm, hadn't he? Surely he had. And men—what was the word the *Merck Manual* used? Detumesced, that was it. Surely after an orgasm a man detumesced, but there Nick was, still hot and hard and huge inside her.

Another of those life mysteries she wasn't going to penetrate right at the moment. Certainly not while Nick was still penetrating *her*.

She snickered.

Nick stirred. "Finding this funny, are we?" She turned her head and saw him lazily smiling at her, sated, and so sexy her heart turned over in her chest.

"Very. Or maybe not funny so much as . . ." She felt her eyes drift up and to the right in contemplation.

"As? This better be good."

Her smile widened. "Interesting."

Nick's black eyebrows rose. "Interesting? That's all you have to say?"

He was looking mock-ferocious and . . . and *hot*. When she used to have girlfriends, she'd hear them say that about a boy and didn't really understand it, but now she did. Oh man, did she understand it.

Nick was the epitome of hot. And the epitome of cool. Both, at the same time, with hot prevailing right now. Hot like a flame, a source of immense attraction and life. His skin was hot under her palms, against her front, against the skin of her thighs. And he was hot in that other sense too. So attractive you wanted to jump him. Tough, fully male, exuding pheromones by the ton.

No wonder women fell for him so hard.

A little bit of her joy dissipated as she remembered the many Dreams she'd had about him with other women. How many women she'd seen him with. Fucking. That was the operative word, of course. It had been clear that it was a physical release because in her Dreams, he never lingered. He got up from the bed immediately after climaxing and she'd seen dozens of women, startled, legs still splayed from the sex, looking at the ceiling and wondering what had happened while in another room Nick was already showering.

Of course she had no idea if her Dreams, those special ones that were so intense they felt like life experiences, were real or if she was crazy. How could she know? Her life became so isolated there was no one to ask. No confidante, only her dementing father.

Nick was frowning now, running a rough thumb between her eyebrows. "Whatever you're thinking, stop it right this minute."

Her face cleared. She'd forgotten how well Nick knew her. It had been so wonderful, being *known* by him. Understood and, well, loved.

No one had known her like that since he'd left. No one. It had been like being encased in a clear bubble. She was in the bubble and the entire world was outside it.

Maybe later she could tell Nick about her Dreams. But then of course she'd have to say that she'd seen him countless times with other women, and that was creepy.

She plastered a smile on her face. "Sorry, just thinking."

"Well, stop that. You think too much. You always thought too much."

She took in his face. When he smiled, the boy in him, the boy she'd known, came through. But when he was frowning, he was all man. Wildly attractive.

Down below, her vagina contracted around him and his eyes widened.

"Distract me," she whispered.

"Oh yeah." The voice was a low mutter and he bent to her. Just as his mouth touched hers, the downstairs bell sounded. Loud. Three ascending notes like the peal of church bells.

Startled, Elle looked to the side, to her alarm clock. *Seven.* Something was supposed to happen at seven, wasn't it? Her head was sluggish, no connections possible. It was seven and at seven . . .

"The food." Nick groaned and rolled out of bed. "I'll get it."

In an amazingly short time, he was dressed, had combed his hair with his hand, and looked entirely normal, except for a slight flush. And, well, the scent of sex that still clung to him. But then

Elle had an extraordinarily strong sense of smell. Not everyone would pick up the smell that seemed so strong to her.

"Okay," she said, but he was already walking out the door.

He had to do this. There was no way she could get dressed and walk down the stairs in less than half an hour. Her legs felt like mush. She was uncoordinated, slightly punch-drunk.

And even if the delivery boy could wait half an hour for her to get her act together, she would scream from every pore of her body—*I just had wild monkey sex!* She knew of no way she could hide it. Not to mention she'd be helplessly grinning like a loon.

So let him take care of it.

Male voices downstairs, the door closing. The clatter of kitchen sounds.

Elle lay there listening, every muscle lax. Someone else was doing something in her house. Someone else was doing things. Company and warm food were waiting for her downstairs and it seemed like such a miracle, something so heartening after long years of silence in her home, and feeling alone every second of every day.

A tear welled and slipped down her cheek, and she dashed it away. This wasn't a moment for tears, it was a moment for smiles.

A deep breath and she threw back the covers, heading for the bathroom on shaky legs, completely, utterly happy.

Chapter 3

Nick paid for the delivery. *Jesus*. His heart had clenched when Elle told Jenny to put it on her credit card. If she had any money on her card, he'd eat his shorts. Elle had no money at all.

The judge's illness had pared them down to the bone. The happy, luxurious home he'd known was no more. Now it was this cold, empty shell. Most of the furniture and artwork gone. The once-glorious gardens abandoned and full of weeds.

And Elle—*Christ*. Thin, drawn, dressed in rags.

Still amazingly beautiful.

He remembered her as a beautiful girl who was heading into glorious womanhood. When he left, he knew that was her trajectory. She didn't worry him at all. Pampered daughter of a wealthy, well-respected man, smart as hell, good in school, gorgeous. He was leaving, but she was moving straight into the best possible life.

Nothing had prepared him for the reality—poor, abandoned. But still stunning. If anything, she was more appealing now. The Elle he knew was happy in the way of people whose lives had shown them nothing but the best of the world. Her looks were spectacular, but on top of that had been all the trappings of coming from a wealthy family—healthy diet, lots of tennis, expensive orthodontics, not a care in the world. That Elle had been a magnet.

But this Elle—this tragic waif—she'd grabbed his heart.

His nuts, too, by the look of it.

Because who could resist this girl—no, this woman—whose gaze was deep with the knowledge of pain and suffering. The fall of the family was all around them, but Elle hadn't complained once about what had happened. It was clear that she'd put her life on hold to look after the judge, but not once had she put it that way. An A-student all the way, she wasn't even in college. From the looks of their finances, college was probably out of the question.

She hadn't had anything resembling a life, let alone the life she should have had.

She'd been a virgin. That had surprised him more than anything, though if he'd stopped to think about it, there wasn't any space in her life for play.

He should have stopped when he found out he was her first. Christ, she deserved better than a mongrel dog on his way out the door. What was the matter with him? He'd long ago learned to control his dick, why hadn't he just now?

Well, there was the fact that she'd looked like some kind of movie star on the bed, long, pale blond hair around her head like a halo but not an angel. Not with that look in her gorgeous light blue eyes, not with her arms up to hold him, not with her legs apart in invitation, puffy pink folds of her sex peeping through the ash brown hair of her mound.

That Elle was pure temptation, impossible to resist. He was no hero. Who was he to turn something like that down?

This Elle was completely different from the girl who visited his dreams. Time and again, he'd had the sense of her being there, with him. Usually at night. More times than he cared to think about while he was fucking.

He'd be with a woman, lost in the sex, and there she was. In his head.

He'd had to learn how to get her out of there, like picking a burr out of your coat. "Nick?" He whirled, saw her in the doorway, and his heart nearly stopped.

Jesus, this double vision he had. The lovely, laughing girl of his memory and this—the stunning woman who'd known tragedy. She'd put on blue sweats—clearly old but clean and ironed. Probably dark blue once, now faded to a streaky light blue that matched her eyes.

Nick manfully kept his gaze locked on her face, but he was pretty sure she wasn't wearing a bra. The feel of her under his hands, the taste of her in his mouth—the memory swamped him.

She walked in barefoot—and fuck him if her feet weren't gorgeous too. Slim, high-arched, with very pretty toes. He nearly sighed because he was fully erect again. He had to feed her before he did anything else. He had to keep his mind on that, not on his dick.

Shit.

Everyone in the Rangers and the guys he'd talked to in Delta knew him as serious and utterly focused. No one would believe he couldn't control himself, keep his dick down. But it was already up, very, very happy to see her. Elle smiled. "Did Jenny have you sign? I'll call her later with my credit card info."

Well, *that* made him angry. It was better being mad at her than unable to resist her. Easier.

"Fuck that," he said, his voice harsher than he wanted. "Did you think I'd let you pay for this meal?" He looked out over the huge dinner table. She hadn't managed to sell the table, obviously. Not too many people nowadays needed tables that could fit dinner parties of eighteen. The food filled half of it. Jenny had gone overboard and the bill Nick had paid wouldn't cover half of it. Jenny's way of helping Elle while salvaging her pride.

Elle's head tilted to the side, pale blond hair covering one shoulder. She frowned. "Why are you mad? Why shouldn't I pay for it?"

"Because you don't have any fucking money, is why!" He had trouble keeping his voice down, keeping his emotions in check. "I'm not going to have you pay for my fucking meal!"

Elle just watched him, head still tilted, as if he were some kind of scientific specimen. Her expression didn't change at his vehemence. She lifted her hands, patted the air, calming down the lunatic.

"Okay, okay. You probably don't believe this, but I actually have the money to cover the meal, but I'll accept your gift. Thank you."

Well, hell. He was all ready to fight it, fight *her*, dissipate some of this tension. And then she turned reasonable on him.

Fuck.

He drew in a deep breath. Grabbed for some control. "The food is still warm. We should set the table and eat. Unless you want to just eat out of the containers?"

"No. We'll eat like normal human beings." Elle smiled and walked to a huge glass-fronted cabinet, which he remembered from when he lived here. They hadn't sold that either. It was enormous and elaborate and he imagined it wouldn't fit the life of modern families. It was the kind of piece of furniture people had a century ago when families were huge. The breakfront was still filled with the plates he remembered—fine bone china with a rose pattern and gilt edges. The service was probably not easily salable either—there were hundreds of pieces.

Elle set the table as the maid used to—with a huge platter serving as a mat, plate, bowl, tons of forks and knives and spoons. Two glasses each. The wine her friend sent went on a silver wine-bottle thingy.

She'd grown up with good wines. The judge had enjoyed his wine and had a famous wine cellar. That would be gone, he imagined.

Elle sighed as she sat down. Nick poured a finger of wine in her crystal glass and some in his. He swirled and smelled and tasted. The judge had taught him about wine and this one was superb.

"Merlot. French. 2011, which was a very good year." Elle smiled happily at him as she put down the glass and attacked the food. "Bon appétit."

The family equivalent of grace. Elle's mother had been half French.

"Bon appétit." Nick smiled back, his earlier edginess and bad temper gone. It was absolutely impossible not to smile at Elle. From the pale, lost waif he'd seen at the cemetery, she'd changed into a woman with flushed cheeks and sparkling eyes.

That was him. It made him uneasy to realize that he was the one who'd made her happy. Good sex did that, he knew. And though it was her first time, she seemed to have enjoyed it. It was physiological. Sex raised blood pressure, got the circulation moving. If nothing else it was a great physical and psychological release.

Sex was good for you, made you smile.

So that was it. That was all it was. Decent sex on a sad day for her. For him, too. The judge had saved his life. He'd been a good man and now he was dead.

Elle tackled the food like she'd been starving. Nick shifted uneasily in his seat. Had she been starving? The idea made his skin prickle with horror. Elle not having enough to *eat*. The very idea was awful. She said she had the money to pay for this meal, but what if that wasn't true? He was going to prowl around until he found her bank account and find out what the situation was.

He'd also find out her bank account number. He had thirty thousand saved up. He had no expenses in the military. He was Special Ops and they were either on a mission or on a training cycle and were fed and lodged. He'd just applied for Delta, a year or two early. If he made Delta his pay would go up. What was he going to do with the money? He didn't want to buy a house, didn't even want to buy a car.

The instant he got back on base he was going to transfer everything he had into her account.

"Oh man," Elle moaned, twirling her fork. "Carbonara. My favorite. Carbs and cream and cheese and bacon. Bliss."

A huge forkful disappeared into her mouth.

Nick frowned, a horrible thought occurring to him. "You weren't *dieting* were you?" She was way too thin. Christ, if she'd reduced herself to this willingly . . .

"No, Nick." Elle shook her head, swallowed, twirled another strand of creamy spaghetti around her fork. "I, um, lost weight because looking after Daddy was hard and I sometimes forgot to eat. I really look forward to putting the weight back on."

He grunted. "Good." And attacked the food himself, appeased. The first bite had him narrowing his eyes.

"Fabulous stuff, eh?" She was grinning at him. "And Jenny sent enough for a platoon. I'll bet you don't eat like this in the military."

"Absolutely not." Christ no. His last op, a three-week training cycle in the Everglades, had been wall-to-wall gummy MREs, where the chicken couldn't be distinguished from the pork or the beef. He'd shat hard little rubbery pellets for the duration. He'd only been back two days when he'd . . . what? Heard her call? Dreamed of her? Whatever, he'd had an irresistible urge to check *Lawrenceonline* and had immediately found the judge's obituary. "When they feed us hot meals, it's pretty basic. Steak and chicken and pork and potatoes. And watery salad no one eats."

"Speaking of chicken . . ." Elle poked her pretty nose in another container and breathed in deeply. "Hmmm. Roast rosemary chicken." She looked up at him. "White meat or dark?"

Your meat. The words were right there on his lips, as a vision blossomed in his head of him eating *her.* Head between her legs, lapping and nibbling.

Oh, ouch. His hard on just got harder.

Elle stopped, fork in the air, obviously tuned into the sudden change of atmosphere. Nick could swear that the molecules had suddenly become charged.

Dial it down, dickhead.

Elle was probably having her first decent meal in weeks, maybe months. She was smiling and there was color in her face. He was not going to ruin that for her because he had a sudden surge of hormones that were shaking his body.

Because, fuck, that's what was happening.

If any of his Ranger teammates realized that he shook when he was next to this girl—now a woman—they'd shit their pants, because a good part of Ranger shooting training was using live bullets, sometimes at very close range.

Nick was known as one of the coolest shooters, almost mechanical in his ability to put the bullet where he wanted it to go, and the way you did that was to be in control of your body.

Not sitting at a table, afraid to get up because you'd hobble with the blue steeler in your pants. *Not* putting down your fork because your hand was shaking so much it fucking clattered against the plate. *Not* being unable to look away from a woman's face.

Any of his teammates seeing him now would report him to the XO.

"Nick, aren't you eating?" she asked. She'd demolished the carbonara and set the bowl aside, and was now demolishing an entire chicken breast with jacket potato. A salad of cherry tomatoes and feta cheese was in a crystal bowl next to her. She'd stopped eating to look at him quizzically. "It's really good stuff."

He pasted a smile on his face, kicking himself for being an asshole. Way to go, douche bag, keeping Elle from her food because you can't keep it in your pants.

"Great stuff," he agreed, pointing with his fork at her. "Now eat."

"Yessir," she said, rolling her eyes, digging in.

Damn straight.

God, it was good to see her, rosy and smiling, so different from the ice white young woman at the cemetery who'd looked as if a truck had run over her. And, well, it was really good to see her, period.

Had he been planning on staying away forever? As the years rolled by, maybe his subconscious had been starting to think of coming back. Briefly. Just a day. He'd stayed away out of respect for the judge, but she was nearly twenty. It's just that he'd been so goddamned busy. To his surprise, he'd taken to soldiering as if born to it. He'd been singled out for Ranger almost right from the start and had barely been folded into the unit when he'd been called in to ask if he wanted to apply to Delta.

Fucking A he wanted to try out for Delta. The shooters. Of all the special forces, Deltas were shooters first and foremost and that was Nick. To his surprise, he'd also had a knack for languages and he'd been seconded to cross-train with France's GIGN and Germany's GSG-9.

He'd been kept busy thirty-four hours a day, totally focused on the job. No room for romance with other women, either. Sex, yeah. There were always women in the bars around the bases, but he didn't have time for anything other than sex. Two fucks in a row was the norm. Three on occasion. Four was a borderline relationship and that was off the cards.

It turned out he didn't have to deal with the judge, after all, and for that he was ashamed of himself. Men didn't wimp out. He'd had no idea the judge had been so sick.

Coming home. When he ran through the scenarios in his head, there'd been various outcomes. The judge kicking him out on his ass, just like last time, only without the money. The judge welcoming him back because, after all, Elle was an adult. The judge inviting him in for coffee, letting him know Elle was studying nuclear physics at Harvard or MIT and didn't have time for a lowlife like him. The judge saying someone had snapped Elle up and she was married with a kid.

That one hurt.

The truth was the one thing he hadn't planned on—Elle still here and the judge clocking out mentally before he did physically.

"Stop thinking that, Nick. Right now." Elle's voice was low, very serious.

Nick's fork clattered to the plate. What the fuck? "Are you a mind reader?"

Jesus. Maybe all those weird dreams he'd had of her were real. Maybe Elle could fuck with his head.

"You wouldn't let me think sad thoughts, so this is payback. And no, I'm not a mind reader. Don't worry about that." She leaned forward on her elbows, tucking a strand of pale hair behind one small ear. "You don't have to be a mind reader to know that you were thinking dark thoughts. Sad thoughts. This house has known nothing but sadness for years now. Sadness and darkness and despair. Daddy was frightened to death when they diagnosed him with Alzheimer's because he knew exactly what was coming, both for him and for me—and it took all my energy, every ounce of it, to keep him cheerful for as long as there was a person inside him that could feel cheer. Daddy left a long time ago. I did my mourning a long time ago. I've had about as much sadness as a person can bear and I don't want long sad faces around me. Now—" She slapped the surface of the table and made the water glass slosh over. "Smile, damn it!"

Nick was so startled he did smile. Showing all his teeth, too.

She smiled back at him, pleased with herself. "That's right, Nick. I knew you could do it."

Oh God, look at her, he thought. Just like his nickname for her when she was a child. *Pixie.* A beautiful little pixie, slightly careworn, perched on the edge of her chair, surrounded by a cloud of blond hair, pale eyes like shards of summer sky, smiling at him.

Irresistible. And he didn't have to resist, did he? Because though by God she'd had a worse time of it than he had these past five years, his life hadn't been all shits and giggles either.

He'd chosen the hardest military training possible, probably the hardest on earth. These past years had been day after day of grueling physical and intellectual training, the only breaks actual field ops, getting shot at, which was marginally better than the rest of it. Lying in swamps in Indonesia for days waiting for a shot at the man who'd planted the Indianapolis bomb. Indonesia had 450 venomous insect species and he'd been bitten by every single one. The bare, arid plains of Tibet, helping train local fighters for the successful coup and breakaway from China. Four months spent fifteen thousand feet up on the Pakistani side of the Himalayas with only goats and four other Rangers for company, fires forbidden, trying to contain the situation, then scrambling to get out when Pakistan blew up.

No, like his little Pixie, he felt it was smiling time. Pleasure time. God knows they both deserved it.

Sex. They both deserved it. The best sex he'd ever had, and the best sex she'd ever had too, by definition. They should have some more of it.

Right now.

Elle straightened in her chair and watched warily as he moved toward her. His very best stealth stalk, trademark Ranger move. "Nick?"

"Elle." The word came up out of his guts, from the very core of him. And he had no further words in him right now, none.

"Nick, what are you do—" He lifted her up out of her chair by her elbows and as soon as she was on her feet, he pulled her top up over her head and tossed it to the ground. "Oh." The one word barely had any breath behind it because what he was doing and what he was going to do was real clear.

If his face didn't tell her, his blue steeler did.

It was a really good thing Elle seemed to be okay with this, because though Nick had self-control up the wazoo—he was nothing *but* self-control—right now control was a pretty shaky thing.

But she seemed okay with him pulling her pants down, kicking them away, and laying her down on a clean bit of surface of that mile-long table that he cleared with his arm. More than okay, actually. He'd barely touched her except to strip her and lay her out like a sacrifice in some weird religion and she was already with him. The left pale breast quivered with her heartbeat. She was breathing heavily, already panting, watching him out of half-closed eyes.

Nick stepped between her legs, reaching out to separate them, but she beat him to it, sliding her legs apart as fast as any soldier responding to a shouted command. He didn't have to shout it, he didn't even have to whisper it. She knew what he wanted.

With one hand, Nick unzipped himself, happy he was in the habit of going commando. He placed one hand by her side on the table and grabbed his cock with the other.

His cock did not like the feel of his hand. It knew precisely where it wanted to be and it wasn't in Nick's fist, which is where it mainly was when he was in the boonies training or on missions. His fist just wouldn't cut it when Elle's pretty little sex was right there, open and glistening, just waiting for him.

He ran an experimental finger down her, just to test the waters and an alarm bell rang in his head, loud enough to catch his attention even when there wasn't much blood left in his head to think with.

She was wet, but not wet enough. Certainly not wet enough for him to slam into her as he had just been about to do.

Okay.

There was an app for that.

He dropped to one knee, leaned forward, heady from the scent of her and placed his mouth between her legs. He didn't kiss her, not yet. He just breathed her in. She smelled absolutely wonderful, of some scented soap with high notes of sex.

He'd once read an article in a magazine in the waiting room of the base dentist. Together with *Field & Stream*, the daily *Stars and Stripes* and *Guns Magazine*, there was also a copy of *Vogue*. The wait was long, and after reading the other stuff cover to cover, he finally started thumbing his way through *Vogue*. There was an article on "noses," expert perfumers who were basically human bloodhounds. He was interested because they'd just had a training session on how smells could give you away in an ambush situation. Scent Management it had been called, and they were taught not to use soap or mouthwash or shampoo forty-eight hours before deploying.

So he'd read the article on how noses could distinguish a thousand scents.

Elle's sex had a smell that was unique, and it went straight to his cock.

She wasn't ready yet, but soon.

He licked her and added taste. *Oh God.* She tasted delicious.

She sighed heavily and he would have smiled if he hadn't been so intent on licking her, tasting her.

He kissed the lips of her sex exactly as if they were her mouth, opening them with his mouth, licking deep inside her. With each stroke of his tongue she gasped, and when he felt her clench around his mouth, he stood up and gazed at her.

Oh, yeah.

Her cheeks were deep pink, as were her hard little nipples. Her mouth looked swollen though he hadn't kissed it yet.

He would.

She looked wanton, spread out on the dark wood of the dining table, pale and slender and so mouthwateringly delectable. He stood between her wide open legs, enjoying the sight of her pretty little cunt, pink and juicy. He ran an experimental finger around her and hummed a little. *Mmm.*

Yeah. She was ready.

Nick leaned down, placing one hand on the table next to Elle's pale breast and the other holding her hip. He didn't need to hold his cock for entry, it knew how to get where it wanted to go all on its own.

He slid into her slowly, the feeling so exquisite he closed his eyes until he was fully embedded inside her.

They both sighed.

His eyes snapped open. It would have been a funny moment but he was beyond laughter, beyond even smiling. He'd fucked way too many times to count, but right now this was the most erotic scene he'd ever set eyes on. Elle's pale, soft skin contrasting with his rough, dark skin, her legs open to him, her pink sex clenched around his cock.

Elle's eyes were half closed, only a shimmering pale blue showing. She was panting slightly, chest rising and falling.

Her arm reached out and wrapped itself around the arm he'd planted next to her, as if to brace herself. She seemed to sense the coming storm. "Nick," she whispered. Her hand tightened on his arm.

It set him off.

Not holding himself inside her for a moment or two, letting her get used to him. Not a gentle in and out, testing her readiness. Nope.

A storm.

His hips slammed against hers with the full strength of his body. He had to hold tightly to her hip or she would have slid to the other side of the table. The room was filled with the sound of his heavy breathing and flesh slapping against flesh and he was mesmerized by the sight of his cock moving in and out of her, fast and hard.

He couldn't stop. There was no mechanism in him that would allow him to stop or even slow down. He was overtaken by some power outside himself that wouldn't—couldn't—rest until he'd reached inside her just as far as he could go, over and over again. And she was with him every step of the way, pale eyes on his, mouth open, bringing in air in great gulps, clinging to his arm, digging her short nails into his skin as hard as she could, fingertips turning white. He didn't feel it—he was beyond feeling anything but the enormous heat centered around his hips as he moved in her as strongly as he could.

Elle's head moved back, exposing that long, white throat—and God how he wished he were a vampire because he'd just sink his fangs into her—and she moaned, then cried out. Her stomach muscles pulled as she clenched around him so hard he felt her cunt like a soft little vise, closing around him, letting go, closing . . .

The heat and the pressure were too much. He leaned forward, head hanging low, not even watching her anymore because everything in him was concentrated on where he was slamming into her, moving as deeply as he could, feeling those soft wet tissues pull him in even more tightly, faster and faster . . .

Until he exploded.

He couldn't have stopped if someone had put a gun to his head. A lightning-fast white hot line running down his spine raising goose pimples everywhere and he erupted inside her, holding himself tightly against her while he jetted endlessly in massive spurts to the tune of his heartbeat. For so long he wondered dimly whether he was emptying out his heart and not just his dick.

It stopped eventually, as all storms do, and he came to, crouched over her, now resting on his forearm, head low over her stomach. He watched a big fat drop of sweat fall from his face onto her pale belly and quiver with her heartbeat.

Finally, he lifted his head to look at her. Her eyes were closed, head turned slightly to the right, unmoving. She looked like she'd died and was this gorgeous, rosy corpse, completely wiped out.

"Oh no, you don't," Nick growled, lifting his hand from her hip to turn her face to him. "Open those baby blues."

Her eyelids flickered and opened slightly.

He tapped her face. "All the way."

Her eyes opened wide, studying his features, then drifted closed.

No way. "You don't get to zone out. Not an option. We've just started, you can't quit on me now."

The corners of her mouth lifted, breath coming out on a long soft exhale. "No energy," she murmured. "Maybe later."

He was buzzing with energy. "Nope. Not gonna let you. Here."

Nick reached over to a big bowl filled with dark chocolate mousse. They'd never got around to it. In reaching for it, he pressed more tightly to her, even though he was only semi-hard. There was a serving spoon in the bowl and he scooped up a dark frothy mass. It smelled wonderful.

He didn't need to prop himself up anymore, so he snaked his other hand around her neck and lifted her head and shoulders off the table, holding the spoon to her mouth with the other hand. "Open up."

She opened obediently, lips closing around the spoon, tongue licking her lips.

Oh God. He surged inside her, moving his hips against hers.

Elle sighed with pleasure.

"Another." He pressed a huge spoonful of the chocolaty glop against her mouth and she obediently opened. "Another."

With each mouthful he got harder. Any man would have to be dead and long buried not to get aroused at the sight of her closing her mouth around the mousse, then swallowing.

"Feeling more energetic?" Nick demanded, pulling almost all the way out, then sliding back in. He was hard as a rock again.

Elle sighed.

Another stroke and her eyes opened. *Oh yeah.* She was feeling more energetic. But it was cold in the room.

Nick pulled her up in his arms and lifted her. Reflexively, Elle's legs tightened around his waist. "We need the bed for this round."

Elle sighed again, smiling, her breasts rubbing against his chest. "Okay." She gestured gracefully with her slender arm at their clothes puddled on the ground. "We should pick those up."

"Uh-uh." Nick started walking toward the staircase. Actually, he wanted to run up, but he had his pride. "For what I'm planning, you won't need any clothes."

Chapter 4

It was the faintest of sounds but Nick woke up instantly, fully awake. He knew that sound, his life was lived by the cadence of that sound. His cell. Between bouts of sex he'd gone downstairs to grab his jeans and shirt.

Elle was sprawled all over him, soft and light, smelling of woman and sex.

The cell's ring had a Pavlovian effect on everyone in the Rangers—every single man sprang to his cell made of a black nonreflective matte material, and it was rare it took more than a second. One second went by, two, three, four . . .

No doubt at the other end a bot was clocking the response time and someone would mention it once he got back to base. But jumping would wake Elle up, and he simply couldn't do it. She was so deeply asleep it was like she was in a coma. Nothing moved, not even her eyes under the lids.

Rangers were taught to move like ghosts, imperceptibly, without making a sound. So now he used that skill to disentangle himself from the sleeping arms of a beautiful woman rather than float in the dark toward a kill.

In an instant, she was clutching a pillow and he was standing naked by the bed, looking down at his display. The words were barely readable. Displays had two modes—nearly dark if a light could betray their position and bright enough to act as a flashlight. The default mode was dark and he left it like that. He could read the text words in dark mode well enough.

Wheels up oh dark hundred. Majestic.

Shit. There'd been talk of this op, not a training mission, coming up. The brass had been waiting for intel from an exfiltrated agent and apparently they'd got it. No one knew where yet, but that was standard—need to know. They'd find out on the plane where they were headed. The only clue they'd have was the gear assigned. Cold-weather gear or hot-weather gear. That would give latitude. Longitude? Who the fuck knew?

All Nick knew was he had to get out of here fast and he didn't want to. He wanted to stay right here, with Elle. Fuck her and feed her and watch roses bloom in her cheeks—that's what he wanted.

He stared down for just a second. She was on her side, one slim arm outside the covers, face in profile, deeply asleep. There was only the dim light of a quarter moon riding high in the sky, but he didn't need light. She was imprinted on the inside of his eyelids. He knew, without seeing her clearly, that her skin wasn't that shockingly white color she'd had at the funeral. He knew the lines of her face had moved into their natural set—smiling. When he saw her at the funeral he didn't need for her to tell him smiling hadn't been a common occurrence in her life.

It was there in her face.

He wanted to stay and make her smile and laugh and make her eat until she put the pounds back on, and he wanted her to feel as beautiful as she was by making love to her as often as his stamina would let him.

That's what he wanted. But wanting and having were two entirely different things.

What he had was a duty to get to Fort Bragg in time to be briefed and gear up. If they were wheels up at midnight, he had to get there by six tonight and it was a fourteen-hour car trip. He'd just have to push it.

He also had two things to do before signing in.

Nick dressed quietly. Quiet was what Rangers did. They were shooters, they were snipers, they were one with the night. Their clothes were dark. They carried nothing that could shine or jingle.

When he was dressed he spent long minutes looking down at Elle, wrestling with himself. There'd been a new rule instituted the year before, after a Ranger let slip to his girlfriend that he was going on mission to Venezuela. The airhead had posted it on her Facebook page and the team was wiped out half an hour after landing.

New rule—only wives could know of deployments and they couldn't know when or where. Wives had had to sign an oath that they wouldn't disclose any intel at all, ever. Girlfriends had to be kept absolutely in the dark.

Giving girlfriends intel wasn't just a felony, it was a felony subject to court-martial. So what Nick was contemplating was something very, very serious and he had to reason it through.

Giving Elle any info whatsoever was wrong, against regulations, dangerous even.

But . . . he couldn't disappear on her. Just couldn't. It simply wasn't in him. She cared for him deeply, even after he'd disappeared on her and left her alone with a sick father. Every inch of her skin, her mouth, her sex—they told him she cared. No one else cared for him, not in the whole wide world. He was respected in the military but he had no close friends and God knows, he didn't have any girlfriends who cared. Just fuck buddies who forgot him the second he walked out the door.

He couldn't leave her without a word, but leaving her word could get him court-martialed.

The battle inside him was fierce but brief. Army vs. Elle. Elle won.

He took an envelope he found on top of her dresser and wrote *Pixie, be back as soon as I can* on the back and placed it on the pillow next to her, fully aware that he was committing a felony. Downstairs he stopped by the judge's desk in his study and memorized her bank account number and the undertaker's phone number. He could do the rest on the road.

His last mission had lasted four days. With any luck at all, this one would be short too. Rangers weren't the ones they sent in to get intel. They were the ones sent in to shoot the hell out of a place and get out fast.

They always got a couple days downtime on return from an op. So he'd come back here, then he and Elle would talk. Work something out, though he had no idea what. But now that Elle was back in his life, there was no question of leaving her again.

In five minutes on his smartphone, he paid the undertaker's bill—even though the fucker was a mercenary son of a bitch and had overcharged Elle for everything. As soon as he had time, he'd transfer what was in his bank account to Elle. The next thing could be done on the way down to Fort Bragg. Shouldn't take more than a quarter of an hour. As soon as it was opening time, he'd stop at the first supermarket he saw.

Man, the thought of her not having food in the house was fucking painful. He'd had to *work* to hide his wince when he saw her cupboards.

Well, those days were over. He was in her life now and she wouldn't go through that ever again.

Nick slipped out the door, quietly closed the front door behind him, not wanting to leave, knowing he had to.

He'd left once and he had to do it again.

No choice.

But this time he'd be back.

Elle woke up late and woke up . . . happy. The past couple of years she'd trained herself to wake up slowly, from dream to sleep to wakefulness, step by step, because when she woke up quickly the effect was brutal. Like waking up to a sword at your throat. She'd trained herself to come up from sleep like a deep-sea diver floating gently up, because if you did it too fast you got the bends.

Sometimes when she Dreamed, those odd states that were more real than any reality—where she could see things she knew she couldn't see in real life—she could transit to wakefulness because it was like stepping from one room to the next, not one world to the next.

Her Dreams were not always pleasant, and that made it easier to deal with. No getting the bends from watching Nick have sex with an anonymous woman and then waking up to the reality of her life. What hurt—like walking over glass—was normal dreams of better times and then waking up to the reality of her life.

The reality of her life had been caring for a broken shell of a man and juggling the dwindling money supply.

Her father was no more. She'd buried him yesterday.

But she didn't mourn him. She couldn't. No one knew better than her what a hell his life had been. She missed the man he'd been before the empty shell took over.

She'd loved him, cared for him, buried him.

Done her duty and followed the dictates of daughterly love.

Now a new life awaited.

She opened her eyes, stared at the ceiling, noticed for the first time that the watermark left by a broken pipe looked like a butterfly. A deformed butterfly by Picasso in his Cubist period.

She'd skimped on food and heat to repair those busted pipes, and now there was a crazed butterfly on her ceiling.

She smiled.

Still smiling, she closed her eyes so she could concentrate better as she took stock of herself.

Wow. She and Nick had made love until past midnight. She'd gone from zero to hero—from no sex to more sex than any woman could possibly handle.

She stretched and felt aches and pains, particularly between her thighs and the muscles of her core. But elsewhere, too. Her mouth felt slightly swollen from his kisses, her breasts still seemed to feel his mouth. The insides of her thighs were stretched from being held open for so long and slightly abraded from his hairy thighs moving between hers.

She felt imprinted with Nick. She could smell him on her, feel him on her. If her body had been a crime scene, they'd find his DNA all over her. Luckily, her body wasn't the scene of a crime but of unimaginable pleasure.

Last night had been a sort of reboot. From an existence of gritted teeth and iron duty, she'd shifted over into a life of hedonism, of pure pleasure. Food had tasted wonderful instead of like glue, the wine had been like some libation of the gods instead of something sour and acidy she couldn't drink.

She'd *slept*. Really slept. Like normal people did, going deep under, then rising refreshed to a normal day.

Oh God. Normal.

Nick had flipped a switch and her life became normal. Not something to be endured but something to be savored. There were things to look forward to. Breakfast for one. She couldn't remember the last time she hadn't woken up with her stomach in a knot.

Now her stomach was this open and friendly organ, making smiling *me too* noises. Rolling its eyes toward the kitchen downstairs because, really . . . she hadn't eaten since last night and it was time to eat.

She opened her arms and legs like a child making a snow angel. Nick wasn't there and since she didn't encounter any warmth, he'd been up for some time. If he was trying to cook breakfast, good luck. She had enough coffee for this morning, a little milk if it hadn't spoiled, and an apple.

Well, they could go into town and have breakfast at Jenny's. And she could thank Jenny for last night's feast. Kill two birds with one stone.

Except for caring for her father, all the old problems remained, the ones that had seemed as insurmountable as the Himalayas. There was a mortgage on the house it would take her twenty years to pay off. Joshua Bent, the owner of Bent Mortuary Services, had told her he'd hold off on sending her the bill for a month and that he'd give her a ten percent discount and stagger the payments over a year, but with all that, an eight-thousand-dollar bill was on its way to her.

But Nick was back, and she felt hopeful for the first time in a long time.

She was drowning in debt but . . . it was only money. She was young and she could work. She had her health, she was smart and good with computers. She'd manage.

And Nick was back.

She could face anything right now. Even a bare kitchen. Because Nick was back.

She threw back the covers and shot into the shower, remembering how the last time they'd made love had been in the steamy confines of the shower cabin. Hot, heated sex under hot water. *Mmmm.* Oh man, she was going to forge a good and sexy memory with Nick in every room in the house, to replace the sad ones.

It was cold in the house, unfortunately. She felt it academically, because she was molten hot herself though it was freezing. She didn't even choose a heavy sweater because, well, . . . Nick downstairs would certainly see to keeping her warm today.

She hugged herself briefly, glad he wasn't seeing this excess of childish enthusiasm because she was totally incapable of suppressing it.

She nearly flew down the stairs, expecting to find him rooting around uselessly in the kitchen, ready to suggest going out for breakfast and food shopping and a walk around town, and maybe even a movie in the afternoon.

She hadn't been to the movies in . . . forever.

The movies, walks in the park, fabulous sex. All those things were in her future. Yes, they were.

She wasn't so relentlessly *alone* anymore, she was part of a couple. One by one her girlfriends had fallen away. It seemed like getting a boyfriend in high school entailed ditching your friends.

And then of course all her high school friends went off to college and were lost forever.

Well, every single bit of it—including college, eventually—was now open to her. She wasn't alone any longer, and the world was full of people to befriend and movies to see and things to do and places to go.

She was poor but she was young and strong and above all, she wasn't *alone* anymore. Nick was with her.

She hugged herself again and went into the kitchen to say good morning to Nick.

Only . . . Nick wasn't there.

He wasn't in the kitchen and he wasn't in the living room. He wasn't anywhere in the house. That huge anticipatory feeling, like a balloon in her heart, deflated. She had so many things to tell him, but above all she wanted to just see him, touch him. And, well—since they'd started—she wanted to have sex with him again. Soon and as often as possible.

She peeked out the living room window, looking left and right. Nick's SUV was gone. Had he parked it in the garage? But it wasn't in the garage either.

Oh. So he'd gone into town without her to do the shopping. Which was nice but . . . she'd rather have gone with him. It was nice of him to let her sleep in, but she'd have infinitely preferred driving into town with Nick and doing some shopping, even if she had to pretend she wasn't using up the last of the reserves in the bank.

She paced the ground floor— kitchen, living room, dining room, study, den, spare bedroom—over and over again, restlessly waiting for Nick. It was a stupid thing to do of course but there was no stopping her. She had all this energy to burn off, this sense of anticipation, as if life wasn't going to begin until it began in his presence. Everything else was fake time, time to be counted off, minute by painful minute until Nick returned.

Time went back to being so painfully slow, as it had in the endless days of her father's illness. The grandfather clock struck every hour, but it felt as if days went by between the hours. Time did that stretchy thing again as she paced the rooms, unable in any way to read or watch TV or listen to the radio or troll the net for entertainment.

Why hadn't she taken Nick's cell phone number? It hadn't even occurred to her. Oh God, what she'd give to punch in a number and hear his voice again, so deep she sometimes felt it in her diaphragm. He'd be in the supermarket or even on his way back here and they could talk of inconsequential things, but she'd have heard his voice and he'd give her some estimate of when he would be back so she could stop pacing and checking her watch and pacing some more.

Time crawled on, one painful second at a time. There was absolutely nothing for her to do. Life with her father had been filled with duty, minute to minute. But now all she had to do was wait for Nick and it was excruciating.

She paced and checked her watch and waited, slowly becoming worried. Had he had an accident? The roads were icy and treacherous still. Was he in the hospital right now, bleeding and unconscious? Should she call the police?

But Nick's driving was almost preternaturally good. Calling the police was over the top, potentially hugely embarrassing if he came in to find her talking to the police.

Because that would be crazy, right?

Over the years of isolation with only a demented shell of a man for company, she'd lost sight of what was normal and what wasn't. Lost her touchstones of normality. But even to her, calling the police when someone was a little late in coming home from shopping seemed nutso. Over the top anxious, even possessive. Not the kind of person any man could possibly want.

No, Nick would come back when he'd finished . . . whatever it was he was doing.

At noon, the doorbell rang and she ran to the front door, smoothing her hair, wiping her palms on her jeans.

Normal, Elle, normal, she chanted to herself under her breath. No throwing herself on him in relief. No asking where he'd been. Just smile and say hello.

But when she flung the door open, it was only a pimpled teen in some kind of uniform. She blinked, stepped back.

He was consulting a clipboard, looking at her, leaning back to look at the pewter street numbers on the lintel. "Ms. Elle Thomason? Of 1124 Linden Drive?" Behind him was a delivery truck, with some supermarket logo on the side.

"Yes?" He had the right address, he just had the wrong house.

But apparently he did have the right house, because the kid signaled someone behind him. "Okay—bring them in!"

Bring them in?

"I'm sorry, I don't understand . . ." And then, of course, she did. Two men ferrying boxes—and boxes and boxes—of groceries carted in on a hand truck. Hundreds of dollars' worth of food.

"Ma'am? Ma'am?" The kid's voice was sharp with emphasis. He'd been talking to her and she hadn't heard him. "We're going to need to know where the kitchen is."

Numb, Elle stepped back inside, lifted her arm, unable to speak. The men passed her without a word, neatly stacked the boxes and went back out for another load.

In the kitchen, Elle opened a box, peered inside. All dry goods. Staples. Pasta and rice and flour and sugar. All kinds of canned goods. Enough to feed a battalion. Other boxes with staples. The next delivery was fresh fruit and vegetables, more than any person could possibly eat in a month. A huge package of every kind of fresh meat, most of which would have to go into the freezer.

The delivery guys had her sign something and left without saying another word. She stood unmoving in the kitchen, up to her knees in food, sick to her stomach, feeling the world spinning around her, feeling the cold creep back into her bones.

Her legs felt weak, no longer capable of holding her up. She reached blindly for a chair when the phone rang.

"Ms. Thomason?" A male voice. She recognized it but couldn't put a name to it.

"Yes? Who is speaking."

"This is Mr. Bent, Ms. Thomason." Silence. "Of Bent Mortuary Services? Your father's funeral yesterday?"

His voice buzzed uselessly in her ear because the truth had hit her like a hammer blow.

Oh God. That chair was necessary. She sat down, barely able to breathe. Nick . . . was gone. It struck her like a blow to the heart, squeezing all the air out of her chest. That was the only explanation for the empty house, the supplies arriving from Morristown, two hundred miles to the south.

Nick was on the road and stopped at the first opportunity to top up on gas and top her up with food. A kind gesture for the forlorn waif.

And now Mr. Bent was calling to say he'd changed his mind and wanted his money now instead of over the course of a year.

Money she didn't have.

It was hard to even think about that through the pain of Nick's departure. Money. How could she think about money with Nick gone? She could barely focus.

Mr. Bent's tinny voice was faint, sounding as if he were calling from the dark side of the moon. No—wait. *She* was on the dark side of the moon, on some cold airless rock spinning in space.

His voice buzzed in her ear again. She couldn't understand the words, but she had to say something.

"Yes, um, Mr. Bent. I'm sorry, I didn't hear what you said. What can I do for you?"

Oh God, she was so intent on not shaking apart there was no room left to consider her words. *What can I do for you?* Well that was a stupid thing to say when the answer was obvious. *Pay your bill.*

He spoke again, words that made absolutely no sense. "What?"

"I said—" And now Elle could hear the forced patience. He was repeating something for the third time. "I said, Ms. Thomason, that full payment wasn't necessary, though I do thank you. We had agreed you could stagger your payments."

"What?" Her head was ringing. Nothing made sense.

"Are you all right, Ms. Thomason?"

No.

"Ah— Yes, of course. I just don't know what you're talking about."

A long sigh. "Your bill has been settled in full. And I wanted to thank you because we had made an arrangement to stagger your payments over a year."

She sat up straight, the words having finally penetrated. "The bill has been paid? In full? Who paid that bill, Mr. Bent?"

He made a startled noise. When he spoke his voice was slow and careful. "You did, Ms. Thomason. Or rather"—the sound of computer keys clacking—"a certain Mr. Ross paid on your behalf. A Mr. Nick Ross."

The cordless handheld slipped from her fingers, clattered to the floor. Mr. Bent's voice rose like a ghost's, calling her name.

Elle wrapped her arms around her midriff, trying to contain the pain inside waiting to spill out. It felt exactly as if someone had punched a huge hole in her, ripping out her heart. She rocked, trying to dissipate the pain.

Of course Nick had paid. He'd come back, briefly. Found her looking like an abandoned stray, bereft of everything, thrown her a mercy fuck, got some groceries in the house, and settled her bill.

Then left, of course. Why would he stay?

At some point Mr. Bent must have hung up because the handset on the floor stopped squawking. At some point, the sun moved across the sky. At some point, she stopped shaking.

At some point she recognized deep, deep in her bones, not just in her head, that Nick was never coming back.

As the light was fading from the sky, it started snowing and the temperature in the house dropped, became colder yet. When her fingers and toes started hurting, she got up stiffly, muscles and bones aching.

She moved slowly, as if someone had beat her and she was nursing injuries. Someone had beat her, of course. Nick. It would have hurt much less if he'd actually taken a baseball bat to her because broken bones knit, eventually. Broken hearts? Not so much.

An animal instinct told her she'd been grievously wounded. Something deep inside her had been broken. She shuffled slowly through the house, touching things Nick had touched.

There was no energy in her to put the massive quantities of food away. Just seeing all that food made her nauseous. She could barely bring herself to look at it. She shuffled out of the kitchen, closing the door behind her.

One by one, she closed every door of the house. All the downstairs rooms, pulling the doors gently closed, hardly realizing what she was doing, knowing only that the house should feel the way she did. Empty and closed.

Somehow it had become dark. She didn't have the energy to turn on the lights. The darkness somehow fit.

She stopped at the bottom of the stairs, looking up. The stairs seemed interminable, like they went all the way up to heaven, though of course there was no heaven. Just the second floor, and her bedroom. The stairs seemed impossible to climb, though she managed it slowly, step by step. She'd been doing *impossible* for some years now and she could do this, even though each step felt like climbing a mountain. Her legs were weak and could barely carry her. Halfway up, she had to sit on a step and rest her swimming head on her knees. After a while, she got up again, clutched the banister and pulled herself up, step by step. Feeling a hundred years old, she finally made it to the top and shuffled down the corridor.

Elle stopped at the threshold of her dark bedroom, closing her eyes and swallowing heavily.

The room smelled of him. Smelled of primal male, of male sweat and sex and some special pheromonal scent of Nick she would recognize anywhere because it had been imprinted on her skin and in her mind.

Oh God. She had to be quick before she broke down and cried. If she fell onto her bed crying, she would never get up. She felt that, felt deep in her soul that if she gave in to despair she would never recover. There was absolutely nothing left in her to resist the darkness. She'd fall into it and never come out.

During the long years of caring for her father, there'd been a wall inside her. Outside she did all the things she should—cared for and loved a husk of a man who didn't recognize her. Who had forgotten how to feed himself and wash himself. Who required the care a baby would, except this was a 190-pound man. Then a 160-pound man. Then a 120-pound man.

She cared for him, dealt with doctors and medical bills and running a household. But there was always the wall she could retreat behind, and behind that wall she was still Elle Thomason, a young girl and then a young woman with a young woman's dreams. Behind that wall, if she could get her father to sleep fitfully, she could read books and laugh at TV shows and get indignant at the news she read off the net.

There was a duty-bound robot in front of the wall, but behind that wall was a person—Elle Thomason.

That wall was shattered and there was no place to hide now. Nothing between her and cold reality.

Elle needed to get away from here. She needed it like she needed air. If she continued staying in this cold, dark, and empty house with her father's ghost and the memory of those few hours with Nick, hours in which she'd felt warm and sexy and alive, in which she'd been a woman and not a pathetic discard, she would die. She'd simply curl up into a ball trying to protect her shattered heart and never get up again.

Her will to live was almost gone and she had to leave this place before it sucked the marrow of her bones.

There was no plan. She was operating entirely on instinct. Some sluggish yet stubborn part of her that insisted on movement, on escape.

Packing—that wasn't hard. Her wardrobe had been whittled down to basics. And she didn't want to carry much, anyway. The down coat with the ripped sleeve she should have worn to the burial, two sweaters, three pairs of jeans, warm pajamas, socks, underwear, boots. Everything fit into a large backpack.

She looked around her room carefully. The bed was rumpled, unmade. It was almost like a religious ritual with her to make up the bed as soon as she got up, but there it was—blankets and sheets tossed every which way. She could see semen stains, and a darker splotch that was her blood. For a second the desire to walk over and bury herself in the bedclothes, curl up on the bed and breathe in the smell of Nick, was nearly overwhelming.

That way lay madness, though. She'd lived far too long with madness, knew exactly where that led. It led to death.

There was no life in here. Just sadness and despair. She closed the door quietly and walked back downstairs.

What else would she need? Documents. She hesitated in front of the study door, then pushed it open. It had been her father's refuge. Later, it became a place of torment as she tried to jam the square peg of their penury into the round hole of her father's endless needs. She swallowed and walked inside.

During her childhood she'd loved coming here. The room always smelled of books and lemon polish and the flowers Mrs. Gooding cut from the garden. Now it smelled of mildew and dust.

She checked for the thousandth time their bank account. There was only a couple hundred dollars in the account, free and clear now that the funeral was paid for. And there was the mortgage. Three years ago she'd had to get a mortgage on the house as her father's medical needs ballooned. The bank director—whose son Daddy had helped keep out of trouble with some minor drug dealing charges—had been very difficult to deal with. She'd gotten the mortgage at ruinous terms and was deep underwater. The mortgage was worth much more than the house.

The house was falling down and needed new plumbing, a new roof, and a new boiler. A new everything, really.

Well, the bank could keep the house. She would simply walk away. Others had done it and she would too.

She needed some form of ID, but what? She'd never gotten her driver's license and had never been abroad, so she had no passport. Rooting through the drawer she touched a small box and brought it out. Her mother's documents. Her mother's passport, driver's license, and Kansas ID. All expired, but still. She looked exactly like her mother. Many people had commented on it. The driver's license photo was from when her mother was thirty-five and Elle studied the photo. Her mother had actually looked younger at thirty-five than she did at twenty.

Her mother had been a lawyer. As a professional, she'd kept her maiden name.

Laura Elle Connolly.

It was doable.

She could even keep her name, say she used her middle name. That's who she would become. Her mother. She'd become Laura Elle Connolly, known as Elle.

The wind rattled the windows and she shivered. It felt like she'd been cold for years. Wherever she went, she wanted the sea and warmth. Either Florida or California. There was a quarter on the desk and she held it in her fist until it warmed up.

Heads, Florida.

Tails, California.

She flipped it, watching it spin end over end until she caught it and opened her fist.

Tails.

California it was.

Two years ago, she'd taken down one of her father's favorite books, a first edition collection of Oscar Wilde's poems. Inside she'd found two crisp new hundred-dollar bills. She'd kept them in the volume, vowing to use them only in the direst possible emergency. Well, that emergency was here. The money went into the backpack.

She hoisted the backpack over her shoulders, walked out the front door, down the sidewalk to the street, and left the keys in the mailbox. The Greyhound bus station was ten blocks away. She'd checked and a bus was leaving for San Francisco at eight P.M., and the fare was more or less half of what she had.

Laura Elle Connolly, known as Elle, walked out of her old house and her old life, turned right, and began the long walk to the bus station and to her new life.

Chapter 5

Fort Bragg
Fayetteville, North Carolina
Three months later

He was wired again, at last.

As Nick Ross limped out of the debriefing room, his cell was slapped into his hand. SpecOps soldiers aren't likely to give away sensitive intel on their cells to their buddies—but just in case any soldier went temporarily bat-shit insane, their personal cells were taken from them before a big op and returned to them after it was over.

He had his connection to the world back now.

It had been a long nightmare of a mission. Three months in the jungle on an Indonesian island waiting for a specific Tango to show up. The Tango was delayed, so for three long, miserable months he and his three teammates lived in trees and camouflaged pup tents, eating cold MREs and taking dumps behind a huge tree root until the MREs got them too gummed up for any kind of bowel movement at all.

They ate badly, slept badly, and lived like wretches, completely cut off from the rest of the world except for the daily encrypted burst that always bore the same message: *nothing*.

Until three days ago when the Indonesian sky practically lit up with the Gotcha! sign as Abu al-Wahishi, promoting his candidacy to replace Osama Bin Laden as King of the Shitheads, continued his worldwide recruiting tour. They'd missed him in Yemen and they'd missed him by an hour in Somalia, but they didn't miss him on Bandar Island. His features were burned into every single team members' brain cells, right down to the inch-long scar down his right cheek, courtesy of a bomb that went off too soon and barely scratched him, and the slightly crooked nose.

Nick had been at the end of his eight-hour stint up a mangrove tree when a ZiL truck drove up and there he was, Mr. Bad Guy himself. Nick had the immense pleasure of watching al-Wahishi through his crosshairs as he got out of the passenger side of the ZiL, stretched and then dropped like a sack of meat where he stood, courtesy of a 7.62 mm cartridge forged in the good old US of A.

One of the reasons they'd been so uncomfortable was that they never made camp. They were prepared at all times to exfiltrate on a second's notice, and after Nick shot the fuckhead right through the bridge of his nose, his pus-filled brain exiting rapidly from the back of his head, they broke camp immediately and made their way to the coast two clicks away.

But not before the guards surrounding al-Wahishi got off several bursts from their AK-47s. Nick's shot had been silenced so the guards weren't firing at any target they could see. They just fired at random, and damned if one bullet didn't tear a chunk of Nick's right thigh away, missing the bone and missing the femoral artery but hurting like hell all the way to the coast, and nearly causing him to pass out from the pain in the Zodiac racing over choppy seas to where a helo waited in international waters to pick them up.

Luckily, he was injected with enough morphine on the helo to make the pain go away and make him a very happy man until he woke up seventeen hours later in the hospital.

He woke up with a heavy bandage around his thigh and in great pain again, but he was told he wasn't going to get any more pain-killers until he was debriefed. Well, now they'd been debriefed and he had been offered pain relief, but he had other things to do.

Something he'd been wanting to do for three months, two days, and seventeen hours.

Call Elle.

He was perfectly within his rights as long as he didn't talk about where he'd been or what he'd seen or what he'd done, which was cool. You don't want to tell a woman you care about that, *Oh, I haven't called but I've been living in a tree waiting to shoot a man's brains out.*

But Elle was smart. She'd made him for a soldier, and she'd understand that he couldn't talk about it. What difference did it make anyway? There were plenty of things for them to talk about and, well, he didn't really plan on talking much. Not for the first couple of days, anyway.

He planned to walk in, take Elle to bed, and stay there until they were both too sore to walk, the spell in bed broken only by eating and sleeping. *Oh yeah.* The thought of that—of taking Elle to bed and staying there for a long, long time—had sustained him over the past truly awful three months.

He was slated to become Delta. Not many Delta Force opera-tors had girlfriends. Most, like him, had fuck buddies who didn't mind if the men drifted in and out of their lives, leaving without a word and showing up again with no advance notice. But some had girlfriends. A couple were even married.

Nick had had no desire for a steady girlfriend but Elle—Elle was different. He didn't know how they'd make it work, but they would. Maybe he could convince her to move down here. There was a state university. Elle had always been an A student, she'd breeze through it, in whatever degree she wanted to get. And Nick could see her every time he came off an op.

That whole coming and going thing—he had to put a little Vaseline on the lens of his imagination because not too many women were happy at the thought of just sitting there waiting for their man to come back, in the hope that he didn't come back in a pine box. But he could convince Elle. Elle cared for him. He'd seen it in her eyes, in her touch.

Oh God. Don't think of her touch. Those three months slapping away bugs and sucking MREs, he hadn't dared think of her because he'd get a woodie and he didn't want to do that on the op. He was living with three other men, elbow to elbow, and he couldn't do something about it without them knowing. Nick had got himself off any number of times with other guys around. They all did. Sexual release was a known stress reliever. But whacking off to thoughts of Elle while the other guys listened and cracked jokes. Nope. Couldn't do it.

But now he wasn't on an op and he was going to see Elle real soon. With any luck he could coax her down here, because the idea of driving the fourteen hours to Lawrence made his leg hurt just thinking of it. But he'd do it if he had to. Or he'd fly to the Kansas City airport, then rent a car to Lawrence.

However it was going to work, he was going to be with her before the sun set.

Oh yeah.

He'd memorized her home number and cell number. He tried home first and got the first of a number of shocks.

This number has been discontinued.

That freaked him. Had her phone been cut off because she couldn't afford to pay the bill? *Fuck!* He hadn't had time to dump money in her account before leaving on the op.

Then he went to DefCon I when he found out her cell was cut off too. *Number nonexistent.*

He Googled her from his cell and nearly passed out from relief when nothing came up. So she hadn't been in an accident. She wasn't—he swallowed around the dry boulder that had suddenly appeared in his throat—dead.

But she would certainly be hurting for money. He'd been planning to do this and was sorry it was so freaking late. Who knew he'd be sent on the longest op of his life? He was going to transfer the contents of his bank account to hers. He didn't need money. It just sat there, this lump in his account. Let her have it.

First, check to see what she had in the bank.

He knew her bank account number. It was a local bank and their firewalls were pathetic. He easily hacked past them and then stared at his display.

Elle had closed her account. Three fucking months ago.

Now he was scared. A quick check showed that the power had been cut off three months ago. *Jesus.* On a hunch he checked the property rolls and stared. The bank owned her home. It had foreclosed on the mortgage that had been placed on the house three years ago. It hadn't occurred to him that she'd have placed a mortgage on the house, but it made sense if she'd been having money problems dealing with the judge.

He winced when he saw the amount. Over a hundred thou. Well, they'd manage.

Or not. Because Elle hadn't been making payments. The home technically belonged to the bank now. Lots of people still lived in foreclosed homes, but not without electricity. Not in the middle of winter. His skin itched with anxiety.

If this were an op he could send a drone over the house, look for signs of life. A tended garden, smoke from the chimney. A drone at night with IR and thermal imaging could see if someone was living there. It could even discern candlelight.

Shit. Not an image he wanted in his head. Elle, huddling in a cold, dark house lit only by candlelight.

There was no question of not going to Lawrence. He had to get there and fast. A quick check and he discovered he could hitch a series of helo rides from here to Kansas City and rent a car from there. He could be in Lawrence by 1700.

The rides were uncomfortable and hurt his leg, but he didn't notice. He just sank into himself as he was carried northwest, running over and over through the same set of facts that made no sense. Or made awful sense, depending.

Because, well, there was another scenario buzzing in his head so loudly he had trouble thinking about anything else. The house and everything connected to it had been abandoned three months ago, exactly when Nick had abandoned her. He hadn't abandoned her, not really, he'd had every intention of coming back, and he'd even left her an illegal note, but the fact of the matter was, he'd left. And though the note was already too much, it didn't exactly give a lot of info.

Abandoned on the lowest day of her life. Left alone in a cold empty house the day after she buried her father. Looked at it that way—well, it wasn't pretty. Because lots of bad things could happen to people felled by a blow when they were already low.

He hadn't been worried about her the entire op. The only thing he'd been really worried about was his usual—a) get the mission done and b) come home alive. Elle had been there like a lollipop he was going to give himself when he'd done his job right.

He'd willed himself into making sure they got their mission done and he could bring his ass home safely, and he knew that as soon as he got the chance, he was going back to Lawrence.

But there was another scenario possible. And in that scenario, Nick leaving was just too much for her to bear and she—

Don't go there.

But he went there anyway.

Because what was burning inside him—so much that he leaned forward in the helos as if he could make them fly faster, and he drove almost double the speed limit once he was on the ground—was a very clear image of what might be in that house that wouldn't show up on IR.

A corpse.

It was nearly dark when he raced up the driveway, stumbled out of the car forgetting to close the car door, and limped as fast as he could to the front door. Nobody answered the bell. At that point, he wasn't expecting anyone to. The front door lock was a joke. Inside of a minute, he was walking into the atrium.

He stepped inside on full alert, every sense alive. There was, of course, no light. Just to be thorough he tried the switches, but of course nothing worked. It was okay. He'd brought some of his kit and part of that kit was a military issue flashlight that lit everything up just fine. Not that there was anything to see. But there was something he smelled. Something awful. Something . . . dead.

Oh God. He'd smelled death before and this smell, thick and rancid, was one of the worst. He followed his nose into the kitchen, heart thundering, and stood on the threshold, flashlight panning over the room.

Not Elle. Not dead. The smell was that of meat that had rotted for three months. Spread out on the floor was box after box of groceries bearing the logo of the supermarket he'd stopped at. A couple of boxes were opened but as far as he could tell, nothing had been put away and certainly nothing had been eaten.

He checked room after room, his feet leaving tracks in the otherwise untouched dust, everything in exactly the place it had been three months before.

The desk in what had been the judge's study showed a neat pile of bills with a checkbook on top. The stubs of the checkbook matched the bills.

The huge standalone safe's door was open. Inside it was completely empty. The judge used to keep significant amounts of cash there. He remembered the time the safe had been emptied because the judge had given him everything in it. At the time, beside the cash, there had been a few gold ingots and stiff engraved documents—stocks and bonds. Now there was nothing.

He checked the rest of the study, but it was totally void of clues.

The stairs were hard for his leg and he climbed like old people did, one stair at a time. He ignored the pain and lifted his head and flared his nostrils, pulling in air, dreading the thought of smelling a cadaver up here. Nothing horrified him the way the thought of smelling Elle's corpse did.

But there was nothing. Just cold, dead, empty air. He checked every room, leaving Elle's room for last. Finally, he pushed open her bedroom door, heart knocking against his ribs, barely able to cross the threshold.

It was exactly as he left it, down to the unmade bed. He flared his nostrils again and thought he could smell those long-ago smells of Elle and sex, though that was crazy, of course.

There was nothing here. Here was where he fully accepted that Elle was gone. She'd always been so neat, and the fact that the room was a mess, hadn't been cleaned up, was like the final nail hammered into a coffin.

He checked the closet, wincing at how few clothes she had. She'd once had the wardrobe of a princess. He used to tease her about her clothes and she'd laughed him off. She'd been young and pretty and rich. Of course she liked clothes. Now her wardrobe was whittled down to a few cheap everyday items and that was it.

He had no way of knowing if she'd packed a bag, no way of knowing what was missing. No way of knowing if she had walked away empty-handed.

There was utter despair here, he could feel it, could smell it over the faint smell of rotten meat coming from downstairs. There'd been brief joy here when they'd had sex, but it had been replaced by hopelessness. Nick could almost see Elle roaming the empty house looking for him.

Not finding him.

He touched the unmade bed, walked around it—and that was when he found his note. On the ground—facedown. Had she seen it? Whether she had or not, she'd let it flutter to the ground, left it behind. Whatever. She hadn't waited for him.

His leg buckled, it simply couldn't hold him up anymore.

He made it to the bed and collapsed.

Elle had no relatives. Nick knew that. No aunts and uncles, no cousins. It had just been the judge and her. He'd got it that the judge's illness had separated her from the rest of the world. If she had friends to bolt to, he had no idea who they were. Her laptop was gone. From what he could tell, it was basically the only thing she'd taken with her.

He had no clue where she was. For all he knew, she was starving in the snow somewhere. That thought was wiped right out of his head, pronto, because it was too painful to even contemplate. But the echo of it remained. One thing for sure—wherever she was, she was hurting.

So was he.

He sat all through the night in the nest of bedclothes they'd made, head hanging low, not thinking, just feeling. Twisting his note in his hands.

Realizing with each painful beat of his heart that Elle Thomason was gone from him forever.

Chapter 6

Palo Alto, California
Ten years later

The view was muddy, as if under water in a swamp. Men moved quickly, their movements exaggerated, like ants in an anthill that a stick has just stirred. A wailing siren sounded, filling the air.

She was following one man in particular, not tall but immensely strong, with thick shoulders and a barrel chest, with three red stars on his collar. He was in charge, his body language that of dominance, the body language of those around him that of extreme subservience.

The man in charge pointed imperiously, but she couldn't make out at what. There were two doors, side by side, and a huge sign in the middle with two arrows, one pointing right and one pointing left. The writing was strange, a completely foreign alphabet, with words running up and down not left to right.

The column of soldiers didn't hesitate. They poured through the right-hand door at a dead run. Disciplined and fast.

I must follow them, she thought, but the scene was already shifting as she moved past the door and down a white corridor. The men were already at the end of the corridor, in front of a steel door like a bank vault. A screen was to the right. It had odd markings. The commander of the soldiers pulled back his sleeve, punched in numbers on a skin keypad, slapped his palm against the screen.

Even over the wailing siren the hydraulic hiss of a releasing lock was loud. Two dull clangs and the door started opening slowly outward. There was a massive change in air pressure from the corridor into what lay behind the door. The air behind the door was at a much lower pressure and it was as if a sudden wind pressed against the soldier's backs, the high-pressure air flowing into the room behind the door.

She couldn't feel the difference in air pressure, of course, but the soldier's uniforms flattened against their backs. One soldier, taken unawares, stumbled.

The bank vault door continued its smooth progression outward. What lay beyond the door would be visible in a moment or two. She mentally leaned forward, anxious. She'd traveled almost ten thousand miles to see behind that door. It reached midpoint and started swinging to the right, and she could see two huge rails with an electromagnetic engine at the back. The soldiers ran into the room and took up stations around the huge piece of machinery, backs to it, rifles pointed outward. Their leader stepped forward and—

BLACKNESS

Deep swirling blackness.

A sickening rush . . .

"—all right?" A tapping of her cheek. "Elle? Elle? Talk to me!"

She was weak, unable to move. Hands, feet, neck—all unresponsive. Her eyes fluttered open to see a pretty face hovering anxiously over her.

"Elle? Can you hear me?"

"Yes." It came out an unintelligible croak. She coughed. "I

can hear you." The features of the anxious face were familiar, they worked together, her best friend— "Sophie." Sophie's face smoothed out instantly, the lines of anxiety disappearing.

"Wow, you scared me. We couldn't get you to wake up." Sophie looked around, tapped on the counter to connect her to the adjoining room where the control panels were. "Dr. Connolly's awake. Did the fMRI show a change of status?"

A disembodied voice answered. "Yes. Subdural involvement. Parahippocampal gyrus lit up like a Christmas tree."

"Thanks, Rahjiv. Save the data and we'll collate with the other data tomorrow. I think we can wrap this up for today. You guys can go home."

"What—" Elle's mouth was so dry she had trouble articulating. "What time is it?"

"Seven thirty, P.M. You've been out for almost six hours."

Elle closed her eyes, trying to absorb that information. Six hours outside her body. This was the third controlled experiment of an out-of-body experience. This time with specific coordinates. She'd gone far away and it had taken her a long time to get there and a long time to get back.

It was all coming back. The injection of SL-61, an experimental drug to enhance psychic abilities. She'd been hooked up to blood monitors, to an EEG, EKG, and a mini functional-MRI. And she was restrained. Before she could think to resent them, fight them, the wrist, ankle, and neck restraints were released with a loud click.

Firm hands supported her back and she fought the dizziness as she sat up. Disorientation, nausea—they were part of the mix. The price to be paid.

"What are the—" Elle's tongue was too thick to complete the words. Sophie held her head and brought a glass of water to her mouth. Ice cold water, going down like a dream. "What are the readouts saying?"

"Brain activity massive. But your body went into lockdown. BP 80 over 60, heart rate 60, temperature 96 degrees. No change whatsoever for the six hours." Sophie's deep blue eyes, warm and sharp, examined her carefully, the anxiety back. "We were really worried."

Six hours. *Wow.* Elle's recorded journeys so far—to San Francisco and to Boston—had taken just a few hours. And she'd never felt as wiped out as she did now. "That new iteration of SL is powerful."

Sophie blew out a breath. "We need to tweak it. Not everybody would react as well as you have."

They were working on ground-breaking research. A young intern on the team joked about working on a project that would win the Nobel in twenty years. No one had laughed.

Elle and Sophie had both earned their PhDs from Stanford—Elle in neurobiology and Sophie in virology—with dissertations that formed the backbone of the Delphi Project. It was run by a small specialized lab called Corona Labs, funded by a major pharmaceutical corporation, Arka Pharmaceuticals, which owned a majority share.

Sophie came from a wealthy family, but Arka had paid for Elle's studies from her junior year on. To pay back her scholarships, she undertook to work for Arka for four years.

The work was fascinating and no hardship, except for the head of the project and CEO of Arka, Dr. Charles Lee. He took a personal interest in the study they were conducting. Very personal. Though he worked at the Arka Pharmaceutical Corporation headquarters in the Financial District of San Francisco, these past few weeks saw him here at the research lab in Palo Alto more often than not.

His interest was keen, almost feverish, and he was pushing for them to keep a pace that was almost unscientific. Sophie had several times gently suggested that "given the controversial nature" of the study, progress should be made step by step, making sure that they were on solid ground before going forward.

They were investigating what used to be known as ESP or paranormal abilities, though the field was now being folded into general neuroscience. Some of their data was irrefutable, but science progressed slowly and there were always those whose entire careers were spent in one paradigm and would fight to the death before admitting that another paradigm could apply.

Elle had tried to recuse herself when an fMRI showed that she had the same enhanced part of her brain that the other test subjects had, but Lee would have none of it. He wanted her as part of the protocol and part of the scientific team at the same time. And then, she and Sophie had found out that a number of the researchers had similar fMRIs.

Elle knew that she was jeopardizing her scientific reputation, but she wasn't unhappy at playing both roles. For the first time in her life, she was beginning to suspect that her Dreams were true out-of-body experiences and not some horrible pathological form of subconscious escape.

That she could think of them as journeys and not as dream craziness was a huge step forward. This had been the subject of her doctoral dissertation, funded entirely by Arka. She'd been very lucky at Stanford in finding a professor who didn't chuck her out for harboring dangerously lunatic ideas.

And then, another miracle in the form of the brand-new Department of Psychic Sciences at Stanford. It was predicated on the existence of extrasensory perceptions, studied at a neuronal cell level, and had been established thanks to a huge grant by Arka.

Elle swung her legs over the side of the cot, carefully planting her feet on the ground and testing whether her legs would carry her weight. She'd nearly given herself a concussion at the last test, trying to stand up and then dropping straight to the floor.

Her out-of-body experiences took an enormous amount of

energy. The enzymes in her body showed that it was the equivalent of running a marathon. In one test she'd actually lost half a kilo.

She tried to stand up but her legs wouldn't hold her just yet. Sophie tried and failed to keep scientific detachment in her voice. She glanced down at her tablet, then back up. "Well?" She cleared her throat, bit her lips. "Did you do it? Did you get there?"

This was the longest trip in Elle's experience, the longest trip in recorded projection history. Halfway around the world, to a specific point Elle had never seen, and could hardly imagine. Merely on the basis of GPS coordinates and a Keyhole 15 photograph of a complex that was mostly underground.

"I did," Elle answered softly. She waggled her head left then right, feeling tendons pop. Coming back was always hard. Much harder this time, considering where she'd gone.

"Yes!" Sophie beamed and held her fist up for a fist bump. Then sobered, looking around uneasily. Every word was being recorded. "Honey, protocol says that I need to debrief you immediately, but you're looking pale. Maybe we could do this tomorrow?"

"No." As long as she was sitting, Elle could do this. She wanted to stick to the protocol as much as possible. Besides, she needed to get something out. Sophie would understand.

Elle closed her eyes, thought back. Unlike dreams, her Dreams didn't recede quickly into forgetfulness. Mostly they were images and they lingered. "Dark," she said softly. "So it must have been night. Everything was strange and different. The shapes of things, the alphabet."

"The one you studied?"

Elle nodded. "Mongolian." She shivered. Her soul or whatever part of her traveled had gone far, far away. She felt lost, disoriented. Completely outside herself. The weakness in her legs was bad enough, but there was also a hollowness inside her chest, as if her internal organs had disappeared.

The disorientation was complete. It hurt to move, but still she lifted her head, trying to focus on her surroundings. As she looked around, everything seemed new. A lab she'd worked in every single day for the past year looked odd, foreign. Different and slightly unreal.

Elle closed her eyes as the room started to revolve, opening them when she heard Sophie's voice.

The protocol called for at least two researchers to be present during debriefing, but they were short-handed because three researchers hadn't shown up.

"And you were—"

"In a facility. A military facility. It looked like a research station." In reporting, she started to come back into herself, the world filling out, becoming a little more real. "I saw the symbol of the Mongolian Defense Force—their army. And there were the red-and-blue flags of the Mongolian Republic on flagpoles."

Sophie was tapping on her tablet. "Okay. Were you following a particular person?"

"Yes. A very broad-shouldered man, of medium height. In a gray and green military uniform. He had three stars on his collar."

"We'll look that up," Sophie murmured.

"Well, he was obviously a commanding officer. He led his men to an attack on the facility. They came in through a river or a deep sewer. I couldn't tell. When the alarm sounded they ran through a lab. But they didn't stay in the lab; they ran out a door on the other side, then made straight for an armored door. They must have been testing hazardous material behind the door because the lab had negative pressure. The soldier's uniforms flattened against their backs as air rushed in. The man had the code. When it opened, he waited while his men rushed in. There must have been twenty soldiers with him. When everyone was in, he closed the door."

"Did you see what was behind the door?" Sophie asked.

"Oh yes." Elle's voice was soft. "A huge piece of machinery. A rail gun. It looked like it might actually be functional."

Sophie's mouth made an O. "A rail gun," she repeated slowly and Elle nodded.

Rail guns were the holy grail of military research everywhere. They were electrostatically charged rails that could hurl projectiles at up to seven thousand miles an hour. It had very few moving parts and, run by electricity, it eliminated explosives, thus rendering it invulnerable to enemy detection.

The idea of rail guns had been around for over a hundred years. It was an amazingly complex piece of machinery. The first power to develop one would have a powerful weapon that could launch devastating attacks thousands of kilometers away and yet remain undetected.

Elle met Sophie's eyes. Both of them had suspected for some time that the research they were carrying out was for military purposes. They'd set up a secure e-mail system to communicate to each other their suspicions. This was more or less confirmation of that.

Elle had been sent on a military reconnaissance.

It was clear to both that they had to pretend they didn't understand the significance of what Elle had seen. They had to get away and discuss this privately.

Elle yawned massively, fists thrust in the air. "Sorry," she said, a sheepish smile on her face. "Really tired."

"What do you need?" Sophie put a hand to her shoulder. Elle was usually famished and thirsty when she came back from a trip of a couple of hours. Now she'd been gone six.

"As usual, I'm hungry and thirsty," Elle said as cover. Food and drink was the last thing she wanted. "And I want to go home. Rest."

"Sure. I'll go get you some more water."

Elle wasn't hungry or thirsty, she was depleted. And she had to go to the bathroom. She took care of her physical needs in the small bathroom adjoining the lab, washed her face, then looked at herself in the mirror.

She looked exhausted, as if she'd run a marathon after a couple of sleepless nights. Her skin, naturally pale, was ice white, lips faintly blue. The harsh overhead light played tricks on her face, turning her light blue eyes the palest of hues. The mirror showed a ghost, even her eyes drained of color.

Was it worth it?

Yes.

Probably.

Maybe.

She was learning to direct her Dreams now, and not be directed by them. Overwhelmed by them. It was why she'd chosen neuro-science—to understand. And as much as she considered herself a dispassionate scientist, a woman driven by a thirst for knowledge, she knew deep down why she was so driven.

To exorcise Nick.

Oh. Good. There was just the faintest prick to her heart when she thought of him, not the massive jolt that thinking about him had caused over these long years since he'd abandoned her.

No, no. Not abandoned her. Abandoning something meant an implicit tie of responsibility, which Nick hadn't had. Hadn't in any way felt. Had made pains to avoid. So he hadn't abandoned her, he'd just left to continue on with his life.

Of which she had no idea, thank God.

Since that horrible day in Lawrence, ten years ago, her Dreams of him had been few and far between and mere flashes, not watching his life, as it had been before. Now she mainly dreamed about him, not Dreamed. And even those were now rare.

Even obsessives lose sight of an obsession when there was nothing to feed it, she supposed. She scrubbed all thoughts of him from her head as much as she could during the day. And her life had kept her so busy it hadn't been that hard. He invaded her head at night, though, in her dreams. There, big as life. So much a part of her mental landscape that much as she tried not to, every other man was measured against his yardstick, coming up short.

Ten years.

She'd accomplished so much since she walked out the door of her home that freezing winter evening so long ago. It seemed she had used up all her bad luck, and it was finally time for the good. On the long bus trip to the coast, she sat next to an elderly African-American lady, Cora, and they became friends. Elle didn't say what had happened, but Cora understood very well that she was running from something. Cora didn't ask and Elle didn't tell.

When they arrived at the bus station in the Castro, Cora's son Darryl was waiting for them. Cora demanded that Darryl give her a job and the use of a room right above the bar-restaurant Darryl ran in the Tenderloin. Elle spent the next five years bartending and working for Darryl. After the first week, he gave her a raise, saying he'd never met a harder worker.

Well, hard work was what Elle did. She'd done it for free before and being paid for it felt like a bonus.

Darryl hadn't always been a model citizen and once he understood she had no real ID, he got to work with his contacts in the underground and soon she had legitimate ID as Elle Connolly, California resident.

She enrolled as a part-time student in City College and aced all the courses, not realizing how incredibly starved she'd been of intellectual stimulation. By the time she got her master's in biology, she had three offers of a full scholarship to Stanford. Darryl always said that he was glad his momma lived long enough to see her graduate. Cora had been there, beaming in her wheelchair at the graduation ceremony.

In college she could no longer ignore her Dreams, and by the time she got to Stanford, she had a professional interest in them.

There seemed to be an unofficial group interested in the neu-
rological underpinnings of paranormal abilities, and to her astonishment, a huge multinational pharmaceutical corporation
swooped in and funded an official research group. A functional
MRI scan showed that the research subjects shared certain com-
monalities.

Like Sophie, Elle signed up as guinea pig and researcher, and
found that many of the researchers had a hot spot in their heads
and abilities they'd learned to keep secret. They were all very keen
on the project and worked long hours, like Elle herself.

This was the fourth time she'd actually put herself into a controlled Dream state during the day, and each time it was utterly
exhausting. Clearly, when she Dreamed at night, her body had
time during sleep to recoup its energies. Blood tests showed a de-
pletion in red blood cells after each Dream.

Sophie came back in, handing her another glass of ice water,
casually touching her arm. Sophie didn't touch people much. Elle
had noticed that. And like herself, Sophie didn't date much. Sophie's hand on her arm was warm, unusually so, and she held on as
Elle downed the tall glass of water.

By some trick, the warm hand and the cold water seemed to
revive her. A little. Enough to smile at Sophie and pretend she was
much better.

"Thanks," she smiled and the worry lines in Sophie's face
smoothed out. She lifted her hand and Elle immediately felt the
cold.

She suspected Sophie was a healer but understood completely
if she wanted to keep it secret for now. Sophie had the same hot
spot in her brain that everyone else in the program had.

"You okay to get home?" Sophie frowned at her, her hand hovering, clearly wondering if she should surreptitiously touch Elle
again. "Do you want me to drive you? I could pick you up tomorrow morning and drive you back in."

"Didn't you say you had some work at home to finish up tomorrow morning?"

"Well, yes. But nothing I can't put off."

Elle stacked her spine. She felt weak and groggy, but she was not going to make Sophie drive in tomorrow morning just for her. "No, I'm fine. See you tomorrow afternoon in the lab, okay?"

Another searching gaze and Sophie relaxed. "Okay. See you tomorrow."

After she left, Elle sat for another ten minutes, then realized she had to get herself home now or sleep over in the lab. It wouldn't be the first time. But right now, she fiercely wanted her little apartment, its familiarity and its comforts.

Elle made it home before collapsing. Just. She walked straight through the door, made a beeline for the couch, dropped purse and briefcase on the floor and fell onto it, rather than sitting down. She tilted her head back, trying to let the past twenty-four hours wash over her.

She had to take a shower and she had to eat, but right now she was too exhausted to do anything but sit there, staring at the ceiling.

It reminded her of her first year in San Francisco, waitressing by day, attending night courses. She'd been younger, though, and stronger. And excited at the thought of getting her degree. Back in San Francisco, she'd been fueled by the energy of exploring the world after so many years in a state of stasis, looking after her father. She'd imagined she would finally start . . . *Life*. Study, find a job she loved and a man she could love. Start a family, just like everyone else.

The study and the job had worked out. The family, not so much.

Actually, she hadn't had much of a love life. To be brutally honest, she hadn't had any kind of love life.

When she looked in the mirror, she saw an attractive woman. Judging by the way men reacted to her, she knew she was attractive to men. In the beginning she went on tons of dates, with every guy who asked her out. She was anxious to start dating because what Nick had shown her was so enticing, she knew she wanted more of it.

Except it seemed that the sex she'd had with Nick was exclusive to him. To her horror, nobody came even close to making her feel the way he did. Elle had actually felt repulsion with a lot of guys, not even wanting to be touched.

She wasn't gay, so that was out. She was a heterosexual lock— and the one key that opened her was gone, forever. So she came home every night to her pretty, tiny apartment and tried not to wish that she were not so relentlessly alone.

She was so tired she fell asleep, right as she was, on the couch, with her coat on. And dreamed.

It was that day again. She'd relived it endlessly over the past ten years.

After months of cold gray weather, it was finally sunny again. The sun shone off the snow and lit her bedroom with a brilliant light that glowed even behind closed lids.

She smiled, yawned, stretched. Dramatically threw the covers back.

Smiled some more. Her body felt sore, used, great. Warm from Nick's touch still. Warm. She was warm down to her bones. Warm and—and light. A great heavy burden had been lifted and she could move with ease.

She opened her eyes and looked at the rumpled bed, the folds of the sheets and covers making dramatic lights and shadows in the brilliant morning light. Things gleamed in her bedroom, the bright sun catching glints in a silver vase, the mirror over the vanity, the brass lamp.

She gleamed. She felt all shiny and new.

And she had a shiny and new love. Nick.

Who wasn't in the bedroom or the en suite bathroom.
Or downstairs.
Her heart was beating fast now, the beat of imminent danger.
The beat of dread. She looked and looked, the drumming of her
heart covering the icy silence of the house. Her cheeks were
wet as she called Nick's name. She swiped at her cheeks impa-
tiently, the beating of her heart so loud her ears rang. . .

Elle started awake, gasping loudly in the silence of the night.
Ashamed that, once more, she'd woken up with tears in her eyes.
She could keep the tears away easily during the day. She'd rather
submit to torture than cry. But at night, in her sleep, she was
caught with her defenses down and she hated it.

The ringing didn't stop. It always took a minute or two to
come back into herself, whether she'd lost herself in a dream, or
a Dream.

She fumbled for her purse, hands awkward and clumsy, another
residue of the dream state. She checked the display and saw the
photo of Sophie's smiling face, hand holding a glass of champagne
high, a picture Elle had taken at the reception thrown by Arka for
the kickoff to the program.

Elle coughed to loosen her throat so it wouldn't sound froggy
and thumbed the off-image button so Sophie wouldn't see her face
with its tear tracks. She'd say she'd just put on a masque.

"Hey, Soph," she said casually. "What's—"

"Elle listen to me because I don't have much time. Put me
on vid." Elle clicked and Sophie's drawn face came on, bobbing
up and down as she moved around her bedroom. She was pale,
sweating, eyes huge and haunted. Her voice was a low whisper,
tone rough with anxiety. She glanced quickly over her shoulder,
then back into the display. "Les and Roger aren't playing hooky.
And Moira has disappeared too. They've been captured and—and

taken somewhere. I don't know where but it's not good, Elle. It's like we're being . . . rounded up!" She was moving frantically, from room to room. "I got a call a quarter of an hour ago from Nancy, who got a call from Moira. It was only a few seconds but Nancy said men dressed in black were in her house. They were armed. She was hiding out in the closet. Now she's not answering, her phone is dead. And Moira, Les, and Roger are unreachable too. Listen, Elle, get out. Get out as fast as you can. I don't know who they are, but it's not good. And Nancy told Moira our sensors are tracking devices. I don't—" She froze. Even Elle heard the sound in the background. Something crashing to the floor.

There wasn't even a pretense at stealth, which frightened Elle even more.

The image on her phone blurred, shadowy figures appearing suddenly.

"Dig the sensor out, dump your phone, and *get out*!" Sophie screamed and her phone went dead.

Elle held her own phone in her shaking hand—a thin slab of transparent plastic that had inexplicably become as dangerous as a rattlesnake.

She opened her hand and it dropped to the floor. It didn't break, of course. It was the latest generation and there were videos all over the net of it working after having been shot with a bullet. It was made of the same polymer as the blast-proof vests worn by bomb squads.

It gleamed there, on the floor. She could be tracked through it. *Get out!*

Good thinking. Get out, escape. But not if she had something *inside* her that could let them track her.

No turning the lights on, but it wasn't necessary. She knew every inch of her home. She rushed to the kitchen, pulled out a small knife she kept razor-sharp, and ran to her en suite bathroom.

It didn't have an outside window, so once she pulled the door shut, no light would betray her if someone was watching outside.

Hurry-Hurry-Hurry! She chanted to herself as she doused her left bicep with disinfectant. She pressed her finger on the almost-invisible dent in her skin and felt it—a tiny chip Corona had said was a biosensor. The biosensors were to be surgically removed after a year and the recordings placed on a graph.

It was randomized. Half the staff of volunteers had taken SL-61, the experimental drug, and half placebos. Elle had no idea which camp she was in, but it made no difference if the sensor was also a tracking chip. It had to come out, *now*.

There was nothing to dull the pain. She had only a rudimentary first aid kit in the bathroom. Above all, she had no time.

Gritting her teeth, she slid the knife into her skin and stopped, brow beaded with sweat, trying to get used to the pain, red hot, almost electric. There was no getting used to it. There was only getting through it as quickly as possible. She turned the tip of the knife and cut at a right angle, then stopped, head bowed over the sink. The pain was so sharp it was nauseating. She waited for the nausea to pass, lifted the flap of flesh she'd cut out, reached into the bloody meat of her bicep with thumb and index finger. It was deeper than she thought and she had to actually dig to find it. Twice she had to stop because she was about to pass out.

Finally, finally, her index fingernail touched the edge of the sensor. She was in almost halfway up the first knuckle. She looked up. The mirror showed her bloodless face, white lips, face drawn in pain. Taking a deep breath, she curled her fingernail under the edge of the chip and pulled.

She screamed, knees buckling. Only her left arm hooked over the bowl stopped her from falling to the floor. That *hurt!* Magnitudes more than cutting into herself. It felt like electrical wires transmitting pain down to her bone.

God. Sophie said to hurry! But she couldn't go anywhere as long as she had this . . . this *thing* inside her. There was a keening sound inside the bathroom and it took her a full minute to realize it was her own voice, panting and sobbing with pain.

She couldn't pull her finger from her flesh because she'd never have the nerve to dig it back in. With her right hand she pulled, harder and harder, feeling the resistance of the chip, almost as if it were alive.

This wasn't working. Was it deeper than she thought? But no, she could feel it. It should have been out by now. With her left hand she pulled a clean washcloth from the counter, stuffed it into her mouth and before she could rethink it, braced her feet and pulled as hard as she could. The washcloth muffled her screams as she bent her head back, incapable of breathing from the pain.

Her head spun, black spots danced before her eyes. She was a whisper from passing out when the chip moved under her finger. She pulled harder, the pain so sharp it felt almost like a living thing, then staggered back when she finally pulled the chip out.

Elle spat out the washcloth, head hanging over the washbasin, her panting loud in the room, trying hard not to throw up. Finally, the room stopped swimming. The tears of pain dripped into the sink, her arm throbbed.

Everything disappeared though when she brought the chip up for inspection. It had the Corona logo of three tiny crowns in one corner. It was a standard chip except for one thing—there were tendrils growing out of it, twisting and curling. *Alive*. Holding the chip close to her eyes, she touched the tendrils with a set of tweezers and watched, horrified and fascinated, as they retracted, as a sea anemone's tendrils would.

The tendrils had grown out of the chip. Whatever was in the chip, it was semi-alive. No, scratch that. Alive.

There was no time now to explore the chip, though. She left it on the edge of the sink, then set about repairing herself. She applied gel from her derma-glue tube that would hold the skin together better than stitches, then stuck on an antibiotic bandage with a painkiller gel.

There. The best she could do.

The pain had powered down to a dull throbbing that hurt like hell but didn't impede her movements. She moved fast now, in the dark, choosing cold-weather sports clothes from her closet. There might be the faintest of chances that Arka had seeded its employees' clothes with trackers, so she chose clothes she'd never worn to work.

Warm cashmere sweater, wool pants, thermal socks, boots, long down coat. In the living room her fingers ran across one of the shelves until she reached a familiar book by feel. She couldn't read the title but she knew what it was. A thick tome on advanced bio-chemistry, guaranteed to spark not an atom of interest in anyone. Inside she'd carved out a hole in the pages large enough to hold cash. She pulled out the entire stash—two thousand dollars. She knew only too well what it meant to be on the road without cash.

She bolted for the window. Sophie's voice had been raw with fear. Sophie was so steady and stable. Hearing that note of panic in her voice had galvanized Elle.

There was no background light to betray her as she peered out the edge of her front window. In the back of her mind, she knew what she wanted to see and she saw it. The small empty garden of the front of her building and the empty street beyond it. It was a dead end street, and she knew every car on it and knew every person who lived there.

Nothing. Dark and silent and safe. Was she overreacting? Had Sophie been somehow having a psychotic episode? And yet, that chip with the terrifying tendrils— Maybe it would be best to dis-appear for a few days. She started to turn away, then stopped as something dark glided into view.

A car she'd never seen before—black and unfashionably huge—

slid to a stop and four men exited. The interior lights didn't come on as they slipped out of the car like shadows. Dressed in black, they seemed to meld into the night, but not so much that Elle couldn't tell where they were headed.

Straight to her building.

The car rolled forward, made a U-turn on the empty street and stopped right in front of her building's driveway.

Her four-story apartment building was built slightly back from the road with a small garden in front. The garden was protected by a chest-high wrought-iron fence with a six-foot gate in the middle.

The four men had black full-face helmets with the dull black lenses of nightvision.

Two of the men moved like shadows to the corners of the fence and crouched, the other two disappeared. Elle had no doubt where they had gone—to the back of the building via the alleyway. As she watched, the two men out front tapped their ear and stood.

It didn't take much to guess what they'd heard. The other two were stationed in the back and they could make their move. In a synchronized flow that would have won medals at the Olympics, the two black-clad men smoothly cleared the fence in a lithe leap and moved slowly, deliberately forward.

Toward the front door. And, eventually to her apartment on the second floor.

Oh my God, Sophie was right!

Elle realized she had seconds to get out. Run and go— She drew a blank. But wherever she was going she had to get there fast. She scooped her purse off the floor and ran.

Her apartment building was part of a complex of four condos, connected by basement corridors invisible from outside the house. Heart thumping, she tumbled down the stairs to the first floor, then kept on going down. She swiped her card past the basement entrance sensor, slapped her hand on the sensor that read the vein pattern of her palms, then let out a sharp exhale as she heard the click of the front door unlocking. The building had excellent security, both digital and bio. She'd traded space for safety. If these men were able to circumvent it in mere seconds, they were very good. Professional. That scared her more than if DOPA addicts were breaking into her home.

Her car was lost to her. They'd parked right across the driveway, blocking her. She had to get as far away as she could on foot, when she could hardly stand.

There was no noise from the building. If they were breaking into her apartment, they were doing it silently. Well, her security was a step down from the building security that they'd laughed at when they broke in.

The basement corridor was long and almost completely dark, the only light coming from dim chemical bulbs every ten feet. It felt like the corridor stretched forever. She leaned against the wall, legs weak, arm throbbing.

It had to be done. The wall at the end of the long corridor looked at least a mile away, receding constantly, like some movie effect. Cold sweat covered her face and chest. She swayed and would have fallen if she hadn't slapped a hand against the wall.

For a moment, for just a moment, she was tempted to simply slide down that wall and wait for whoever was up there to make it down to the basement. If they were thorough, they'd check the building plans on record. The underground connecting corridor was a feature of the building.

If she didn't move, they'd come for her and find her.

Three people were missing from the program—four now, with Sophie—and it was very likely they'd been abducted by whoever had sent the men who were right here, at this very moment going through her house. Whatever they wanted, it wasn't good.

Sophie had risked precious minutes warning her. Had maybe compromised her escape to warn her.

Go, Elle told herself. And a couple of seconds later, her feet obeyed.

She was gasping with fatigue when she reached the end. She stopped, leaned against the wall, catching her breath. It was so awful, the drumbeat of imminent danger sounding in her head, but her body unable to obey. Stress and danger hummed in her, but she could barely stay upright.

Every minute spent here increased the chances of her being found. If the men in black came down to this basement corridor she'd be the easiest prey on earth. She'd read somewhere that the latest generation of stunners could kill or maim at five hundred feet.

She straightened away from the wall and turned, her feet moving in a maddeningly slow shuffle.

There were two exits, one up the building stairs that led to the front door and one that let out the side of the building. Instinct had her taking the side exit. She opened the side door cautiously and peeped out. There was absolutely no one in sight.

How much time did she have?

Even if they circumvented her personal security system as easily as they did the building one, surely it would take some time to establish that she wasn't home? A few minutes at least.

It would have to be enough.

She knew her neighborhood well enough to make it through backyards, going as fast as she could, until she finally came out onto another section of town. On foot it took about ten minutes. By car it would take longer, even if they knew where she was. As it was, when they discovered she wasn't home, they'd probably cover her neighborhood in a grid search, which would take time.

Elle exited the warren of backyards and service alleys into an entirely new neighborhood. Not a savory one either.

Great, because maybe they wouldn't look for her here.

Elle stopped, leaning against a broken street lamp, catching her breath. She needed a plan that covered more than the next five minutes, but it was eluding her. Pain and adrenaline and exhaustion were blocking her thought processes. She needed a safe place—but where?

An expensive hotel was out. So were the three or four hotels that the company habitually used for visiting professors, because the men after her would have that list. And of course they'd know if she used her credit card.

Think Elle! She clung to the lamppost, head down, trying to reason her way through this. She was so very tired. The test session had drained almost every ounce of energy out of her. Then the shock of the phone call, the pain of digging around in her own arm, of pulling that chip out, the terror at seeing those men in black after her . . .

This is what Jane Macy must have felt like after her breakdown. She'd had a psychotic episode after a test and had disappeared. The company had cited privacy issues when Elle asked about her.

Why was she thinking of Jane?

Oh! The memory popped into her head, clear and complete and she pushed off from the lamppost with a surge of energy she knew was the last of her reserves.

Jane had had an affair with a married guy, a lawyer working for one of the many venture capital firms in the area. His wife was really powerful and could do some serious damage to him if she found out.

The one thing everyone knew about the wife was that she really liked being rich, disliked even seeing poor people. She wouldn't travel through poorer sections of the cities she visited on business trips, and had her drivers make great circuitous loops to avoid even the sight of the poor.

So Jane had found a tiny motel in the poorer part of town that didn't ask questions, didn't take down ID and took cash.

Elle remembered the name of the motel and knew where it was.

It was walkable, just. If her strength held out. And she'd have to walk through more backyards and back roads, because she had to assume there would be cars on the streets looking for her, and cameras they could hack.

The one thing that had been clear when Arka started up the research project was that Arka was awash in money. It had money to burn, and if it sent out its full security force, she was in real trouble.

She couldn't think beyond finding a place to rest, so she pushed off and began the long trudge to the motel that asked no questions.

Arka Pharmaceuticals Headquarters
Financial District
San Francisco

Dr. Charles Lee watched the video of the debriefing of Dr. Elle Connolly for the fifth time. Dr. Daniels hadn't been at all thorough and would be reprimanded, but what shone through was that Connolly had penetrated the secret lab at Bayankhongor, apparently during a training session. There were twenty three-star generals in Mongolia and Lee would show Connolly photographs but he was almost certain that the three-star general she'd seen was General Yisu, the head of Mongolian Special Forces.

And the secret camp, whose coordinates he'd given to Connolly, was working on a rail gun.

Surely that would buy him some time with the Chinese Ministry of Science and Technology?

Resentment swelled in his chest at the thought. Though he'd emigrated with his family to America at the age of seven, his heart had remained back in the homeland. He'd raced through school and university and had risen quickly up through the ranks of Arka with one thought, and one thought only. Coming back to Beijing a conqueror, bearing the key to making China the uncontested sole superpower in the world, and taking his rightful place at the top of the government hierarchy.

He'd started by working with General Clancy Flynn, using black funds from the U.S. military, then funneling the results to Beijing. The response had been immensely gratifying. A byproduct of one of the research projects was a cancer vaccine. He'd sent in a black ops team run by Flynn called Ghost Ops—men whose pasts had been erased, men who no longer officially existed—to destroy the lab where the vaccine had been developed, then sent the vaccine to Beijing. The top tiers of the Chinese government were all now vaccinated and a mass vaccination of the forty-million-strong armed forces was under way.

The Ghost Ops team had been accused of domestic terrorism, forevermore criminals in the eyes of the U.S. government.

Flynn had been only too willing to sacrifice his black ops team. Lee understood that Flynn resented the Ghost Ops leader, Captain Lucius Ward. Lee didn't care either way. It seemed to him the squabbling of children. What he had got out of the operation was four elite warriors to experiment on.

Because his ultimate goal was the creation of a super soldier. Tougher, faster, smarter. With better eyesight, better hearing, greater healing abilities, faster synapses. Captain Ward and the three Ghost Ops soldiers that had been caught—another three had escaped and were still at large—proved recalcitrant in the extreme, however. In the end, Lee had decided to sacrifice them, harvest the brains and study the effects of the drugs he was testing.

The captain and the other three soldiers had been rescued before they could be sacrificed, and Lee had lost a great deal of research that had been in their bodies and would have been evident in their harvested brains.

He had a new protocol now and was working with the funds funneled to him by Clancy, now retired and the head of a security company.

Clancy wanted better contractors to make more money.

Lee wanted to change the world.

Right now, though, their goals meshed.

Back in Beijing, Lee had enemies, men who resented his grow-ing power. They were sabotaging his plans, mocking him behind his back while he was an ocean away in California.

So he'd decided to make *himself* smarter and faster and stron-ger, to be living proof of the validity of his Shin-Li project, Project Warrior. He'd been injecting himself with diluted versions of the experimental drug. It worked, it worked wonderfully well. Though he gave no outward sign, he felt immensely stronger mentally and physically. In the mirror in the morning, he could see muscle defi-nition in his chest and arms. It was growing increasingly difficult to tear himself away from his naked image in the mirror.

He *felt* different. Lee was an observer, a scholar, a scientist at home in the world of learning. He often thought he would have been an excellent court scholar in the time of Confucius. He was used to studying the world dispassionately, his only passion that of making it back to Beijing a victorious man, the architect of a new world order.

But now—now he felt like he could take on the world himself, single-handedly. He'd been willing to forge a new world with his mind and scientific training, but now, oh now, it was like he could do it physically.

And now he had an even stronger tool. Literally revolution-ary. His special Delphi Project, named after the oracle in ancient Greece. A handful of men and women with special powers they tried to hide and suppress. But you can't hide from an fMRI. He'd gathered them together to study their capabilities and replicate them. He'd expected the project to last at least a year, right up to the moment he expected to defect back to Beijing. But his hand was being forced. The Ministry of Science and Technology in Bei-jing was about ready to close the door they'd been holding open for him. And that moron Flynn, who was funding both programs, was increasingly shrill about wanting results.

Beijing and Flynn wanted results?

He'd give them results.

He was rounding up the subjects with special powers. He'd infuse them with massive doses of SL-61 and he'd find the secret to developing super warriors who could fly, who could throw fire projectiles halfway across the world, who could read minds.

Project Warrior was on an accelerated schedule and, he thought as he made a fist, admiring the muscles in his forearm, so was he.

Palo Alto

There it was. Probably the only motel in the area that didn't belong to a chain. It didn't seem to belong to anyone, really. The once bright green façade was faded to a light pea green. Most of the plants in the courtyard were dead and the bright red neon sign advertising V CANCI S sputtered and fizzed.

It wasn't much, but Elle had to hope it would offer her shelter and protection for a few hours because she didn't have the strength to go one step further.

Walking into the dirty, dusty lobby Elle realized she was overdressed for the place. Her big down coat was expensive, as were her boots and purse. Luckily, the young guy behind the counter looked either half asleep or like he'd just taken two tabs of FeelGood.

They turn the cameras off, Jane had said. Still, Elle kept her head down as she registered, pushing across the counter a hundred-dollar bill for the sixty-dollar room. "Keep the change," she muttered, eyes down. A none-too clean hand with cracked fingernails made the bill disappear and a scratched card key appeared.

A bored voice said, "Down the hall. Take the right corridor." She walked away, trying to keep her knees stiff. If she fell down or fainted right in the lobby that would make her memorable.

Or not, considering the type of motel it was. Maybe they had drunk or drugged ladies falling down all the time. Elle kept her eyes down on the stained plaid-brown-on-brown carpet, putting one booted foot in front of the other, a huge noise roaring in her head, brightly colored spots in front of her eyes. If the room was far away, she wasn't going to make it.

Luckily the room was close by, just around the corridor to the right. She held the card up to the sensor with one hand, and balanced herself against the door jamb with the other. She felt more than heard the clunky *click* as it opened. In a normal hotel, by law the card would log her name and time of entrance and eventual time of exit in the central computer, but Jane had said this kind of place didn't go in for niceties.

Elle stumbled into the room, pulled the door closed, walked to the window, and closed the blinds. She leaned against the wall next to the window and finally her legs gave way, simply wouldn't hold her up any longer. Her purse *thunked* to the floor as her knees buckled.

She slid with her back to the wall down to the dirty carpeting, clasping her arms around her legs, leaning her head forward until it rested against her knees.

Trembling started from her legs, traveling up through her body like an electric wave. She sat there in the dark, arms and legs shaking, a deep chill in her core, riding out the storm.

She lost control over her own body. It shook and shivered and panted and she could do nothing to stop it. It was physical and mental and spiritual. It was as if she'd come up against some inner boundary, a place where everything had to stop because she could go no further.

Had nothing left.

Could barely breathe, let alone plan the next step.

She sank down deep inside herself, the world slowly turning black.

And it was because she was so weak and so depleted, because she reached some dark place of despair that held her deepest truths, that it slipped from her.

Something she'd sworn she'd never do, something that in any other moment she'd rather die than think, came welling out.

From deep inside her, it came. Totally unstoppable, torn from her.

A call so strong it was a scream inside her head.

Help me, Nick.

Chapter 7

Mount Blue
Haven
Northern California

Nick Ross bolted up in bed on a gasp, heart drumming against his
ribs, sweat popping out all over his body. Clapping his hands for
the light, he threw back the covers and rushed for the door. Remembering at the last minute that he was naked.

In a fever of impatience, he turned back and hopped into the
clothes he'd thrown onto a chair an hour ago. His usual—black
jeans, black sweatshirt, black combat boots. Without bothering to
lace his boots he raced outside.

Usually, he got a rush when he walked outside his door. He'd
rather die than say it, or even show it, but he loved Haven. He
and his teammates were on the run from the U.S. government:
fugitives, outlaws. They'd built a secret city and somehow a community of misfits had gathered around them. He and Jon Ryan and
Mac McEnroe didn't even question it after a while. People came,

always on the run from something bad, and the three soldiers protected them.

It was a mountain—a forgotten, hollowed-out silver mine that had been turned into a thriving community of runaways and outlaws. Like Hole in the Wall in the old west, only high-tech. The community was circular, built inside the mountain. Every time Nick stepped out from his quarters, he always paused along the balcony that ringed the huge open atrium below. His community, his people. Gave him a rush, every time.

Except now.

He'd pressed their emergency button, the one that had never been used up until now, connected to Jon's and Mac's rooms, before bolting out the door. Jon's room was on his floor, Mac's was two stories up. He ran straight to the end of the corridor and when he passed Jon's door he bellowed, *"Jon! Situation room, stat!"* He banged his fist, hard, on the door, then hit the stairs at a run. The elevator would be too slow. He took the stairs four at a time and at the end simply vaulted over the bannisters down to the floor below and ran for the situation room.

The doors of the room were biomorphically programmed to open for him, Mac, or Jon, but it took two seconds to process and he had to stand there, three feet out, practically hopping in place, fear and panic prickling along his nervous system, until the door whooshed open.

He rushed inside and skidded to a stop, looking around wildly for something—anything—that could help.

Their situation room wouldn't have been out of place in the New Pentagon. They had it all, including holographic monitors showing every inch of the security perimeter around Haven. If a jackrabbit shat in the woods, they knew about it. They were illegally linked into every overhead satellite, and at any given moment one or two of their almost invisible drones was dropping visual, IR, and thermal images onto their servers. That kind of intel would be considered a security breach serious enough to warrant a court-martial, but since the entire U.S. military was gunning for them, and a court-martial had found them guilty of treason in absentia anyway, they figured why not. Their server farm, hidden in the mountain, was one of the largest in the world. They had serious crunching power at their disposal.

Not to mention serious firepower. The armory would do any military installation proud.

None of it helpful at the moment because what Nick really, *really* needed was—

What?

Fuck. He didn't know what he needed, but he needed it *now.*

The door whooshed open, Jon came in at a run. Wheeling to a stop, he checked the monitors—which showed acres and acres of nighttime mountainside. Utterly peaceful, utterly normal, utterly calm. Sensors blinking green. "What the fuck, Nick?" Jon's bright blue eyes narrowed as he glared at him. His blond hair was tousled, shirt buttoned wrong, sweatpants hanging off his hips. He looked around again at the monitors, brought his gaze back. "I repeat—what the fuck?"

It took every ounce of his self-control, but Nick managed not to twirl around, hands on head, looking for something that could be an outside sign of what was going on inside. His heart was pounding, adrenaline running through his system and he had nowhere to go with it. Nothing to hang this huge flaming ball of desperation on.

He tried to speak, but his throat was too tight. On the second try he got it but what he wanted to say was so enormous his voice cracked. "She needs me. She's in danger and I have to get to her now, and I don't know where she is and she fucking *needs* me." Normally he would have been ashamed to death that his indrawn breath sounded like a sob, but right now he didn't give a fuck. It didn't matter. Nothing mattered but Elle.

Jon's eyes narrowed further. "Who needs you? What are you talking about?"

All Nick could do was stand there and pant, fists clenched so hard the knuckles were white. Ready to fight Jon, ready to fight the world if it could help her, but it wouldn't. He couldn't help her until he knew where she was and what she needed.

"Elle," he said simply, because with all the thoughts swirling in his head, that was the only thing that stood out. That made sense. Elle.

Elle. In danger. God. He couldn't even stay in the same room with that thought.

Jon shook his head and turned gratefully when the door opened. Mac walked in, arm around his wife. His pregnant wife. The pregnant wife Nick had woken up. Both men were now glaring at him. Catherine McEnroe was an incredibly special woman and Mac wasn't happy that she'd had her rest interrupted. Even pregnant, she worked tirelessly as a doctor taking care of their little community. So, yeah, interrupting Catherine's sleep was a big no-no.

Everyone treated Catherine with kid gloves. Even Nick, who liked her and respected her. But Elle—Elle trumped Catherine any day.

He didn't give a shit about anyone's sleep if Elle was in danger.

"Elle," he repeated, his voice raw.

"L?" Mac asked, frowning. "The letter?"

Jon took it up. "L for link? L for lonely? L for—"

"Elle." It was the only thing he could say. His head was going to blow up. Every single danger hormone in his body was awake with nowhere to go. He was a guy built for action, and he always knew which action to take. To be so primed, so pumped, so fucking scared and dying to race to the rescue but have no idea *where* was driving him bat-shit crazy.

His fingers beat a harsh tattoo against his thigh and his foot was tapping. Jon, Mac, and Catherine simply stared at him. He knew what they were thinking—Nick Ross *agitated? Scared?* What was that about?

Nick didn't do agitated and scared.

"Nick," Catherine said gently and took his shaking hand in both of hers. Mac tensed. Everyone knew Nick didn't like being touched. But this wasn't someone he didn't know entering his personal space. This was Catherine, and her touch . . . soothed. Calmed him, just a little.

She held on to his hand, watching his eyes. After a moment she nodded. "It's her, isn't it?"

His head jerked awkwardly, neck stiff with tension.

Catherine had something. He didn't know what, nobody knew what really, but she had . . . something. If she touched you, she understood you. And, lately, if she touched you, you felt better. Which explained why her husband, Mac, the toughest, meanest son of a bitch on the planet, was walking around with a goofy grin on his hard, ugly, scarred mug.

Nick had wondered about that. About being married to someone like Catherine. Someone who understood you inside out with a touch. Understood you and loved you.

Elle had loved him. It had been clear in her eyes, her voice, her face. She'd loved him and he'd lost her and—Oh God, she was in danger. She needed him and he didn't know how the fuck to find her.

He shivered, turned his sweaty face to Catherine.

"Yeah. She's the one you felt when you touched me." A few days after Catherine somehow found them in Haven—a place three experts in security had hidden carefully away from the world—she'd touched him and understood that he'd lost someone, that he was worried sick about someone.

She never went there again and neither did anyone else.

But now it had to come out.

He grabbed Catherine's hand, barely noticing Mac and Jon exchanging looks. "Read me," he whispered urgently, clasping her hand hard between his trembling hands. "Tell me where she is. What's happening to her. I got a call for help and I don't know where she is and, *Oh God . . .*"

Nick's throat closed tight. Nothing more could come out. He clung to Catherine's hand as if it were a lifeline. A raging river was tumbling him over and over down an endless descent into hell and only her touch could make sense of it.

Catherine was shaking her head slowly, eyes on his, face sad. "I am so sor—" She stopped, breathed out, tilted her head. Even though she was looking straight at him, her eyes grew distant as if watching something a thousand yards away. Her grip tightened, her hand warming up until it felt red hot in his cold ones.

"Elle," she whispered and Nick broke out in a cold sweat. He was shaking, could barely breathe.

"Yeah," he said hoarsely.

"What?" Catherine blinked.

"Elle, Elle, *Elle*," he shouted.

Mac's jaw tightened. Nick didn't give a shit. Mac could shove it up his ass if it bothered him that Nick was shouting at his wife. Because Catherine knew something and something was better than what he had right now, which was a shitload of nothing. No intel, no idea where she was, nothing but ashes in his hand and his head exploding from the need to get to Elle as fast as humanly possible. Wherever the fuck she was . . .

He had no idea. But maybe Catherine did. He stepped closer to Catherine and Mac took a step forward too. Jon grabbed Mac's arm and shook his head.

Well, fuck.

Nick wasn't going to hurt Catherine. If Mac used his brains instead of his dick, he'd know that. But Nick wasn't letting Catherine walk away without finding out what she knew, however the hell she knew it.

"That's the name you said." Nick ground his teeth at her blank look. "Just now. Just now you said Elle. That's the name of my— The name of the person I need to find."

His throat was so tight. Just hearing her name after so many years—he couldn't think straight.

"Elle," she said softly.

Nick nodded, like some big dumb animal that couldn't speak. Elle.

Catherine was focusing on him again. Her other hand came up to clasp his in a tight grip, warm and soft. Something to cling to in the painful darkness of his terror.

"That's the one I felt, right, Nick? The one you lost?"

He nodded again. Tried to speak. Failed.

"You care about her." It wasn't a question.

Oh God, yes. He nodded again, jerkily. Found his voice. "Where is she? She needs me. Now. I have to get to her, right now." He was vibrating with tension, ready to take off anywhere Catherine said.

There was sadness on Catherine's beautiful face. She tightened her clasp. "Oh Nick. I'm so sorry. It doesn't work that way."

An icy chill worked its way through his veins and he realized he'd been subconsciously counting on Catherine to do her woo-woo stuff. Point him in Elle's direction so he could race to her. "Then how the hell does it work? Can you tell me that?" He stepped even closer to Catherine, right in her face, his voice rising.

Out of the corner of his eye he saw Jon grab Mac's arm again. Not even Jon could stop Mac if Mac didn't want to be stopped, but Mac got himself under control. Nick wasn't going to hurt Catherine, but he *was* going to question her.

He was staring wildly down into Catherine's eyes, as if he could will the information on Elle's whereabouts out of her, drag it out of her through her skin if necessary. But staring was an act of aggression. They'd been taught that, at the beginning of their careers as soldiers. Body language had been a big thing. How to silently threaten, how to pass unnoticed, how to reassure.

He didn't want to scare Catherine.

With a wrench, Nick turned his gaze away from Catherine and stared blindly at the room. Their war room, they called it. With everything you needed to go on an op. Just as long as you knew where you were going, of course.

As soon as he knew where to head, Nick was going to grab Jon, drag him to their ultralight stealth helo, and take off.

Nick was the team driver. If it was anything that traveled over land, Nick could drive it as fast as it could go over any terrain. Jon was the pilot. Their little helo could make it anywhere in the Continental U.S. It was the dead of night. Little Bird could silently land in any private airfield without detection. They could fuel up and be gone before anyone knew they were there. They'd done it before.

Nick didn't even want to think what would happen if Elle were OUTCONUS. Didn't want to go there. Couldn't.

She'd called out to him. That had been a distress signal he'd heard in his head, loud and clear. Surely there was—was a *range* for that sort of thing? Surely he wouldn't have heard it if she were in Europe or Africa?

The signal he'd got was loud and absolutely urgent. She was in danger *right now*, and if she was across an ocean she was fucked and, *oh God* . . . He couldn't wrap his head around that thought.

Elle dead, Elle dying . . . he couldn't do this. Simply couldn't.

Catherine's sympathetic face—he couldn't look at that either. His eyes roamed the big room, partly to distract himself from that awful panicky desperation that gripped him, so he could function on some basic level, and partly to see if something in their gear-packed room could help.

Huge holographic monitors ringed the walls. They had tiny drones of their own hovering 24/7 over a ten-square-mile radius

surrounding Haven, and thus had a 360-degree IR view of everything. Highly sensitive motion sensors and sound sensors. If a fly
farted anywhere near them, they knew about it. Their computers were illegally hooked into the Keyhole 15 satellites and they
could get real-time intel on more or less anything happening in the
world, particularly in the Fucked-Up Latitudes.

All Nick needed was a location and he could zoom in on her.

A location he didn't have.

So the holograms, the satellite feeds, the vast crunching power
of their servers—their server farm was bigger than the Pentagon's,
bigger even than Amazon's—couldn't help. Behind the titanium
door on the left-hand wall was an armory that would do a Delta
team proud. Nick had been Delta, and there were a few extra
goodies in there that even Delta hadn't had.

If there was an enemy, they could take them out, no question.
They had the tools and the determination to protect what they had.

Hell, Mac had a wife and a baby on the way to protect. Mac all
by himself was a war machine.

So they had the stuff to get there, wipe out the opposition, and
come back in stealth.

He, Mac, and Jon were really good at slipping into places
and extracting things and people. They hadn't been Ghost Ops
for nothing. They were Ghosts because everything about their
past had been erased. Wiped clean. They didn't exist anywhere
on earth. And they were Ghosts because they had been trained
to move with stealth. When they didn't want to be found, they
weren't.

Even here, creating a community of geniuses and misfits, they
hadn't been found.

Taking stock of the war room calmed Nick, just a little. When
he found out where Elle was, there'd be firepower and the will to
use it. He didn't care if she had a fucking army after her.

But where was she?

It was a male operator's paradise, full of high-tech gear and comms. With a woman's touch in the far corner. Catherine had been a researcher before going on a mission to find a man she'd never met, Mac. She'd been sent on that mission by their former commander, Captain Lucius Ward, the man they thought had betrayed them.

Ward hadn't betrayed them. He'd been betrayed himself and had lost his health and his sanity after a year in the hands of monsters. They'd gone to the rescue of the captain and been astonished to find three of their comrades who had been experimented on until they were nearly dead.

Romero, Lundquist, and Pelton had lost almost a third of their body weight, had been crisscrossed with surgical scars, and had lost the ability to talk when they'd been brought back to Haven.

So Catherine was caring for them, bringing them back to life, while trying to figure out what had been done to them. That something was very, very bad.

She was a neat woman so her corner wasn't the mess that their space was, but she'd obviously been interrupted. Maybe by her husband Mac carrying her off to their cave. They disappeared together a lot.

A big briefcase had toppled on Catherine's desk, paperwork spilling down out of it like a glacier's moraine. She was researching what had been done to their teammates and the captain. A series of glossy company brochures and prospectuses cascaded down. He stared at the pile of documents.

Catherine's soft voice cut in.

"What? What is it, Nick?"

She repeated whatever it was she'd said before. Nick saw her mouth move but couldn't figure out the words. He was staring at Catherine's corner of their war room. He couldn't tear his eyes away. It was as if a spotlight had lit up her briefcase.

She said something else and Nick tried really, really hard to concentrate. But it was useless. He'd focus on her, then his mind and his eyes would wander.

A slap to the back of his head nearly sent him spinning to the floor. "Focus, you dickhead," Mac growled. "Catherine's trying to help your sorry ass."

Nick breathed in, breathed out. Without moving his head, his eyes slid back to Catherine's corner. Catherine's arm snaked out and it took him a second to realize that she blocked her husband's arm.

"Wait, Mac," she said, tilting her head to look at Nick. "Is something happening?"

Was something happening? Fuck if he knew.

"Why are you staring at my briefcase, Nick?"

"Huh?" He felt so stupid. Usually he was quick. His usual response to things was at lightning speed. He was on alert, always. Nothing ever took him by surprise. He was reacting to danger before most other men even realized it was there.

Now he felt slow, sluggish. Thoughts occurred to him slowly, as if they had to take a huge trip to get to his head. It was as if his head were taken up by a computer virus slowing everything down.

Soft warmth on his cheeks. Catherine's hands on his face. "Look at me, Nick."

He looked at her, though his eyes swiveled. She shook him lightly. *"Look at me."*

Reluctantly, he tore his eyes from the corner and looked into her eyes, fiercely focused on him. "There's something over there that is sparking something in you. What is it?"

He shrugged. "Dunno," he mumbled. And he didn't. He had no idea what was in Catherine's briefcase and he didn't care. And yet, his eyes slid back to the corner.

Another slap to the back of his head he barely felt. "Nick," Mac growled.

Catherine rolled her eyes. "Stop that, Mac. You're not helping. Step back."

And Mac stepped back.

Amazing. Even with everything roiling inside him, Nick marveled at Mac's obedience. Nobody gave Mac an order, ever, except their former captain, Lucius Ward. Ward was still too sick to give orders so Mac was still God. He was 6'4" of pure muscle and meanness who turned into a house pet when his wife spoke.

Catherine didn't stop to savor her victory. Mac had more or less rolled over for her the instant they met, so she didn't fully appreciate having a killing machine like Mac obey her. She walked to the corner, stuffed everything back into the briefcase, and brought it over to Nick.

His eyes followed her every step of the way.

She replicated the spill of documents on the table in front of Nick.

He greedily eyed everything, unable to take his gaze off perfectly ordinary pieces of paper and some glossy brochures.

"Nick." Catherine put her hand on his once more. It was a deliberate move and not even Mac objected. Catherine had some kind of secret power, some woo-woo thing that scared him and everyone else because it wasn't woo-woo. It was fact. If she touched you, she knew what you were feeling. And lately, terrifyingly, if she touched you, she knew what you were thinking.

Must be scary shit to be married to someone who could walk around inside your head but Mac looked pretty happy about it.

"Nick." Catherine's hand tightened and Nick tore his eyes away from the briefcase. "Talk to me. Tell me what happened. What has you so upset?"

"Upset." A sound came from his throat that was more an animal sound than a human one. "Upset is spilling soup, missing a train. Elle's in *danger*. I'm not upset about that, I'm scared out of my fucking mind!"

He was sweating like a pig, heart pounding erratically. He felt like a machine that was broken and shaking to pieces.

"Okay. Okay. Calm down. You're not helping her by panicking." Catherine put her other hand around his. Nick wanted to snarl at her, but with his hand encased in hers he actually felt his heart rate starting to slow. Something was working. "Tell me exactly what happened."

His heart gave a huge pump. His voice rose. "She's in trouble. She somehow contacted me after all these years and she's in trouble! In danger!" His gaze slid back to her briefcase. It glowed, as if in a spotlight.

"No, Nick." Catherine's voice was soft but firm. "You're not telling me what happened, you're telling me your reaction. You were sleeping? Nick!" Her voice sounded like a slap. "Look at me!"

He slid his eyes to her, reluctantly.

"You were sleeping?"

"Yes." He had to force the word out through a tight throat.

"Something woke you up?"

"*Elle!* She woke me up! Oh God, she . . ."

Catherine gave his hand a shake. "Focus hard, Nick. You're not helping Elle at all. She's in trouble and she might die because you can't focus on anything but your feelings. I can feel you—you are one big wave of panic and fear. That is not going to help Elle. You can only help her if you remain calm and focused. Forget your feelings. Focus on the situation. Focus on helping Elle."

Fuck. She was right.

Focus.

Nick took in a huge gulp of air.

He hardly recognized himself. He'd been a Ranger, he'd been Delta, he'd been Ghost Ops. No one had ever had to tell him to focus. He was nothing but focus. Brutal and unyielding. On a mission, he was pure cold steel.

Now he was trembling, sweaty, mind flying into a million tiny pieces.

"Come on, Nick." Catherine looked serious, frowning. "Help me here. Help me help you."

His eyes slid back to the briefcase. It gave him something. Some sense of calm, a point to focus on.

"Let's go back to the beginning. Look at me, Nick."

Damn. His eyes swiveled. "Looking."

"You were sleeping. Were you dreaming?"

Had he been? Yeah. He'd been dreaming of Elle. Of the last time he'd seen her. And goddamn if it hadn't been a wet dream. He'd woken up with a hard-on that he lost the second he got the danger message. No way was he going to say he woke up with a hard-on. Not in front of Catherine. Or Mac or Jon for that matter.

"Nick? Dreaming?"

"Yeah," he muttered.

"Of her? Of Elle?"

"Yeah." His jaws clenched.

"Was there something different about the dream?"

He was checking her briefcase, but swung his head to her at the words. "Different how?" He couldn't help himself, help his suspicious tone.

She kept her voice soft. "Do you often dream of her, of Elle?"

No! The word was right there, in his mouth, filling his mouth. No, of course he didn't dream of Elle. That would reveal a weakness. A man was weak in sleep, couldn't control himself. So, no, he didn't dream of Elle. He didn't dream of anything, fuck you very much. His dreams were his own goddamned business.

"Yes," he said.

She nodded. "And this one had a different flavor?"

Well, he'd woken up with a woodie, if that's what she meant. He'd woken up in a sweaty panic.

"Close your eyes, Nick."

"What?" *Christ*. Time was this big heavy thing swirling around a drain. Elle was in danger, in danger *right now*. He didn't have time for this shit!

Nick shifted on his feet. He wanted to pull away from Catherine, run for the door, but . . . he couldn't free himself.

He was strong. He'd been strong all his life. He'd been in the military for almost half his life and every single fucking day he'd trained for combat. He was a shooter. He'd shot several million rounds in his life. His hands were strong. Once he'd tested at 180 pounds on the grip-strength test. He could crush Catherine's hand in a nanosecond.

Except . . . he couldn't. He couldn't pull free from her.

"You are scared and you want to spring into action." Catherine's eyes exerted a pull as great as her hand. He couldn't look away from her. "But you have no idea where to go. I'm trying to help you, Nick. If Elle sent you a message, she also sent you the way to find her. So you need to listen hard to what she tried to tell you. Now *close your eyes*."

There was no way to disobey her. He closed his eyes.

"Clear your mind," Catherine said. "There's only Elle, and the message she sent you. That's all there is in the world. She's in trouble and if she called for help, there's a way to find her in her message. So think carefully. You were dreaming about her. And you heard a cry for help. Think back to that cry."

Nick nodded, thought back.

"You were dreaming about her, about Elle. Then the dream changed, correct?"

He nodded again. *Exactly*. That was exactly it. It was as if Catherine had been there.

"All of a sudden, it lost that dreamlike feeling and become real. Something you could touch and feel."

"Yes." That had been exactly it.

"You woke up and felt the danger."

His eyes opened. "Yes." All over his body, every cell prickling with it. Even before he heard the words, the call.

"Did you *see* her?"

Did he? Nick dug deep. There was this huge overlay of sweaty panic. He had to get rid of that, try to remember. His jaw clenched. "Yes, I think—I think I did."

Another squeeze of his hand. "What did she look like?"

"Older." The word popped out as the images in his head suddenly coalesced. "Tired. Scared. She had— She had her hair all in her face," he said suddenly. "Short hair. Chin length. She always wore her hair long—" A sudden flash of memory of Elle's hair trailing over his stomach like a pale waterfall nearly killed him. "But it's short now. All in her face, messy-like. She's bleeding—" Mouth dry, he tried to swallow. "From a cut. It's deep. She's— She's worried about it. But not because of the cut itself. There's something else about the cut, but I don't know what." He found himself rocking in distress. "I'm not understanding this."

"Okay," Catherine suggested gently, "don't worry about the cut right now. Put that aside. Is she sitting or standing?"

What the fuck difference did it make? Still— "Sitting," he said, decisively. Suddenly, the knowledge was there, in his head. A picture of Elle, face in her hands, shoulders sloped in despair. The despair colored the air around her, was deep and dark. *Oh Elle.* "She's sitting on the floor, back to the wall."

"What's the room like?"

He hadn't even thought of that. Everything had been centered on Elle, in danger. He concentrated harder. "Not a—a house. Or at least her house. I don't get that impression. Everything feels cheap, slightly dirty. Not like her at all." The last time he'd seen her, she'd been absolutely broke, but even then everything had been clean. Threadbare but clean. The place she was in felt dirty and downscale.

"What is she seeing, Nick?"

He screwed his eyes more tightly shut. What was she seeing? He had no idea.

"Dunno. Walls. A bed. But— it feels strange to her, not familiar."

"Like a—a hotel?"

Jesus, yes! "Yeah, like a hotel. Or . . . she's on the first floor. Maybe a motel?"

"Do you have a sense of what it looks like from the outside? If it's an unfamiliar place, she'll have noticed more about it than her own home, which would be so familiar to her. So think. Reach in through the scream for help to see if there's more information there. There will be. You just have to find it."

Damn. Catherine was making sense. But it had been like one huge powerful pulse, strong enough to wake him, to panic him, but no hidden messages.

Nick waited, sweating, then shook his head.

"Think back to the dream. Just before it faded. Can you try to remember what was there before that beacon lit up to call you to her? I'm sure there was an image that must have bled into the beacon. When she called for help, it must have been part of the call. That's the only way it would work. Any call that strong, to wake you up from a distance, would have information in it. Hidden, maybe. Or rather the beacon call was so strong you can't perceive the other data in it." She looked swiftly at her husband, then at Jon, the team cybergeek. "Think of it as—Jon, what do you call it when information is hidden but not encrypted in a computer message?"

"Steganography." Jon was watching everything soberly. His default emotional mode was manic, teasing, but he wasn't teasing or facetious now. He was dead serious.

"Steganography, right." Catherine turned back to Nick. "Think of it as what you'd call intel hidden in a message. She'd have some sense of where she is in the call for help if you got the sense that she wasn't home. If she were home, that would be background noise for her. But if she's away from home, on the run, that would be part of the emergency call."

Put that way . . .

"Think back. You got this call. What did it feel like?"

What did it feel like? It felt like shit—Elle in danger and he didn't know how to help her. "Like Elle threw a rock at my head. The way you do at a window. Then screamed for help."

Catherine was listening to him with every fiber of her being, concentrated wholly on him, holding his hand. "That feeling you had. The feeling that she wasn't in her home, in a familiar environment. That came from her, from Elle. She wasn't beaming that at you, but it was in the message. She must have come to the place from somewhere else. So, in your head, try to spool back, as if it were a tape on rewind. Just slide your finger from right to left in your head. Picture it, Nick. Sliding your finger, going back in time."

Her voice was almost hypnotic. Her gray eyes were glowing as if a lightbulb had lit up behind her eyes.

"Back, Nick," she murmured. "Slide it back. I'm there with you."

He slid it back. Back . . .

Catherine's eyes dimmed. She tightened her hand on his. "I'm reading *you* too much, Nick. You're like a foghorn while I'm trying to listen to music. Calm down, cool it. You're deafening me."

Nick didn't have to look to know that Mac and Jon were exchanging glances. No one ever had to tell him to cool it, ever. He was nothing *but* cool. Cold as ice. Elle was the only thing that had ever wiped away that cool. He had shed tears exactly once in his lifetime—sitting on the edge of Elle's bed back in Lawrence, knowing she was gone forever.

And now.

Knowing she needed him and being unable to help because he was a mess inside.

"You are a cool, calm, still lake," Catherine said. "Emotionless, inert."

He was a cool, calm, still lake. Emotionless, inert.

"I'm feeling it," Catherine said softly. Her hand on his glowed with warmth. She was somehow reading him. Reading Elle through him. "Fear. Not yours, Nick. Hers."

"Panic," he said and swallowed.

"Yes." Catherine's eyes were closed now, her voice a whisper so low he could barely hear her. "Panic. She's on the run. Running away from . . . I can't tell. Men in black suits, with—" She stopped, the dreaminess in her voice gone. She looked over to Mac and swallowed. "I've been around you guys long enough to recognize it. She's being pursued by men wearing combat gear, fully armed, with nightvision."

Nick froze. He could almost hear Jon and Mac stiffening with attention. Catherine had just described soldiers. Or if not soldiers, then elite corporate security. Either way bad news. The worst news possible. Trained men gunning for one woman.

Calm, still as a lake . . .

"Men are coming for her, outside her house." Catherine breathed in and out, somehow glowing once again.

Nick picked up. He was getting images, flickering as if in an old-time movie. Fragmented—there and not there. Yet somehow he could follow because there was the essence of Elle there, and he could follow Elle to the ends of the earth.

Nick spoke. "Those guys in combat gear, they're coming fast. Co-ordinated. But she's been warned. She's somehow wounded, in her arm. There's pain that she is blocking out. She grabs her bag and runs out and down, down—down a set of stairs, past the ground floor, down . . . There's a long dark corridor, very long. She runs to the end of it, goes up the stairs, out into a backyard. She cuts across a number of yards; she knows where she's going. She runs as fast as she can until she stops. Clings to a lamppost. The street is—

anonymous. Just normal houses, not too rich, not too poor. She runs again, as fast as she can, down dark streets with nothing remarkable to identify them. The houses are getting poorer, though. The streets are darker. She's afraid. It's a bad part of town. But I don't know of what town. She stops, winded. She's looking at a building. Very shabby, faded green façade. There's a neon sign, VACANCIES. The first A and the E are burned out. I can't make out the name. She's feeling—not safe so much as anonymous. She signs in, pays in cash, leaves a false name. Have no idea what it is. She fades in and out."

"Did you get a sense of where she is, Nick? Where this hotel or motel might be?"

Nick's free hand clenched. *Well, fuck. If I knew that, I wouldn't be here, twiddling my freaking thumbs, I'd be on my way to her, wouldn't I?* But he couldn't say that. Couldn't speak disrespectfully to Catherine. First, because Mac would flatten him. Second, because he liked Catherine. And third, because she was trying to help. "Don't know." A shudder ran through him at his own words. "I don't know."

"Ah, but you do," Catherine said, her voice gentle. Nick's hand jerked in hers. "Listen to your body, Nick."

What the—

"Your body is talking to you. Listen to it."

His eyes popped open, slid over her face to the briefcase. Slid back. Nope. His body was telling him jack shit.

Catherine let go of his hand and pulled her briefcase toward her, pulling out a wad of paperwork, a sheaf of what looked like lab reports and some glossy thick paper, brochures of some kind.

For some reason, her movements fascinated him. He watched, almost enthralled.

"This has been calling to you. You haven't been able to take your eyes off it. There's something here that is of importance."

Catherine began methodically placing the paperwork in neat

piles all along the ten-foot-long table filled with holographic monitors that served as command central.

Nick watched as she butted the lab reports into a neat stack, another set of printouts of God knows what, then she started fanning the brochures and prospectuses, leaving each company logo clear.

One suddenly lit up in his head as if a spotlight shone on it.

"That!" he shouted. His shaking finger pointed.

"What, Nick?"

He stood up, rushed to the fanned-out glossy company brochures. His finger landed on one in the center. Three stylized gold crowns. Corona Labs—BRINGING THE FUTURE TODAY.

"This," he said, finger tapping. Each time he touched the paper it seemed to get warmer.

This turned out to be the brochure for a new company.

Catherine picked it up, showed it to her husband. "I thought I knew more or less all the research labs in the country, but this is a new one." Mac turned the glossy paper over in his big hands. There was a videolette loop embedded in the paper, all the rage nowadays. Some smiling woman in a lab coat endlessly raising a test tube in triumph, putting it down, raising it . . .

Nick was shaking with tension. The logo, the name Corona Laboratories meant nothing to him, but still they shone in his mind.

In a corner he could hear Jon restlessly tapping on the light keyboard—a projection of heat-sensitive light on the table. Jon's fingers were a blur.

Mac handed the brochure to Nick. "This mean anything to you?"

Nick took the thick glossy paper and studied it carefully. The smiling woman, raising her hand with the test tube and putting it down in an endless loop was completely unfamiliar to him. He studied the text—

Corona Laboratories—Bringing the future today.
Corona Laboratories is an offshoot of several highly

successful research labs, dedicated exclusively to the
study of neuroscience . . .

Technobabble.

Nick flipped back and forth. The brochure was one of those folded into thirds. The videolette on the cover. Opening it, company data on the left-hand side and what they called the "core mission" in the center. The right-hand leaf was taken up with the premises of the company—a crystal Buckminster structure aboveground, extensive skylights set in some grassy meadow. Underground it was huge.

He didn't give a shit about any of it. This fucking brochure had practically reached out and grabbed him by the balls, so why wasn't he getting what it was supposed to tell him?

He looked it over again and again, even flipping it upside down, which did nothing but give him a headache. The reflection off the glossy paper nearly blinded him. He narrowed his eyes.

Catherine was watching him closely. "What, Nick?"

He shook his head, like shaking off water. A sharp movement.

The contact info—the address seemed to leap out at him.

1657 McGraw Drive, Palo Alto.

Palo Alto.

"Hey!" Jon shouted just as Nick dropped the paper as if it burned his fingers.

Jon swiveled the screen. He'd turned the hologram function off, the screen was showing a newspaper article with no photographs. "Corona Laboratories was bought a year ago by none other than Arka Pharmaceuticals." He turned to Nick. "Whatever it is that's calling to you, buddy, it's no good."

Arka Pharmaceuticals had kept their former commander and three of their teammates prisoner, conducting experiments that would have done the Nazis proud, for over a year. The year he, Mac, and Jon had been in exile, convinced their commander had betrayed them. Lucius Ward hadn't betrayed them. He'd been betrayed himself and had paid a terrible price.

Catherine had worked for a company owned by Arka and they still had men out looking for her. Arka was a multibillion dollar company with a whole board full of people who would testify that it was run by angels. Nobody would ever believe that an Arka-run lab had tortured highly-decorated soldiers. Nobody would believe that they would kill Catherine on sight.

Of course now she was in Haven, their high-tech community of misfits where, like everyone else, she fit right in. She was now revered, actually, as the community doctor. Not to mention the fact that she had Mac guarding her day and night, and if anything ever happened to Mac, then he and Jon would step right in. Both of them would give their lives to keep Catherine safe. Arka wasn't getting its hands on her.

And now Arka was somehow involved in a threat to Elle too. She was under threat right now and he didn't know where the fuck she was, except that she was in some seedy motel with a faded green façade . . .

"Palo Alto!" Nick shouted and all but smacked himself in the face. Somehow hidden in the distress call was the image of Corona Laboratories. Maybe she worked there, maybe she didn't. The fact was that Corona was mixed up in the threat to her and Corona was headquartered in Palo Alto. The city was less than an hour away by helo. "She's got to be there, that's why I couldn't keep my eyes off that goddamned brochure. Jon—"

But Jon was grimly tapping on the conference table surface, connected to four monitors. "On it," he said.

Nick rushed to his side, skin prickling. He'd been paralyzed with fear, but now urgency rushed over him like a flood that had been dammed up but now released. Elle was in Palo Alto! He knew it, could feel it. He'd been blasted with a distress signal but with no way to know the point of origin, and it had been driving him insane. Elle could have been in New York, Alaska, fucking France. All places it would take him hours and hours to get to. But she was in Palo Alto and their helo could get him to her in less than an hour. Oh Jesus . . .

Jon had pulled up a Google map and was checking a list of motels. It was painstaking work because it wasn't like facial recognition with known parameters. A faded green façade wasn't much of an identifier and they needed night shots to see a sign with a letter missing.

"Go to a forty-mile perimeter," Nick said and the first screen zoomed out. "Go dark." Jon tapped the table and all the screens showed night shots, most illegally hacked from the Keyhole 15 satellites, some from their own drones.

The second screen was flashing hotels and motels. They stopped at a shot of a building with a neon sign flashing VACA CIES. Nick studied it. A tall red brick relic from the thirties, it looked like. A distinctive tattered awning over the entrance. It felt dull and lifeless. Wrong, in every sense. He shook his head. "No."

Ten minutes later they had it. A low building set in a depressed-looking strip mall. V CANCI S a neon sign posted on top of a pole advertised.

"Day shots coming up—now!" Jon switched the screen and, yes, there it was. A low-lying building once painted green, now faded. The address was underneath—2442 Century Way. The GPS data was there, and it gave distance from landmarks around Palo Alto. Nick was an excellent orienteer. He could get to the place on the monitor blindfolded. Now that he knew Elle was there, he'd walk over glass shards barefoot to get there. The screen shot pulsed with meaning. From the depths of his being came the certainty. Elle was there, in that building, right now.

If she wasn't dead.

"She's there!" he shouted. "I can feel it. Jon, start Little Bird up!"

Jon could start Little Bird up from a remote that was kept in the armory. On mission it was set on the inside of his wrist with derma-glue. If he started it up now, Little Bird would be already firing up its rotors by the time they made it down to the hangar.

Nick was at the door, but he was alone. No Jon.

He looked over his shoulder, wild with urgency. Now that he knew where Elle was, the rush was in his blood like a fever. Even this extra minute might mean the difference between life and death for Elle. What the fuck was Jon waiting for?

"Jon!" he said sharply. "Come on!"

But Jon was shaking his head and if Nick didn't know better, if he didn't know that Jon didn't do emotion, he'd swear he saw sadness in Jon's eyes. "Can't." His voice was lifeless, dull. "Little Bird's rotor head is broken. I went down to Sacramento to an aviation parts dealer today to steal a new one, but I haven't had time to install it. It'll take a couple of hours at least. I'll step on it, you know I will, but I'm working alone. The only other guy who knows enough about it to help is Pelton."

Catherine gasped. Pelton, one of the men they'd rescued from Arka's dungeon three months ago, had only recently come out of a coma. He was in their infirmary, flat on his back still, IVs running in and tubes running out. No way was Pelton going to be any help.

Well, fuck it. Nick wasn't going to waste any time with regrets. It was what it was. "Send me a drone over the motel! I'm taking the hovercar!" he shouted over his shoulder as he ran for the hangar.

Chapter 8

Arka Pharmaceuticals Headquarters
San Francisco

Former General Clancy Flynn twirled a huge gold ring around his meaty finger, blew out a breath, tugged at his tie. It was a red silk Valentino tie that went nicely with the tailored suit, which was obviously bespoke. No designer made that size.

Dr. Charles Lee suppressed a light shudder.

Flynn became more disgusting every time they met. It was as if Flynn were on this hugely accelerated Bloat Program. He'd put on ten pounds every time they met. He was now at least three hundred pounds. The very weight of Flynn's flesh had assumed a gravity of its own and it was dragging him down. Though Lee kept his office at a cool and constant 72 degrees, Flynn was sweating, his own flesh acting like a heat generator. His heart had to beat twice as hard to get blood around all that meat. His sweat stank—a rancid odor that was stronger than the men's cologne he wore and the smell of expensive laundered material swathing his grossly huge body.

Flynn was a heart attack in waiting, except he had to wait to have it until Lee's program was complete.

Flynn ran a very successful and lucrative security company founded on the contacts Flynn had made in his twenty-five years in the military. Flynn was very greedy. Lee's program was the key to great wealth, but they'd had some stumbling blocks. Quite a few, actually. The last one cost over a million dollars. But Lee now had something even bigger than the former program, which had aimed at augmenting the aggressiveness, muscle mass, reflexes, and IQs of soldiers.

Flynn was financing the secret program in order to have the best private security company in the world. Lee had his own agenda: he was planning on turning the forty-million-man Red Army of ordinary soldiers into the equivalent of forty million Special Forces soldiers.

Lee was very close to that goal. He'd had annoying setbacks and on one memorable mission run by Flynn's company, Orion Security, in Africa, the entire team had gone rogue. Well, Lee had adjusted the doses and several other missions had gone very well indeed.

Most of the progress had been made thanks to experiments conducted on the four elite soldiers over the course of a year. The former Ghost Ops soldiers that had been captured in the Cambridge lab conflagration.

Flynn had been particularly happy to know that the main test subject was Captain Lucius Ward. Apparently, Ward had shown Flynn up several times while they were both serving and Flynn had wanted payback.

Well, Lee was a scientist, not a butcher. However, Flynn's enthusiastic support *had* made him push the boundaries. A little. Ward had had over forty surgeries and had been slated for destruction when he and three other soldiers from his elite unit had been rescued by forces unknown.

A party to the rescue of the men had been identified as a female research scientist who worked for one of his labs. The woman, Dr. Catherine Young, was brilliant. Cameras had caught her image. He didn't need to put her features through facial recognition software, he knew her well.

After that daring rescue, Young had disappeared off the face of the earth. Lee had put his entire security apparatus to the task of finding Young, but they were stymied. She'd somehow gone beyond their reach even though he had vast resources to throw at the search.

How could a nerdish scientist who didn't have much of a life outside the lab completely disappear?

He wanted Young because she'd taken four promising soon-to-be cadavers from his research, but also because she had something he desperately wanted. Something in her brain. What was in Young's brain—and in the brains of a number of people Lee had rounded up—was much more valuable than increasing Flynn's bank account. Increasing Flynn's bank account was a mere byproduct of the Warrior Project. And, anyway, if everything worked to plan, Flynn's bank account would soon be seized by the Chinese Finance Ministry.

After the invasion of the United States.

A drum of fat, heavy fingers. Flynn's jaws flexed as he suppressed a yawn.

Well, if Flynn was bored, Lee would soon cure him of that.

Flynn shot his wrist out and showily checked the time on his new gold Rolex. It was a Trasparénce, the new line introduced last Christmas. The dial was a blank pure crystal screen to everyone but the owner. The screen was set to the owner's retina and would show the time only to the owner.

No one will ever steal your Rolex. The ads had been everywhere. The watch cost $130,000.

How Flynn loved his expensive toys.

"It's four P.M.," Flynn growled. "I interrupted negotiations with members of the Libyan regime to come here because you said it was so goddamned important. So I'm here. What is it? I need to be back in Virginia by eight." Orion consulting had a FastJet company plane that could fly in the stratosphere at 1000 mph. It could cross the country in two hours, coast to coast.

"Watch," Lee said simply, and flicked on the array of four holo-monitors. He saw Flynn move his head from monitor to monitor. Before Flynn's gaze reached the last one, Lee started talking.

"This is the secure lab of a small research company we bought about a year ago. It carries out legitimate research on vaccines, but there's a separate lab that only carefully selected researchers can access and they are carrying out an entirely different kind of research. This is linked to the research at Millon Laboratories, which we had to shut down after the unfortunate incident."

Each monitor showed a patient lying unconscious on a gurney, with an IV line that ran into the back wall. It wasn't readily discernible on the screen, but each patient was in a nearly indestructible and completely transparent cage made of graphene. The patients were young, in their midtwenties, evenly distributed by gender. Two men, two women. There had been ten, originally. Six had been sacrificed.

"What you're seeing is people we discovered by hidden fMRIs. Each has a zone of their brain—the parahippocampal gyrus—that lights up, particularly under thermal imaging. It is a part of the brain that is undiscovered territory. We are uncertain as to its function, but in these specimens the parahippocampal gyrus is unusually active and seems to correspond to unusual . . . abilities the specimens have."

Flynn checked his watch again. He'd never been interested in the science itself, only in the results. And the results had to be of use to him and to his company for him to be interested. Well, he was about to get an eyeful.

Lee tapped his finger on the table. He was so used to the light projection keyboard's settings that he didn't actually have to have the light projection on. It was a minor ploy, but to an ignorant outsider like Flynn, it would look like magic.

The commands he gave changed the nature of the liquid being pumped into the patients' systems. From a powerful narcotic to a powerful stimulant. From zero to hyperawareness in a minute.

"I'll remind you of the thrust of the main project," he said softly. "We are perfecting a system that will improve the motor skills, neural response times, muscle mass, eyesight, and hearing of soldiers, sometimes by a factor of 300 percent. Essentially, we will create supersoldiers who will be stronger, faster, and smarter than any other soldiers in the world. There will be no warriors that will be able to defeat your men, General Flynn."

Lee never used Flynn's former title except when he wanted to make a very strong point. And this was one of those times. He could actually hear Flynn's breathing speeding up, becoming loud in the silent room. The moron was getting excited, exactly as if he were seeing a naked lady. Lee refrained from shaking his head at how pitifully easy to manipulate Flynn was.

"But—" And here Lee turned to Flynn and looked him in the eyes, distracting him for the minute it would take for the super-stimulant to hit the specimen's bloodstreams. "But I think we can take it one step further. In addition to superstrength and speed, we can add superpowers."

A crease formed on Flynn's fleshy face. Superpowers. That was crazy, right? Lee could almost read Flynn's thoughts.

Only it wasn't.

He had four more specimens he'd caught recently, being prepped. He very much suspected that one, Sophie Daniels, was a healer. That would be a battlefield power to reckon with.

Lee gestured toward the monitors and watched Flynn's face as he took in what was happening.

Almost to the second, all the patients bolted up in bed. Lee had calculated body mass in the ccs of stimulant he pumped into them, so it worked on each individual at the same time. Every specimen was brought abruptly and rapidly into consciousness, with no self-defense mechanism.

It was spectacular.

"Fuck." Flynn breathed as he leaned forward. Lee could have easily "pushed" the holograms closer to him, but it was better this way. Make him work for it. Flynn's eyes were bright with the reflected light of the monitors and he was watching with his whole body.

Cell number one: male, 23 years of age. The instant consciousness hit him, he levitated a foot above the bed, the sheet dangling from the sides of his body. He sat up, looked around with a frown, and his body floated gently back down to the surface of the bed.

Cell number two: male, 27 years of age. He bolted up, face angry. The bedside cart flew violently against the wall and shattered. Flynn flinched. It was hard to watch. The walls were powerfully strong yet completely invisible. The cart shattered against a wall they couldn't see.

Cell number three: female, 21 years of age. She lay unmoving, only her open eyes showing that she was awake. Suddenly, a fire bloomed in the corner of the cage, burning brightly, fiercely, seeming to gush out of the floor of the cage. Just as suddenly it stopped, collapsing in on itself, leaving only blackened stains crawling up the invisible walls.

Cell number four: female, 25 years of age. Only her head turned as she looked at the corner where the invisible cameras were. Her eyes were flat and black.

Flynn gasped, a harsh intake of breath. His eyes widened, bulged.

Lee's hands went to his own throat, as if he could tear it open with his hands before it closed up completely. Then it closed tight. No air coming in, no air going out. His chest heaved use-lessly trying to suck in air that couldn't reach the lungs. It was as if he were being hanged, something tight and hot around his neck, tightening, tightening . . .

The world shimmered, the edges of objects limned with violent color, then the colors draining away, leaving everything gray, be-coming darker. Edging into blackness.

Lee couldn't think, couldn't reason. What he did he did out of sheer instinct, recognizing in the flat black gaze from the moni-tor what was happening. His right arm flailed uselessly, he was a foot away. His body wouldn't obey him, he couldn't move his legs. All he could do was collapse, and in falling, reach for the control button that would open up the hidden IV bags of the powerful narcotic.

His finger tapped on a point on the desk as he focused fero-ciously, as if seeing through a tunnel growing ever smaller. The force around his neck tightened, pressing against his Adam's apple, starting to crush it. He tapped, tapped, head lighter and lighter, starting to black out . . .

And the force around his neck abruptly ended, like a noose that had loosened. Lee jolted, fell into a chair gasping. A hoarse chok-ing sound was on his left. His neck hurt but he turned to see Flynn on his knees on the floor, head hanging down, face splotched with ugly purple-red stains. One hand went to his throat as he brought air into his lungs in long loud gasps.

"Jesus!" It came out a hoarse whisper. "What the fuck was that?"

Lee couldn't speak yet. His shaking finger pointed to the holo-monitor showing cell number four. His trembling hand stayed in the air until he could speak. "Her." He coughed as he tried to make his voice stronger. "She can . . . somehow . . . reach out. Touch . . . people. Things."

Flynn turned awkwardly until he was sitting on the floor, back to the wall.

"Well, fuck." His lungs bellowed in and out. His breathing became a little less labored. His complexion was back to his usual florid red without the purple. "Is that what you're working on? People—things—like *them*?"

Lee needed to choose his words carefully. Flynn was his lifeline. His source of money. If it was cut off he couldn't continue his research. He would never make his way back to China as a conqueror.

But though he knew that, some essential bit of oxygen had cut off his good sense.

"Yes." Crazily, he smiled. "Once we can control them, extract from them the essence of their powers via spinal fluid and inject them into our superstrong and supersmart soldiers—the sky's the limit."

Damn! He was supposed to approach the whole subject gingerly. Lee knew only too well how crazy his plan sounded. He had complete faith in it, but to an outsider it would reek of insanity.

And here he'd blurted out the project bluntly to a man who had no imagination and no sense of grandeur. A man who dealt exclusively in dollars and cents and believed only in what he could touch.

So he was very surprised when Flynn reached into his jacket pocket and pulled out a platinum bump card. He tapped on it. "Give me yours," he wheezed.

Lee had to stand up, unbutton his lab coat to get at his wallet. His legs would barely hold him. He gave Flynn his own bump card. Flynn tapped the two cards together. When Lee looked at the card again, he could barely believe his eyes. Flynn had just transfer-bumped fifteen million dollars into his card.

Flynn looked up at him, heavy brows frowning. "Control them."

Lee nodded.

"Then use them."

Oh, yes.

Steadier now, Lee stood and looked at his specimens, now comatose on their beds, the only signs that something had happened
were the steel components of the crash cart scattered on the floor
of the cell of number two and the black scorch marks on the invisible wall of number three's cell.

He'd hated his American childhood, ripped from what should
have been his Chinese destiny. But he'd loved American comic
books as a kid.

Protocol One, the Warrior Project, would create supersoldiers.
Forty million Chinese Captain Americas.

But Protocol Two, the Delphi Project, would go one step further.

It would create an elite force of X-men.

Hunkered down in the dark, Elle buried her face in her arms.

She was the very picture of helplessness and she hated that,
hated it. But there was no choice. The escape from her apartment
had eaten into her reserves so deeply she had none left.

There was possibly some kind of scientific ratio to be studied—
the further she went in her projections the greater the energy ex-
pended. It was an entirely new field of scientific research, one that
she'd happily devote her life to, only it wasn't going to happen.

What was going on at Corona? Sophie's panic call and the men
in black. What was happening? Elle wished she could call some
of her other colleagues, to see if this was companywide, but a cell
was a huge arrow in the sky pointing down—*here she is*!

Sophie'd said to leave hers back in her apartment and she had.
The latest generation of phones had an off button for localization,
but she didn't trust it. Not if people with guns were hunting her.

She shivered. Was it cold in the room? Her whole body was
trembling and she felt ice cold. There was no way to tell if it was
shock or the temperature in the room. Maybe shock. She understood perfectly the physiology of shock. She'd come out weakened

from her dream state, had had to perform minor surgery on herself and then go on the run. All the peripheral blood had rushed to her core to maintain vital organs alive.

Everything in her was cold, even her brain. She was used to being able to think herself out of difficult situations, but it was as if someone had thrown a blanket over her brain and it moved sluggishly, as if stumbling in the dark.

Right now, she needed to analyze the situation carefully, start making plans. She'd disappeared before—surely she could do it again. But no thoughts appeared. No analysis, no strong sense of reasoning her way through as she'd always been able to do.

Instead, with her last reserves, her entire being had sent out what could only be a distress call. Just to show how crazy she was, she hadn't even sent it out to any of her coworkers.

Nope, she'd sent it to Nick. Who could be anywhere in the world.

Nick, whom she hadn't seen in ten years and would never see again.

Nick, who wherever he was, wouldn't care.

Insanity.

These past years of hard work, rewarding work, making new friends, entering the exciting world of scientific research—she'd tried so very hard to forget all about Nick. Every girl got her heart broken by a handsome man, right? Nothing new about that. Happened to everyone. Whole days, then whole weeks would go by when she wouldn't think of him and then *wham*! A smell, a taste, a sound—it was always something. It would remind her of the years they spent together—or worse, remind her of the night they spent together.

And it was enough to set her off.

Her heart would clench, a cascade of hormones, bad ones, the ones associated with fear and loss and pain, such as CRH or cortisol, would flood her system. Before she knew the words, she understood the mechanism.

And now that she knew the words, now that she'd made this her field of study, she thought she'd banished her ghosts. Her ghost. Nick.

She'd made a successful life for herself, rarely thinking of him. And yet at the moment of her direst need, who did she think of? Nick Ross. *Damn* him! Wasting time wanting him was dangerous. Folly of the highest order.

Though there really wasn't anyone to call. Maybe that was it. Most of her friends were fellow research scientists and, lately, members of the experimental protocol. There was no one capable of fighting those men in black, certainly not the men she knew.

Slope-shouldered, nearsighted men, pale and thin. No. Paul Mela, Alex Karras, or Thomas Chu—even if she could contact them, even if they came, they'd be massacred.

She'd been right not to call them.

It was so hard to be in the dark, in every sense. She'd seen the men and disappeared. She needed more information. A scientist dealt with data, and she had none.

What was happening?

Could she—*dare* she check?

Elle was only beginning to test the boundaries of her gift. Today's projection of herself halfway around the world—that had been the first time she'd tried to deliberately project herself to an unknown place far away. It had left her so depleted she'd felt half dead.

She could do short distances. She'd tested that, over and over. But she didn't have total control over where she went. It was like being in a Porsche with only the accelerator, no brakes and no steering wheel. Heady and dangerous.

Those men had moved with the professional grace of athletes or military men. They were heavily armed. She needed to know where they were.

The decision was made.

She slid down until she was lying on her back on the dirty carpet, grabbing a pillow from the bed and putting it under her head. Close to the floor, the smell of grime intensified. She shut it from her mind, along with the lumpiness of the carpet and the lint she could see under the bed. She wasn't here for comfort, she was here for safety. A little dirt and a few smells were a small price to pay.

She closed her eyes and willed herself to start shutting down. Slow down her pounding heart, will her hands to still, her breathing to slow.

It was all so very new. She'd only gone on four voluntary trips before. All her life, her Dreams had taken her away when they wanted, where they wanted. There'd never been any question of directing herself, projecting herself where she wanted to go.

Hell, she'd been twenty-one and still heartbroken over Nick before she realized that what happened to her sometimes wasn't merely crazy dreams. It had been in San Francisco, working hard to pay tuition before the grants and scholarships had kicked in. Desperate for reading material, she'd taken the bus to Clement Street and gone to Banana Split, a huge bookstore with tons of used books and a friendly staff that didn't mind if you spent hours there. On the second floor, browsing the Paranormal section she'd seen a book, dusty and badly printed, and it had changed her life.

A simple title—*Astral Projection*. But she'd recognized instantly that it spoke directly to her, to what she'd always been able to do but had been unable to recognize. She learned she wasn't alone. A number of people were able to astrally project, and Elle started to make it her business to know everything about it. That semester, she switched to biology, aiming at a PhD in neuroscience, and it had led her straight to Corona, which was studying extrasensory powers.

Until she'd actually enrolled in the Delphi Protocol, she'd never been able to control her projections. They just . . . happened.

Maybe more when she was stressed than when she was relaxed, but there'd been very little relaxation in her life after her father became ill, so that wasn't a big help.

Some nights her trips were brief. A few minutes in an unfamiliar landscape and then she'd be back. One constant was that the longer the trip, the more exhausted she was when she woke up.

The Delphi Protocol was controlled in every aspect. From the drugs in the IV line to the monitors checking her status. And still, she'd been told her vital signs had gone dangerously low in today's experiment. What would happen if her vital signs started plummeting? She was alone here. She could lapse into a coma, even die.

But she could die, anyway. Those men had been armed and Sophie's call had been a panic call. Sophie had said some people had been killed. In all likelihood, for whatever reason, something highly dangerous was going on and it was entirely possible that the men in black had orders to shoot her on sight.

So staying here, alone in the dark, wasn't going to save her.

They'd know she hadn't hailed a taxi and there was only so far anyone could get on foot. If they had the right resources they would find her, no question. She'd signed in under another name but presumably they'd have a photo of her. That bored and stoned young man at the front desk might remember her.

They could break in her door at any minute.

The Delphi Protocol had been exact and precise. Elle tried to duplicate it, though she had no equipment at all except her body and her mind. First, she'd been told to lie flat on her back, arm out for the IV. Silly as it seemed, she lay there flat on her back and put her arm out from her body. There hadn't been a pillow so she removed it from under her head.

What had Sophie done next? Inserted the needle. It was the new generation of hypodermics—thin as a human hair while inserted, it expanded once in a vein. It hadn't hurt at all going in, and she'd felt only the lightest whisper of sensation when it expanded.

But the drug had burned a little when it started flowing in her veins.

Corona had refused to give the exact molecular structure of the drug, citing patent concerns, but Sophie had told her that though she didn't know its exact composition either, it had been tested thoroughly on animals and had never caused an adverse effect.

So Elle lay still and imagined the whisper of the superthin needle being inserted into the vein of her right arm, the slight sensation of fullness as the needle expanded, the feeling of warmth as the drug began to course through her system.

There must have been a light sedative in the drug because she had instantly relaxed and had felt so light that it was as if she floated an inch or two above the mattress.

She felt herself relax, as if she'd been perfused with the drug. It had been a wholly pleasant sensation and she willed herself into feeling it. Feeling weightless, as if gravity had suddenly been revoked. So light that she rose a little, hovered, then continued up, up, up . . .

It was pitch-black outside, the darkness broken only by the few intact streetlights. Palo Alto was a prosperous community, and further east she could see well-lit streets and cars whishing by, brightly lit storefronts and restaurants and bars. But in this small corner of town, darkness reigned.

Few cars passed by on their way to somewhere else. Nobody was walking on the sidewalks, which were narrower than normal, cracked in places from the roots of the big, old, unpruned trees lining the street the motel was on.

Elle drifted over the rooftops, all sense of anxiety gone. It was peaceful up here in the chill air, under the star-filled sky. The moon had set. The brightly lit center of town was aglow in the distance, like a huge campfire. Two streets over, where the shops started selling something other than cheap clothes and liquor, some young kids spilled out of a bar, reeling in the street, shouting. They were drunk and laughing. One kid, tall and lanky, bent over from the waist, hands on knees, and threw up in the gutter. They all laughed harder.

Students, she thought with an inward smile. Always the same . . .

What was that?

Thick, untrimmed bushes across the street two blocks down from the motel quivered, as if a wind had passed through. But it was a windless night. Two men stepped out, clad in black, black mask, black goggles. Black holsters with thick black handles sticking out of them.

They didn't speak, instead communicating with hand signals, easy to follow. Two more men stepped out from the bushes another block down and they met up with the first two.

The men were utterly silent, almost invisible in the blackness of the night. Nobody noticed them. One man, taller than the rest, pointed his finger at one of them, then pointed the finger down the street, at the motel whose flickering sign could be seen. The man who'd been singled out pulled off his mask and pulled a windbreaker from a side pocket. In a second, he looked almost normal.

Maybe an observant person would notice a bulge on his hip, but the stoned guy at the front desk wouldn't notice if a grenade went off right beside him.

The man in the windbreaker walked down and across the street, stride easy and relaxed. Guy crossing the street to a motel.

The other men melted back into the bushes.

Elle followed the man into the lobby where the night clerk was gently dozing, a *Justice League Dark* comic draped across his chest. His mouth was open and he was snoring lightly.

At the sound of the bell over the door ringing, he gave a slight start and opened his eyes. They were unfocused. When he saw the man in the windbreaker he smiled. "Hey, dude."

"Hey." The man dug into his pocket. "I need to ask you a question. I just had a fight with my girlfriend. A big one." He winced and gave a rueful smile. "She's right and I was wrong and I need to talk to her now that I've sobered up."

The clerk waggled his head. "I hear you, man."

The man in the windbreaker placed a photograph on the counter and tapped it. "That's my girlfriend. She isn't with any of her friends, so I'm making the rounds of hotels and motels. I really need to talk to her. Did she check in here?" A hundred-dollar bill slid across the counter and disappeared behind it.

"Pretty, pretty lady." The clerk smiled dreamily.

"Yeah. That she is. So . . . you seen her this evening?"

"Yeah, man. Came in about two hours ago."

The man in the windbreaker slumped in relief. "Thank God! I was so worried that she was walking around in the dark. What's her room number?"

That rang a bell of alarm. The clerk's eyes opened wide. "Hey, man. Sorry. I'm not supposed to—"

Another hundred-dollar bill slid across. "I really need to talk to her. Tell her how much I love her."

The bill was pocketed. "Awww. Okay. I can tell you're a good guy. She's in room number nine. Down the hall and to the right. She's checked in until—"

Elle watched the man pull a stunner from his holster, set to green. Lethal charge. In a second, he'd pulled it, placed it against the clerk's heart, and pulled the trigger. He turned around before the clerk fell to the floor and gestured out the door.

The three other men came at a dead run while the man in the windbreaker shot out the lights in the lobby. The only illumination came from the clerk's old-fashioned flat computer monitor, which illuminated the scene with an eerie pale glow.

Without speaking a word, the man in the windbreaker pointed down the hall, then gestured right. The four men pulled their stunners, all set to yellow, a voltage guaranteed to knock out a bull, and moved silently down the corridor toward Elle's room.

Where her defenseless body waited, unable to wake itself up.

Chapter 9

The hovercar had been tested at 200 mph. Nick pushed it to 160 off highway in hovercraft mode. Coming down off Mount Blue, Nick had to be careful not to ram into trees. The hovercar responded like a dream and he speed-slalomed his way down the mountain.

Once he was off the mountain and into the flatlands, though, Nick took off, paralleling the interstate, sailing over ditches and fences. The hovercar had excellent forward radar and he swerved around obstacles the hovercar couldn't clear. When the quickest way forward was the interstate, he simply jumped the guardrails, went to wheel mode, and flew down the fast lane. The hovercar was invisible to radar and not too visible to other drivers. By the time a driver could flip him the bird, he was twenty miles away. He could outrun any police car. And frankly, he didn't give a shit about anything except getting to Elle as fast as humanly possible.

Jon was in contact over the comms link. He was making good progress fitting a new rotor head. Mac was giving a hand and he estimated he could be in the air within the hour.

Maybe, just maybe he could get to Elle and save her from

whatever danger she was in. But there was no one in the world who understood the underlying principle of the universe—shit happens—better than Nick Ross. He wouldn't feel anything like relief until he had Elle with him, in his bed, in Haven. Surrounded by a mountain and sensors and trip wires and drones up the wazoo. And once she was in his bed in Haven, he'd keep her there for the next week. Maybe more. Not only to bed her, but to *feel* her, touch her, reassure himself that she was safe and with him.

And she'd stay that way for the next hundred years.

But first, he had to find her.

He had no idea what that distress call was about, but it had been *potent*. A blast of pure terror. He'd woken up, heart pounding with fear. Up until about an hour ago, Nick would have said he didn't know fear, but now that was a lie. Sheer bone-chilling terror had infused every cell of his body when he'd received the blast in his head.

Nothing like that psychic blast had ever happened to him before. Well, except for Catherine somehow reading through touching him that he'd lost Elle and mourned her. Which made sense because Catherine had the gift of reading people and missing Elle was in his blood and bones, not just in his skin.

As far as he knew, Nick had no gifts beyond strength, a good aim, and an ability to fight. Certainly nothing woo-woo. He'd fought and worked like a dog for everything he had, no "gifts" at all. So receiving that blast from Elle had been completely off his radar.

It wasn't a dream and it wasn't craziness. It was definitely Elle who'd contacted him, no question. The blast had had Elle in it, unmistakable. Fear, yes, but gentleness and smarts in a mixture that was simply her. He hadn't questioned it for one second.

So here he was on the interstate going as fast as humanly possible to get to her.

Traffic was getting intense on the approach to Palo Alto, requiring all his attention, when Jon's voice sounded in the comms button behind his ear. "Yo man," he said. "Check the drone monitor."

Nick glanced down to his left and froze.

Fuck!

Faint lines moving toward the motel, almost invisible. The men on the screen were wearing stealth combat gear, but Haven's drones combined IR and thermal imagery that made visible what would have escaped the drones' technology if the two sources hadn't been combined. Four men, moving slowly and carefully down the street where Elle's motel was. The street was dark, every other streetlight was burned out. When they were still, the men disappeared, but when they moved, he could see—just barely— their outlines. They moved like fighters. That and the fact that their signature was mostly cloaked was enough for him.

They were operators and they were dangerous and they were out for Elle.

He checked the GPS and saw that he was five minutes out. *Jesus.* He moved the accelerator stick to its maximum power and shot forward, leaving a wake of startled cars behind. As he zoomed down off the interstate ramp as fast as the vehicle could go, straining forward as if he could personally make the hovercar go faster, he kept checking the drone monitor.

Three of the men disappeared into a dark spot by the side of the road that was clearly bushes. One man pulled off his face mask and his head bloomed bright red in the thermal images. As Nick watched, he pulled on a windbreaker and made his way across the street, a shimmering red man shape, head twisting, checking the road for traffic.

There was none. The place was deserted. It looked like the motel was half deserted too, to judge by the empty parking lot. And whoever was in that motel, including Elle, would be no match for the four trained men who would converge if they discovered Elle was staying there.

Nick studied the maps, calculating a trajectory that didn't include roads. He didn't need roads, he just needed a path that didn't have barriers over one meter high. He could do it, just, in hover mode. Haven had rules against using hover mode in densely populated places. Hovercars were military secrets. He and Jon had liberated two hovercars from a base in Nevada and appropriated them for their use. They were particularly useful in winter on Mount Blue when the roads were snowed in. Using hover mode in towns would raise interest and maybe alert military authorities, and that was the last thing they wanted.

But this trumped everything. Danger to Elle? No question.

Nick switched to hover mode and pressed the stick forward to maximum speed. He had seen a path, but it ran through backyards and between houses. He'd leave a trail of broken branches and disrupted flower beds behind, but he didn't give a shit. Arrowing his way to Elle took every ounce of expertise he had and then some, like slithering down a rubble-strewn mountainside at top speed, but he had no choice.

Though he was moving at top speed, taking insane risks, he always kept an eye on the drone monitor. He was two streets down when he saw the lights in the lobby of the motel dim and a figure with a flame red head appear in the doorway. The thermal image cooled as the man pulled his headgear back on. When he gestured, three ghost images crossed the street.

Fuck-fuck-fuck! They were honing in for the kill!

Not if he had anything to say about it.

By the time they entered the lobby, Nick was at the corner of the cross street. The hell with security. He braked hard and abandoned the hovercar where it was. Who cared if anyone saw it? The only important thing now was Elle, Elle, Elle. The thought that he'd lost her for ten years and that he might find her now, dead body already cooling, made him break out in a sweat.

His heart was pounding, which was a good thing and a bad

thing. A good thing because it meant more blood to the extremities together with a decent dose of adrenaline which would speed up his already-fast reflexes and shut down pain for a while if he got shot.

A bad thing because above 120–125 beats per minute fine-motor skills began to degrade. He was going to shoot to kill, and he wanted to hit what he was aiming at.

The only way to slow his heart rate down was to breathe deeply and force it down. He and Mac and Jon had trained for this, though what they did you couldn't train to do, you had to be born to do. Training only took natural abilities up a notch.

So he spared a second, two, for deep breaths and a conscious tamping down of his body's fight readiness.

Then he ran.

Just as he took off, he could hear a murmur from the open door of the hovercar. Jon's voice. Well, whatever it was Jon had to say could wait because Elle had about a minute left to live.

Afterward, he couldn't remember closing the distance between the hovercar and the lobby of the motel. He jumped out of the hovercar and then a second later he was wrenching open the door of the lobby, barely casting a glance at the body of the night clerk whose legs he could see sticking out from behind the counter.

He didn't need to know where Elle was. All he had to do was follow the last of the men, who was at the end of a corridor, turning right. Everything in Nick screamed to run full tilt into them and mow them down, but though there was no contest between him and four other men—no matter how good, no matter how well trained—he had no idea where Elle was. Once he was in combat mode his senses narrowed; he couldn't take the fuckers down and at the same time ensure that Elle wouldn't get caught in the crossfire.

Nick sprinted silently to the corner and caught the last guy around the neck in a chokehold, yanking him back into the main corridor. The stunner made a light buzzing sound so he pulled his Glock 32 with the silencer, rated at two decibels, less noise than an exhale. He nudged the ballistic mask up with the muzzle, shot the man right between the eyes, and eased him quickly down to the dirty carpet.

One down.

He peeked around the corner and saw three men congregated at a door. They'd found Elle's room. Elle was behind that door. They wanted to hurt her, maybe kill her—and that wasn't going to happen. Not even if there were a hundred of the fuckers.

The man with the windbreaker, clearly the leader, had grabbed a key card and waved it in front of a monitor set in the wall to the side of the door. In a second, the door to Elle's room would swing open. The card didn't take immediately and windbreaker guy waved it again. Nick could hear the faint click of the lock disengaging and watched as the guy at the door brought his stunner up.

They were covered in LocTite, head to toe. Nick's stunner couldn't stun through the suit designed to dissipate beams; and his Glock, powerful as it was, would break a bone or two but wouldn't penetrate. Nick wanted these fuckers *dead*.

It would have to be done the old-fashioned way. By hand.

Nick was good at combat strategy. In an instant, the whole thing was planned to the second; he didn't have to think at all. It was like a geometric equation, moves calculated and precise.

He ran full tilt into the corridor, a swarming mass of muscle and deadly intent. Planting his right hand on the wall next to the last guy, he pivoted, lifting his body, putting his entire weight behind the kick to the head. The man fell like a bull in the slaughterhouse, but Nick was already at fuckhead number two, dropping to the ground, scissoring his legs between the man's legs, throwing his entire weight into his elbow, which he drove straight into the middle of the man's face. Bone crunched and blood sprayed. The leader had turned around, aiming his stunner at the ground but

Nick wasn't there anymore; Nick was aiming a kick at the solar plexus, something the LocTite couldn't protect against.

The man fell, temporarily paralyzed, without breath, and that was fine because it allowed Nick to finish all three of them off properly with three hard head-twists. He lifted each head slightly to make sure that the spinal column had been severed from the brainstem, because he wanted these fuckers to *stay* dead.

The instant he finished off the third, he ran into the room and his head nearly exploded with panic when he saw it was empty.

She wasn't there! Elle wasn't there!

Where the hell could she be?

The dead guys thought she was here, so he'd assumed . . .

Had she escaped? There was one window that gave out into a courtyard, but it had been painted over a billion times; and if it had once been designed to be opened, that day had long since passed.

He pulled with all his strength, then desisted. If he couldn't open it, Elle couldn't either.

Oh God, oh God. If she'd escaped, how could he find her, how could he protect her if he didn't know where she was?

Think!

Not on the bed, not out the window, maybe the closet? Nick yanked open the plywood door and stared inside at the tiny space full of empty misshapen wire hangers.

Not there . . .

And that was when he saw her. Lying faceup on the floor, one arm outstretched, pale as ice. Unmoving, unbreathing.

His heart stopped. Simply stopped for a long horrible second.

He was too late.

Somehow they'd killed her.

He hadn't been able to save her.

All his life, all he'd ever wanted was to keep Elle safe. And now he'd found her after all these years and she was dead.

He took a shaky step forward then sank to his knees . . . to be near her, and because his legs simply wouldn't hold him up. He felt hollowed out, totally, completely empty. Incapable of thought or action. Merely a bag of skin holding in guts and bones.

He wanted to gather her in his arms, but his body wouldn't obey him. He gave the order but nothing happened. His entire body was lax, as if it had simply given up. As if it had died but hadn't told him yet.

But he wanted to be closer to Elle, so he did the only thing he could think of—he toppled forward onto her, hoping that his limbs would recover and that he could gather her in his arms and weep over her.

She was cold, so very cold and still, rocking gently when his full weight fell on her, but not gasping or jolting.

His face was cold. That was the way he understood that tears were tracking down his cheeks. He didn't wipe his face—he couldn't. All he could do was watch the tears as they plopped on her neck.

One large teardrop had fallen on the pale skin just above the collarbone. It quivered, stilled, quivered, stilled.

Her heart was—it was beating! He shifted his head so his ear was right over her heart and . . . there it was! The faintest of heart-beats, thready and faint but regular. His head moved up and down gently on her chest. Her chest was moving—she was breathing. She was *alive*!

She wasn't conscious, her eyes were unmoving behind her lids and her breathing was shallow, but by God she was breathing and she was alive.

A bolt of energy shot through him. Now that he knew Elle was alive, he could do anything. Strength returned to him in a hot rush. Nick gathered Elle's limp body up in his arms and stood up. He studied her face hungrily, wanting to understand what the past ten years had been for her.

She'd been just as he'd described to Catherine. Older, even more beautiful.

She'd been a beautiful girl and she was now a stunning woman. That glorious pale blond hair was cut short, waving around her face like a halo. He hefted her in his arms. She was easy to carry, but she'd put on some weight. The last time he'd seen her she'd been frighteningly thin.

Why was she here? Where had she been? Who was she now? And above all, who were those men gunning for her?

Only one way to find out.

Nick lay Elle gently on the bed, two fingers to the wrist pulse and waited. Sixty beats per minute. Okay. Now to frisk the fuckers who'd wanted to kill her. Or kidnap her. Either way they weren't going to do anything now.

Nick went out into the corridor, pulled off masks, and took snapshots of the four faces. They were slack in death, but Haven's facial recognition software would identify them soon enough. He kneeled by each body and frisked them, but wasn't surprised to find nothing at all. Their LocTite suits were top of the range, but nothing that couldn't be bought if you had the money. Weaponry ditto. No pockets, only holsters and a knife sheath. The knives were Gerber Mark IV, black oxide, brand-new.

Everything was brand-new. The LocTite suits didn't have a scuff on them and looked like they'd never been cleaned.

Nick gathered their nightvision goggles, stunners, guns, knives, and wristwatches in a small nylon bag folded in his backpack. The cells he put into another bag that emitted a strong masking signal so the cells couldn't be traced, and then went back into Elle's room.

She was still out. That worried him, but there was nothing he could do for her except get her back to Haven as fast as possible and have Catherine examine her.

The bud behind his ear buzzed. Jon. He'd forgotten all about

Jon trying to contact him as he was getting out of the hovercar. He tapped a point on his wrist, opening the connection.

"Sitrep!" Mac barked. "We saw the four bad guys on our monitor. Status?"

"Dead," Nick replied, walking out of the motel with Elle in his arms. "Put me on speaker." Now he could communicate with Jon and Catherine too. All three had been waiting in the war room for him. No way would they be able to go back to bed.

"What's wrong with her, Nick?" Catherine's voice was gentle. She was the only person on earth who understood what Elle meant to him.

"I don't know." Striding toward the hovercraft with a limp Elle in his arms, Nick's voice came out hoarse and strained. "She's alive, that's all I know. I'll get back as fast as I can so you can examine her."

"About that, Nick . . ."

Jon cut in. "I'm in the helo, coming down. Meet me at Cache 4D. We'll put away the hovercar and I'll fly you back. Tomorrow night I'll come down with Eric and he can drive it back."

"Thanks, Jon," Nick choked. His knees nearly gave out with relief. Haven kept caches all over the state. He wouldn't dare abandon the hovercar, but Cache 4D was a large storage unit nearby. Haven owned the entire unit via seven shell companies, and it had a helipad disguised as a loading apron. With any luck, he'd have Elle back in Haven in under an hour.

He opened the passenger door and gently lay Elle in the seat, clicking the biomorph scan and getting out of the way. Once scanned, in case of an accident, a jet of instantly hardening foam would envelop her, set to the exact specifications of her body. Once the scan was complete, he reached into the compartment under the dashboard and brought out a paper-thin thermal blanket. He'd heat the seat too. He lay his hand against her cheek. She was still so cold. Whatever was wrong with her, surely heat wouldn't hurt?

To his astonishment, a soft hand cupped his and he was looking into Elle's beautiful light blue eyes.

"Nick," she whispered, eyes wide, looking shocked. "You came. I called you . . . and you came."

He turned his hand to clutch hers, loosening his hold when she winced. He kept staring into her eyes, completely unable to talk. He opened his mouth to speak and nothing came out.

He thought he'd never see her again. He thought he'd live his life to the bitter end full of regret and fear for her. He'd joined Ghost Ops because without Elle the fact that the old Nick Ross had to disappear off the face of the earth meant nothing to him. Ghost Ops soldiers could have no loves, no attachments, and that suited him right down to the ground. Elle had taken all of that away.

And now he'd found her, against all the odds. She was here, right now, watching him out of those beautiful, expressive eyes. Nick, who always knew what to do, who always had that next step mapped out, and the one after that and the one after that . . . he couldn't think. Couldn't talk.

Elle slid her hand from his and touched his face. "I can hardly believe you're real." She looked around, blinking. He knew she could only see a dark street and the inside of a strange-looking car. "Is this a dream?"

Nick leaned forward and kissed her. Very quickly, because she was weak and they had to go now. But it served an important purpose. Those lips were very real. Elle was real.

"No dream. But we have to get out of here fast, honey. Some bad guys were after you, and we have to go right now."

Her brows drew together, a faraway look coming into her eyes. "I saw them," she said in a whisper. "I saw them coming down the street, coming to the motel. And I saw"—she focused on him, searched his eyes—"I saw *you*, Nick. I thought I'd gone insane. What happened?"

"Later. I'll explain everything later." Much as he hated leaving her, forsaking the touch of her, Nick moved away, sprinted around the front of the hovercar, slid into the driver's seat. "Hold on tight." He put himself in wheels mode and took off north, just as fast as the hovercar could go.

"Where are we going?"

Nick slid his eyes over to her. *Goddamn, she is beautiful.* He knew she was beautiful but when he thought of her, it was the golden waif he remembered. Lost and thin and frail. Lovely, because nothing would change that perfect bone structure and coloring, but soft and vulnerable. Sitting next to him was a woman who would turn heads every time she walked down the street, but who looked strong and capable. Though bruised and dazed, she was composed.

When he found himself sneaking peeks at her, looking at her elegant pale hands folded in her lap, memorizing that perfect profile, following that long white neck down to where her coat fell open to show a V-neck sweater, he realized he could crash them at the speed he was going. So he gripped the accelerator stick with white knuckles and turned his face resolutely forward.

"We're going to a place no one will find you, honey," he said grimly. "I'm taking you home."

Was it magic? Was she a witch? Had she somehow conjured Nick from thin air? Was she still in Dream mode?

Well, that she could answer. There was very little sensory input in her Dreams, her projections. Even when her spirit hovered over that facility in what must have been the Free Republic of Mongolia, an ice-bound facility on fire, she'd felt neither heat nor cold.

But now she felt it all. The cold as she came up to find herself in a strange type of car with the door open and Nick—*Nick!*—bending over her. The touch of his hand to her face, his fingertips rough, the touch soft. *A kiss!* A kiss she actually felt and not the thousand kisses she'd dreamed of over the years until she forced herself to stop. Those had been Nick's lips on hers, no question.

This wasn't a dream, this was real.

And this wasn't the Nick she remembered, not at all. That Nick had been like a young panther. A man, yet with traces of the boy in him. This dangerous-looking Nick had no boy in him at all. He was hard, scarred, bulked up even more. His face was harsh, lean, the skin weather-beaten, pale lines fanning out from his eyes. She knew he was thirty-three, but he looked older.

They were driving at an impossible speed, though she felt safe in Nick's hands. He clearly knew what he was doing. And though the vehicle they were in was odd, it seemed to respond well and hug the road tightly even though they must have been going well over a hundred miles an hour.

Anything she had to say would have to wait, because Nick needed all his attention to drive.

He said he was taking her home. Where no one would find her.

Where was home? North, clearly. They were up on the freeway, heading north. Elle didn't really care where they were going, as long as they were leaving danger behind.

She tried to think about the situation, about the warning Sophie had given, about the tracking device, but it was no good. She was exhausted. Completely depleted. She couldn't reason in any way. All she could do was live each second exactly as it came up, with no past and no future.

It was frightening as hell to be in this state. She'd been yanked back just as the men in black on the street had stopped at her door at the motel. She'd seen Nick, but there were no emotions in her Dream states. She'd simply recognized him, somehow known he was there for her. He followed the men into the lobby, down the corridor, and then it was all mostly a blur.

Except for one thing. When Nick stepped into her room, there were four corpses in the corridor.

She'd seen that very clearly. He'd dispatched the men coldly and mechanically, like a surgeon excises a cancer. She'd never seen anyone move like that—blinding speed and power and violence, and at the end, four dead bodies.

She shivered.

Nick flicked a glance at her but said nothing. He reached for a button on the strange-looking console and the air in the cabin warmed up even more.

They sped in the night. There was very little traffic. The few cars on the road seemed to be standing still as Nick flew past them.

Elle looked out the window and thought she recognized a few landmarks. What difference did it make? They were going where Nick wanted to take her.

He swooped down from the interstate on an exit ramp. They'd passed the signs too fast for her to make out exactly where they were. He threaded a fast, complex route through a number of side streets until they reached what looked like a dead industrial park.

At the end of a trash-strewn street was a gate and Nick headed straight for it at top speed. Elle barely had time to gasp as the gates slid open just in time for them to sail through. She turned in her seat. Behind them, the gates were closing fast. Everything about the place spelled abandonment, but those gates had worked perfectly. Nick stopped the car and tapped a point on the console.

"On site," he murmured and she looked at him, startled.

"Roger that," said a disembodied voice, deep and loud and clear. "Incoming, ETA five minutes."

Nick looked over at her and ran the back of his index finger over her cheek. "Hang in there, honey. We'll be home soon."

She was a fool, because just the sight of him in the penumbra, face strong and sober, voice tinged with tenderness, nearly undid her. This was so dangerous. He'd brought her to her knees ten years ago. It had taken years to recover.

Granted, she wasn't the naïve and needy young girl she'd been then, but he still had the power to affect her deeply. If some-one had asked her, she'd have sworn that Nick Ross was dead to her and yet here she was, shivering and susceptible all over again, melting at his touch.

Never again.

She stiffened, pulled back.

She'd projected twice in one day. She'd been pursued by men who had taken many of her friends prisoner. She was lucky to be alive. She had Nick to thank for that, but that didn't mean she owed him anything but gratitude.

Certainly not love.

When she pulled back, Nick's face turned blank and his hand dropped. His voice was brisk and businesslike. "I need to get the hovercar under cover. Can you stand?"

Stupid question. Or maybe not so stupid.

Elle pushed down on the floor with her legs. They didn't tremble. Okay. Good to go.

"Yes, I can."

"Good girl." In a second he was at her door and helping her down. Elle moved slowly. She wanted to make sure she'd been right about being able to stand. The idea of fainting was too awful to contemplate. She wasn't weak and needy. She wasn't the Elle he'd left. She was strong.

It was just that it had been a very bad day.

Her legs held, thank God. Nick handed her her purse. "Look up."

A wind had suddenly blown up and she wondered if she heard right. "What?"

"Look up." Nick put a finger under her chin and tilted her head back. "Our ride's here."

Oh my God. A helicopter! Coming down almost right on top of her, and she hadn't heard a thing! The helicopter was barely discernible in the gloom and the cockpit was dark. Instead of the deafening roar of helicopters in the movies, it barely made a low buzzing sound as it veered off a few feet and neatly landed, like a cat after a jump.

"Come on!" Nick practically picked her up and hustled her over.

The helicopter looked eerie—made of some sleek dark matte substance with no apparent windows. Just as she determined that there was no way in, a door slid open showing a dimly lit interior. Four steps unfolded from the side.

Elle walked up into the cabin and sat down in one of the seats. Through the open door she could see Nick driving the odd car into what looked like a warehouse and then running back. He leaped into the body of the helicopter without using the steps, shouting "Go-Go-GO!"

The steps retracted, the door closed, and the helicopter lifted off abruptly, leaving Elle's stomach behind. It was utterly quiet inside the body of the helicopter. In every film she'd ever seen, people wore headphones to mask the noise, but inside it was like a cathedral.

There was no way to see outside the helicopter. There were, though, four big monitors showing what looked like the view outside—the brightly lit interstate off to the right, and infrared images, thermal images, and GPS coordinates on a moving map.

They were continuing their way north, the destination a blue cross to the northeast. Elle couldn't make out where they were heading.

"Name's Jon. Pleased to meet you." A partition had slid to one side and the pilot stuck his hand through. Elle awkwardly reached forward to take it. "Really glad Nick found you before his head exploded."

The hand was big and tough and belonged to a man who looked like he'd just come in from surfing some big waves. Though it was freezing cold outside, he had on an unbuttoned aloha shirt over a blindingly white T-shirt. The aloha shirt had bright blue parakeets flying among bright yellow palm trees, echoing his bright blue eyes and long sun-bleached hair.

He had a big black gun in a well-used shoulder holster.

Everything about the man was breezy and easygoing except his ice blue eyes, which were cold and hard, and his gun, equally cold and hard.

"Pleased to meet you," she said. She looked at Nick, then back at Surfer Jon. "Thanks for the rescue."

Jon winked and one side of his mouth turned up. "Any time. Rescuing beautiful women seems to have become our latest pastime."

"Jon . . ." Nick growled.

Jon rolled his eyes and cocked his head to one side, contemplating Nick. "Dude, chill."

"Where are we going?" Elle tried to keep her voice calm. The only answer was silence.

The question had to be asked. With every passing minute, Elle felt her strength returning. She'd just been rescued, it was true. But it was also true that she was in a helicopter going God knows where with two men, one of whom had just murdered four other men in a terrifying display of surgically precise violence.

Nick.

Forget that she'd known Nick very well once. She'd grown up with him. But then he'd disappeared, made a brief appearance in her life and then disappeared again.

She had no idea who he was now. None. For all she knew he was as dangerous to her as the men he'd killed. And Jon? With his happy turquoise and yellow shirt and the charming smile? And who was now ferrying the three of them God knew where?

He looked dangerous too.

So—what were her options? None, as far as she could tell. The helicopter was sealed tight. Even if she could somehow overpower two visibly strong, armed men—which was crazy—she'd have to learn to pilot a helicopter before it plunged to the ground. Which was insane.

Door number one was closed, which left just door number two.

Do nothing and hope she survived.

Nick tried not to stare at Elle. He really did try but it was impossible. Lucky thing she wasn't looking at him. In fact, she looked everywhere *but* at him.

She was feeling stronger. When she first came to, she looked as if it took everything in her just to keep upright. Now she kept her back stiff and kept herself turned away from him.

It wasn't just hurt feelings. She'd been plunged into a new world—his world—like plunging into an ice cold lake. Dangerous men had come after her, and though she hadn't seen him actually kill the four men, he knew he had the stench of murder on him. Elle had always been spookily aware of things, as if she were plugged into some other system of information. He wore what he was like a cloak around him. He and Mac both were uneasy in the civilian world. People parted for them, instinctively, and were usually agitated without knowing why. Sheep backing away in distress from the disguised wolf.

Jon on the other hand was just as dangerous but managed to conceal it for a little while with his garish shirts and predator's smile.

Elle sensed what Nick had become. She didn't like it, but he didn't give a fuck about that. She'd get over it.

Against all the odds, he'd found her. He thought he'd spend the rest of his life alone, but he'd found her. He wasn't ever letting her go. She was his until the end of time.

So she could hold herself stiffly away from him and she could not look him in the eyes and she could feel unease, but in the end it didn't make any difference at all. She was going to Haven with him and staying there.

Elle was watching the monitors, doing her best to ignore him when the map monitor winked off.

"Nick." Jon's voice drifted back from the cockpit. "It's time."

Oh, shit. He was frozen. How could he do this to Elle?

"Nick." This time there was pure steel in Jon's voice. Nick knew that if he fought Jon on this, Jon would turn the helo right around and head back to Palo Alto.

Elle turned and finally looked at him, a question in her eyes. He hated this, simply hated it. Nick picked up Elle's hand and faced her squarely. "Honey, I'm really sorry. Believe me when I say it's for your own good."

He reached behind him and slipped a hood over her beautiful, astonished face. He held her hands with his because he'd have fought fiercely anyone who put a hood over him. It was the ultimate of insults, and if she'd struggled with him, slapped him, kicked him, he'd understand and simply take it.

She did none of those things and he realized how much he underestimated her. Elle was nothing if not smart, and she knew she was no match for him physically, in any way. And certainly no match for him and Jon. The only intelligent thing to do was endure and that's what she did.

She sat stiffly, hooded head turned toward the front, dignified and completely still. Her hands were as stiff as wood in his.

Nick had never loved her more.

And he knew that with each passing minute, she hated him more and more.

Luckily, they were close to Haven. Jon was flying the helo at top speed now. It was a cloudless night and they were off everyone's radar. Soon they were on the home approach.

Mount Blue was a black shape against the starry sky. Below them, he knew, a large metal plate was extending out from the base of the mountain, providing a landing platform. Four minutes later, Jon landed perfectly on it and shut down the quiet engines.

The metal plate started retracting with the helo into the huge hollow structure invisible to the outside world.

Mount Blue. Haven.

Home.

A tension Nick had refused to acknowledge lifted from his shoulders. Elle was safe here. Everyone was safe here.

This was their refuge and the refuge of the family of misfits and talented outcasts they had gathered around them. He and Mac and Jon. Ward and Lundquist, Romero and Pelton. The entire Ghost Ops team had been sent to destroy a lab in Cambridge they'd been told was secretly weaponizing *Yersinia pestis*, bubonic plague. Only there was no secret project. A team of soldiers had been waiting for them to take them out. They'd been accused of high treason and had escaped on the way to a court-martial in Washington.

There was no way anyone could hold a Ghost Ops operator prisoner.

On the run from the entire U.S. government and bitter about their betrayal at the hands of Ward, a man they all worshipped, Mac, Jon, and Nick had found refuge on Mount Blue in northern California, inside an abandoned mine Mac had explored as a child. They holed up here, and damned if soon a community hadn't congregated around them. The community was turning Haven into the most comfortable high-tech lair for people on the run the world had ever seen. They were becoming self-sufficient in everything: energy, Internet, food—you name it.

The best thing was that the entire community was funded by two Latin America drug cartels. Jon, who had a personal crusade against drug dealers though no one knew exactly why, had spent two years undercover in the biggest Cartagena drug cartel walking a tightwire, pretending to be an emissary from California's dealers. He got enough intel, while burrowing deep into their finances, to put three hundred men away forever.

Whenever Haven needed anything, they just skimmed off the

Caymans and Aruban bank accounts of the cartel, leaving bread crumbs and footprints back to one kingpin after another and enjoyed it greatly when some scumbag took the blame and got whacked.

One less fuckhead on this earth, Jon had said. In the meantime they all had black credit cards in false names with several million dollars behind them.

The platform stopped moving and they were inside the hangar. It was an immense space two hundred feet high. They kept all their vehicles and drones and the helo here.

Elle couldn't get down out of the helo hooded, so Nick simply picked her up by the waist and swung her out. She didn't resist, but as soon as her feet hit the ground, she stepped back, away from him.

Oh no you don't, Nick thought.

These security measures were standard practice and necessary, he knew, though he regretted bitterly having to treat Elle like this.

The thing was, he, Mac, and Jon had become the front line of defense for a community of vulnerable, talented people that trusted the three outlaw soldiers to keep them safe. The three of them took that trust seriously. Everyone who came was vetted. If they passed, they could stay. If they didn't pass, they were given a big dose of Lethe, an amnesia drug, and left down in the valley without any memories of the hidden city inside Mount Blue.

Nick knew that if Elle somehow didn't pass the test, he was going back into the world with her, even though he was hunted by the U.S. government and there was a huge bounty on his head. He'd take his chances. Elle was not leaving his side, ever again. And he was never leaving hers.

Nick and Jon exchanged a glance. *No talking.* The rule for those who came to them but weren't of them yet. Any voice would echo in the huge chamber. Nick simply put his arm around Elle's waist and started walking to the elevator, Jon keeping step.

The elevator was a miracle of technology. The elevator lifted two thousand feet in the air so smoothly that it was entirely possible that Elle didn't realize she was in an elevator.

The elevator, together with most of the infrastructure had been designed by a talented engineer, Eric Dane. Eric had spent years writing report after report about the structural weaknesses of the Bay Bridge in San Francisco. When the '21 Halloween quake struck the bridge, collapsing and killing forty people, Eric's reports vanished and he was blamed for the collapse. A multimillion-dollar lawsuit was filed against him but there was no one to sue.

Eric had made it to Mount Blue, where he built them a comfortable, beautiful impregnable fortress. Haven.

There was no elevator *ding* at the top, just a silent opening of doors onto Haven's atrium.

If they weren't outlaws, and if Haven were a public place, the atrium would win a slew of city design prizes. A huge airy plant-filled plaza filled with terra-cotta pavestone paths winding through unexpected small squares with a flower bed here and an organic tomato patch there. There were benches and flowing metal-and-wood sculptures by the famous sculptress Kloe, on the run from her very rich and very abusive husband.

Overhead was an invisible arched roof made of graphene, one molecule thick, studded with tiny solar panels that provided light in the evening and helped keep the atrium at a steady 72 degrees all year round. The atrium was ringed with balconies, behind which were offices and homes. Some housed families and some, like Nick's pad and Jon's pad, were glorified bachelor officer quarters, though more spacious and definitely better-looking. Whenever a space needed decorating, everyone turned to Nancy Parsons, whose decorating firm was destroyed by her husband and partner, who ran off with every cent and the secretary, leaving Nancy holding a sackful of debt her husband owed the mob, no way to pay for it, and the mob on her heels.

On the third floor was their war room and Nick and Jon made their way through the paths of bright vegetation. It was four A.M., too late for the owls and too early for the larks. Mac and Catherine would be up, though, waiting to debrief.

Even if there had been people, not many would think twice about Nick and Jon marching a hooded figure across the great plaza. At one time or another, many honored members of Haven had been marched hooded up to the war room.

Another elevator let them out onto the third floor. Nick kept his arm around Elle to guide her and also . . . because.

Because he was still finding it hard to believe that she was here, with him. Pissed at him, sure. She had every right to be. But against all the odds she was safe and alive, and that's how she was going to stay. He'd found her, he'd fought for her, he'd waited for her for ten long years. She was his.

Jon went ahead, his biomorphic profile opening the door. Elle's wasn't programmed in. Yet.

Elle sensed that there was a threshold and she stopped dead. The war room was straight ahead of her, the corridor behind. Her new life, her old life. Straight ahead of her Mac and Catherine were waiting, as Nick knew they would be. They'd stayed awake all night, even Catherine, who was three-months pregnant. She wouldn't leave Mac, who wouldn't go to bed until his men were home. Mac wouldn't even have tried to convince Catherine to lie down because she wouldn't and he knew that.

To one side was a serving cart with a number of dishes with silver covers.

Stella. Bless her. She'd once been a world-famous actress until a stalker slashed her face to pieces. No one at Haven even noticed her scars anymore because everyone loved her. She was smart and kind and ran the extraordinary communal kitchen with a lot of help. No one ever wanted to get on her bad side because access to Stella's cooking was basically access to heaven itself. On the run and hunted, the people of Haven ate better than most millionaires.

From here on in, Elle was his and he was going to take care of her and that included feeding her. Before bedding her.

At the thought, his dick swelled.

Shit.

After long years of training, his dick had learned to obey him. It didn't get out of control anymore. In fact, it had been so obedient the past couple of years it was practically dormant. Ghost Ops had taken every ounce of attention and energy he had. Then they were on the run and in hiding, so bedding a woman became this huge energy suck. Not only because he had to plan the exit before the entry, as always, but now also because he had to work really hard not to leave a clue as to who he was. That involved having fake docs on him at all time, and it involved remembering his fake name and fake legend, exactly as if he were working undercover.

If anyone figured out a way to fuck without leaving DNA anywhere, he'd have been right on it.

It was exhausting and a lot of work for a one-night fuck, because two nights was pushing it. Jon didn't seem to have any problems. From what Nick saw, Jon got laid a lot on a regular basis and had no problem whatsoever with telling the women lies.

For Nick, it got very old very fast.

So, now his dick was waking up and smelling the roses. Or at least smelling Elle. Because over the smell of her fear and exhaustion was the smell of her. Something fresh and springlike and absolutely unmistakably *her*.

No other woman in the world smelled like her. Looked like her. Was her. Which explained the half-woodie in the presence of Jon and Mac and Mac's pregnant wife, though he knew better.

Nick put his hand on the small of Elle's back and she stiffened again, which was enough to take the starch out of his dick. She was disoriented enough without coping with his horniness.

Nick laced his hand with hers, ignoring the fact that she didn't close her hand around his, keeping it loose. He tugged and she walked forward, turning her head slightly at the drop in air pressure as the door shut.

Mac, Catherine, and Jon were standing in front of her, Catherine with a welcoming smile. Mac didn't do welcoming smiles, but at least he wasn't scowling, which was something.

Nick whipped the hood off Elle's head, her pale hair lifting slightly with a crackle, then falling back down in light shiny curls.

"Honey," he began, but Catherine gasped.

"Dr. Connolly! You're the one Nick went out to rescue?"

"You know me?" Elle asked.

Three deep male voices echoed. "You know her?"

Chapter 10

Lee suddenly stood up. "I need to check something," he said and walked out the door. But not before Flynn saw the sweat beading his forehead.

Something was wrong with Lee. Seriously wrong.

Former General Clancy Flynn had watched him carefully all day. Lee was a slick one, always cool and calm and emotionless. Two of the secret programs Flynn and his company had financed had earned him a lot of money in return. And the new one was going to be a bombshell. Creating faster, stronger, smarter soldiers was every general's dream, but it was the private sector, and Flynn's company Orion Security in particular, that was going to make it a reality.

They were close. There'd been a trial in Africa, where Orion had a potentially huge contract to guard a convoy conveying diamonds from a rich mine in the rebel-army infested interior to the coast. At first it had worked like a dream. He and Lee had watched as the team moved with increased precision and speed, like a well-oiled machine. Visibly enhanced, a joy to behold. And then the breakdown where they self-immolated.

But those first hours were promising. Lee said he had pinpointed the problem—a question of dosage—and one trial had gone very well and another trial was scheduled for next week.

But this new development . . .

If Flynn hadn't seen it with his own eyes, he would never have believed it. The *potential.* There was no limit to what he could earn with enhanced soldiers with powers like those.

Lee was onto something that would change the world, if it didn't kill him first.

If Flynn didn't know better, he'd say Lee was drunk. But Lee didn't drink, he was a teetotaler, something Flynn couldn't understand. The world was full of pleasures Lee seemed immune to. He was a driven, dedicated man and he was falling apart.

The signs were clear.

Lee had spent the entire time drumming his fingers restlessly on the desktop and jiggling his foot. He'd swallowed often and adjusted his shirt collar as if it were too tight, though actually it was loose. Lee had lost at least ten pounds since the last time Flynn had seen him.

But more than anything else there had been a barely contained excitement about the man, which was totally unlike him. Flynn had known Lee for a long time. He'd commissioned research from Lee's company back when he'd still been in the military. He believed in Lee so much, he dipped into his own company's pockets to keep this line of research going when he retired. It had been banned by the government, but what the government didn't know wouldn't hurt it.

"Human experimentation" was a big no-no in government labs, but that was bullshit in Flynn's opinion. Portable weaponry had gotten about as lethal as it was ever going to get, and there were limits to the use of the big bombs. The last frontier was human enhancement, which was going to make all the difference in the coming resource wars.

Lee had always been cool and rational. The ultimate scientist, though Flynn had always suspected Lee had another agenda. Not money, which puzzled him. Because money was the best motivator there was. Lee liked money well enough, but mainly he saw it as a tool to help him continue his research. He himself lived simply. So money wasn't it. Whatever it was, as long as it didn't impede the ultimate goal, Flynn didn't give a shit.

But now whatever it was that was driving Lee was messing with him—with the man Flynn had just given fifteen million dollars to.

If what Lee was working on panned out, the history of soldiering would be changed forever and Flynn would almost overnight become one of the richest men in the world. If it didn't pan out because Lee went off the reservation, then Flynn was out a shitload of money and the promises he was making to potential clients would turn out to be so much hot air. And a couple of those clients were not men you could lie to and walk away from alive.

Whatever happened, he needed to stick around for a few more days to make sure Lee wasn't going to make fifteen million dollars go up in smoke.

He tapped his ear. He needed to check in with headquarters.

"Yessir." Oh yeah. Melissa, his new secretary. Efficient and pretty and eminently bangable. She could roll out of bed after two hours of fucking him and coolly plan his next day's schedule while he was still gasping on the bed.

"Yeah, Melissa. I know I said I was coming back today, but I need to stay. Block out the next two days and cancel my flight back to Virginia. Tell the pilot he can stay at the Marriott until I need him."

A pause and then Melissa's throaty voice. "Done."

"I'll let you know when I'm arriving. And, Melissa?"

She recognized that tone and her voice dropped even lower. "Yessir?"

"Don't be wearing panties when I arrive."

Flynn disconnected with her throaty chuckle ringing in his ears.

Mount Blue

Elle found herself in a warm embrace, short but heartfelt. The woman embracing her was slender, so the slight protuberance of her belly could be easily felt. She was pregnant, and there was no doubt whatsoever who the father was. He stood right behind the woman with a hand on her shoulder.

They made a strange couple. Beauty and the Beast. The woman was very pretty, with shoulder-length dark hair and gray-blue eyes, and the husband . . . well, the husband was huge and ugly and frightening. Those were the only words that really fit. He was the tallest man in the room—though both Nick and Jon were tall men—and would be in just about any room. His face was hard with a nose that had been broken several times, what looked like a knife scar on one side and a burn scar that had melted the skin on the other. His eyes were cold and hard. This was a guy you wanted to avoid if you knew what was good for you. That didn't stop the woman from gently stroking the huge hand on her shoulder and giving him a quick loving glance over her shoulder.

He smiled down at her and the entire arrangement of his facial features changed. He didn't turn warm and cuddly, but there was no doubt what he felt for the woman. Elle herself would have been frightened to be in the same room as the guy, but love was love. What could she say? She'd been in love forever with a man who'd abandoned her twice, so she was no one to judge.

This woman knew her, which was eerie bordering on creepy. "How do you know my name?" Elle asked as the woman took her hand.

"Chicago, May 2022, the annual meeting of the American Neuroscience Academy. Room B. Your paper on 'Immune Markers in Trance States' blew us all away." The woman shook her hand gently then let it go. While Elle's hand had been in hers, there had been a weird flash of warmth, something gently blooming then fading. It might have been coincidence, but she felt a little stronger too.

Chicago, May 2022. "You were there?"

"I was." The woman smiled softly. "Though I read the entire paper later because I had to leave halfway through and go to Room C. To deliver my own paper on 'The role of Kir4.1 in Oligodendrocyte Myelin Formation'."

Elle gasped. "Dr. Young! Dr. Catherine Young!" This time Elle was the one to grab a hand. She pumped it up and down. How amazing to find her here! Catherine Young was a legend who was doing cutting-edge research into dementia. Unlock dementia and you unlocked a number of secrets of the brain. "What a privilege! I've followed your work these past years with a great deal of interest. Particularly your work on the gamma secretase activating protein in translating ribosome affinity purification. I know you're applying it to a study of dementia, but really, it could be extrapolated to association cortices in the parahippocampal gyrus."

Dr. Young leaned forward. "Oh, I know! I was studying the dementing process, but your findings are important in gaining a clearer understanding of immunoreactivity. When we used immunofluorescence assays—"

"Did you use the Coons and Kaplan technique?"

"We did. It's old but it is reliable and stable. I know some are using the new Hunter and Florheim technique, but—"

"Whoa!" A deep voice interrupted. Elle turned her head to see Nick with his big hands up in a time-out gesture. "Some pity for the non-geeks here. And especially pity for two certain non-geeks who are starving because they just saved a certain geek's ass."

Elle felt anger shoot through her whole system. "That would be me, I suppose?"

Nick nodded. "That would definitely be you, *Dr. Connolly*. No wonder I couldn't find you. You'd changed your name." His jaw muscles visibly moved. "I imagine that there's a mister Connolly somewhere. Or, knowing you, another Dr. Connolly."

Elle's own jaw tightened. Nick sounded angry. As if she'd done something without asking permission. *How dare he!* She narrowed her eyes. "No mister, no doctor. Connolly was my mother's name. I took it after—after."

"What? What?" Nick's eyes widened and he got in her face, jaws working. She could actually hear his teeth grinding. "You changed your name? You fucking changed your fucking *name*? Do you have any idea how fucking *hard* I—"

"Nick." Dr. Young's husband landed a very heavy hand on Nick's shoulder and dug his fingers in. Nick's face showed nothing, but those hands looked extremely strong. It was entirely possible that he was doing some damage to Nick's shoulder. The man shook his head. "We don't talk to women like that in Haven, Nick. We don't talk to anyone like that. You should be ashamed of yourself."

Nick shrugged his shoulder and the man lifted his hand. Nick was glaring at her and she glared right back. Of all things, she hadn't expected this. *He* was mad! At *her. The nerve!*

Anger, red hot and painful, boiled in her chest. Elle turned to the other woman in the room. Dr. Catherine Young could be trusted to be rational. "Dr. Young, please tell Nick—"

Dr. Young lifted her hand. "Please, Dr. Connolly, call me Catherine."

One big breath. Two. *Manners*, she told herself. "And you must call me Elle, of course."

Catherine nodded and smiled. They could have been in a drawing room over tea instead of some hidden location with three frightening men and one world-class scientist. "Well, Elle. We should make some other introductions. You've met Jon."

Jon gave an ironic smile and a two-fingered salute off his forehead. "Ma'am."

Elle inclined her head. "We've met. As a matter of fact he rescued me."

"*He* rescued you!" Nick said heatedly. "He didn't do anything but fly the helo! So how the hell does he come off as the big rescuer? *I'm* the one who—"

"And this is my husband, Mac." Catherine's voice was soft, but she managed to run right over Nick's rant.

"Ma'am." Mac had the deepest voice she'd ever heard. It was a rumble she felt in her diaphragm rather than heard. He reached over, engulfed her hand in his, squeezed gently for a second, then let her hand go. Which was nice because he could have crushed it easily and Elle needed that hand.

Catherine hadn't mentioned last names at all. Interesting. Well, if she couldn't know names, could she get some info on other things? "Nice to meet you all. So. Where am I?" she asked.

Silence. Utter silence. That was interesting too.

"I'm sure Nick will bring you up to speed eventually, Elle." Catherine smiled at her. "But in the meantime, you must be exhausted and you must be hungry. So before we show you to your room . . ."

"*My* room," Nick interrupted angrily. "My room. She's staying with me. In my room."

Another moment of perfect silence.

"Elle?" Catherine asked softly. "Are you okay with that?"

She had no idea what to say. None. All of a sudden she was aware of her immense exhaustion, like a living thing weighing down on her. A huge boulder that weakened her knees and seemed to dim the lights in the room.

This was Nick, the man she'd loved almost her whole life. And this was Nick, who'd abandoned her the day after she buried her father. And this was also Nick who by some crazy tangled reasoning in his mind had decided he was angry at her.

That was enough to make up her mind.

"No," she said decisively. "Could I have a separate room?"

How she was going to deal with Nick from here on in was something she was going to have to face in the future, but right now, she was at the end of her physical and mental resources. Having a fight with Nick was utterly beyond her.

Nick's eyes bugged. *"What?"* His deep voice rose an octave. "What? What the fuck? Of course—"

"Nick. Stop that right now." Catherine Young seemed to be about half the weight of Nick and she had a soft voice, but that voice stopped him dead in his tracks.

His mouth closed with a snap, lips pressed together as if he had to work to not talk. But his eyes were still wide and a little wild. He huffed out a big breath like a bull.

He wasn't liking this. Not one bit.

Good.

"Well, first things first. I'm not letting you go to your room before getting a bite to eat." Catherine gently steered her toward a cart, pulled a chair from a desk and sat her down. Mac pulled something down from the wall, detached it, pushed a button, and it magically unfolded into a table that connected to some hidden seam in the service cart with a distinct click. It was a cue for everyone to grab a chair and place it around the table.

"Guests first," Mac said in his deep bass. Which was kind but also served to remind everyone that she was the outsider here. Mac and Catherine started lifting covers off the serving plates and the room filled with the scent of delicious food.

Nick sat his chair right next to hers, so closely his shoulder brushed hers as he piled food on a plate and set it in front of her. "Eat," he commanded.

Everyone was looking at her expectantly, as if they'd never seen a person eat before. Elle waited a second, fork poised above her plate, watching them watching her.

Nick nudged her plate closer. "Eat," he repeated.

She ate.

All it took was a bite or two for her eyes to open wide with astonishment. As a scientific experiment she took a bite from everything on her plate and confirmed her first hypothesis.

"This is the best food I've ever eaten," she blurted. They'd been watching to see her reaction to the food. Catherine sat back and looked at her husband and Jon with a smile. Both men nodded. Nick didn't meet their eyes because his were fixed on her in an unblinking stare.

Everyone but Nick was transferring food to their plates. Nick's plate remained empty as he continued watching her. It didn't intimidate her, though. She'd suffered worse things than having someone watch her eat. Not to mention the fact that eating this amazing food was no hardship.

Huge ricotta raviolis with a wild mushroom and cream sauce, the most succulent *tagliata* in the history of the world, dusted with arugula and parmesan flakes. The lightest possible fried artichoke slices. Sautéed escarole with plump raisins. Frisèe salad with hot bacon. Steamed broccoli with garlic and a balsamic vinegar reduction. A freshly baked ciabatta to soak everything up.

Simple fare, done absolutely perfectly.

Nobody talked. Nobody should. The food was a religious experience and required proper worship. Elle had eaten a couple of times at Chez Panisse before Alice Waters retired, and this food was arguably better.

There was tiramisu—what looked like the platonic ideal of tiramisu, frothy and creamy and chocolatey—in a big glass bowl in the corner. Just for encouragement.

When she was stuffed, Elle sat back. "Is this a secret five-star restaurant? The kind that never advertises and you have to be a foodie and pass a test to find? Though"—this with a slanted glance at Jon—"hooding clients is taking it a bit far."

"Good old Stella." Jon had eaten with unswerving fervor and wasn't finished. He heaped a third helping of everything onto his plate. "I love her experiments, but when she does the basics . . . man. No one does it better."

"Stella?" This Stella person was obviously the chef.

Jon grinned. "Yeah, you wouldn't believe who the cook is. She's—"

"Jon!" Mac's deep voice was like a whip lash. Jon's blond eyebrows shot up.

"We might want to discuss this, and other things, tomorrow." Catherine placed a hand on her husband's huge one and gave Elle a smile.

There was another painful silence.

Secrets. Deep secrets that weren't going to be shared with her. *O-kay.*

Nick had spooned some of the tiramisu onto a dessert plate and put it in front of her. "Eat."

Elle set her teeth. "Is that all you can say? Eat?"

"Oh no." Nick gave a smile that showed his own teeth, but wasn't friendly. "I've got a lot of other things to say, but not right now. Later. When we're alone."

Curse her fair skin. Heat rose from her chest and she knew she was turning pink. Because it was very clear what he meant.

And curse her obsession, because instead of making her angry that he was assuming she'd just sweep aside ten years of abandonment to go to bed with him, her body reacted to his words and to the images his words conjured up with enthusiasm, completely out of her control.

Right now, with Nick so close to her, his shoulder rubbing hers, his body heat like a force field around him, his fierce eyes locked on hers—her body remembered what it had been like to make love to him.

She'd spent the entire night with him in a state of arousal, just like now. A flush of heat prickled through her body as if she'd suddenly stepped out into the blazing sun. Her breath grew shallow, her breasts felt heavy, swollen.

Her sex . . . wept with pleasure. Incredibly, it suddenly felt as if Nick's penis were in her and her sex clenched around it, stomach and groin muscles pulling hard. Her heart was knocking against her ribs so hard she was sure someone could hear it.

Certainly Nick could. Or he could hear something because his gaze narrowed and tightened, his nostrils flared, and two white lines of stress appeared around his mouth. His eyes were focused on her face then abruptly dropped to her chest. It would be pointless to cover her breasts with her arms, he'd seen her hard nipples.

Oh God, this was so humiliating. It was like being stripped bare of all defenses, rendered down to bedrock, open and vulnerable when she'd worked so very hard all these years to make herself strong and protected.

All it took was Nick's presence and she morphed back to that helpless, grieving girl who'd been full of hopes and dreams for one night.

What a triumph it must be for Nick. That he could disappear for ten years and she'd still be so lovesick his mere physical presence turned her on more than any number of courters ever could.

Nick didn't look triumphant and cocky, though. He looked stressed, almost in pain.

"Goddamn it," he said suddenly, grabbing her hand and standing up. He walked fast to the door, pulling her stumbling behind him.

Elle looked back and saw Catherine half rise and her husband reach out to her and shake his head. She sat back down, looking troubled, and then the door opened and Nick pulled her into the corridor as the door slid closed behind them.

Elle stopped, frozen. The first thing to strike her was the smell. The smell of a vast garden, of lush vegetation, sweet and fresh.

The corridor was curved, one of many circling a huge central space filled with plants. Trees, bushes, flowering plants, leaves thick and glossy, thriving. The space was . . . amazing. Huge, like a city square, rising up to a ceiling. Or—a roof? A transparent roof studded with bright lights against the black night sky.

Down on the ground level someone walking on a path looked up and waved at Nick, who paid no attention to anything but getting them to the elevator at the end of the corridor.

She stumbled again, but instead of stopping, Nick put his arm around her waist and speeded up.

Elle didn't know where they were going but wherever it was, they were going there fast.

Nick barely made it to the quarters Red and Bridget had just vacated because they had a brand-new baby. The first Haven citizen.

He felt like any minute now something would explode. His head. His skin. His cock. Something. Just itching to go up in flames. Something inside him that couldn't be contained and was ready to blow.

He had to draw in a deep breath to be able to function even on the most basic level.

He tapped on the wall beside the door and a keyboard lit up. He turned to Elle and tried to keep the rasp of strong emotions— anger and relief and, well, horniness—from his voice. "For the moment, this is where you'll stay, if you don't want to stay with me." He ignored the huge pump of his heart that those words and the very idea created in him—that Elle, finally with him again, wouldn't want to stay with him, be with him. He punched in a four-digit code. "I'm putting in a temporary code. 1993, your birth year. You can change it later if you want."

He looked at her, the implication a dark cloud between them. She might change it and not give him the new code.

The door whooshed open and he held his hand out. She ignored it. She crossed the threshold and he marched in right behind her.

That lovely face turned indignant. "I don't know if I made myself clear, Nick, but I do not want to sleep with you."

As soon as the door slid shut, he backed Elle up until her back hit the door with a thud, then moved in close. He was behaving like a real dick but he couldn't help himself. No way he could have stayed in the war room eating and talking with Elle right beside him even one second more.

Right now she was here, with him. So close he could touch her if he dared.

Nick slammed his hands on the door right beside her head. She was caged in by him, though he wasn't touching her anywhere. If she really wanted to get away from him, he'd let her. It would kill him, but he could do it.

He hoped.

He wasn't touching her anywhere, but it was as if his skin had developed some other sense or was able to reach out to her. He dipped his head, his nose shifting her hair away from her ear. "You don't have to sleep with me, but damned if I'm going to leave you alone in here. You were comatose when I found you. You've been through hell. If you need something in the night, you don't know how this place works. You won't know how to call for help. And I'd just stay awake worrying about you. So if you don't want me to touch you, I won't. But I'll be goddamned if I leave you alone here." He pulled away and looked down at her.

Jesus, why did she have to be so fucking beautiful? She was even more beautiful than the last time he saw her. Over-the-top gorgeous, supersmart. A doctor no less. Someone Catherine admired, and Catherine was one of the smartest people Nick knew.

Nick had thought of Elle almost every day since Lawrence. He'd memorized her. The last image of her sleeping in bed was one he'd carried inside him for ten years.

The supersoft pale blond hair like a cloud around her head, the light blue eyes that looked like shards of summer sky, the high cheekbones, the shape of her head, that narrow torso, the puff of pale hair between those long, slender legs . . . every inch of her was in his head.

But there was a new Elle now, all grown up; and if anything, she was even more perfect than the young girl. He eagerly drank in all the new details of this new Elle because though she was never leaving his sight again, if he could help it, life had this funny way of whacking you in the head.

He would have sworn he would live the rest of his life in Ghost Ops. When his past had been wiped out and he'd taken the oath, with Lucius Ward and Mac McEnroe as his commanding officers, he knew this was to be his life forever more. And then Ghost Ops died, its forces scattered, accused of treason. What he thought would be an undying commitment proved to be short-lived.

So, yeah, you never knew.

So he drank in every detail of Elle because life being what it was, she could disappear on him in a heartbeat.

Her skin was still ivory perfection. The few lines around her eyes did nothing to detract from her beauty. She'd filled out so she no longer had that lost-waif look. She looked strong and capable and held herself with authority.

God, he loved that.

He was just barely keeping himself from touching her. He had to keep his hips pulled back because his dick was pressing against his pants. It wanted to be inside her. Smart dick.

He could barely remember his last hard-on. Some waitress down in Bakersville. She'd been nice enough. Lonely, like him. The signs had been unmistakable. Nick had become the world's greatest expert on lonely and could sniff lonely people out in a crowd. They'd gone to a nearby motel and she'd been older and more used up than he thought, and his cock had gone a little limp. She noticed, had smiled sadly, and started buttoning her blouse back up.

Nick had willed his cock back up and forced himself to give her an extra good time and afterward, when she'd left at dawn, he'd stared at the ceiling until the sun rose over the windowsill, thinking of absolutely nothing at all.

That had been six months ago and he hadn't had wood since. Hadn't seen a woman who even vaguely interested him, and hadn't jerked off.

Right now, it felt like his cock would never go down, ever again.

He bent again, his lips almost but not quite touching that long, pale slender neck. "So like it or not, Elle, I'm staying here. I'll sleep on the couch, I'll sleep on the fucking floor, I don't care. But you're not leaving my sight."

Elle gave a long exhale.

"You bastard." Elle's voice was the barest whisper.

"Yeah. No argument there." There wasn't. He was literally a bastard. He doubted his mother even knew who his father was. Apparently there'd been plenty of candidates. But over and above that, in Ghost Ops you lied and cheated if that's what it took to get the job done. He'd been undercover and lied about himself so much it was hard to remember what was the truth. He and his teammates fought for survival not for goodness. There had been very little of that in his life. The judge and Elle herself had been the only good people he'd ever met.

So yeah, he was a bastard.

He turned his head so his ear was close to her mouth. "So in a second I'm going to step back, though it'll cost me, and let you settle in. But I'm not going anywhere and you'd better get used to that. Because from here on in, I'm sticking to your pretty tail."

Her skin flushed. He could almost feel the heat. She pulled in a deep breath and gave him a hard shove. If he didn't want to move, no shove of Elle's could ever make him move, not even an inch. But he stepped back.

"You bastard!" Her pale blue eyes shot fire. "You son of a bitch!

You leave me—twice!—without a word and now I'm supposed to let you just stick close to me? Until the next time you leave?"

Nick fisted his hands in her soft pale hair, pulled her head back a little and kissed her. Finally. It was what he'd been craving since she'd woken up in the hovercar. Not before. Before he'd been too wild with terror to think of kissing her. In fact, if he'd thought of it and if he believed in God, he'd have taken a vow of chastity in exchange for a living, breathing Elle. He'd have given anything up, promised anything on earth to find her alive. Kissing her had taken a backseat to that.

But he hadn't promised anything to anyone. He'd found her, saved her, won her. Fair and square.

Her mouth still tasted wonderful—fresh, clean, enticing. She was holding herself back, her mouth cooperating but the rest of her stiff and unyielding. She stiffened and shoved him again, sliding away from the wall.

He was angry, frustrated, still humming with adrenaline. He wanted to hold her, protect her, fuck her. But even through the huge waves of emotion roiling through him, emotions he hadn't the foggiest idea how to handle, a small part of him, the non-dickhead part of him, rejoiced.

This was the real Elle now. She'd somehow regained her footing. He'd found her nearly dead, she'd been hooded, taken to an unknown location, met people she'd never seen before and who held power over her. She'd been beaten down, just a little.

But this Elle—she didn't do beaten down. She stood absolutely straight, high color riding her high cheekbones, light blue eyes narrowed so that only a pale blue gleam showed, her face, her entire body, stiff with dignity and resistance. This was the woman she'd become. Strong and in control.

He stepped back, hands up because she looked like she was about to attack him. Nick wasn't afraid of anyone on earth in hand-to-hand combat. Except Elle. Because to save his life, he couldn't lift a hand against her. If she were armed and shot him, he'd be unable to resist.

He was really lucky she wasn't violent by nature.

"I didn't leave without a word," he said softly.

Her face sharpened. "What? What's that supposed to mean?"

"I left you a note. I suspect you didn't see it."

Her nostrils flared. "Stop jerking me around, Nick! Damn you!"

"I said I was coming back. And I did. I came back. I thought we would be gone for a day or two, but it turned out we were gone for three months. But I left you a note."

"Yeah," she sneered.

His jaws clenched hard. "Yes. I did. And you know what?" He tapped her on the chest with a finger. "I risked everything to leave you that note. It was a court-martial offense. Only married opera-tors can tell wives that they are going on an op and you weren't my wife. If my commanding officer found out I'd left a note to some-one who wasn't a relative, I would have been fucked. So leaving you that note was a *big fucking deal.*"

She punched him. It didn't hurt but did take him completely by surprise. "I didn't find any note!"

"No, it fell to the floor because you threw back the covers when you woke up."

Her eyes opened wide. "How the hell would you know that?"

"Because I came back for you. You're not listening, Elle. I left the note on my pillow, but when I came back it was on the floor. You didn't see it. You didn't see it and you didn't trust me to come back, and you left. And I have spent the past ten years worried sick about you." *And she'd changed her fucking name!* He was still mad about that.

"Oh no, Nick Ross." Elle moved away from him

Oh no, you don't, he thought. *You don't get to hold back.*

His hand on her cheek brought her face back to him. "Look

at me, honey. I'm not lying. I'll never lie to you. I got a text from my superior officer that night. We were going on a secret mission. And though the U.S. military has divorced me and would probably kill me on sight, I still can't tell you where we went or what we did. But I was under direct orders to leave immediately and not tell anyone where I was going or even that I was going on an op. I thought it would only be for a few days, but we ended up staying three months."

Elle brought her hands up. They were shaking. "Don't," she whispered. "I can't deal with this now."

The flush of anger had gone from her cheeks, leaving her icy pale. He didn't ever want to see that color on her face again, and here he was the one who caused it. Shame made him step back.

"Okay. You don't have to face anything right now except shower and bed."

"I want to sleep alone, Nick."

"You will. I'll bunk on the couch."

"Alone."

"Not going to happen. Sorry. I'm not going to leave you alone. I won't touch you unless you want me to, but I'm not leaving." Their eyes met and held. She was strong-willed but so was he.

She made a sound in her throat and looked away.

Damn straight. She wasn't going to win this one.

Nick pointed. "The bathroom's through there. You'll find everything you need. You'll find clean tees in the dresser drawer. They'll do for a nightgown until we can get you some clothes. Now I'm going to lie down because I don't know about you, but I saved someone's life tonight and I'm goddamned tired."

He could hear her teeth grinding. No matter. He went to the closet, pulled out a blanket, placed his boots next to the couch, lay down and pulled the blanket over him and, closing his eyes, turned over.

He didn't watch but his hearing was just fine. He heard her take a shower, pad across to the bed, and slip under the covers.

The bed was comfortable, he knew that. It was the same make as his own, and it was great. She didn't resist more than a few minutes. He heard her breathing slow down and almost felt her tumble into a deep sleep.

He waited half an hour then threw the covers off and padded barefoot to the bed. He'd dimmed the lights to the faintest of glows, just enough so if she woke she wouldn't be in complete darkness.

There was no question of sleep. He felt like he'd never sleep again. Every hormone in his body that governed sleep, hope, happiness, and sex was pinging around his system and he had nowhere to go with it. He hooked a chair with his foot and sat down by her bedside because the only thing that could calm him was looking at her.

Elle.

After ten years—fifteen if you counted from the day the judge kicked him out—she was here, with him. He'd lost hope. He'd resigned himself to that aching emptiness he sometimes let himself feel, knowing it would be forever. To his dying day, he'd be alone in the most elemental sense of the word.

The closest he had to a place in the world was here, Haven. He respected Mac and Jon, he liked Catherine and the misfits making up Haven. That was going to be the extent of his relations till the end of time. Everyone at arm's length, no one close.

And now . . . Elle.

She was pissed at him. That was cool. It didn't make any difference to him because he had her again. That particular warmth that only she could give—it was back again. She'd slipped through his fingers once but she wasn't slipping twice.

He sat next to her, watching her pale profile, watching the

covers rise and fall, knowing he was going to be next to her for the rest of their lives and felt something he hadn't felt in a long, long time. In fifteen years, actually.

Happiness.

Her eyes fluttered once, twice, opened. If he hadn't been staring at her face, he'd have missed it. But he hadn't been able to look away from her all the while she slept. Outside on Mount Blue, dawn had come and gone and it was late morning. If he hadn't wanted to guard her sleep, he'd have tapped a button and turned the walls into giant monitors and watched the dawn with her.

It would happen.

Elle frowned, light blue eyes flickering from him to the room like bolts of lightning in the dim light. Nick tapped and the ambient light came up slowly, so she could see more than the dim shadows of the furniture.

She hadn't had the strength to notice much last night, but now he watched her take in her surroundings.

The room was nice. Everything in Haven was nice. They had supertalented people who'd designed the spaces and he and Jon were master thieves. They'd stolen furniture from the finest designers. The room was spacious, beautifully appointed, a delight for the senses.

Elle's gaze rested thoughtfully on everything in the room, taking in the luxurious feel of it. Finally, her light blue gaze rested on him.

"You," she said. Nick couldn't figure out the tone of her voice. One thing for sure, though. It wasn't enthusiasm he was hearing.

He leaned forward in his chair, placing a hand on the mattress. "Me."

There was maybe half a foot between them, but it felt like oceans, like whole valleys and planets were between them. Nick couldn't stand it for one second longer. Talking things over would come later. The words would only confirm what already was.

She was his. He was hers.

He leaned forward and touched his mouth to hers.

He could taste the surprise. Now he wanted to taste the heat. He'd been a good boy. He'd waited. He'd fed her, let her sleep. But the control was fraying because just watching her sleep, he'd wanted her like his next breath. He leaned against her fully, bringing her arms up and around his neck. She resisted but he kissed her harder—and felt the exact precise moment when her resistance broke. She tightened her arms around his neck, nearly choking him, and lifted herself up into him so her breasts rubbed against him.

Oh yeah.

He ate at her mouth, pressed against her harder and felt his mind blur. There was no strategy now in his movements, no feeling his way forward. His body took over completely. He hadn't been celibate these past ten years, but it felt like it.

He panted as he pulled her T-shirt up and off, then unzipped himself. He slid under the covers and shifted her leg with his hand—remembering clearly how soft she felt—and his rock-hard cock found its unerring way inside her. He pushed hard, mind blasted by all that softness and heat and— He stopped.

"Oh God," he wheezed. There was barely enough oxygen to breathe, not much making it to his head, but what he was feeling was unmistakable.

Buried deeply inside her, Nick lifted his head and looked down. So beautiful, like an otherworldly creature, an eye magnet for men and yet . . .

He moved his hips forward, as if testing her.

"No one else has been here." Nick stared into Elle's pale blue eyes as he said this, and her eyes flared. "No one, ever, has been here but me."

Her mouth opened and closed. There was no way for her to lie because her face, her eyes, her whole body was open to him.

It was too much. His hips started hammering against her, lifting her with each stroke and he could feel her emotions pounding inside her, finding release in the sex. It was fast and hard and intense and couldn't last and it didn't. One last stroke that drove her almost to the headboard and he started coming like a train, moving hard inside her all the while, coming in hot pulses that felt like his spinal cord had liquidated and found its way to his dick.

And at the very last minute, when he was crushing her against the mattress, head down on her shoulder, sweat coating his body, he felt it. That sweet little cunt, clenching around him in white hot pulses, milking him. *Oh God, yes.*

At the end they lay there, plastered together, Nick still panting.

Elle punched him in the shoulder and burst into tears.

"Shh, shh." Nick kissed her neck, that soft spot behind her ear. Her mouth, briefly, because she punched even harder when he kissed her lips. "No, honey, no."

He settled more deeply against her. He'd lost part of his erection. The days in which he could come two, three times in a row were gone. But his dick didn't want to leave her in any way so there was enough blood in it to stay in her.

He was careful not to slip out. No, no. If he could, he'd stay in her forever.

She was crying silently, head buried in his shoulder, trying to stifle her sobs but failing.

It broke his heart.

He held her close for long minutes, knowing it would be best for her to get it out of her system. When she calmed, he eased away so he could look at her. She turned her head away and he gently tilted her face back to his.

Even after crying, she was the most beautiful woman he'd ever seen. How could that be? She'd been rescued at the last minute, been hooded and taken to a place she'd never seen before. She'd had the shock of seeing him after ten years. He'd fucked her near to death. She'd had a storm of tears.

And still she looked beautiful. Her eyes didn't swell, her nose didn't turn red. The tears simply dried on that pale ivory skin like shards of crystal and, *oh* . . . It almost hurt to look at her.

He was lying with his entire weight on her, cock still in her. What he had to say required saying not only with words but with his body. He knew that at some primal level she would hear and feel the truth.

"I never left you."

She was watching him carefully out of those pale blue eyes. Listening to him. Feeling him. A big lie is told with words but told with the body too. Tiny signals of falsehood, many imperceptible. But they were touching each other all over. He was inside her. His body had the stillness of truth.

Her eyes searched his. "I thought you'd left me. Again."

Nick closed his eyes in pain. "I know, honey. I realize that. There was nothing I could do. I made it up to Lawrence the instant I got back but—you'd left."

"That night," she whispered. "I left that night. I felt like I'd die if I stayed one more minute."

His heart clenched as he thought of her—poor and abandoned, striking out on her own.

"Because it was the second time you'd left me." There they were. The words he'd been dreading.

Because there was no way he could tell her the truth—that the judge had sent him away. Nick knew the judge had been absolutely right to do what he did. But Elle wouldn't see it that way. She'd watched her father decline badly and he didn't want to add anger to her memories of her father. The judge had been a good and noble man who'd had to bear a lot at the end of his life.

Wherever the judge was, his daughter wasn't going to resent him because he'd sent Nick away.

Nick lifted himself up on his forearms and looked down at her. At this woman he loved with all his heart. He'd loved her these past ten years and he'd love her until the day he died.

Which might be tomorrow.

He cupped her head in his hands and opened himself.

He was good at lying. Good undercover agent. He never saw a need to tell anyone what was going on inside himself. That stopped right now, because Elle had a right to see inside him because she was inside him.

He looked her in the eyes and opened his soul.

"I can't tell you why I went away that first time. I could lie to you and you'd believe me. I'm really good at lying. An ace at it, in fact. But I won't lie to you. I will never lie to you for the rest of our lives. But this one thing—I can't tell you and you will have to accept that."

She thought about it long and hard. She didn't even pretend that she wasn't. He watched her work her way through it, knowing what he was asking her.

"You won't lie to me?"

Nick dipped his head, kissed her shoulder, lifted his head again. "No, not ever."

"You'll tell me what's going on here? In this place?"

For the first time since he'd found her, he felt like smiling. "Oh yeah. Because this is your new home. You're going to live here with me and the others for the rest of your life."

She sighed and he could feel her acceptance in her voice, in her skin, in her heart. "Tell me," she said. "What's going on here?"

Nick rolled them to their sides because it was going to be a long story, and he didn't want to separate his body from hers. He wanted to stay with her, in her, as long as he could.

And he told her. Everything.

Chapter 11

At noon, Nick left her at the door with a kiss and an enigmatic smile. "Go do your thing, honey," he said.

The door slid open, he gave a little push at the small of her back and she moved reluctantly forward.

And found herself in an utterly familiar environment.

Mini electron microscopes, ELISA arrays, titrators, chromatographs, handheld MRIs . . . the works.

A lab. And a well-equipped one at that. It was chilled and smelled like every lab Elle had ever worked in—of disinfectant and ozone. And like every lab she'd ever been in, it spelled order and reason in a disorderly and unreasonable world.

She felt herself relaxing even before Catherine came to her with a smile and a white lab coat held over her arm. "Hi, I hope you rested well. That was some trauma you went through." She leaned forward and gave Elle a quick kiss on the cheek. As before, a rush of warmth went through her at Catherine's touch.

Catherine held out the lab coat, which fit Elle perfectly. Putting on the lab coat was like putting on a magic coat of armor. Elle felt herself again, in her element again. In control again.

Catherine smiled gently and Elle had the impression she understood exactly what she felt.

"Stella said she'd send breakfast up to you and Nick. Did she?"

Elle didn't blush. It hadn't been in any way a suggestive comment, any kind of observation about her and Nick. Catherine simply wanted to know if Elle was comfortable, had had breakfast. Elle relaxed even further.

"Breakfast. Well. I don't know if what this Stella sent up could really be called breakfast. Breakfast is usually coffee and yogurt, so breakfast doesn't quite cover it. I think 'feast' would be a more appropriate term. And 'delicious' should be in there too."

Catherine's smile was blinding. "That's our Stella."

"I know you're not supposed to tell me who she is." Elle cocked her head. "Jon seemed to think that I would know who she is if I heard her name. But I'm not up on trendy chefs. As a matter of fact, since Alice Waters retired, I don't think I know the names of any chefs at all. And certainly not a Stella."

Catherine hesitated a beat. Big secret. "Sorry," Elle said. "I guess that's none of my—"

"Stella Cummings." Catherine dropped the name like a stone in a pond and Elle's jaw dropped along with it.

"Stella Cummings the *actress*?" A legendary actress, two-time Oscar winner, the first when she was a child. The youngest Oscar winner ever. Considered one of the most beautiful women in the world. Word had it that she'd been attacked by a stalker and disappeared. Every once in a while there was a Stella sighting—like there used to be Elvis sightings—but they always turned out to be fake. "She's *here*?"

Catherine took her hand and once more that weird warmth rushed under her skin. "Yes, she's here. It's a long story, but the essence is that she was in serious danger and she found refuge here. A lot of people have found refuge here, including myself. This is—for want of a better word—a community. We call it simply the Haven. We grow our own food and are almost completely self-sufficient in terms of energy. We don't need the outside world. And some, including myself and definitely including Nick, Mac, and Jon, are on wanted lists. It's a long story."

"Nick told me some of it," Elle said quietly.

"Good. Then you'll understand that we want to keep our existence quiet."

"Absolutely. I do too. Not to mention the fact that I had four men out to get me. And they would have if Nick hadn't come."

Catherine showed Elle to two small armchairs, a surprising addition to a lab. No armchairs in Corona Laboratories, that was for sure. But through the open door, Elle could see what looked like a small and very well-equipped infirmary, so it was possible that the lab doubled as a place where patients could talk to the doctor. There was so much about this place that intrigued her.

They sat knee to knee, both bending forward slightly. Something about this place—its beauty, the sense of order, the kindness she was being shown and—let's admit it—Nick's presence all relaxed her. The usual reticence Elle felt with people she didn't know, and often with people she did know, fell away like an old, uncomfortable garment.

Elle always gave partial accounts of herself, cutting out whole sections and most particularly the section where she went elsewhere when she slept. Only at Corona, working with Sophie and the others, did she feel she could let her powers unfurl.

Catherine managed to make her feel as if she were wrapped in a warm bubble of trust and understanding. "About Nick," she said.

"Yes."

"He got what he described as a call from you last night. It was a strong and irresistible message that he felt came from you. I can tell you that he absolutely believed you called for help and that he was in a frenzy to get to you."

Elle nodded. The difficult part was right ahead. She was going to have to convince Catherine that she'd somehow contacted a man who was far away. A man she hadn't seen in ten years. She sent him a huge SOS and managed to let him know where she was without using a cell or a Personal Communicator. Just through the magic of her crazy head.

Any person on earth would consider her nuts. Elle was fully prepared to undergo a long, slow process to convince Catherine that she wasn't crazy, she just had this crazy power. All the scientific evidence she had that she wasn't a lunatic was back in the lab, so she had to replace graphs and videos with words.

Elle drew a deep breath. "Okay. There are a few things I'm going to have to say, which you're going to find hard to believe. Really, really hard."

Catherine gave a faint smile. "Try me."

Elle's stomach hurt and she had to consciously slow her breathing down. She knew everything there was to know about the physiology of stress and anxiety. Her body was trying to give her enough oxygen to deal with an upcoming trial.

"I can astrally project. It's an old-fashioned term for an out-of-body experience. I've always had this . . . talent. Ability. Call it what you will. When I was a child I used to have what I thought were very vivid dreams, and when I had my special dreams I would wake up very tired. In my dreams I roamed around Lawrence, Kansas, where I grew up. Sometimes I'd see my father playing poker with his buddies, sometimes I'd see schoolmates or other people I knew. The dreams increased in frequency around the time my mother died, when I was six. Sometimes I'd have several a week. I think my father thought I was always tired because I was sad at the loss of my mother and he was right, in a roundabout way. Nick came into our lives soon after my mother's death and the dreams stopped for a long time. Then Nick suddenly disappeared and my father became ill with Alzheimer's. It was . . . a bad time."

Catherine nodded. "As you know, dementia is one of my main fields of study. It's awful when it happens to someone you love."

Elle bowed her head.

"So," Catherine said, "when Nick disappeared and your father developed Alzheimer's you . . . projected more often?"

She nodded. "All the time, it seemed. I was exhausted because I Dreamed all night. To me, those are Dreams with a capital D, to keep them distinct from the normal dream state, because those Dreams aren't—aren't normal."

Catherine made a noncommittal sound in her throat.

"And yet—and yet I swear to you that every word is true—I have the capacity to project myself outside my body. I know how crazy that sounds, but—"

"Oh!" Catherine's eyes rounded with surprise. "I believe you. No question."

"You do?" Elle felt her own eyes round with surprise.

"Yes." Catherine leaned forward and clasped her hand around Elle's wrist, as if it were a shackle. A warm, soft shackle. That rush of warmth began, tingly and somehow pleasant.

Catherine closed her eyes. "You're frightened of the men coming after you. You're worried about your good friend." She frowned. "Sophie?" Elle nodded in surprise but Catherine couldn't see her. "She's been taken somewhere and you have no idea where and you don't know what's happened to her. Through all of this, you're scared and also overwhelmed with joy that you're with Nick. You have loved him . . ."

"Forever," Elle said softly. "I've loved him forever."

"Yes. You have loved him forever." Catherine nodded and opened her eyes. When she lifted her hand, it felt as if a light had gone out. "I'm an empath. For most of my life I thought I was a freak. Unlike you, I never thought to scientifically study my gift. I thought of it as a curse. Reading people is not always a barrel of laughs."

Elle nodded. "I'll bet." She leaned forward in her chair again. "So you—you're working on your power. Is *power* the right word? We were calling them Perceptual Studies. Just to—you know—give it a name."

"It's not a bad name. Ultimately, your study was funded by Arka, wasn't it?"

Elle nodded.

"We recently rescued a number of men who had been involuntarily enrolled in a series of studies carried out by Arka. Jon has hacked into their computers and I have access to all the data. I'll enjoy going over it with you."

"They also funded a study at Stanford that was the precursor to the Delphi Project. The Delphi Project is a study of extrasensory perception. We were coming up with some interesting theories."

"Would you like to continue your studies here?" Catherine waved a hand. "We have a good lab here and we have access to every single piece of equipment you could possibly need. We have unlimited funds and can acquire more or less anything we need. What's not available commercially, well, we use the five-finger discount."

"I'll bet that's Jon too."

"Bingo."

They smiled at each other, then Elle's smile faded. "I have a lot of data with me in a pen drive and I know where to access more. But more than anything, we need to find Sophie and the others. They are being rounded up by Corona goons and nothing good will come of it."

"No." Catherine had sobered up too. "Corona is Arka. Nothing good can come of Arka kidnapping people." Her pretty jaw set. "I have four men I'll introduce you to. The ones who were brought here half dead three months ago. They'd spent a year in a high-tech lab that was essentially a prison and were experimented on. I've never seen anyone with as many surgical scars as their leader."

"Lucius Ward? Nick told me about him."

"What was done to him and to his men was criminal. If they've started kidnapping people, it means that whatever is going on is coming to a head and we must stop them. We have to get your friends out."

"Catherine . . ." Elle hesitated. "I once went to an Arka lab. It was scary. They had vast security resources. They had guards everywhere and the labs had high-tech security with a number of backups. I don't know if we can mount any kind of offensive move."

"Oh my dear." Catherine patted her hand and stood up. "We have something far better than security goons. We have the entire Ghost Ops team, right here. I'd pit them against any foe on earth. They are invincible." She leaned over the table, pressed a button and spoke quietly. "Mac? Can you and the guys come up? There's something we need to talk about."

Arka Pharmaceuticals
San Francisco

Four vials. One, two, three, four.

Lee studied the brushed aluminum vial holder on the pristine surface of his huge desk. He could see its upside-down reflection, as if it continued on down into the nether regions of his desk. He carefully pushed a button on the side of the holder, entered a code on the keyboard that was projected onto the surface of his desk, and heard the satisfying hiss of a vacuum seal being broken.

The container was manufactured by a subsidiary of Arka and not only met ISO Standard 900012 for the containment of biohazardous material, it doubled the standards. It was unbreakable and unbreachable. You could take a mallet to it, you could run a tank over it. It would not break and it would not open.

If civilization were to suddenly stop, a thousand years from now whoever inherited the earth—Lee's guess would be rats—would find the container intact and rub their paws over the slightly raised Arka logo and wonder in their little rat brains what was inside.

Power. That was what was inside. Immense power. Power to change the world and it came from him. He'd done this.

It seemed insane that he was about to unleash all this power and not take it inside himself. Not become immensely powerful himself.

The Warrior project had gone through so many iterations he'd almost lost hope, but then Edison himself had said that a scientist never failed. He just found the ways an experiment didn't work.

Since he was a small child torn from his homeland, China, and dragged to the country he detested, the United States, Lee had dreamed of coming back to his homeland a conqueror. It was clear to anyone who had eyes in their head that China was the world's foremost superpower now and Lee intended it to remain so for the next thousand years. It was the oldest civilization on earth and had been dormant far too long. But its long sleep was over and now it would take its place as the leader of mankind.

It would manufacture not only superior products but superior humans. Starting with him.

Three months ago he'd gone down to the secret underground labs at Millon Laboratories, a small high-tech company Arka had purchased. He'd found it best to carry out the research Flynn was paying for in scattered small-scale labs of companies he held a majority share in. No one knew about this research. Certainly not the board at Arka. It pleased him no end that he was beating American capitalism at its own game. Preparing for its future destruction under its own nose.

And yet, Lee's contacts in Beijing had told him that his time was running out. When Lee had first contacted his childhood friend, Chao Yu, who'd risen high in the ranks of the Ministry of Science and Technology, his friend had been enthusiastic, and had taken the Warrior Project directly to the minister himself, Zhang Wei.

Everyone in the Ministry had been hugely excited, but the excitement waned as Lee kept coming up against problems. The science was impeccable. There had been sporadic successes but not replicable enough to bring to Beijing. All he needed was the money to institute testing on a larger scale in order to speed the process up. He needed Flynn's money.

Lee hadn't planned on showing Flynn the paranormals, but he'd had his hand forced. Flynn had been impressed and doubled the funding, but it was almost too late. The window of opportunity back home was closing.

And that was when it occurred to Lee that he would be landing in the Fatherland with a terabyte of encrypted data, a case full of vials, and some video footage, nothing more. Chao Yu was a scientist and could be trusted to break the data down and explain it but that could take time. Days, weeks, even months. He didn't have weeks and months. Time was tight and he needed to arrive with a visibly functioning program, ready to be up and running as fast as doses could be manufactured.

Manufacturing, distributing, and injecting the doses to the military would already take six months. They needed to start right away and he needed to be credible right away. He himself had to be a walking advertisement for Project Warrior.

So he'd started experimenting on himself, in minute doses, and the results were overwhelming. He felt stronger, faster. He *was* stronger, faster. The other day he had clocked himself at under a three-minute mile run. He'd never been a runner, never been an athlete, and he'd casually broken an Olympic record.

He'd never felt better, stronger, more clear-headed. But it had taken months for the dosage to take effect. Speed was an issue, both in the lab and in the field. The effects had to be immediate. So he'd been experimenting with a fast-acting virus as a vector. It had worked wonders on animal trials.

Lee missed his soldiers fiercely. He needed Special Forces soldiers for the trials, but though he'd broached the subject several times with Flynn, who would have access to plenty of specimens as an ex-general, the cretin had refused. The theory was that any Special Forces soldiers, either on active duty or retired, would be missed.

He'd made an exception for the Ghost Ops soldiers who'd been captured, because they were not on any official lists. Were, in fact, officially nonexistent. On the subject of more soldiers to experiment on, Flynn had been unyielding.

A sudden rush of rage shook Lee—a hot course of hatred pulsing through him. It felt good, it felt right. Flynn had blocked him every step of the way. The original plan had been to celebrate the Chinese New Year in Beijing, as a newly minted senior official of the Ministry. The Chinese New Year had come and gone. He'd stood in the dark in his penthouse apartment on Market Street listening to the sounds of the annual Chinese New Year parade. And now with the new deadlines, it was entirely possible that Flynn's hesitations and penny-pinching would cost Lee his chance.

The hatred felt right, felt good. He clenched his fist and imagined it curled around Flynn's fat neck, crushing the windpipe, watching with glee as that already purple face turned blue, anticipating the tiny snap as the hyoid bone broke.

Lee could do it now too. One-handed. He'd surreptitiously tested his grip on a dynamometer, and he'd hit two hundred pounds, the most the machine could measure, halfway through the test. In all likelihood, he could tear Flynn's throat out with one hand.

The thought pleased him enormously.

Oh yes. He was going to be a walking advertisement for Project Warrior.

He broke the final seal on the container and watched as curls of smoke from the dry ice rose together with the central cylinder. It stopped with an audible click, gyrated 90 degrees, and the three vials automatically emptied into a single syringe that had been pushed up from the side.

Beautiful piece of equipment. America still did this kind of thing so well, so elegantly.

Lee picked the syringe up with his right hand and turned it until the hair-fine needle pointed at the ceiling. He rolled up his shirtsleeve and placed his left arm on the desktop, admiring it. His suits hid the fact that he'd developed superb muscle definition over the past month. His arm now was lean and hard with veins carrying oxygen to the newly forged muscles.

He smiled as the needle painlessly slid into the vein. Lean, mean fighting machine. With a double PhD.

The new dosage with the viral component—SL-62—spread warmth throughout his system, like a healing balm. He felt good, more than good. He felt *great.*

A few more tweaks and they'd be ready to roll. They would have been ready six weeks ago if that fucker Flynn hadn't been so pissy.

Lee recoiled for a second. He couldn't remember the last time he'd used the word *fucker,* or even thought it. It wasn't him. Or at least it wasn't the old him. The new Lee could use whatever word he wanted. Fuck them.

He stood up, strength infusing his system. His vision was blurred, though when he took off his glasses, he could see perfectly. It was raining outside and dark, even though it was still early afternoon. But light bloomed in his eyes and he could make out figures in front of the Ferry Building, almost half a mile away.

He stretched and smiled. He felt great. Just great.

Mount Blue

They filed into the lab one by one. Mac first, then Jon, then Nick.
And there she was, sitting in the lab in a white coat, looking so
beautiful she took his breath away. But more than beautiful, she
looked . . . right. As if she were born to be sitting in their lab in
Haven.

She and Catherine had been conferring, heads together, serious but clearly in tune with each other. Two beautiful women—
though, however pretty Catherine was, she couldn't hold a
candle to Elle—one dark-haired, one fair. The smartest women
he'd ever met, dealing with some very nasty shit without breaking a sweat.

Nick went over immediately to Elle and sat down next to her.
He picked her hand up, kissed the back of it, then leaned over and
kissed her cheek.

He totally ignored the stunned expressions on Mac's and Jon's
faces. They looked as if Nick had sprouted wings and flown loops
in the air.

"Hi, honey." He smiled. He felt new muscles in his face because
sure as shit he hadn't done much smiling these past years. He'd
never been a smiler. But seeing Elle sitting there, now officially
a part of Haven and officially his—well, that was worth a smile.
"Everything okay?"

She sighed and leaned into him. *Oh yeah.* Nick put an arm
around her and didn't know who was more comforted. Him or
her. Whatever was coming, they'd face it together.

"We need to talk," Catherine announced. "Because there's
something we're all going to have to decide. I'm going to let Elle
talk, but first I think you all should know something about her.
You know that I am an empath? That I can read emotions and,
lately, thoughts? Though—trust me on this—I make a real effort
to stay out of your heads."

Nick and Jon chuckled. Right now if she was in Nick's head she'd back out fast, blushing hard. Because a part of him was sitting there ready to absorb information. A briefing. This had all the hallmarks of a briefing and he'd been doing briefings all his adult life. So he was paying attention but there was another bit of him free to just . . . play.

Think about other things.

Like, how incredibly soft Elle's hand was. And her cheek. And her neck. She was just so fucking soft all over. It seemed impossible to him that human skin could feel that soft. How he'd loved kissing her all over, moving his mouth down over her pale breasts, heartbeat showing in the left breast, his hand moving down over that flat belly, down to the cloud of light brown hair covering her sex . . .

"Elle?"

Nick started slightly. *Fuck.* He had the beginning of a hard-on. *Christ. Bad news.* Mac and Jon were as observant as any two men could possibly be. Had they noticed? Nick crossed his legs uncomfortably, glad that he was too tanned to blush. Not that he ever blushed, but still.

Catherine was standing in front of them, holding her hand out to Elle.

Shit. Nick had completely zoned out. If Mac knew, he'd have his ass.

Well, Elle was moving to stand beside Catherine, so he wouldn't be tempted to think of how very, very soft she was between her . . .

"You know me, of course. My name's Elle Connolly." He still couldn't get used to that name. And it still bugged him that she'd changed it. "I'm a biologist with an interest in the biology of the human brain. There's one other thing about me you should know." Elle glanced at Catherine, who nodded imperceptibly. "I can astrally project."

Whoa. Nick sat forward with a frown. *What?*

Jon leaned forward too. "The fuck?"

Catherine held up her hand, palm out. "I know this is going to be hard to absorb, but you've taken me on board, so this should be a bit easier to swallow."

Damn straight it had been hard to swallow that Catherine could read emotions by touch. Nick and Jon had been hostile to her, though happy for Mac that he'd found someone who could put up with his ugly mug. But when Catherine came to them with some totally crazy story about Lucius Ward being held prisoner in a clinic in Palo Alto and wanting them to rescue him . . . well he and Jon had nearly mutinied.

Lucius had abandoned them. Betrayed them for money and left them for dead on a bogus mission that had blown up in their faces. The three of them, Mac and Nick and Jon, had taken the fall for blowing up a lab. Their intel—false of course—had been that the lab was brewing a weaponized version of bubonic plague. A nightmare. One of the many nightmares Ghost Ops had been set up to avert. They'd gone in, blown up the lab, killed what turned out to be totally innocent scientists and had been taken down and accused of treason. Lucius had disappeared and they read afterward that he'd had a big financial stake in the lab's rival. So they'd been sold out by a leader they revered.

That was what they knew, it was the new bedrock of their lives and here Catherine came leading Mac around by the dick with some cockeyed story about Lucius not betraying them after all that only a shit-for-brains who was getting laid like nobody's business—that would be Mac, who in his previous life had been as unassailable as a stone cliff—could believe.

What was the proof?

Catherine had touched Lucius and had somehow learned the truth. So they had to go risk their lives on a wild goose chase on the say-so of some dame. True, she'd found them, when the entire U.S. government and its military hadn't been able to find them. But still.

Both Nick and Jon had been about a hair from pulling a gun and tying Catherine up—probably having to shoot Mac in the process—when she'd touched them.

Nick had never known anything like it. It was as if an entire world was there, in her touch. And she knew everything about him. It just slipped from his skin to hers. Everything he'd kept absolutely hidden for almost ten years—it was somehow right there for Catherine to read.

She didn't know Elle's name and she didn't know the details but she caught exactly his sorrow and his deep desperation at not knowing if Elle was alive or dead, sick or well. Happy or needing him. She'd known all of that at a touch. And she knew something about Jon as well, though he wasn't talking and neither was she. But whatever it was she'd found out, it hurt and it was true.

So, yeah, Nick and Jon were going to believe her if she talked about woo-woo stuff. Mac wasn't an issue. Catherine could say that the moon was a hologram and Mac would believe her.

There was silence in the room. Nick frowned. "What does that mean exactly?"

This time Elle spoke. "It means that I have out-of-body experiences during sleep. Except I'm not really asleep when that happens. It's more like a coma. I had an EEG of my brain during an out-of-body experience and it almost flatlined. It's only in the past year that I've tried to analyze this as opposed to hating it. Three months ago I enrolled in a program to study what used to be called paranormal abilities. The study was funded by Arka Pharmaceuticals."

Nick's teeth ground and Mac issued a low growl. Arka Pharmaceuticals had kidnapped and tortured Lucius and three of their teammates—Romero, Lundquist, and Pelton—nearly to death. So anything connected to Arka was pretty much on their shit list.

Elle pressed a button, the lights dimmed and a hologram lit

up. There were ten faces in two rows of five. Nick saw Elle in the second row. "These are the people who were originally enrolled in the program and two of us, myself and Sophie Daniels, drew up the experimental protocol and oversaw the tests."

Elle manipulated the tiny remote and the hologram showed low buildings in a green sward. "This is the campus where the tests were carried out."

"Wait!" Jon was frowning ferociously. "Go back."

"Okay." Elle obediently went back to the previous 'gram. "Here?"

"Yeah. Third from the left, top row. Who is she?" Nick looked over. Jon was grim-faced, practically vibrating with tension, which was totally unlike his usual cool surfer–dude persona. Actually, Nick had never seen him tense, ever. Not even under fire.

Did he know the girl?

Elle smiled at Jon. "Sophie Daniels. She's one of my best friends. We did our graduate studies together at Stanford, only she studied physiology. She has a master's in that and is working toward a PhD in virology."

Jesus. These brainy women.

"Did she have a—a power?" Jon sounded like he was choking, and Nick understood where he was coming from. Women already had all sorts of powers without any of the woo-woo stuff. But these chicks had real powers and their men would just have to suck it up.

Elle pursed her lips. "Not that could be tested, though we were only at the beginning of the trial. But—" She hesitated. "She's a healer. She never talks about it, but I saw her close up a nasty wound with her touch. It comes with a heavy price, though. She was weak for days after that." Elle hesitated. "Corona didn't know. Nobody knew. But she passed an fMRI screening test and was enrolled in the program. Like me she was also tasked with recovering and collating data."

Jon's jaws were working. "Isn't it unusual to have test subjects also running the test?"

"It is, yes." Elle agreed. "And later on, for publication purposes, that would have been a big problem. But that's what Corona insisted on and they were paying the bills. So there was that anomaly. And this past week there were others."

"Such as?" Catherine asked.

"I don't know. It's as if the program itself developed a fever. We were asked to do three times the testing we were doing before in half the time. Results were to be sent directly to the coordinator's office instead of being collected and collated on a weekly basis and then passed on. And then"—Elle stopped and looked at them each in turn—"and then people started disappearing. One, then two and three a day. The protocol stipulates that the test subjects show up at nine A.M. every morning, but we started having massive no-shows. Sophie and I called their cells and home numbers but got no responses. Yesterday—no, two days ago—there were only four of us, plus Sophie. I was being tested and Sophie oversaw the testing. When I got home, I got a panic call from Sophie saying that we were being rounded up. They were after her and were coming after me. I guess you know the rest."

Oh yeah, they knew the rest. Nick's fists tightened. They'd come after Elle. They were dead men walking.

Elle's voice softened, became pleading. "I know you guys are . . . in hiding here. I know these people"—she gestured to the hologram of ten faces—"are complete strangers. But they are not strangers to me and they are being held against their will. And I fear that they are being hurt or . . . worse." She drew in a deep, steadying breath.

Unlike the war room, which was always kept dim, the lab was brightly lit. The overhead light lit Elle's hair into a shiny pale halo around her face, but beneath the halo was no angel's face.

In his heart, in his head, Nick had kept an image of Elle that no longer existed. For so very long, in his head she'd been the young, pampered girl of a wealthy father who led an immensely sheltered life. Then that image had been exchanged for an exhausted waif of a girl, overwhelmed by her father's illness, almost on her last legs.

So in his head Elle was vulnerable, requiring his protection. That's the thing that had driven him so crazy—or, well, crazier— all these years. Elle, alone in the world. Alone in a world of predators. He knew precisely how cold and cruel the world was, he'd known since he could walk and talk. He knew that the weak were crushed, whether you were a good person or not.

Elle was a good person. He knew that, deep down inside. Nothing would ever change that because it was in her bones. When she was a girl, she'd go out of her way to do casual kindnesses completely unaware of how unusual that was. The gardener who came twice a week always got a glass of iced tea. A kid next door had tragically developed leukemia and Elle would go over to read to him all through his chemo.

A good heart and weakness equaled disaster. Danger with a loud siren attached.

The Army, Rangers, Delta, and then Ghost Ops. Nick's whole adult life was making sure he wouldn't be weak. Making sure he could defend himself with every weapon known to man and failing weapons, with a rock or his fists. He'd had to defend himself plenty, because the world was a shithole.

What possible defenses could Elle muster against the world? She'd taken off with no money and no friends and that thought had been like a spike being hammered into his head, every single fucking day for ten fucking years.

The images came to him nightly.

Elle, alone and penniless in some dump of a town.

Elle hitchhiking and ending up in a car with a guy with a knife.

Elle walking alone through the wrong part of some city, a gang of rapists trailing behind her.

And always, always the image of her helpless and alone.

Well, she might well have at some point been helpless and alone, but she sure wasn't anymore.

The women he was looking at was beautiful, yes, but visibly smart. It was there in her sharp light blue eyes that took everything in, there in the strong bone structure of her face, there every time she opened her mouth. Strength and discipline were in every line of her body.

And, shit. A PhD from Stanford. They didn't give those away in cereal boxes. And Stanford was expensive. Over $100K a year the last he heard. So she'd either earned that money or been given scholarships or a combo of both. Either way, she was a woman to be reckoned with.

And if the idea of the pale vulnerable waif broke his heart, this strong, confident woman melted it. She didn't need him, not in any way. She'd made her way in the world just fine without him.

But if she'd have him, he was hers to the end of time.

So, yeah, he was in. She wanted her friends rescued? Whatever she wanted, he wanted to give it to her.

"I'm in," he said.

"Me too." Mac's deep rumble came with a nod.

"Oh yeah," Jon breathed.

Elle studied the faces of the three men and one woman before her. Catherine was with her, no doubt. That in itself was a minor miracle. That she'd risk her man, Mac, for people she didn't know.

Nick was with her. He'd made that clear this morning. It frightened her to think that if she ordered him into a minefield, into the pit of hell, he'd go. That kind of power scared her and she didn't know if she'd ever get used to it. She'd been alone for so long the idea of having a man like Nick right beside her, ready to do what she asked, was powerful but terrifying.

She might be leading him and Catherine's husband and surfer dude to their death.

Sophie and the others might be already dead. Corona might use them to set a trap for her. But there was no way she could leave the others in the group helpless and on their own, and there was no way she could rescue them on her own.

So she studied the faces of these three men who were going to have to risk their lives to save some pretty odd people and might lose their own in doing so.

She studied their faces for weakness or doubt and found none.

Elle gestured at the hologram. "I'm asking you to rescue these people, who are in terrible danger. There was an urban legend making the rounds of the Corona researchers that a new method of distilling parts of the brain into a liquid that can be injected has been developed. That a couple of people have been 'harvested' already. That's the charming term used in science, by the way. Harvesting. As if people were crops. There were rumors of a previous study group that disappeared. I didn't pay much attention because there are constant rumors making the rounds and many of them are silly." She stopped, drew in a deep breath. "But now. . . I'm not too sure it's silly. I think it might be true. I think that the people ultimately running the trial have gone insane and there is no telling what they'll do, the lengths they'll go to for results. There's something behind this I don't understand. Sophie and I both felt it, but we were so taken up in the results of the tests we decided to let it go. It was just a feeling, after all."

"But you were right to feel uneasy," Nick growled.

"Yes." Elle felt a spurt of relief. He understood. "We were right.

I have no idea where to go from here. I don't know where the subjects were taken. The entire area is studded with labs. Arka owns a number of them. The labs would be underground and would probably not be on any schematics. Actually they could be anywhere. We are not even certain the lab would be in Palo Alto. They could have been taken anywhere in a van."

The thought terrified her. Sophie and the others taken somewhere where they couldn't be found, like cattle to slaughter.

Mac spoke, in his deep, gravelly voice that sounded like it came from underground. "Do you have any clues at all as to where they might have been taken? How about other labs that were cooperating with the program? Do you have a list?"

Elle shrugged. "As far as I know, no other labs were involved. I have the e-mail of everyone and I've started a program on my computer to search their e-mails for the names of other labs, but so far nothing has come up."

"The tracking devices?" Catherine asked. Elle had told her about the device she'd pried from her arm.

The men sat up straighter. "What tracking device?" Nick demanded.

Elle held her arm out, pulled up her sleeve and pointed to the bandage. Nick was going to be so mad at her. When he asked about it this morning, she'd simply said that she'd cut herself. "All the members of the trial group were injected with a microchip. We were told that it was to monitor our vital signs. Each week we held our arms over a reader where the data was downloaded. But Sophie said to cut it out of my arm when she called to warn me, so I did."

"And you were going to tell me about this when?" Nick's jaws flexed. She shrugged.

"Do you know where the database is held?" Jon asked. Nick had said that Jon was their cyber expert.

"Sorry, no." Elle shook her head. "It would presumably be in the company database, except I suspect now that the entire project was off the books. In which case it will be in an encrypted file on someone's laptop. I don't even know whose."

"We'll go over satellite images of last night. See if we can find any useful images." Nick looked at Mac. "Did we have any drones out?"

Mac shook his head.

"Damn." Nick beat his fist lightly on his knee. "And we can't send them out now until we have some idea of where. Though it sounds too late for drones, if they are all underground."

Oh man. Elle understood his frustration. How could they rescue the group if they didn't know where they were? If the group hadn't been split up. If they were still alive.

"Okay," Mac said decisively. "I'm assigning tasks. Elle, write up everything you know, absolutely everything and go over it with Catherine and make sure you keep an eye on that troll of yours that's going through the e-mails."

"I designed a program that will generate passwords on the basis of keywords. It will generate over a billion and can be sent in one packet to try a massive decrypt just as soon as we have someone's computer to hack," Jon said. Elle blinked. *God, a program like that could earn millions in the outside world.*

She nodded. "That would be really useful."

Mac continued giving orders. "Also go over satellite shots. Make sure you include Keyhole 15 over a 48-hour spread over the entire Palo Alto area. They might have started rounding the test subjects up early."

Elle barely stopped from gasping. The Keyhole series of satellites was top secret. Top-top secret. Like having-to-kill-you-if-you-discover-anything-about-it secret. She only knew about it because an analyst who had a crush on her told her about them. She'd gone to the darknet to research it. The rumor was that its lenses could read the numbers on a credit card in moonlight. "You can do that?" She couldn't stop herself from asking Jon. "Hack into Keyhole?"

"Oh yeah, he can." Mac did something to his face, moving a muscle or two around in an odd configuration that in anyone else might have been a smile.

"We need to go to Elle's house and find that tracer, download what was on it and reverse engineer it. Would that be possible, Elle?" Jon asked.

She thought about it. Well, if Jon was that good, it was a possibility. Each tracer would have a set of basic instructions and would be programmed to emit a signal. Catch that signal and scan for other signals . . . She nodded. "Yeah. If we can hack into the basic underlying protocol, maybe we can locate the other devices, unless—"

"Unless they're all dead," Jon finished grimly.

Oh God. Elle put a hand to her stomach. She looked at Jon. "And—And suppose the house is still under surveillance? I have no idea if they have enough security personnel to post a guard at each empty house, but it seemed like there was plenty of money available. They just might do that."

"I'd welcome that," Jon said, bright blue eyes suddenly dark and flat.

She shivered. The men who'd rounded up her friends, were keeping them prisoner and were perhaps planning on killing them were evil and she was happy to help in engineering their downfall. She should be happy she had these tough good guys on her side. But that fleeting expression on Jon's face . . .

"Okay," Mac said in his deep bass. It was extraordinary. Every time he spoke Catherine just *glowed*. As if his words were lightbulbs that lit her up from within. "It looks like we've got our team and our assignments. So let's get going."

"Not so fast, Mac. Aren't you forgetting something?" A deep voice Elle had never heard before.

The effect on Nick, Mac, and Jon was electric. All three shot to their feet with blinding speed, chairs scraping on the floor. They stood almost quivering to attention, arms stiffly up in a salute, astonishment on their faces.

Catherine stood frozen. Nobody had heard the door behind them open, which already struck Elle as strange. That anyone could get the jump on Nick, Mac, and Jon seemed outlandish.

That the person who got the jump on them was an old, old man leaning heavily on a cane and on a tall woman seemed impossible.

"Sir!" Mac barked, echoed by Nick and Jon.

The man had once been tall and looked as if he'd been strong. Now he was stooped and his skin hung loosely on his big frame. He moved slowly, as if every step hurt, which was probably the case because Elle had rarely seen so many surgical scars as this man sported over his big bald head, running down to disappear into the large sweatshirt that billowed on him.

The woman by his side had the most extraordinary face. It was. . . It was beautiful, but it looked as if Elle was seeing her through a kaleidoscope, lozenge-shaped pieces of her face almost but not quite fitting together. And yet the woman moved with the grace of beauty.

The man shuffled his feet, leaning heavily on the woman, moving steadily until he stood by Catherine and Elle. He leaned over and Elle heard him whisper to the woman supporting him, "Thanks, Stella." She threw him a blinding smile, her face stretching in odd ways across the white lines crisscrossing her face. His smile in return was tender. There was a flash of something there for a second, and Elle wondered if he was as old as he looked.

Stella! In an instant the kaleidoscope twisted and righted, and Elle could clearly see who she was. Stella Cummings. Once the most famous actress on the planet, deemed one of the most beautiful women in the world, now Haven's chef. Elle was so busy gaping at her, wondering if she dared ask for an autograph because Stella in *Nobody But Me* had given her courage and hope five years ago when Elle had gone through a bad period, that she barely noticed the three men following the old man into the room.

They were visibly young yet they moved as if they were older than the first man. Big-boned but thin, faces emaciated, hollowed out with suffering. They looked like a strong wind would blow them over, but there they were, shuffling forward behind the older man like wraiths following a ghost.

Stella left the old man for a moment and crossed the room to kiss Elle on the cheek. "Welcome to Haven, my dear." Elle blushed with pleasure. Stella Cummings, kissing her on the cheek!

Stella went back to the old man. A ghost of a smile crossed his face.

"At ease, men," he said. His voice was hoarse as if he didn't use it much. He had trouble articulating. But he continued, each word coming out painfully, though he didn't stop until he'd said all he wanted to say. "I understand we've got a chance to grab the motherfuckers who fucked with us—" His dark eyes scanned the room, alighting on Catherine, Elle, and Stella. "Pardon my language ladies," he said solemnly.

"We're scientists," Catherine said. "I think fuckers is the correct technical term."

Another ghost of a smile. For a fleeting second, Elle could see something of the man he'd been, hidden deep behind the shattered exterior. And that man had been . . . handsome. Yes, she could see it now. And Stella saw it too. Certainly her eyes never left his face.

"We want payback," he said simply.

The two badly injured men nodded their heads jerkily. They clearly had little motor control. "P-P-P-Payb-b-b-ack," one stuttered. He had a big perfectly round keloid scar right over where the neocortex was. Someone had punched a sensor right into his brain.

All three men were becoming white-faced with the strain of standing up, and the man with the sensor scar was trembling. They didn't look as if they could face breakfast let alone a mission. She looked around. No one was saying anything about their obvious physical condition. She waited another second but there was only silence.

O-kay. She would have to be the bad guy.

"That's very kind of you," she began gently, "but perhaps—"

The elderly man turned his head painfully and fixed her with a look. For an instant Elle wanted to step back, the power of that look was so great. It was a banked power, a power linked to a damaged body, but inside that man strength and intelligence glowed and gathered.

The words came slowly and painfully. "I understand there are people in their hands. They will experiment on them and then they will kill them. I do not want to live if we can't make an attempt to rescue them the way my men rescued us. We aren't physically capable of going on the mission with you, Mac." His already hoarse voice broke and he hung his head down as if someone had cut a tendon. Then his head rose and his black eyes glowed with strength and purpose. "But we are perfectly capable of manning the war room and providing intel. So we will rescue those people. Together. Hoo-yah."

"Hoo-yah!" A chorus of seven men's voices, all strong and true, rang out.

Chapter 12

One entire wall of Lee's office was a huge glowing hologram. Along the bottom of the hologram ran a series of data packets, including the date: three months ago.

Millon Laboratories at Palo Alto. Before the facility had been destroyed. Lee clenched his fists at the memory. Catherine Young had suddenly risen up and bit her employer in the ass. She'd taken a huge bite out of him and had almost brought his entire project down. Years of work nearly destroyed because of one woman and the faceless men who'd helped her.

He had a small part of the attack on tape, though it had been mostly destroyed by something the faceless men had done to his security system. His very, very expensive security system.

It still burned.

He'd recognized Young immediately of course, brazenly breaking into his facility with the use of a cloned pass.

The lab had been hidden and illegal, given the type of testing that had gone on. He'd had to go in and complete the destruction she'd wrought so that when the authorities came to investigate, he'd been able to plausibly state that the extra underground floor was merely equipment storage space. There hadn't been any technical experts in the law enforcement team, luckily. But he'd had to buy off the three technicians who'd worked on the floor, and it had cost him. Money, time, effort.

Flynn had placed him under pressure, then Beijing had placed him under pressure.

That's not how science worked. Science proceeded at its own stately pace. Putting pressure on the scientific process was an abomination. This was something nonscientists like Flynn were simply incapable of understanding.

What Lee was working on had the potential to change the world forever, as momentous as the harnessing of electricity. More so, even, as it would change the nature of a part of humanity. This was not something that could be done in a hurry and sloppily.

Injecting himself with SL-61 had been a stroke of genius, because he felt stronger and more intellectually acute than ever. He felt, for want of a better word, invincible.

There had been a missing element, though. An element he'd discerned in an animal experiment on the hidden Level 4 the night the laboratory was destroyed.

How he'd loved Level 4. It had been his very own reign, a place where he held the power of life and death, a place where he created living organisms. A place where he'd been a god. He'd carried out extensive animal testing on Level 4 that would have been illegal under the Animal Testing Bill. The experiments might have been illegal according to a bill passed by a lobby of fanatical men and women who cared more for dumb creatures than for science, but they had been necessary. He'd been testing iterations of SL that would increase strength and speed and intelligence.

He and the SL drugs had been conducting a kind of dance. Two steps forward and one step backward, then three steps forward and two steps backward, then one step forward and three steps backward. Then ten steps forward.

Of course, it was immensely complex, as he was effecting change at the cellular level and trying to make it stable. He was speeding up evolution itself, something no one else in the history of the world had ever attempted. And he was *succeeding*, damn it. Every single trial that ended with a problem also unveiled a new possibility.

It was impossible to explain to that moron Flynn. To his astonishment, though, it also proved impossible to explain to the Ministry of Science in Beijing. Nobody cared about the process, about the secrets to life itself, which he was unlocking. All they cared about were tangible results. A drug that would increase the capabilities of soldiers in the field, that would prove stable over time and that was cheap to produce.

In any hands but his it would have been impossible.

Up to that point there'd been fifty-nine iterations. Nothing compared to Edison's 10,000 failed attempts. Lee had only tried fifty-nine times, but that fifty-ninth . . .

Deep below the earth, in the animal lab, Lee had found part of the key to changing the world in an animal cage housing a bonobo. There'd been ten bonobos, big, healthy apes genetically predisposed to peaceful behavior. SL-59 had had a negative effect on nine of them. They'd turned listless and died.

But the tenth . . .

Lee watched the holographic recording. He'd been watching it over and over again while poring over the analyses of the blood and brain tissue. He'd gone back postmortem to the original MRIs and had discovered something that had escaped his researchers' notice—a slight anomaly of the hypothalamus and increased temperature of the periaqueductal gray of the midbrain. Both qualities had increased notably after administration of SL-59.

In the hologram, so clear someone else in the room would have difficulty in distinguishing between now and three months earlier, he stood before a transparent Plexiglas cage, watching the beautiful animal inside.

The hologram clearly showed all the data contained in the data infocubes at the forefront of the cage. Gender, genetic history, MRI and CAT scans, IQ test results, dosages, and times of injections of SL-59.

The other bonobos had been sitting in their cages, movements slow, eyes lifeless.

Bonobo Number Eight, though. Ah, he wasn't sitting listlessly. No, he was upright, well-balanced, brown eyes sharp. In the hologram, Lee stood studying him and it was clear that the animal was studying him right back.

The camera had been at Lee's back so he couldn't see his own face but he knew that he'd glanced down to see the EKG tracing at that point. Bonobos were peaceable within their own groups, but grew agitated in the presence of other species.

Number Eight's heart rate remained unchanged.

Amazing. Either the bonobo had developed an ability to control its own heart rate or an instinctive fear had been overridden by the drug. Perhaps both. And then something remarkable had happened. The animal had checked Lee's hands for weapons and his eyes for intent. There had been no mistaking the raw intelligence in the animal.

They had stood there for a minute or two, gauging each other, two beings on either side of a species divide.

Then the bonobo had smashed itself against the Plexiglas trying to get to him, beating itself into a pulp.

But those few minutes had been enough to give Lee an insight into attenuating the intensity of the violence while retaining the intelligence, and that insight had led to a virus-borne bit of genetic engineering that he thought represented the breakthrough they needed.

SL-59 hadn't worked and SL-60 hadn't worked. But SL-62 . . . ah. And an hour ago he'd injected himself with the drug.

In the hologram he watched as the bonobo killed itself against the glass in a frenzy of ferocity. When the animal finally lay on the straw-covered floor of the Plexiglas cage, a ruined sack of broken bones, Lee hit rewind.

He stood and watched, once more, that moment in which he and the bonobo faced each other down.

As he watched that moment again, he felt strength course through his system, oxygen flowing deep and rich in his veins, bringing blood to his muscular system. He felt each muscle almost separately, felt how well each muscle fit together with the others to form a strong and powerful whole. Though he was on the twenty-second floor of a skyscraper in the Financial District, he felt as if he were barefoot in the jungle, connected to the earth through skin and blood and bone, taking strength from the earth, giving it back.

The hologram switched off and he went to the window to look out over the city. He lifted his hand and placed it against the glass and it was as if his hand passed through the glass, out into the city, reaching down to the tiny people below, hurrying to get out of the inclement weather. He could swat them away so easily. Such ants, all that toiling and striving so essentially meaningless. Puny and weak and craving direction.

Soon their lives would be harnessed to a greater good instead of being so random.

He would head a triumphant army of supermen. Hadn't mankind always dreamed of this—of a superior race that would come and lead? All those legends of the gods with immense power over the earth and its creatures—surely their species knew it was always going to end up like this? All Lee had done was speed up the process and place its agency in the right hands.

Of course, he had the power of the gods too. He could feel it, feel vitality run through him, feel his muscles and sinews reknit into a more powerful whole. Feel his brain rewiring itself. His eyesight was so acute he thought he could see individual strands of hair in the ant-people down below on the street. His hearing was so keen he could hear the centralized air system's gentle hum. It had started to snow, a bit of sleet mixed in, and he could hear each spicule ping against the window panes. He could hear—

The door opening.

"Goddammit, Lee," Flynn's grating voice boomed. "What the fuck were you thinking—"

A hot mist rose in Lee's mind when he heard Flynn's voice. The prick. The fucking *prick*. Every cell in his body pulsed with raw, red hatred.

Lee flew across the room, grabbing something shiny off his desk, hand punching forward. Flynn's eyes bugged as he looked down at himself, at the very small shiny handle sticking out from his chest. The handle belonged to a pure titanium letter opener that was deeply embedded in his heart.

He was dead but he didn't know it yet.

Flynn stood, staggered, righted himself, watching as a big red flower blossomed out from the handle, covering his pristine white Armani shirt. He staggered again, fell to one knee, head hanging. Straining sounds came from his throat, though he wasn't able to formulate any words.

Good. Flynn talked too much anyway.

Part of Lee admired the fact that from six feet away, having had to turn around, pass by his desk to pick up the letter opener, he'd still instinctively been able to punch it straight between the ribs and bury it directly into Flynn's heart.

Lee stood above the man, watching as the other knee gave out and he fell prone onto the floor. Flynn's heart continued pumping blood for another two minutes, then the flow slowed then stopped.

Lee looked at his reflection in the window, brightly lit against the snowy night sky as darkness descended in his mind. His eyes were wide, a slight smile on his lips. He watched for a moment, his ability to recognize the creature in the reflection draining away as quickly as Flynn's blood had drained from his body.

Lee looked around, not recognizing anything familiar in his surroundings. He moved into a slight crouch, hands pulling up toward his chest, hands open like claws. Walls . . . he had to get out. Move. His body craved movement, craved blood. It was sheer chance that he moved toward the wall with the door and not to one of the other three walls. He walked forward and the door, biomorphic and primed to recognize his profile, opened.

He didn't question that. There was very little reasoning ability left in him, just enough to recognize a door with an image of stairs and to realize that it led to an exit. The stairs led to the outside world, a world that awaited him.

He started loping for the stairs.

A woman stepped out from a door. Her eyes widened when she saw Lee, a binder dropping from her nerveless fingers. "Dr. Lee—" The tone was a question, but it was never answered. Lee jumped to her, hands out to hold her shoulders still as he sank his teeth into her neck. In two strong bites he'd chewed her ear off, then dropped her at his feet, bleeding and twitching.

Out. He wanted to be out. He was strong and he wanted—no he needed—to hunt. To kill.

He scrambled down the stairs while he still recognized the concept of stairs. By the time he reached the lobby teeming with people he'd lost the concept. But it didn't matter because there was plenty of meat here.

He still recognized the concept of prey.

In the hallway, the woman slowly rose. She raised a hand to the side of her head and frowned. Pain, wet . . . She had no words for the sensations she could only feel. Her hands drew up to her chest, formed claws. Kill. She wanted to kill. There was prey around, she could smell it. Unsteady but unyielding, she loped down the corridor where two creatures had appeared.

Prey.

Mount Blue

"Eat," Stella Cummings said, pushing a plate of potato gratin across to Lucius. A very small portion, since he'd only begun to tolerate food. She looked across at him, tortured, suffering yet upright and determined. Any other man would have died a hundred times with what had been done to him. What had been done to her by her stalker was a fraction of what had been done to him, and it had almost destroyed her.

He was an extraordinary man.

"That's all you ever say to me. Eat," he replied, dark eyes fixed on her. "You'd think I was five years old."

Even in his weakened and emaciated state, Lucius Ward was a man to be reckoned with. She definitely didn't think he was five years old.

"Eat," she repeated and smiled at him.

His face suddenly sharpened. His huge hand covered hers. "God, Stella. You are so beautiful."

You are so beautiful. She'd heard versions of that phrase all her life. The word had been *pretty* when she was a child actress but turned into *beautiful* right about puberty. Through some accident of bones and hormones, she hadn't gone through an awkward pubescent phase at all. She'd continued working as an actress all the way through. By the time she was thirty-five, she'd made 120 films and had been considered one of the most beautiful women in the world.

What had that gotten her? Not much, besides more work. And more work. The men who'd courted her had courted the face, not the person behind it. When they discovered that her life was work, work, work, and very little play, the infatuation disappeared.

It certainly hadn't brought her love.

And now the face was gone.

"Not so beautiful anymore, Lucius," she said without any sadness. Crazily, her lost beauty had freed something up in her. Everyone in her life now liked *her*, not her face. Liked Stella, the member of an underground community and not Stella the remote movie star.

She was no movie star now. She could never be in the business again. The stalker had sliced her up too badly. Ninety-seven slashes all over, fourteen to her face. One slice had gone right through her cheek, making it impossible to smile on the right side of her face. She looked like someone had put her into a kaleidoscope and shaken it.

His hand tightened on hers. "Beautiful," he repeated forcefully.

Oh God.

Sex, love—those were things that had completely fled her life after the stalker. There'd been lots of sex before, though not love. But afterward, both had been out of the question. She'd taken refuge in anonymity while her scars had healed as much as they ever would, cooking near Mount Blue in a small diner belonging to the cousin of her former housekeeper. She'd needed to do something, something tangible, with her hands, the way she'd needed to breathe. And Elena had sent her to her cousin, where she'd buried herself in the kitchen in the back and started creating. The greasy spoon became a diner and was on its way to becoming a restaurant when the news told her that her stalker had escaped.

She'd been on a break, chatting with a customer, a good-looking, mysterious guy who showed up from time to time and who never told her his name. If there was one thing Stella had learned in her life to respect it was privacy. "Don't ask don't tell" covered a lot of things, not just one's sexuality. She didn't want to talk about herself and he didn't want to talk about himself, and that suited them both.

And then the news flash—Steve Gardiner, stalker, slasher, and all-around psycho, who'd convinced the judge to put him in a mental institution instead of the deepest darkest cell on earth, had escaped.

She'd been talking to Jon when she heard. Suddenly she began to shake all over, the trembles coming from deep in her core. A fear so great she couldn't move, couldn't breathe, couldn't think.

He'd taken one look at her, seen how terrified and broken she was, and simply brought her up to Mount Blue, to Haven, where she'd joined the community of misfits and runaways and had been happy ever since.

Here in Haven she'd found companionship and purpose. But love? It hadn't even occurred to her that she might find it here, of all places.

She looked down at the large hand covering hers. She remembered well that terrible night three months ago when Lucius and Miguel Romero, Larry Lundquist, and Bob Pelton had been rescued from a lab that had been like something out of a Nazi concentration camp and brought to Haven. The four men had been starved, full of surgical scars, so weak they couldn't walk. It had taken Catherine a week of IVs just to get them to be able to sit up in bed.

That's when Stella had taken over, making it her personal mission to get them to eat as much good nourishing food as they could hold down.

Particularly their leader. Lucius Ward. *Captain* as Mac, Nick, and Jon called him.

Their respect for him had been evident in every line of their bodies, and once she got to know him, even the terrible tortured version of him, a strong man who had been rendered down to bedrock, she understood why. This was a formidable man in every sense.

She'd seen him put himself together inch by agonizing inch. If Catherine said to walk ten steps, he'd walk fifty. Grimacing with pain every inch of the way.

And though he never smiled and the lines in his face clearly showed he'd never been a smiling kind of man, his face lit up when she entered a room.

So, yes, wow, sex seemed to be on the table.

But something needed to be said first. "You don't have to call me beautiful, Lucius," Stella said gently. "I know I'm not beautiful, not any longer. And if you don't care, I sure don't."

While she talked his dark eyes roamed over her face, over every inch of it. It was something she was used to. When she'd been beautiful, men had stared openly at her, as if she were something rare and different, belonging to a different species. After she'd been sliced open, people had stared for a different reason, the way you'd stare at a train wreck.

One of the many things she loved about Haven was that no one seemed even to notice her scars.

Lucius smiled, pulling at the burn scar on his right cheekbone. He brought her hand to his mouth and placed his lips in the palm of her hand. He kept it there for a long time, so long that she moved the tips of her fingers over the skin around his mouth, feeling a few scars, feeling the small bite of his heavy beard.

He finally lowered her hand to the table, but kept it in his.

"I never missed a movie of yours. I think I've seen every one since you were a kid. You had a rare beauty and a rare talent. But I find you more beautiful now and your talent is one that everyone here appreciates."

"I know they appreciate it." She smiled at him. The compliments on her cooking were frequent and fervent and she understood completely. Before she arrived and reorganized the communal kitchen, Mac had cooked. Every person who told her that had winced.

He was searching her eyes again, a look so penetrating it was as if he were walking around inside her head. "You don't believe me when I say I find you more beautiful than before."

She kept an easy smile on her face. "Lucius, it's not necessary for you to say that. I don't need it."

"I know you don't. But I need to say it. Stella—" he stopped. Licked his lips. Swallowed. Looked down at their linked hands, then back up at her.

If Stella didn't know better, she'd say he was nervous. But that was impossible of course. Mac, Nick, and Jon were three of the toughest men on the face of the earth. Capable and brave and determined. They had defied—were still defying—the U.S. government and the entire military. They were unbreakable men and this man, this man holding her hand, was their commanding officer. Had led them into battle. That kind of man didn't do embarrassment.

And yet . . .

"Stella, I have something to say." His voice, already hoarse, had roughened. "And I'm finding it . . . I'm finding it hard."

"I'm listening, Lucius." She couldn't imagine it hard for Lucius to say anything.

He drew in a deep breath. "I'm falling in love with you. No, scratch that. I am in love with you. Since the moment I saw you when we were brought into Haven."

Oh God. Tears pricked her eyes. Lucius and the three others had been carried into Haven because they'd been unable to walk. All four of them had been on the verge of death. She remembered Lucius clearly lying on the gurney in the infirmary, a wounded and broken man. It had hurt to look at him, a clearly once-strong man who'd been tortured almost to death. Catherine had had a near-death experience herself and was in a coma, so it had been up to Stella and their two nurses, Pat and Salvatore, to take care of everyone.

After the attack, Stella had had four surgeries and had spent months in the hospital. With nothing else to do, she'd observed the nurses and had a pretty good handle on what to do.

Lucius had opened his eyes briefly when she approached him on the gurney. "We'll take care of you," she whispered. He'd nodded and passed out.

That was the first time he set eyes on her.

Since then, she'd looked after him. Not out of pity, oh no. Partly out of rage. She'd been subjected to insane violence too, just as he had. The violence of the cruel and cowardly. She knew exactly what that was like and the idea of a man like this, a combat hero, who'd dedicated his life to his country, being tied down like an animal and tormented—it drove her half crazy.

But the real reason she'd looked after him was that she'd seen right through the naked, half-dead man who'd arrived in Haven and saw, very clearly, the extraordinary, strong man he'd been. His courage and strength had been clear to her from the start. He'd been smart and strong and brave. Handsome, even, as she'd been beautiful. And then they'd fallen into the hands of monsters. But she came out of it and he was coming out of it, and in watching him put himself back together, she'd lost her heart to him.

He reached out a hand to her face, finger trying to trace the worst scar of all, running from her left eyebrow down to the right jaw. The one that had taken sixty-four stitches to close. She was lucky to have a functioning eye.

Instinctively Stella reared back. No one had touched it since the surgeon had taken out the stitches.

"No, no," he whispered. "No, darling. Shhh. Let me touch." His finger, slightly rough, traced the deep white scar over and over again, slowly, from end to end.

That had been the first slash, the stalker having taken her completely by surprise. Her entourage had known for years that she had a violent stalker. Nobody told her, the idea being that she'd "lose her focus." And they'd lose their gravy train. The stalker had sent her menacing letters, horrific gifts, had made threatening phone calls. All intercepted. The man she'd considered her personal assistant was a bodyguard. His dead body had been found just outside her bedroom door, lying in a pool of blood.

It was the cut that had hurt the most, slicing her face and her life in two.

Lucius's touch was so gentle, his eyes so understanding. They just sat there in the quiet room, his finger tracing her worst nightmare from temple to chin. His thumb wiped away the fat tears that welled from her eyes.

His eyes—they *knew* her somehow. No one had known her. Her fame had been like a stone wall between her and the rest of humanity. Even her lovers pleasured her body without ever touching her heart. They didn't want to touch her heart, anyway. That had always been very clear.

This man, with the ruined face and broken body, this man touched her heart.

A sob escaped her, quickly stifled. She never cried, ever. The tears were . . . a mistake.

"Hush, darling," he said, that deep voice so tender. "I haven't finished talking yet."

She nodded, throat too tight for words.

"I love you, Stella. I know I have nothing to offer you, not even myself. I can barely stand upright. I have no career, no place to call my own but here. I am a hunted man, together with the others. Should we be caught, we'd be court-martialed, but I don't think we'd make it to a tribunal. They'd shoot us first. I don't have anything resembling a future. I'm not even fully a man again. But I swear no one else could ever love you like I do. Someday I'll be whole. I believe that completely. It won't be today and it won't be tomorrow. But, do you think—do you think you could wait for me?"

That strong, scarred beloved face was open for her to read, to see his anxiety. Those dark eyes were locked onto hers.

The tears were falling freely now, catching on her upturned lips. She cupped his face with her free hand.

"I'm not going to wait for you, Lucius." He flinched and she clutched his hand harder. "I don't have to wait. I'm already yours."

"Do you think Jon will find a clue in Elle's house?" Catherine came out of the bathroom with perfumed steam billowing behind her, like some goddess coming out of the mists of time.

Billowing steam, goddesses, mists of time. *Christ*. Mac didn't recognize the thoughts in his head these days. They were totally unlike the thoughts of Mac BC—Before Catherine. He seemed to be having a lot of those thoughts nowadays, though.

Everything in his life had changed since Catherine, not least the small bump showing in her belly. When he saw it, when he touched it, his heart gave a huge kick in his chest. His child. Their child. Though Catherine was his heart and life, this child would be his only blood relative in the world. Just thinking about it gave him the shivers.

Catherine walked to their bed, smiling sadly. If anyone knew what it was like to be hunted down by the goons of Arka Pharmaceuticals, it was Catherine.

Mac held his arms out and grunted with satisfaction when she went into them. The world was fucked-up almost beyond repair, but when his arms closed around his wife he could almost hear an audible *click*, as if a piece of sophisticated machinery were working well.

He ran a hand down her dark, soft hair. "If Jon doesn't find what we need tonight, we'll just attack it full bore tomorrow. Everyone will pitch in. We'll figure it out."

Looking down, he could see her smile, felt her head nod against his shoulder.

She wasn't quite convinced. True, there were only a few of them against a huge multinational corporation, but they were the best. And they had two secret weapons—Catherine and Elle.

Between them the two women had about a billion advanced degrees and they were highly motivated.

"I appreciate what you and Nick and Jon are doing." She looked up at him, cupped the burn scar on his face. As always, when she touched him there was a sensation of deep warmth and well-being. And something else. Her eyes opened wide because she also got a blast of the surge of lust that took him. It wasn't anything new, he felt a low-level desire whenever she was around and they were alone.

Like now.

She was pregnant and worked hard at the infirmary, so Mac tried really, really hard to keep a lid on it, or at least keep his dick down. If it were up to him or his cock, she'd be flat on her back all night and most of the day. But he loved her too much to act on his lust every time he felt it. She never said no, but he could read her like a book now. If she was tired, faint bruises appeared under her gorgeous silver eyes and that ivory skin became even paler. That was when he really stepped back. And he knew to keep it tucked in his pants when she was absorbed in a task.

She was worried now, that was clear. He smoothed out the furrow between her eyebrows with his thumb. "We have to do this, honey," he said gently. "For Nick, if nothing else. Because he'd go it alone if he had to and we simply can't let him do that."

He could understand her worry. They would risk their lives for strangers. If the three of them got caught they'd be executed. They were all real clear on that. But more important than that, if they got caught or if they died, Haven would die, and not well. The small community they'd gathered around them was precious to him and to all of them. They were moving toward complete self-sufficiency, but it was still dependent on what Ghost Ops could steal or liberate from the outside world. It was dependent on Ghost Ops for protection and direction. If the three of them were gone, Haven would die.

And his child would grow up fatherless.

Mac squelched that thought immediately. Catherine was way too perceptive for him to allow something like that in his head.

"I know we need to rescue them," Catherine said quietly. "No question. And not just for Nick, for us." She searched his face. "We need to do this. I feel it very strongly."

Man, when Catherine felt something strongly it was as true as true could be. But what she felt wasn't making her happy. The lines between her brows were back and her mouth was turned down.

Well, Mac had a cure for that. "You feel it strongly, huh?"

His tone must have tipped her off because her head tilted and eyes narrowed as she studied him. "Mac," she said.

He waggled his eyebrows. "I feel something strongly too. Here." He grabbed her hand and placed it right over his dick and ah, man. It happened again. He'd been semi hard and at her touch, at that massive warmth he always felt when she touched him, he turned hard as steel. "You can feel it."

Her hand cupped him. "It's quite a . . . sensation," she murmured.

Mac thrust himself further into her hand. "Yeah. I have a strong feeling you should be doing something about this. Forget about those other guys. Rescue *me*."

Catherine laughed and pulled him down for a kiss. She looked excited and happy, just what he wanted.

Mission accomplished.

"We'll get her back," Nick said quietly and Elle looked at him in surprise. Knowing how protective he was, she imagined he'd try to distract her, with sex probably, because she was apparently easily distractible that way. With him, at least. But Nick went right to the heart of what she felt.

"God, I hope so." She twined her hands and pulled them apart, an old trick. "I can't bear the thought of her in their hands. Sophie's nice. Good and gentle, you know?" She looked up at him.

His face was tender. "I know. Like you, like Catherine. Would it help you to know that Jon and Mac and I haven't failed a mission yet? Except for the one where we were betrayed."

Elle smiled. "Actually, it does help." And it did. If anyone in the world could rescue her colleagues and her best friend, it was Nick, with the help of his friends. Lines of friendship becoming lines of salvation.

They were sitting up in bed, Elle leaning against Nick's strong shoulder. Finding comfort from just the physical contact. He placed his hand over hers, lacing his fingers through hers.

"Let me show you something," he said quietly in her ear.

"To distract me?"

"Yeah, that too. But also because it's beautiful and we should take time to notice beautiful things."

Elle twisted her head around to look into his face, eyes wide. Nick, a philosopher?

His mouth quirked. "You don't have to look at me like that. I'm not an animal."

She cupped his face with her free hand. "No, you're not." As a matter of fact, he had being a full human being down pat. It was a new way of looking at him, and it hit her heart with the force of a blow. He looked tired, new lines in his face. He, Mac, and Jon were hunted men and yet instead of thinking of keeping themselves safe, they protected an entire community.

He had taken her problems entirely upon his shoulders so naturally that only now she realized he'd done so.

Elle had been almost blinded by her sexual attraction to him and the very strong emotions he evoked in her. She'd seen him as almost superhuman, something more than a man. And he was, but he was also a man. Who presumably felt tired and despondent, who might be sad that his life as a soldier had been trashed, who felt the weight of responsibility for the many souls in Haven who depended on him and his teammates.

But he never let that show.

She saw the full man now. With all his many strengths and very few weaknesses. She was one of his weaknesses.

"Show me," she whispered. If there was something beautiful he wanted her to see, she wanted to see it.

"Okay. Brace yourself."

Nick reached for something, pressed something, and Elle's breath caught in her lungs.

The walls of the room simply . . . disappeared. It was as if the bed had been magically transported into the forest by a benevolent wizard. All around them was deep snow in the moonlight, a bright moon barely visible among the clouds. It had snowed earlier and the forecast was for more snow. For now, though, the scene was calm and gentle. Picture-postcard perfect in an imperfect world.

"Like it?" Nick's deep voice was right against her ear and she shivered. Everything felt so . . . magnified. The beauty of the scene—their bed magically transported to an enchanted forest— the love she felt for the man beside her. The intense affection she was starting to nurture for the outlaw community she'd joined.

"I love it. How did you—" Her voice caught because he was kissing the oh-so-sensitive skin behind her ear and because his hand was smoothing up her thigh, taking her nightgown with it.

"Hmm?" he purred. She felt the vibration of his naked chest against her back. Nick slept naked, which she thought was a bit of overkill. He was a temptation dressed. Naked, he was simply irresistible.

"How did you manage to make the walls disappear?" Because that was a bit much, even for Nick. Even for Haven.

"They didn't disappear. They turned into monitors. What you're seeing comes from remote cameras we have ringing Haven. It's one specific spot, one of my favorites. But later we'll program it to other spots you might like. This scene is real time, but we could show a recording. Sunrise or sunset." His hand found her core, one rough finger circling her opening. Her head fell back against his shoulder. "Anything you want, honey."

"Oh God, Nick."

"Yeah? Is this what you want?" One big finger slid inside her and she shuddered. Ten minutes ago if anyone had asked her, she'd have said she wasn't up for sex. Too tired, too tense, too scared. But that was then and this was now. All her troubles and worries coalesced somewhere outside her. Maybe swirling in that glorious landscape outside. They were still there, but far away. They'd come back of course, but for now, she was concentrated on her body. On the feel of a naked Nick against her back, his finger stroking heat inside her.

He bit her. Lightly. Not enough to hurt but certainly enough to galvanize her, like a jolt of electricity. She broke out in goose bumps and could feel her sex become wet, more open to him.

"That's right, honey," he murmured directly in her ear and she shivered. "Think about this. Think about me doing this to you." The finger slid in deeper, slid out, slid even further in. "Don't think of anything but this."

"Speaking of thinking . . ."

She jumped when his thumb circled her clitoris and his hold on her tightened. She could feel his erect penis against her back, but he made no move to enter her. Just held her and touched her and bit her and licked her, all the while his finger moving in her now-slick folds with a light sucking sound and everything she was, all her senses swirled inward in an ever tightening circle until with one last stroke of his thumb, she fell over the edge, tightening around him endlessly as her climax took over.

"Oh," she sighed.

"Thinking what?" That deep voice in her ear. She shivered.

"What?"

"Thinking. You said speaking of thinking . . ."

Mmm. Thinking. Now that was a pointless activity right now, when every cell in her body felt replete and swollen. She sighed again.

Nick nudged her shoulder with his. "You were going to say something."

"I was. I got distracted."

"Focus."

Focus. Easier said than done while he was cupping her breast. But the thought had been important— "Oh."

"Yeah?"

She turned to face him, placing a hand against his cheek. The slight bristle of stubble tickled her hand. "I should shave."

"Yes, you should, but that's not what I wanted to say. Catherine told me that she suspected that sex, really, really good sex, which I gather is the kind she and Mac have, increases her power. That she thinks sex made her slightly telepathic, more so with Mac."

The smile broadened. "Sex, huh?"

"Really, really good sex," she said primly.

"We'll see about that." Nick slid out from behind her, eased her down in the bed. He kissed her, endlessly, one hand cupping her head, the other stroking her sex. She was very wet, almost embarrassingly so. He circled her with his finger, dipped into her. She was almost hyperaroused from the climax. The feel of his rough finger against her sensitive tissues was almost electric in its intensity.

He took his hand away but before she could object, he curled her hand around his erection. *Oh God.* It felt so *good.* Hard and hot, the skin almost velvety. She pumped her hand up and down, feeling the effect on him. His breathing speeded up, his mouth bit at hers, the hard muscles of his back became even harder.

"Put me in you," he whispered in her mouth.

Elle shifted, opened her legs further, brought him to her and nearly cried out as he slid into her, hot and hard and deep. They both stilled for a moment, as if moving would be sensory overkill.

Nick raised his torso up on his forearms and watched her eyes as he started moving in her. Slowly at first, watching every inch of her face as she watched his. How wonderful to watch him, to see the pleasure she gave him while feeling the slow honey of the pleasure he gave her. She locked her ankles in the small of his back, loving the feeling of his hard, thick muscles moving against her, in her.

She moved to kiss his sweaty shoulder, eyes closed. *I love you so much, Nick*, she thought and he suddenly stilled.

She opened her eyes to find his face slack with shock. His eyes glowed with an eerie light, skin tight across his cheekbones, neck tendons taut with tension.

"I love you too, Elle," he said. She brought her hand to her mouth in shock.

I heard you. In my head. His voice. Inside her head.

I hear you too.

Nick kissed her savagely, slamming into her almost violently. Hard, fast, furious, as if he were trying to crawl inside her body, as if he could physically make them one.

Now, Nick.

His movements became even faster as they clung to each other desperately and just as desperately climaxed. She could feel her internal muscles clenching hard around him, as if to draw him even more deeply inside her.

He slumped on her, limp and sweaty, holding her so tightly she could barely breathe.

When he whispered *sleep* in her head, she did.

Sleep took her like a beloved friend and she fell endlessly into its embrace. Images bloomed, bright and surreal, the stuff of dreams.

And then—and then she Dreamed.

She flew high above the earth, pure being, unrestricted by the rules of space and time. No emotion, just purpose, arrowing straight to a city by the bay, to invisible cages and the desperate faces of friends held by monsters, friends who had lost hope, friends who called to her . . .

She bolted up in bed. Nick sat up too, turning a sober, serious face to her.

"I know where they are," she said and he nodded.

Palo Alto

Jon crouched in the bushes a block from Elle's home. He checked his handheld. It had a special screened monitor that was visible only to him via a lens on his nightvision binoculars. It emitted no light that could be seen by anyone else.

He checked the images sent by the overhead drone. First, he checked himself, pleased but not surprised to see that he didn't show up on any part of the spectrum—not visually, not in IR, and not in thermal. He was covered head to toe in stealth gear that wouldn't be available to civilians. Technically, it wasn't available to him either. He'd liberated it from a military installation in Texas.

The drone showed that the neighborhood was empty, no security goons held behind to keep an eye out for a lone woman scientist who might want to go back to her home. Pity. He'd have welcomed a fight.

These were the same fuckers who had tortured his commanding officer and three of the best teammates in the world. Jon had to stop for a second to breathe his rage back out. Rage did no one any good. Just when he thought he had himself under control, though, a vision of Elle's friend Sophie flashed in his head.

She didn't look like Catherine or Elle, but she had their look—smart, gentle, guileless. Someone who worked for the good of humanity. And beautiful, on top of that. The world didn't grow too many women like that and now she was hunted, too.

She, too, could end up like Lucius—a tormented animal, a lab rat hounded to death.

Goddamn.

He waited another second to get himself back under control. That was a surprise. Jon had plenty of self-control. He knew exactly what kind of face he presented to the world. Relaxed, cool, hip. Mac and Nick—now, they looked like warriors. Cold and tough and fearsome. Not Jon. He cultivated that loose, friendly look. Those who didn't know him probably thought he mellowed out on drugs. They couldn't know how much he hated drugs. And they couldn't know he was a soldier who had killed many times.

Jon kept himself detached, doing what he knew had to be done, but more like a pest controller stamping out cockroaches than a man on a crusade.

He didn't feel cool or detached when he thought of Sophie Daniels in the hands of the men who'd tortured his commanding officer and his teammates, though. He felt white hot rage, so powerful it distorted his senses. *Fuck this*, he thought. *Get yourself under control.* He wasn't doing anyone any good wallowing in his emotions, imagining even now Elle's pretty friend strapped down to a table, being cut, being hurt . . .

Shit.

In Ghost Ops they'd been taught to control their autonomous system. They were shooters and could slow their own heart rate down to take the shot. He crouched for another full minute, eyes closed, slowing down his breathing, taking down his heartbeat, resolutely not thinking of pretty Sophie Daniels being hurt.

So he could go after the fuckers who'd taken her and rip their hearts out.

Okay.

His eyes popped open and he moved forward like a laser beam focused on the mission.

The neighborhood was a quiet one of apartment buildings. He ghosted from bush to tree to car, certain that no one saw him and certain that he wasn't showing up on any surveillance video. When he had Elle's small house in sight he stopped and tapped on his handheld. This was his own invention—the electronic equivalent of radar to detect any hidden detonators or trip wires around the house. It had a radius of 500 meters and when the monitor remained blank, he moved forward.

He could be fast now. He got past the front door security and climbed the stairs to the second floor. In a moment, he'd picked Elle's pathetic lock and was inside her apartment.

It had been trashed, just as Catherine's house had been trashed. It had been done systematically, almost scientifically. Everything breakable had been broken, everything soft had been slashed, everything electronic had been smashed.

Well, she wasn't coming back here. That door was closed forever. She was with Nick and Nick was part of Haven on Mount Blue. Jon snapped a few photos for Elle, sent them to the war room, then moved into the bathroom. Sure enough, there it was, on the sink. The sensor that had been in Elle's arm. The goons who'd trashed her house had simply left it there. It wasn't going to take them to Elle, it wasn't going to take them anywhere but her empty bathroom.

He picked it up with tweezers Catherine had given him and studied it, wincing when he saw blood and bits of flesh clinging to the tendrils underneath the chip. That must have hurt like a bitch to pull out.

The chip itself was tiny, a hard composite shell presenting no visible opening. It was a radio transmitter, sure, but presumably it had to have a facility for a physical data dump. He brought the chip close to his goggles, tapped the side, turning them into powerful microscopes and, *Ah!* There it was. The tiniest of portals and, *Yes!* He had the fuckers.

He had the thinnest fiber-optic thread in existence and with the help of the tweezers he fit it into the portal and started downloading. The data started appearing immediately on his monitor. First physical data going back three months covering every aspect of Elle's body and then, at the end, a code connecting this tracking sensor with every other. Ten other sensors, for the ten other poor sons of bitches who were in the hands of monsters, including Sophie. Six codes were inert, which probably meant the poor fuckers were dead.

He overlay the data for the four live codes onto a GPS map and stared at the screen for a full minute, breathing in and breathing out. When he was sure he had his voice under control, he tapped his comms unit and spoke.

"I know where they are."

Chapter 13

San Francisco

At five A.M., still three hours from daybreak, the helo landed silently on the rooftop of the Arka building, forty stories up. Though it had stopped snowing and the sky had cleared, Nick was sure no one saw them. The only way they could have been detected was if someone on Market Street was looking up at the night sky and saw the stars eclipse for a second. And even then, it could be a passing cloud. A *fast*-passing cloud.

Jon had flown back to Mount Blue to pick them up and fly them to San Francisco. He'd hovered for just a moment over a rental unit in Cow Hollow and Mac had rappelled down. Mac was now on his way in a big dark van they had stashed there and would park around the corner of the front entrance of the tall, slender white building housing Arka, because they had hopes of finding the live bodies of Elle's friends somewhere inside that building.

They had no eyes into the building, none. Jon had failed to break into the building's security, a first. The only thing they had was the building's schematics, on record in City Hall.

So the building on Battery Street was impregnable in terms of intel. All they could do was break in and hope for the best.

Not the smartest infiltration plan they'd ever come up with. But it was the only one they had.

Elle had put herself under. She said she'd be waiting for them at Arka and that she would contact him telepathically. When she said that, Mac and Catherine hadn't blinked. If Elle couldn't establish contact, he and Jon were fully prepared to find the prisoners and fight their way out however they could. Mac would join them if necessary.

It wasn't a suicide mission. It wasn't. Nick kept telling himself that.

He glanced over at Jon. This was exactly the kind of mission that would appeal to his sense of the absurd and he expected to find a half-smile on Jon's face. It wasn't there. What was there was grim purpose and that surprised him.

Nick hated going in blind. They all did. The less intel you had, the greater the fuckup potential, in a situation where fuckup was a synonym for messy death. Though Jon had managed to get the schematics of the building, it was missing whole floors, which was illegal. Every blueprint lodged with the city's Building Inspection Service had to be complete as to architecture and infrastructure, but somehow Arka had greased some palms and various floors were blank. It wasn't even clear if they had electricity. And the building stopped at the ground floor, which both Catherine and Elle said made no sense. So there were subterranean floors too.

How many?

Who the fuck knew?

Nick's jaw was so tight his temples hurt and he realized how much it sucked to go into battle when you had someone you love waiting for you back home. Ghost Ops made a hell of a lot of sense. They'd been screened, carefully chosen, so that no one had anyone waiting back home for them. Not a woman, not a child, not a dog, not even a fucking goldfish—and Nick got that, got it deep in his bones.

Because wanting to come back, wanting fiercely to hold on to whoever was waiting for you after the op, was the surest way to take your mind off the op. And taking your mind off the op was like taking a gun to your head and pulling the trigger.

Fuck.

Operational readiness was a physical attribute, sure. Train, shoot, train some more, shoot some more—until it was all automatic and you reacted faster than you could think.

But you had to think. You had to plan out your moves in constantly evolving situations that were never, ever, ever like the pre-op briefing. No battle plan ever survives contact with the enemy. Shit happens, and when it does you adapt.

You had to be wholly one with the op in your head. No thinking of anything else. Forget the fact that he'd left a white-faced Elle behind, doing her damnedest—as Catherine was doing with Mac— to be upbeat and brave. Terrified he wasn't going to come back.

And the shitty thing was—he was terrified too.

Well, fuck again.

A warrior couldn't have thoughts like that messing with his head. He had to be down with the mission, and ready to die.

Nick wasn't ready to die. Not even close. He wanted to live with Elle for the rest of his life. In Haven, on Mount Blue. Soon they would become completely self-sufficient and they could just turn their backs on the broken world and live in happy isolation. Living the rest of his life with Elle— Oh, man. Waking up next to her, eating with her, sleeping with her.

Fucking her.

The thought jolted him. First, because it shot a crude rush of heat through his system; and second, because for the first time in his life he realized he'd been making love to Elle, not fucking her and . . .

Oh, shit. This was it. He wanted that for the rest of his life.
He wanted her. He needed her.

Nick. . .

"The rooftop door is open." Jon's flat voice broke his pity party and suddenly Nick was back, focused and ready to get the job done.

He checked the rooftop carefully, dialing down the aperture of the NVG. There was some light coming from the aircraft warning light atop a pole that jutted fifty feet in the air above their heads, and it blinded him.

Nick. . .

The field was green, flat. He reconned in quarters—a quarter of the field of vision, blink, another quarter . . .

There it was. The rooftop door. Open, just as Jon had said.

He looked over and their eyes met. *That's not good.* They might as well have spoken the words aloud.

Nick. Something's wrong.

Nick jerked as he realized Elle had been trying to contact him. She'd done it! Elle had said she'd try to go under when they landed on the roof of the Arka building.

Nick. . .

For a second Nick forgot that they were on the top of a building with serious security trying to rescue four people who were God knows where and in God knows what condition. What did it matter? Elle was here with him.

And now he felt her completely, like a gentle hand petting him, a steady warmth in his head.

"I've got Elle," he told Jon.

Jon's mouth tightened. "Yeah? What's she say?"

"That something's wrong."

Jon's response, almost scripted, should have been, *No shit, Sherlock.* But he didn't say that. He didn't say anything. He just tightened his mouth again.

In a moment they were both in a crouch, weapon in hand,

moving toward the open door from two different directions. It if was a trap, maybe one of them could survive.

Elle followed him in his head, utterly quiescent, instinctively understanding that he couldn't deal with distractions.

They reached the door. It was open only an inch and behind the door it was dark. Jon flattened himself on the right side, weapon shouldered. Nick waited a moment, trying to hear what was on the other side.

No one there, a faint voice whispered in his head.

Well, if this was going to work, he was going to have to trust her.

He kicked open the door, jumping over the high barrier designed to keep heavy rain from seeping into the stairwell, landing lightly on a landing, weapon up, completely ready to face the enemy—

Who wasn't there.

Nobody in the stairwell. Elle sounded uncertain. Puzzled.

Nick peered over the banister at the endless flights leading downward. There were faint emergency lights on the landings, but they were no help. The bottom was down there somewhere but invisible.

Arka headquarters covered all the floors from the twenty-second floor to the ground floor.

Nick jerked his weapon and they fell into a rhythm, Nick treading lightly on the edges of the steps, covering the field of fire below them, Jon moving down backward, covering the field of fire behind them. Both weapons up, fingers on the trigger button. They could switch from stunner to bullets in a fraction of a second.

Go on.

On the twenty-second floor, the door to the floor was ajar. Up until now all the doors had been closed, a keypad on the wall next to the door. Nick took point again and slowly opened the door with the muzzle of his weapon.

Jesus! A man was lying on the floor, a pool of blood around his head. A clerical worker, dressed in a white shirt and black slacks. He was lying on his side, one arm at an unnatural angle.

His throat was torn out. Something—someone?—had taken a huge chunk out of his throat and he'd bled out.

He's dead.

Nick nodded at Elle in his head. Yeah. No need to reach down with two fingers over the carotid to check.

His eyes met Jon's.

Nick! Behind you! Elle's voice screamed in his head and he turned just as something came at him, a beast making terrifying animal noises, a creature with blood smeared over its face, hands up and reaching for him. It made a wild leap and it—

Fell to the ground in a lifeless heap, half its head shot away. Nick had opted for good old-fashioned bullets.

"Jesus!" Jon's voice came out a harsh whisper. They'd both taken a knee, ready to deal with other crazies who might be coming, but there was no one. Nick focused on the man who'd attacked him and rose slowly. He hadn't noticed many details—too busy killing the fucker—but now he walked over to the carcass. The . . . man was covered in blood and had—*Jesus.* Nick bent over. Did he have a human ear in his mouth? While attacking, the man had seemed all teeth and claws, but disregarding the blood and the human ear between his teeth, he looked like an executive. An out-of-shape executive who probably took a golf cart around the course twice a month just before a hearty lunch at the club.

He was chubby. His once white, now red shirt strained at the buttons around his belly. He was balding. His suit was good quality and his shoes were shined—and he'd come at Nick like a maddened grizzly bear.

Nick. . .

Yeah, honey? He thought it abstractedly, trying to puzzle out the two men, two members in good standing of the office drone class, one maimed, the other . . . maimer? Nick nudged the first man's head with his toe, turning his head this way and that. The ear in the other man's mouth wasn't his. It was someone else's.

So this thing, whatever it was, wasn't limited to these two.

Nick, get in the elevator and go down to the second sublevel. Now. Elle's voice was more than a whisper now, and there was urgency in it.

He turned to Jon. "Elle says to take the elevator down to the second sublevel. Now."

Nick didn't know Jon that well. When the shit had rained down on them in the Cambridge Lab—belonging to the same company that was raining shit on them right this minute—he'd been on his second Ghost Ops mission. You go into battle a lot with someone and come out the other end alive, a bond is forged. After only two missions and the third one gone to shit . . . well, Jon could easily question the order.

Jon didn't hesitate.

They both ran for the elevator and Nick punched in –2. The lights flickered, cut out, came back on.

"The fuck?" Jon said.

Nick shook his head. He had no idea.

Hurry, came Elle's whisper in his head.

A click, then Mac's voice. "In position."

Nick tapped his ear. "Roger that." He flipped to Haven. "Catherine. How's she doing?"

Elle's spirit was here in a way Nick couldn't explain but knew was true. Her body, however, back in Haven, was in a sort of coma. Though Nick knew, rationally, that she was safe and in Catherine's hands, the irrational part of him wasn't happy with the situation. Whatever part of Elle was here couldn't be shot and killed, but there was something going on that scared him down to the marrow of his bones. There was evil here. He'd been in lots of places where the forces of darkness operated. Where hatred and greed and lust for power were powerful motivators and he could deal with that. All warriors faced the worst of human nature and fought it. That's why they were warriors.

But there was something about what was happening here that scared the shit out of him and he wanted Elle far, far away instead of here. In spirit rather than in body, but still.

Catherine's calm gentle voice came on. Jon didn't react and Nick realized that she'd switched on just his channel. "Elle's fine. Vital signs are stable. I'm at her side and won't leave until she wakes up or until you guys get back."

Muscles loosened in his body. Catherine would stay by Elle's side.

Don't worry about me. The tone in his head was stern. *Pay attention. You're going to have to act fast.* There was silence for a second in his head, and just as the elevator reached the second subbasement level with a ping, Elle reappeared. *Two . . . things. Right outside the door!*

Just before the door swooshed open, Nick tapped Jon's shoulder and crouched. Jon followed his lead and dropped. "Two. All eyes," he whispered and then the doors were open and they both moved forward, Nick right, Jon left and—

Oh God!

It was a massacre.

Dead bodies everywhere in the corridor, everyone in white lab coats stained with blood. Rivers of it. Some had been torn apart, not by knives but by what looked like bare hands.

The coppery smell of blood mixed with the tang of urine and the unmistakable stench of feces—the smells of violent death.

The linoleum floor was slick with blood, the white walls were stained with it, there was even spatter on the ceiling.

Nick!

Two . . . things came barreling around the corner, blood-spattered, mouths open, hands up into claws. They came as fast and as aggressively as any soldier, only these weren't soldiers. Nick and Jon hesitated because these were clearly civilians. Or had been civilians.

A man and a woman in once-white lab coats, now stiff with blood. The woman was young, Asian, pretty. Or had been pretty. Now her face was contorted with inchoate rage as she sprinted screaming down the corridor, leaving the man behind. The man was thin, his lab coat flapping around his thighs, just as blood-stained, just as altered. He was balding with a comb-over hanging down over his eyes which bounced as he lurched down the corridor.

"Jesus," Jon whispered. The man was running—trying to run—on a broken ankle. It was as if he didn't feel it, didn't even perceive it. It looked like all he felt was raw rage as he dragged himself as fast as he could toward Nick and Jon.

There was nothing human in their eyes, pupils expanded almost to the edge of the irises so that their eyes were black. The woman gave a banshee shriek and leaped, claws out . . .

Nick. . .

Jon took out the woman and Nick the man, red mists formed a halo around their heads, two perfect head shots so close together they sounded like one.

Down the corridor, to the right.

"Down there, to the right," Nick said and it took effort to keep his voice steady.

Nick and Jon shared a quick glance then made their way forward, stepping over the woman whose brains were scattered over the floor and the wall. Her hands were still arched in claws. The man had fallen backward, blood seeping from the back of his head. The broken ankle was a compound fracture. White bone stuck out from the gray sock and the foot, connected only by skin, lay flat on the ground.

Pick up his pass.

Nick bent to unclip the pass from the pocket of the white lab coat. For a second, Nick studied the small sharp hologram of a successful middle-aged researcher with a kind smile. His eyes flicked to the still-grimacing face of the dead man. If he hadn't been looking at the dead man and the hologram at the same time, he'd never have believed they were the same person.

Hurry.

Nick had to tuck away the utter dread he felt and concentrate on the mission. Of all the horrors of war he'd seen, this was undoubtedly the worst. Perfectly normal lab drones who'd suddenly turned ferociously feral.

He waved his hand forward and then right and he and Jon started forward at a trot, both of them sniffing the air. Something was burning. They started running. Being trapped underground in a fire was a nightmare. It had already happened to Nick in Cambridge and he wasn't eager to repeat the experience.

They turned the corner to the right and saw a long corridor with a wall at the end. No doors. No elevator. Thank God at least it was free of bodies. They picked up their pace and just as Nick was thinking of slowing down to see if the badge would open something—

Hold the pass up—

The door at the back of the corridor opened up with the sucking sound of a seal being broken. A wind at his back cooled the sweat from his body. This part of the building had negative pressure. A lab dealing with hazardous material.

This is it. I'm going ahead. . .

Nick felt Elle's presence as a faint glow in his head, growing fainter. He didn't have time to worry about that though because he was looking at a series of transparent boxes. No, he thought, the hairs on the back of his head rising. Cages. Transparent cages.

For humans.

Ten of them, seven empty.

All around, monitors and holograms and equipment he had no name for. The room had the ozone smell of electricity and there was a faint hum of working equipment.

Suddenly, Jon took off, walking fast down an aisle, looking sharply into each cage.

The first cage had a tall dark-haired man in it who studied them, then opened his mouth. He was shouting, banging his fist against the cage, but there was no noise. He pointed desperately at a console in the middle of the room and Nick went over to stand in front of it. The man made an O with his fingers.

A button.

Nick looked down, frowning. There were five buttons. Black, white, red, yellow, blue. He looked up at the man who mouthed *red* and he pushed the red button. With a hiss, the doors opened and three figures stepped out of their cages.

"Sophie!" Jon shouted. "Sophie Daniels! Where is she?"

"Sorry, man." The tall dark-haired man shook his head. "They took her away and she hasn't come back."

Jon's face was frightening, bright blue eyes like shards of ice.

One of the women—short, with frizzy red hair—spoke up. "Are you here to rescue us? Because we really need rescuing. And something really creepy is happening inside the building. If you're here to rescue us we need to go, right now."

"Not without Sophie," Jon said, mouth a grim white line.

Nick held up a hand. "Elle sends us." There was a low murmur among the prisoners. "We've got a van outside if we can find our way to it."

"Where?" the other man asked. He looked about twelve, with blond dreadlocks, but he must have been at least eighteen. Elle said everyone had had to sign an informed consent release.

"On Bush, between Sansome and Battery."

"I know a secondary way out," the kid said. "It'll take us right there."

They all looked up as the lights flickered, went out for two seconds then came back on. They were dimmer now. The building was on the generator.

"Dudes," said the kid, young face utterly serious, "we gotta go."

"Not without Sophie," Jon said, face set, nostrils flaring.

Honey? Could use a little help here.

Checking.

Nick took Jon by the arm and tugged him toward a corner. "Elle is looking for her. But if she's not here, we gotta go, like the kid said."

Jon huffed out a loud breath, like a bull. He angrily shrugged off Nick's hand. "Okay," he said through gritted teeth.

A siren sounded. Loud, like an air-raid siren. The former prisoners looked at them, faces pale, pinched, anxious. Nick understood completely. They had a stab at evading being treated like rats and then killed and they were being forced to wait. The redheaded woman let out a sob, then stifled it.

Honey?

She's not here, Nick.

"Gone." Nick met Jon's eyes. "She's not here. Elle looked for her but she's gone."

Jon stood, practically vibrating with tension, punched the side of a piece of equipment and turned to the prisoners. "Do we need to take anything?"

The dark-haired man thought, then shook his head. "If anything, you should download the data from the server. But that would take at least half an hour."

"No." Jon's eyes narrowed. "Not half an hour." He placed his top secret 100 terabyte flash drive into the side of a processer and switched it on. The sirens were booming now and the smell of smoke rose in the air. He pulled the drive out. "Done."

"Wow." The kid's eyes rounded. "How did you do that? I mean—"

You have to get everyone out now. Follow Les, the young kid. He knows how to get out. Go now!

"That's it, let's go." Nick started herding them toward the door, Jon standing guard. He had his rifle up, shouldered, the scope down, out of the way. The scope was a Warren 509 and could pick out rocks on the moon, but was worse than useless in close quarters.

Trying one last time to—

The voice in his head disappeared. Elle, whose soft presence inside him had been so incredibly reassuring, had winked out, leaving emptiness, coldness. Desolation.

Jon stuck his head out in the corridor, then motioned everyone to get out.

Nick stood there, like a moron. There was nothing to tap to get her back online, nothing to switch back on. Elle had disappeared and he didn't have a fucking clue how to get her back. He missed her desperately and recognized now how much it meant to him to have her inside him.

One thing was for sure—he wasn't moving from where he was without her.

A click, then Catherine's voice. She sounded rushed and there were beeping machine sounds in the background. "Nick?" She was trying to sound calm but panic was riding her. "Nick, Elle's vital signs are gone."

He tapped his ear. *"What?"* he screamed. "What the fuck do you mean by that?"

Her voice was steadier. She'd put them all on the same channel and Jon turned his head to him, eyes wide in alarm. Yeah. Jon understood.

"I'm not getting any vital signs. Heart, brain, lungs. Stopped. Can you feel her?" Catherine asked. "Is she still there with you?"

"No!" No, no he couldn't feel her. No, she wasn't here with him. All he felt was cold isolation, not that warm connection that had accompanied him into the building, like gentle hands caressing him. Nothing—just blankness.

Fuck!

He turned around in despair. There was nowhere to look for her, nothing he could do to find her. Her body was two hundred miles away and her spirit was . . . *where?*

He turned and turned with nowhere to go, sweat breaking out all over his body, heart pounding beneath his rib cage. He must have looked like a madman, but he didn't give a shit.

"Hey man, let's go," Jon shouted over the alarm. He was outside the door, the prisoners uneasily congregated around him. "She's not here, we're wasting time."

The emergency lights flickered and went off, casting them into utter darkness for a couple of seconds. When they came back on they were even dimmer than before. Backup power was fading fast. And the smell of smoke was stronger by the minute.

Mac's voice came on. "I've got what looks like fire on the eleventh and tenth floors. Fire engines are coming down Market. People are staggering out of the main entrance. We've got to go. That includes you, Ross."

No, that didn't include him. Damned, if he was going anywhere without Elle. Except Elle was back in Haven—

He heard a dull thump in his ear. "I'm defibrillating her, Nick." Another thump. "But it's not working. The EKG spiked but is flat again."

"Try again," he snarled and he heard another thump.

Silence for what felt like five centuries but was probably only five seconds.

Then Catherine came back on. "She's dying, Nick. There's nothing I can do." Catherine's voice was sorrowful. He could hear the steady hum of machinery that should be beating, together with her heart.

"No!" he screamed. Panic pounded in every cell. He'd never

known panic like this. He didn't know what the fuck to *do*. He'd been trained, and trained hard, to face any kind of danger. Bad guys with guns, ambushes, firefights—you name it, he knew what to do. But what the hell to do now, with a dying Elle two hundred miles away and a missing Elle right here—he had no clue. He met Jon's eyes. "I can't leave her. I can't. Get out of here."

"Dude?" The young kid stepped forward. He pitched his voice so it could be heard over the sirens. "You're looking for Elle Connolly? Right?"

Nick jerked his head up and down. His throat was clamped shut.

"She could astrally project. That's an electromagnetic phenomenon. There's a Faraday cage four doors down. It says Lab Four on the door. Maybe—"

"Nick." Catherine's voice choked. "Oh, Nick I am so very sorry. She's gone. Elle's gone."

"And we have to go too." Mac's hard voice didn't betray anything, just resolute purpose. "You have a mission, soldier. Get out. Now."

"*No!*" Nick screamed again and for the very first time in his life, he disobeyed direct orders. He waved at Jon. "Get these people out and into the van! I'll be right behind you."

Elle wasn't gone. Elle couldn't be gone. He'd just found her, after losing her for ten years. This wasn't happening. He was going to hop into the van with the former prisoners and Jon and Mac, and they were going to drive as fast as the van could carry them to Mount Blue and away from this place with the stench of human sacrifice.

And Elle would be waiting for him, just as she'd be waiting for him every single day for the rest of their lives. She'd welcome the kid, the dark-haired man, the woman with the frizzy hair to Haven, and they'd stay. Of course they'd stay. They were renegades and they had special powers, so they would fit right in, particularly with Catherine and Elle around. Woo-woo stuff was the staff of life on Haven now. There would be kids born who could levitate and travel in time and heal, and their kid would be one of them.

Because he and Elle were going to have kids, no question. He'd never wanted children. Why bring a kid into the world? The world was broken and there was no fixing it. Except—Elle wasn't broken and neither was he. Their kids would be strong and talented and smart.

And he wanted them. He wanted it all. He wanted the fights they'd have and he wanted the makeup sex. He wanted to watch Elle bloom with his child as Catherine was blooming with Mac's child. They were creating something in Haven. Nick had no idea what, he was a soldier for Christ's sake. What did he know? But Catherine knew and Elle sure knew. He wanted to be there and he wanted her by his side.

She wasn't dead. He wouldn't let her be.

Jon was herding the fugitives down the corridor to the right and he looked back at Nick. What Jon was doing was a two-man job. It should have been one man taking point, the other watching everyone's six. It was almost impossible for Jon to do it alone. Their eyes met and Nick couldn't see any censure in Jon's gaze. He was doing what he had to do so Nick could do what he had to do.

Teamwork.

That's what he had with Elle, goddammit. They were a team, a couple. The two of them *belonged* together. Always had, always would. Nick's vision blurred and he swiped at his eyes. Goddamned smoke.

He took off in the opposite direction.

"*Nick!*" Mac roared. He was watching their movements on his handheld and he saw Nick move in the opposite direction from Jon. "You head back right this second!"

Nick turned the sound down.

He pelted down the corridor as fast as his legs could carry him.

It wasn't the thought of Mac waiting or Jon and the fugitives that drove him. It was the thought that maybe just maybe he could save Elle. Crazy as that sounded. There was a 99 percent chance it wouldn't work, but that was better than 100 percent. Because 100 percent meant Elle was lost to him forever—and he couldn't, *wouldn't*, accept that.

Lab 1, Lab 2, Lab 3 . . . Lab 4— There it was! He was running so fast he skidded as he turned into the laboratory, frantically looking for a Faraday cage. He hadn't paid much attention in high school physics and though he'd caught up in the military, he knew he'd never seen one.

The lab was huge and filled with equipment. He raged his way to the end wall, smashing equipment out of his way with his rifle butt without finding anything that even vaguely resembled a cage. He slid to a stop at the far wall, chest heaving, vision blurred looking around wildly.

He recognized one piece of equipment in ten. Everything here was Geekland stuff, hard metallic shells hiding mysterious workings inside and— *Oh shit-oh shit-oh shit* . . . He didn't know what he was looking for.

In a rage, Nick kicked over some free-standing pieces, watching them shatter, bits of Plexiglas tinkling to the floor, dials rolling— and there it was. He stood, panting, looking at a metallic cage. A Faraday cage, it had to be. He stared at it like a dumb beast, tears and sweat dripping down his face—he had to shake himself into action because every second counted.

Go-Go-GO! Pulling a grenade out of his combat vest, he tossed it at the metal cage and ducked down behind a big piece of equipment with two huge centrifuges on top. After a second that felt like a century, the grenade exploded, spewing metal shards everywhere, some embedding themselves into the wall behind him.

Nick rose out of his crouch to look at the smoking mess, ready to scrabble around in the debris looking for something that would lead him to Elle, when he heard Catherine's gasp in the ear bud.

"Oh my God! She's just opened her eyes! Nick! Elle's opened her eyes, now she's closed them again, but the EKG is showing a heartbeat! Oh my God, she's *alive*!"

"Get your ass out here NOW!" Mac was screaming in the ear bud as Nick shot out the door into the corridor. *Oh yeah—getting out now!* And with Elle alive back in Haven, getting back there as fast as humanly possible.

He leaped over the bodies in the corridor, taking the emergency stairs up to the first floor in case the elevator wasn't working due to the fire and, slamming the panic handle on the fire door, ran down the corridor that would take him to the side exit.

He had tunnel vision. Not good. They were trained to avoid it because it could spell death. Just seeing right what was ahead of you without opening the senses completely was bad. But his head was taken up with getting out to Mac, getting the hell out of San Francisco and getting back to Haven—and as always when a soldier isn't paying attention, shit happened.

A body slammed into him from the side. A nightmare, with sound effects. And, he saw in a second, a fucking *woman*. Makeup smeared all over her face, a bib of blood down her once-white lab coat, snarling and growling, low terrifying animal noises. It took Nick one unforgivable second to flash onto the fact that, yes, this was a woman, but yes, she was fucking trying to kill him.

In that second, around 120 pounds of snarling female slammed him to the ground and she started trying her best to bite his face off. Before her mouth, tinted red by lipstick and blood, could reach his face, he shot an elbow to her nose and shoved her off. Whatever it was she was on, it was a painkiller because anyone else would have been doubled over in pain. Her nose was smashed flat against her blood-spattered face. But, no, she scrabbled for purchase, lifted up, and launched herself at him.

Jesus.

Nick sidestepped and did the only thing he could—he slid his stunner out of his holster, flipped it to a stun level just short of lethal, and zapped her. She thudded to the floor.

"Nick!" Mac screamed.

"Coming, boss." Nick tried to keep his voice steady but he was unnerved. He shot through the big lobby, leaping over dead bodies, and out the big glass doors. "Had some problems, but it's—" He skidded to a stop and looked past the corner, out to Market Street.

Market was a scene of utter chaos. Two overturned cars just outside the new headquarters of the Bank of China lay crushed like beetles. Two bodies were sprawled in the street, but the injuries weren't due to a car crash. One body had a missing arm, torn off not sheared off, the missing limb two feet away. The other body—Jesus. Nick looked away. Half its face had been mauled, as if the man had encountered a bear.

No bears on Market in downtown San Francisco.

A fire was burning the Facebook building, flames distorting the Plexiglas structure. People were exiting screaming from the building. Four men were tearing each other to pieces on a nearby corner.

Someone grabbed Nick's arm, hard, and he was thrown into the van. Jon. The instant the door closed shut Mac took off.

Nick turned a blank face to Mac and Jon. "What the hell is going on?"

Mac didn't answer. He was too busy slaloming between car wrecks and the few cars that were on the road. The traffic lights were out.

A heavy thud and a man bounced off their van, bloody fist raised in rage. He was an office drone in a once-good suit and trendy haircut, and he snarled at them like an enraged baboon.

"Let's get out of here," Jon said grimly and Mac pressed the accelerator shift forward as far as it would go, turning right at the Ferry Building, speeding toward the Bay Bridge.

"Oh yeah," Nick said. "Let's go home."

Mount Blue

It was raining. How annoying, all those drops of rain on her face. *Drip-drip-drip.*

Elle lifted a hand to wipe them away, but her hand was heavy, like it weighed a hundred pounds. Something caught her hand, something warm and hard. Something that anchored her mind, which felt like a balloon cast free to rise in the sky.

The soft touch of something on her cheek. Lips? More rain.

Her eyelids fluttered.

"That's right, honey," a deep voice said right in her ear. "Open those beautiful baby blues."

She did. Nick's face was pressed to hers. His cheeks were wet. His voice sounded normal, almost cheerful, but his face was pale with deep white brackets around his mouth.

"I remember," she croaked. Her voice was hoarse, almost painful, as if she hadn't spoken in years. She blinked once, twice, looked around. They were in the infirmary. She was on a gurney. Catherine was standing a couple of feet away, Mac's big arm around her shoulders. Standing next to them was Les, her colleague and fellow test subject, face pale against his blond dreadlocks. Together with Moira and Roger.

Les smiled faintly. "Welcome back, Connolly."

She managed to nod, though her neck hurt.

It all came back in a rush, the memories, black and painful. "I remember. I was going ahead of you to see if there were any more prisoners. There weren't, but I saw victims of violence on the floor, as if a particularly vicious army had swept through. I couldn't believe what I was seeing. Then I passed by something, I heard a click and then everything went black."

Les looked angry. "It was a trap, set just for you. Or for those who can astrally project. It traps your electromagnetic field in stasis and your body starts dying."

Nick drew in a deep breath, looking even more stressed. He screwed his eyes shut. "You did die." He opened them again and looked at her fiercely. "Don't you ever do anything like that again."

"No," Elle croaked and a funny cough came out of her throat. A laugh. "I won't."

He pulled his head back a little and stared in her eyes. "You're staying right next to me for the rest of our lives. I am never letting you out of my sight again. Ever."

"That could get awkward." Elle wanted to roll her eyes, but was afraid it would give her a headache. "What about going to the bathroom? Or when I watch the eighteenth season of *Fashion Runway Reality?*" She smiled at Nick's wince. It hurt to smile, but it was a good hurt.

With each passing second she felt stronger, better. She had no intention of dying again, ever, because it *hurt.*

"God, Elle," Nick whispered. His eyes dropped to her mouth and just like that, strength rushed back into her body and with it heat and sex. The promise of sex, anyway. She felt too weak for it but the way he made her feel, she'd be up for it soon.

He bent and kissed her. A mere brushing of lips, a token kiss. The kiss you'd give your sick grandmother.

Oh no.

She'd almost died here and she deserved better. Even that chaste touch of his lips against hers gave her strength, gave her power. Her arm lifted, snaked around his neck and held him to her. She opened her mouth under his, licked the seam of his lips. She could feel, taste his surprise. It only lasted a second though because he pressed down more firmly against her, mouth open now, tongue exploring . . .

"Get a room," Mac's deep voice, laced with humor, made her start. Nick's mouth lifted from hers. She held out her hand. Nick took it and pulled her upright.

"Gladly," Nick said and looked at Catherine. "Can we go?"

Elle blushed bright pink. Nick's meaning was very, very clear.

"Elle?" Catherine was trying hard not to smile. "How do you feel? Any dizziness?"

How did she feel? She felt *great*. Completely utterly fine. She swung her legs over the edge of the gurney and did a quick internal check. *No dizziness. No weakness. No pain* . . . Nothing but a sudden embarrassingly strong sexual desire. She met Nick's eyes and nearly fainted when he smiled at her.

Oh yeah. I feel just fine.

"Hey." Jon walked in. Something about his tone caught everyone's attention. Mac's arm tightened around Catherine's shoulders. "Get this."

Jon tapped the console and the large central monitor pinged to life. The picture was shaky and it took a second to absorb the scene. The chyron below read—BREAKING NEWS. SAN FRANCISCO.

Anderson Cooper's sober, handsome face filled the screen. Behind him, a cityscape on fire.

"Hello, this is Anderson Cooper reporting live to you from a military vessel anchored off Oakland, California. Behind me you see San Francisco. Or what was San Francisco. Now it is a smoking ruin, the only lights those from raging fires. Explosions flare over the city. There is a pall of thick smoke over the city that impedes aerial views. CNN has learned that Marines are stationed on the San Francisco side of both the Bay Bridge and the Golden Gate Bridge and the National Guard is stationed at the bottom of the peninsula, roughly following the line of Market Street. There are no official comments as yet as to what is happening, though most commentators suspect an epidemic of some sort. It seems the entire city is in quarantine. There has been no word from the mayor of San Francisco, Meghan Murray, or from Governor Spielberg. Calls to their offices have gone unanswered. Speculation that—*Jesus Christ! What's that! Grab him! It! Don't—"*

The screen went dead.

Silence.

Elle suddenly gave a cry. She'd completely forgotten.

"What, honey?" Nick was immediately at her side.

Elle didn't have time to answer. She pounded a light keyboard and sagged with relief when she saw what was on the monitor.

"What?" Nick said again.

Elle turned to the room. "Sophie and I had a secret method of communicating. Two invented email addresses. We set it up so we could talk about our boss behind his back. We knew that something was wrong at Corona and needed a way to get in touch with each other. I'd completely forgotten. Sophie's okay for the moment. But she's in trouble."

Elle stepped back and let the others read the body of Sophie's e-mail to her. Nick wrapped a heavy arm around her shoulders and she leaned into him, into that strong warm body. For comfort and for strength.

> *Elle, I think Arka has bioengineered a virulently contagious virus that takes out the neocortex and activates the limbic system. If you're reading this, then you'll know that the virus has been unleashed. I hacked into the files and I discovered that there is a vaccine. There was so much chaos that I was able to steal it. I have a refrigerator case of 200 vials of vaccine. The electricity has gone out and I don't think the coolant in the case will last much more than 96 hours. I'm in my apartment on Beach Street and I*

*don't dare go out. These . . . creatures are running
around in the street. All I can do is stay locked up in
the apartment and hope that you, or someone, can
come for me.*

*If you're reading this, Elle, send someone. This vac-
cine is our only hope.*

Soph

Elle's heart was pounding as she looked around. Nick, Jon, Mac,
Catherine, Stella, Captain Ward, the other three wounded men.

Jon suddenly made for the steel vault door that she knew was
their armory.

"Jon?" Nick frowned. "What are you doing?"

The vault door opened and Jon disappeared inside. He came
out a minute later, armed to the teeth. "I'm going to rescue Sophie.
What the hell do you think I'm doing?"

Nick's arm lifted from her shoulder and Mac stepped forward
too. "We're coming with you."

"No." Jon stood in the doorway, still dressed in his black stealth
suit. He was bristling with weaponry Elle didn't recognize. "I'm
taking the helo. This is a one-man job. You guys get the lab ready
to produce more vaccine."

He stopped in front of Elle and put a hand on her shoulder. "I'll
bring her back to you Elle. That's a promise."

He ran out the door.

Nick held Elle. "When Jon promises something he delivers,
honey. Let's get going. We have a world to save."

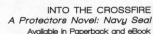